T.A. WHITE
Rules of Redemption
The Firebird Chronicles

Copyright © 2019 by T.A. White

All rights reserved. No part of this publication may be reproduced, stored or transmitted in any form or by any means, electronic, mechanical, photocopying, recording, scanning, or otherwise without written permission from the publisher. It is illegal to copy this book, post it to a website, or distribute it by any other means without permission.

First edition

*This book was professionally typeset on Reedsy.
Find out more at reedsy.com*

Contents

CHAPTER ONE	1
CHAPTER TWO	18
CHAPTER THREE	38
CHAPTER FOUR	56
CHAPTER FIVE	69
CHAPTER SIX	85
CHAPTER SEVEN	104
CHAPTER EIGHT	121
CHAPTER NINE	136
CHAPTER TEN	153
CHAPTER ELEVEN	174
CHAPTER TWELVE	193
CHAPTER THIRTEEN	207
CHAPTER FOURTEEN	226
CHAPTER FIFTEEN	250
CHAPTER SIXTEEN	267
CHAPTER SEVENTEEN	286
CHAPTER EIGHTEEN	305
CHAPTER NINETEEN	324
CHAPTER TWENTY	340
CHAPTER TWENTY-ONE	356
CHAPTER TWENTY-TWO	374
CHAPTER TWENTY-THREE	390
CHAPTER TWENTY-FOUR	406
Discover More by T.A. White	413
About the Author	414

CHAPTER ONE

The burned-out wreckage of the alien spaceship drifted in a halo of its own debris. Its end had been violent, full of fire and carnage as it entered its death throes. The scars of the ship's final battle were visible in the gaping wounds dotted throughout its carcass.

At least half of its body was missing, bits of debris floating in a mass around it. What little remained intact was riddled with scorch marks as it tumbled slowly through space, the story of its end visible to all who neared.

Kira's breath remained steady as she drifted closer to her target, the void of space a relentless presence all around her.

The dead ship was one of many in a debris field spanning thousands of miles. A relic from a battle fought over a dozen years ago, it was the perfect monetary opportunity for the very few brave or foolish enough to attempt salvaging it.

This particular ship was smack dab in the middle of the field. Kira hoped the increased risk of its location meant great reward since most salvagers were smart enough to keep to the outskirts to avoid puncturing the outer hull of their ships.

"Stay alert, Kira. My calculations place the chances of a suit puncture at seventy-six point four three percent."

"We've been over this, Jin. The upgrades to my suit mean I can withstand anything smaller than my fist," Kira responded. It wasn't quite combat grade but it was better than anything her fellow salvagers might have. "The new radar we picked up will detect anything within ten meters."

Jin sniffed, the sound insulted. "That thing is at most ninety-seven percent accurate."

Kira ignored the grumbling. Her friend had fought the radar's purchase and had been grumpy about its presence ever since. Kira didn't care. The new radar would be a valuable tool, especially if they continued going after ships other salvagers were too afraid to attempt.

"The radar isn't going to replace you. It simply frees you up to concentrate on more important tasks," she told him in a soothing voice.

She flicked on the propulsion unit, grinning as the thrusters kicked online. She loved this feeling—the abrupt jolt that took her from drifting aimlessly to becoming the guide and navigator.

She easily dodged the bigger pieces of debris as she wound her way to the misshapen hulk waiting for her.

"I still think we should have gone after the ship the Sweet sisters told us about. This one has disaster written all over it," Jin groused.

"If we'd done that, we would have had to fight off those same sisters once we finished the salvage. You know they have a habit of stealing other people's work," Kira explained again. "Besides, I'm pretty sure this ship is warrior class. An elite or superior at the least."

"That makes me feel a lot better," Jin said sarcastically. "It's not like they don't have a high mortality rate for salvagers."

"You're doing a great job in boosting my confidence with this conversation." Kira's voice was dry.

"It's my job to notify you of the potential risk in any salvage operation."

Yes, and Jin was scrupulous about doing his job. Even when she preferred he didn't. Like now, while she was drifting through the void, a few thin layers between it and her.

Kira maneuvered around another set of space junk. Looked like a bulkhead, probably one of the reasons the lower half of the ship was

CHAPTER ONE

gone.

"I'm approaching the main body," Kira said, the banter of earlier falling away as her focus turned to the job.

"What do you see?"

"The control room looks intact. A few of the weapon chutes are visible."

The main bridge would have been in the upper middle part of the ship, behind several bulkheads. She'd been right. It was definitely a superior class.

During the height of the war, it would have sent the human fleet scurrying. Nearly indestructible, its defensive and offensive capabilities were among the best their enemy, the Tsavitee, had. No doubt it had been responsible for sending more than one of the Consortium's ships to an early grave along with any unfortunates among the crew.

This one would have been considered midsize—not quite a dreadnought. Though next to Kira's form, it seemed massive.

She knew the specs for this ship, had studied them and others like it. It would have had a crew of about a hundred aboard when it was destroyed. A hundred of humanity's enemies eliminated in one of the bloodiest battles of a decade-long war.

Built from a dark metal, it nearly blended in with the black of space. Ominous and foreboding, the ship's lines were full of sharp edges. If it had been intact, it would have bristled with weapons capable of tearing her small ship apart. Kira didn't know if the feelings she got from it were based in her own perceptions and history or because the ship was a graveyard for those who never made it out.

"Any of the cannons look salvageable?"

Kira magnified the ship in her viewer. It was difficult to tell, since it continued to rotate along the same lines it would have when it died.

"No, they're torn to bits. There are pieces here and there, the rest of the parts are likely floating around me," she said.

3

"Do you think they're worth salvaging?" he asked.

"Not on this trip. I'll focus on the main body for now. We can mark the location and return for the rest."

"All right, I'm ready for you to begin your approach. Remember, these ships tend to have nasty defenses. Try not to trip them this time."

"I haven't forgotten."

"You say that, and yet you always seem to find trouble." His voice was tart. "I'm not coming to get you this time."

"Don't worry. I don't expect you to. Just make sure to keep the *Wanderer* out of danger," Kira said. Before he could respond, her voice turned businesslike. "Beginning my approach."

"Your trajectory is good. You should reach the ship in four minutes and ten seconds."

Kira maneuvered closer, her heart rate remaining steady despite the danger. She'd made it three meters when her proximity alert went off, the screen in her mask flashing red. She hit her thrusters, shooting left. A silver shape sailed by her.

Guess that meant the ship's defenses were intact. A grin took over her face.

When they finally cracked this nut, they were going to make a mint. Enough for a new food synthesizer capable of making food that tasted like food and not the chalky crap she was currently living off.

"What was that?" Jin asked.

"Nothing," she told him, her voice distracted.

The weapon chasing her through the wreckage looked like a long silvery ribbon. It moved as if it were organic, darting around pieces of metal with a lithe, sinuous glide as it followed Kira. It reminded her of Earth's eels. She'd never seen one personally but she'd seen pictures in books and in video.

This thing moved in much the same way, as if it was swimming through space. If it caught her, it would wrap around her before

CHAPTER ONE

yanking her apart. That was if it didn't burn through her suit first.

"Is that a strigmor eel?" Jin's outrage was clear even over the comms.

Kira didn't bother denying it, too busy trying not to fly headfirst into any wreckage.

"How did you set off the ship's defenses?" he cried.

"Little busy here." Kira thrust down, the eel just missing her.

"Did you not cloak? I told you how important it was to cloak," he wailed.

"I cloaked," Kira said through gritted teeth. She veered to the ship. Maybe it wouldn't follow her inside.

"Don't go inside the ship. That's a horrible idea."

An instant later a second proximity alert went off, alerting Kira to another eel heading her way.

"Told you." Jin's voice was smug.

Kira ignored him, dipping down as she zigzagged recklessly through wreckage capable of cutting her to pieces if she ran into it.

She rounded a piece of particularly large metal, the first eel right on her tail, the second peeling off to try to trap her from the other side. She flicked her eyes up and to the left, blinking twice to trigger her defensive flares. Hundreds of tiny lights, each one a metal ball bearing no larger than a marble, streaked out from her suit.

The first eel flew into them, the balls attaching to its skin in a big clump. Seconds later they burst, splitting the eel in half.

Kira shot away from the wreckage, just in time for the second eel to come up from underneath. She darted through the deadly obstacle course, the eel no more than a few lengths behind her.

Her new suit with its upgrades was a blessing now. It was its own miniature spacecraft, capable of the flexible maneuvering a ship would never have been able to replicate. She'd designed it to her specifications, sourced every piece of it. Now it was making all that time, effort, and money worthwhile.

The viewscreen expanded and contracted as she searched through the wreckage for the perfect spot to take out the other eel.

There. Two long pieces of wreckage floated together, connected by a thin beam. That was perfect.

Kira veered for it, hitting her turbos and increasing her speed. The eel fell back slightly. Enough for her purposes.

She darted between the two sheets, brushing against one side and leaving several sticky charges on it before moving to the other side. The maneuver was performed in seconds.

She hit a hard reverse on her thrusters, gritting her teeth as the suit shuddered to a stop. She turned on her back to face the opening she'd just flown through and waited.

The eel didn't disappoint, sailing into the small space, its body slithering toward her as it spotted her.

She smiled at it. "Hello, beautiful."

She lifted her arm, lining up the shot as it prepared to dart after her. She fired, a blue light streaking toward the eel. It easily dodged, moving to the side as the light missed it.

Her smile widened. She kicked her thrusters online, using them to send her rocketing away from the eel, her eyes locked on it.

The light hit the sticky charges. A force punched Kira in the chest, then the metal around the eel imploded, warping around it and killing it.

Kira continued her backward glide.

"The eels have been neutralized," she said.

"Good, now that you're done playing, maybe you can get to work. You have four hours of air left and it'll take you nearly that long to get close again," Jin said.

"Roger that," Kira said.

She flipped around so she was facing the ship again. This time she was more cautious in her approach, maneuvering so her path mirrored the space junk orbiting the wreck. It meant a less direct trajectory, but it was safer.

An hour later she finally floated into the hull of the ship through one of the holes on its exterior without setting off any other defenses.

CHAPTER ONE

"Jin, you there?" Kira asked once inside the ship.

No response came. It wasn't a surprise really. They'd been prepared for it, and given this ship's defense measures were still online, it was nearly a given. The Tsavitee ships had some type of mechanism that disrupted communications. Even after all these years, Consortium scientists couldn't figure out how it worked.

Either way, it meant Kira was on her own.

The inside of the ship was as dark and oppressive as the outside, a tomb that hadn't been disturbed since the day it was destroyed. Twelve years of silence and solitude, everything in the exact same state as the day it had stopped.

Kira's forehead wrinkled in disgust at the thought of what could be floating unseen next to her. It could be stray metal, the bodies of the crew, or one of the nasty little surprises the aliens liked to leave behind. One never knew, and Kira had encountered all of the above at one point or another.

Kira wasted no time, flicking on her suit's headlamps. She'd turned them off during her approach. The beams from her helmet and shoulders pierced the black. Despite being high-powered, they did little but create thin slices of light in the oppressive blackness. Helpful but not nearly enough.

She unhooked one of the industrial glow lamps from its slot along her side, breaking it against the cold metal and giving it a shake before letting it go. It bobbed to the end of its string, the soft light illuminating the space in a way her suit lights could not.

She grimaced in distaste at the sight of the ship around her. It didn't matter how long she'd been doing this—a Tsavitee ship always gave her the creeps and left her feeling like she was walking through maggots. Still, they helped keep her in business, so she'd table her dislike until she was in her own bunk.

She fired her thrusters in a small burst, propelling herself slowly along the long corridor. In a human vessel, she would be in what was referred to as the lower aft section. It was a term originating from humanity's seafaring history and one they'd adapted once they began to move into space.

Kira couldn't be sure, but if she had to guess she'd say this part of the ship would have been used as quarters for the infantry landing parties. It'd probably also been home to the nasty little monsters and toys they created for the specific purpose of doing as much mayhem and destruction as possible.

For that reason, Kira moved carefully as she headed for the engine room, judging it as the best place to find something worth salvaging.

The government paid top dollar for intact engine parts. They'd been working on reverse engineering the Tsavitee technology, which had given their enemy the advantage.

Even nine years after the end of the war, the government was still having trouble getting their hands on working engine parts.

For all that they were the scourge of humanity, the Tsavitee had been smart. They'd had crew members ready to sabotage the engine and prevent anybody from recovering their technology once the rest of the ship members were dead.

This ship's destruction had been swift and unexpected. Kira's hope was its demise had taken the crew off guard.

She jerked as a shape floated out of the dark, distracting her from her thoughts. The body of a Tsavitee rotated toward her, its face blank and locked in a look of horror, knowledge of its imminent death written there.

The Tsavitee had many forms, depending on its position in their ranks. This one would have been infantry, humanoid in appearance with two legs and two arms, a head with eyes, nose, and mouth. That's where the similarities ended.

This one was larger than any human by at least a foot, its form hulking and muscular with skin the color of graphite. She judged him as in the lower ranks given the visible tusks and the stunted horns curling up from its head.

The horns and fearsome appearance were how they came to be

called demons by the human fleet. In a way, they did resemble the creatures of nightmares from old religious texts.

In their own language, Tsavitee meant scourge. That's what they had been to humanity. A devouring horde appearing out of nowhere and decimating humanity with the most bloody and savage war in history.

Like some plague born from the void, they had swept over more than one human colony leaving nothing in their wake but charred remains.

The death toll had been in the millions. Any progress humanity had made in the centuries since they'd started space flight was wiped away in a few years.

Earth was among those hit with humanity's homeworld reduced to a shadow of its former self. Since then, humans had reclaimed Earth but the cost had been great.

This debris field with its hundreds of dead ships had been the turning point. It should have been humanity's end, but instead, by some miracle, they'd salvaged a victory, stopping the Tsavitee and destroying the backbone of their fleet.

There might have been battles after this one, but this was where historians would point to as the beginning of the end.

Many believed the Tsavitee were gone now, never to return to this region of space, but Kira had her doubts. While the Tsavitee had been beaten, they had not been eliminated.

They were a deadly force, almost single-minded in their purpose. Beings like that weren't going to give up. No, they would withdraw, analyze the data, and then return stronger than ever.

It was one of the reasons the scientists needed to understand as much as they could about Tsavitee technology; Kira securing a decent payday as a result, was a bonus.

Half an hour ticked by as she twisted her way through the corridors, many of which had collapsed into a floating obstacle course. Luckily, she was small, and her suit was among the best, giving her an advantage other salvagers lacked.

She passed several more corpses on her way, careful not to disturb them. They might have been the enemy, but this was their tomb. It was best to leave the dead to their restful peace.

Large tears in the wall gave her glimpses of the wreckage floating outside.

When she finally found the engine room, it was in shambles. Her hopes the crew had spared the engine were in vain. There would be no recovering a fully functional engine, the holy grail for any salvager.

All was not lost, however. The crew would have been in a rush, knowing death was imminent. They wouldn't have had time to do a thorough job.

That's where Kira came in. She was good at finding the spots they'd missed.

She pushed off the floor, floating up as she checked the fuel cells first. Just one of those in half-decent condition would keep her solvent for months.

She worked through the room, her hopes falling further and further as she moved.

"Couldn't have made things easy for me, could you?" she asked the body of an engineer as she pulled it from where he'd been wedged in a small recessed part of the engine.

So far, she'd only found two cells semi-intact. Not quite the score she'd been hoping for.

She gave the engineer a push, sending him floating in the opposite direction before moving into the tight spot.

"What's this?" she asked herself, staring at an intact compartment.

She got out her tools, careful as she took the compartment apart. Surprised pleasure suffused her as she revealed what was inside. A fully intact piece of their engine drive. Rare and valuable. She suspected there were three more like it in the compartments to her left, each one slightly bigger than her fist.

CHAPTER ONE

She studied the first with a frown. In its casing, it was stable, but removing it without the proper shielding would cause it to degrade. If it degraded past a certain point, it would cause a catastrophic failure resulting in an explosion.

Good thing Kira planned for everything.

She pulled a glass-like tube off her suit, removing each piece of her find and dropping it into the tube before closing it and pressing the button on top. It lit with a soft blue glow.

The cylinder had been developed specifically for this purpose. It would keep the elements inside from destabilizing long enough for her to get it to her buyer.

Inside, she danced a little victory dance. A score like this would keep her floating for a good year or more.

Next, she moved to the other end of the engine compartment, removing some of the electronics and stripping the wiring. The metal would fetch a nice price even if the original purpose was fried.

Each item she removed was stored in a bag at her side.

On this first trip, she was mainly doing reconnaissance, cataloging items of value and identifying the equipment she'd need to salvage when she returned. Only small items, or those considered too valuable to leave behind, would be salvaged on this expedition. A find like this could take years to adequately strip.

When she judged the engine room sufficiently deprived of the things she could carry in the small sack at her side, she headed for the command center in the foredeck. Buried in the most protected part of the ship, each command center looked and operated a little differently.

One thing remained the same—it was the military and strategic mind of the ship, a source of valuable intel if the Tsavitee ever decided to return.

This command center was in the shape of a hexagon with no exterior windows. On a human vessel, there would have been countless screens keeping track of conditions and data as circumstances changed. Not so for the Tsavitee. Another mystery to go along with all the rest. No one knew exactly how they flew their ships or sent orders out to their troops.

Kira floated to a stop at the door, careful now she was here. She wouldn't put it past the Tsavitee to set traps for the unwary. She'd seen it before.

She peered inside, her headlamps illuminating the large room. Parts of the space shimmered, giving her a glimpse of a strange, silvery cloud of dust floating inside.

Razor ash. Damn.

The captain of this ship had been smarter than she'd given him credit for. He'd read the signs of where the battle was heading and then deployed defensive measures to secure the information housed in this room.

Razor ash wasn't anything to fuck with. It was diamond-hard, capable of cutting through damn near anything, including her suit.

If even a few specks attached to her, she would decompress within seconds. The suit might be able to repair minor tears, but once the ash got inside, it would eat away at the lining and destroy any electronic circuits–to say nothing of what it would do to her flesh.

It wasn't a pleasant way to go.

The captain and his officers were buckled into their seats, their clothes ragged and their flesh pockmarked from the razor ash.

Kira hovered in the corridor as she considered her options.

The ash didn't have the same tracking system as the eel. It was meant to stand sentry, forever sweeping through the room on the lookout for intruders. Otherwise, it would have locked onto her already. As long as she didn't disturb it, she should be safe enough.

A smarter person would have turned around and left. The haul at her side was plenty.

She pushed off the wall behind her, plotting a course through the room to maximize the chances of avoiding the ash. Lucky for her, it had settled against the far-left side before snaking along the ceiling

CHAPTER ONE

above, leaving an open path from the hall to the captain's chair.

Kira wanted whatever the captain had deemed important enough to set the ash as a permanent watchdog.

She slowly floated through the room, careful not to use her thrusters. The energy signature their use would throw out would have the ash locking onto her within seconds.

She arrowed toward the console in front of the captain, judging it as the most likely to contain useful information.

She checked the ash's progress. It was stationary, but that could change at any moment.

Satisfied she was safe for now, Kira stripped the metal housing from the console, exposing its innards. The information stored in the chips inside was protected by several layers of metal sheeting. It would take time to reach the bits she wanted.

She was halfway through when the ash rippled, sliding through the room as it drifted into a new pattern.

Kira worked faster as the ash floated closer.

Almost there. Almost there.

Kira pried the metal loose, using a pair of force grips to wrench it free, much like a can opener would, the unique alien metal folding under the force and exposing the circuitry inside.

A sheet of razor ash moved in front of the door, cutting off her escape. She grunted as she reached in and started pulling pieces free, storing each one in her bag as the leading edge of the ash slid closer and closer.

Looked like it planned to settle right where she was.

It was inches from her helmet when she pushed off the floor, sliding to the left and away from the first edge of the ash. The move took her deeper into the room.

The ash settled into its new pattern, completely shrouding the doorway.

Kira huffed at the sight. She was well and truly trapped.

She flicked her eyes to the right, bringing up her stats. One hour and sixteen minutes of air left. Under normal circumstances, it should have been plenty to get her to the *Wanderer*.

Waiting the ash out would be her preference. Maybe it adopted a new pattern every hour.

Kira sighed. Her luck had never been the best. If she were wrong, she would have wasted valuable time when she could have been escaping. If she died from asphyxiation, Jin would probably follow her into the next world just to laugh at her.

Time for a new plan.

She pressed a button on her suit and swiveled to face one of the far walls. From what she'd seen on the way in, this wall was unlikely to be a bulkhead. It'd be thinner than the outer walls and would make a perfect spot for a new door.

She unhooked one of the tools, flicking a button. The laser torch ignited, a blue-white light flared out, blinding against the darkness as she set it against the metal.

The razor ash rippled, sensing the disturbance in the small space. A tentacle reached out from the mass as it snaked toward Kira.

Kira kept one eye on the approaching mass as she burned through the metal, counting down the seconds as death advanced on her.

She finished cutting a small door out of the metal, sinking a savage kick against the wall. The sheet popped out, the edges glowing red-hot from the torch.

Kira didn't waste any time, pushing off as she flicked her thrusters on.

This was going to be close.

The ash missed her by millimeters as she rocketed down the hallway, searching for the quickest way to space. She needed out of this ship five minutes ago.

Up ahead, a dark cloud swarmed out of a hallway, eating through one of the dead crew as it raced toward Kira.

She arrowed down a corridor to her left, cursing her luck. It had found its way out of the room a lot easier than it should have.

CHAPTER ONE

That meant it was programmed to search and destroy once triggered.

Lucky her.

Kira spotted a hole in the hull and shot toward it, the ash only feet away as it chased her through the ship.

She turned her thrusters on maximum, pushing for more speed. She needed every bit if she didn't want to die an ugly death in the next few seconds.

Kira darted through the hole, barely clearing it on either side. She was already broadcasting before she was clear. The message was set on a loop in case the Tsavitee ship was still playing havoc with her comms.

"Jin, get the ship ready. I'm coming in hot."

* * *

"What do you mean it's broken?" Kira stared into the innards of the ship's engine.

"Someone decided to haul tail for the ship dragging two eels and a crap-ton of razor ash. You're lucky the damage was this minor," Jin snapped. "If I wasn't the amazing pilot I am, the ship and you would have been toast."

"If you were so amazing, the ship would never have been touched," Kira muttered to herself, prodding the offending part.

"What was that?" Jin's voice was sharp.

"Nothing."

"That's what I thought you said. Nothing." Jin's voice trailed off as he turned away from her.

"Can't you fix it with one of the 3D printers we have on board?" Kira complained.

That's why she had paid an arm and a leg for one after all—to make the necessary repairs when they were in the deep of space.

"No. Someone decided not to pay the tax on the last batch of material, so I don't have enough to fabricate what I need."

Kira looked away. She was that someone. In her defense, the tax had been increased nearly fifty percent this last time. It was robbery, pure and simple. They got away with it because most ships waited until the last minute to order the raw materials they needed for the printer. The station was one of the few in several million miles that looked the other way on some of the salvagers' less-than-legal business endeavors.

Kira rubbed her forehead, trying to soothe away the headache beginning to sink its claws into her.

"Even if we did have the material, it wouldn't matter. That part is highly technical. It's impossible to replicate. I can fabricate a workaround but it has a limited shelf life. Once it goes, we'll barely have sublight speed."

Which for a ship out on the edge of nowhere could be a death sentence.

Kira's headache got worse.

She let out a frustrated sigh. "Alright, let's route to Omega Station. We can get the part we need there."

"Can't," Jin said, his voice slightly tinny and flat.

"Why not?"

"Because the part we need is at O'Riley Station."

Kira stiffened, turning to look at her friend. Jin hovered several feet above the deck, his spherical body no bigger than her head. His shell was an out-of-date military grade drone coupled with all the advances she could get her hands on. Although his parts might be metal and hardware, his mind was pure organic sapience, with all the pitfalls that might bring.

"You can't tell me Omega doesn't have what we need."

Jin was the cool voice of logic and reason in almost any situation. But every now and then, he developed vexing opinions. When he did, things tended to go very badly for Kira.

It was on the tip of her tongue to ask what he was up to. She

CHAPTER ONE

refrained. If she were wrong, the question would offend him, and she'd have to live with a grumpy drone for the next few days—one with control of the ship's internal sensors including temperature and hot water.

"I've already checked the catalogs we downloaded during our last stop. They were out then and weren't due to be replenished for several months. We'd be stuck in port while we wait for the next shipment of spare parts," he told her, a soft whir sounding as Jin turned to face Kira, a small lens observing her.

Kira knew he'd done it for her benefit, turning his "eye" on her so she'd know he was serious. She'd upgraded pretty much every part of him herself. There were over a hundred small cameras installed on his exterior to help him "see" and analyze the world. The lens was a joke between the two of them taken from an old Earth show he'd since adopted into his personal habits.

"We'd be okay short-term, but eventually it would fuck up the entire engine. You don't want to be out a few hundred million miles from the nearest station trying to replace it, would you?"

It was a rhetorical question. As the person who handled their money, he knew exactly how much they had in their accounts and it was nowhere near enough to outfit an entirely new engine.

She growled in frustration. "This had better not be you meddling in my life again. You know how much I hate that place."

He started for the door. "Maybe you should be more careful in your flight maneuvers then."

She threw a wrench.

The wrench froze three inches from him. There was a slight whomp as he tossed the wrench back toward her.

"At least this way, we'll get top dollar for the wreckage you salvaged instead of having to go through a middleman," he said, his voice trailing behind him as he left the room.

Somehow, his silver lining didn't make Kira feel any better.

17

CHAPTER TWO

Kira vibrated with impatience as she waited for the airlock to open. Jin was busy on the bridge, completing the docking checklist required of every ship prior to its passengers disembarking.

His job was made more difficult by the fact they'd chosen the cheapest option for a berth. It meant they docked on the outside of the station, lining their airlock up with one of many on the station's underside. It was less expensive, but it came with more security checks.

They could have chosen the more expensive route of docking on the flight deck on the interior of the station, but Kira had rejected the option before Jin could propose it.

They couldn't afford to waste the money. Besides, this option allowed for a quick getaway if necessary. She had a past on this station. Coming back here even after years away was tempting fate.

She fidgeted with the sleeves of her hoodie, pulling it over her hands. She was dressed simply in a pair of utilitarian cargo pants that fit nicely while giving her freedom of movement. A camisole and thin hoodie completed the outfit.

She was average-sized for a woman, barely hitting five feet, seven inches. She had a runner's frame, lean and lithe, with muscles stretched over her long lines.

Despite her apparent slimness, she possessed a hidden strength, surprising many an enterprising salvager seeking to take advantage of her. They saw the delicateness of her features, the burgundy color

CHAPTER TWO

of her hair and gray-purple eyes that changed colors in a certain light, and made certain assumptions.

Assumptions she was happy to disabuse them of.

Jin floated toward her.

"You finished?" she asked. She was already itching to be gone, mostly because she wanted this trip over and done with. The sooner she got on the station and finished her task, the sooner she could return to the safety of the *Wanderer*.

"All done," he chirped. "The station's AI was extremely slow. It's long past due for an update."

"You didn't talk to a human?" Kira asked.

"They ask too many questions. I hacked the station and dropped our application directly into their systems. We should be good to go."

It seemed her friend had thought of everything.

She folded her arms across her small chest and turned to the airlock as he took up his customary spot, hovering to the left of her head. His small form nearly brushed against the hair she kept cut just below her chin. It waved around her face like miniature tentacles, one of the reasons she kept it short—the better to contain its madness.

"Remember the rules, Kira. Don't draw notice if you can help it. Don't start fights. Don't give people a reason to look twice at us," Jin warned.

"I got it the first time." And the second. And the third; to say nothing of the fourth. At this point, Jin was beginning to sound like a broken record.

"I want to make sure. You have a tendency of forgetting when it suits your needs," Jin said as the airlock hissed open.

Kira hesitated to step off her ship. Jin had nothing to worry about. She had no interest in bringing attention to them. Her entire way of life counted on staying beneath everyone's notice. She hadn't come this far to throw it all away.

"In and out. No problem," Kira told herself.

"There better not be," Jin snorted. "Without that part, we won't make it to the next station."

Kira ignored him and stepped into the docking tube, her plain black boots echoing softly around them as Jin whirred at her side.

* * *

"It's so different," Jin said in awe as he took in the station. "It looks nothing like it did during the war."

Gone were the utilitarian gray walls and narrow spaces she remembered from her previous visit. They'd been perfectly functional—sterile, not a small scrap of color to soften the place. Now, the station looked elegant and timeless, bright spots of color saving it from being too monotonous.

Peacetime had been good to O'Riley, taking it from an obscure military outpost to a thriving hub of trade and government. The central area where warships had once docked for servicing was now an open-air market. The atrium slightly resembled a beehive, with dozens of levels of terraces clinging to the edges and a wide-open space in the middle of the station where several varieties of small ships floated from level to level like bees sampling the different delights.

The ships were personal cruisers, not meant for actual space travel. Some resembled old Earth sailboats, complete with a mast and sail to catch the wind currents stirring the interior of the atrium. Air gondolas also navigated the space, carrying couples intent on a romantic tour of the beehive. Still other ships were built for speed and zipped through the air with reckless abandon.

Kira even saw a few hoverboards staying close to the terraces as hoverbikes made the journey from below to those terraces high above.

A long tram crossed from one side of the atrium to the other. It rushed over an open drop, the floor of the station far below it.

CHAPTER TWO

Above it all was a large dome where dozens of bright UV lights meant to imitate a miniature sun twinkled. Those lights were the reasons for the small trees and planters filled with thriving flowers and bushes that lined the walking paths which bustled with business. High-end merchants had laid claim to the physical shops set along the walls, while smaller vendors plonked their mobile carts wherever they pleased—including the middle of the walkway

In a way, it was genius, forcing tourists to stop and look as they threaded through the maze the carts turned the walkway into.

O'Riley was a shining gem of human ingenuity. Class and privilege shone from the carefully crafted engineering marvel. The station was an emphatic statement, saying this wasn't the backwater of the galaxy anymore. The war might have humbled humanity, but it hadn't broken them. They rose from the ashes to rebuild better and stronger than ever.

Kira and Jin shuffled along the terrace as Kira tried to tamp down the irritation of being surrounded by so many bodies. She'd forgotten how crazy this place was, the press of humanity almost claustrophobic.

For someone used to the quiet of a small ship, this place was a madhouse. A dizzying confusion to senses adapted to solitude and plain walls.

Chaos hammered at her. Voices, sights, sounds–everything drawing her nerves tighter and tighter.

She took a deep breath and then another before she pushed everything away, concentrating on centering herself in the here and now.

Kira spotted a kiosk and strode over to it as Jin flitted from one thing to another. He didn't have the same issues with crowded places as she did.

"Look, they're selling candy globes," he crooned. "Can we get one?"

"You don't have taste buds," she told him.

"But you do," he said hopefully.

She paused and gave him a frown. "I'm not eating that crap just so you can ride my senses. You can do that when we get to the *Wanderer*."

Jin was an oddity among oddities. Unique in a universe full of unique things. He was machine but not. Artificial but real.

One of the many things he had discovered over the years was an ability to tap into Kira's senses—taste, smell, touch, sight, and hearing. It allowed him to experience the world on a more human level, turning it from logical data to something tangible he could feel and almost touch.

"Please."

"That stuff tastes like crap."

"Come on, just one thing," he pleaded.

"What happened to in and out?"

They both stopped when they reached the kiosk, each going silent as they took in the image displayed on the front—a soldier in a Hadron class combat suit riding a waveboard into the upper atmosphere. Emblazoned on the person's uniform was the image of a bird on fire. Behind the soldier, just breaking through the clouds, were ten more in a perfect V formation. The air was filled with fire as wreckage rained down around them, ships above dying as Tsavitee ground artillery picked them off one by one.

Under the image was emblazoned, "What difference will you make?"

Kira swallowed painfully, unable to move, the sight locking her in place.

The Wave Runners were a specialized and elite military unit, bridging the gap between combat suit and aircraft. The hoverboard under their feet made them faster and more maneuverable than any ship ever could be.

They were a product of the war. Their tactics had evolved to meet the Tsavitee's superior forces head-on—the suits and board compensating for human weakness. Humans might never be as strong or fast, physically, as the Tsavitee, but they were smart and

CHAPTER TWO

adapted even under the worst of circumstances. The Wave Runners were perhaps the best example of that.

Jin tapped the screen. The image changed, the station's map and directory appearing.

"Let's concentrate on getting what we need," he said in a quiet voice.

Kira nodded, feeling numb, the earlier argument forgotten as she reached out and began scrolling through the directory.

She hesitated over the name of one vendor. In the description line, it said ship parts.

"Not that one," he said, seeing where she'd stopped. "Their parts have a reputation of breaking as soon as the warranty ends."

She grimaced and continued her search.

"And you can eat and walk," he offered, returning to the former topic. "No reason to stop."

Her sigh was heavy and tired. It was easier to give in. "Fine. One thing."

He let out a happy cheer.

A small smile lifted Kira's lips as she continued to swipe. A familiar name flashed by.

Vander's.

She knew that place. It had been in business when she was a soldier. Back then, they'd offered tech the military didn't provide. They were expensive as hell, but their stuff had been some of the best.

She read the description and smiled. Seemed they hadn't changed much in the years since.

"That might work." Jin leaned over her shoulder. "I wonder if Roxy still works there."

An explosion rocked their terrace from above before Kira could respond. She dropped into a crouch, her heart in her throat as she reached for a weapon she didn't have. Station policy prohibited carrying any type of projectile weapon while in dock.

Screams tore through the air around her as bits of a gondola fluttered down.

She ran to the edge of the terrace, craning her head up as she looked for the source of the explosion.

The bright lick of flame drew her eye as the sail of a small five-seater caught fire two terraces above. The rear third of it looked like a mangled mess as the boat struggled valiantly to stay afloat. Even as she watched, the forward mast snapped. Its engines gave a high-pitched whine as it slowly began to list.

"We don't have to get involved," Jin warned. "Station personnel should respond momentarily."

Kira remained motionless for an interminable moment, her focus glued to the small craft as it tilted further, the engines sputtering.

The craft's engine gave another choking roar. The boat broke loose from its mooring and began to sink. Seeing that, those around her panicked, pushing and shoving, as they fought to get out of the way in case it crashed into their terrace.

"Jin."

"I've already contacted station security. They'll be here in ten minutes."

Kira could see how it would play out.

In five minutes, probably less, the engines would cease function entirely. What was left of the sail would hold for a short time before the weight became too much and it snapped. After that, the craft would either complete its plummet, be torn apart by the winds on the interior of the honeycomb or explode when the fire reached the battery cells.

Station personnel would arrive minutes too late.

The craft rotated, giving Kira a glimpse of those inside. Two children pressed against the windows of the cabin, their mouths open in silent screams, their faces filled with terror.

"Kira."

Kira was moving before he could say more, running parallel to the craft as it began drifting, sinking as smoke billowed out of it.

"Wait for me," he called after her.

CHAPTER TWO

She didn't listen. She needed to time this perfectly.

The small sailboat picked up speed in its descent. It drew level with their terrace, missing it by inches as it fell.

She hit the end of the terrace and leaped, free fall and gravity pulling her down, her heart reaching for her throat. She didn't have time to calculate or second-guess. She hit the bow of the sailboat hard, rolling to a stop as it rocked precariously under her.

She recovered, throwing herself back to rebalance. Without the fully functioning engines and the sail, her extra weight could force it to roll.

"Sloppy," Jin chided, appearing over her shoulder.

"Yeah, yeah. Some of us don't have antigravs."

Jin made a small sniff to convey his opinion on that statement.

Kira ignored her prickly companion. "See what you can do about this thing."

He didn't answer, already heading for the engine.

She entered the main cabin.

Two children huddled behind the pilot seats, peeking over the edge at her with large, wary eyes.

Their clothes were expensive and made from a material Kira didn't recognize.

The boy was around thirteen or fourteen, his guarded expression making him seem older despite the faint remnants of baby fat around his cheeks. In a few years, when time and age had refined the lines of his features, the girls would swarm him.

His top lip trembled as he fought to project a strong front.

The other child was much younger, seven or eight. Her eyes were scared, evidence of tear tracks on her face. Her pale, white-blond hair was tied with a silver ribbon. She looked like a doll, pretty and delicate.

"Is there anyone else here?" Kira asked, making her way toward them even as the cabin bucked and swayed under her feet.

They didn't answer, holding silent and still as she examined the cabin.

A charred body was curled in on itself on the floor behind the children's seats. Black scorch marks climbed the walls to the rear of the cabin. The poor bastard must have tried to protect the children from the fire.

Kira could tell there would be no saving that person.

No one else besides the children was present.

"Come on. We have to go."

Neither child moved.

Kira scowled at them. Time was of the essence. She didn't have time to console them or win their trust. She reached around the boy and plucked the girl up. She sensed she was the key to getting the other one to cooperate. Kira held the girl to her chest as the boy babbled at her in a strange language, his voice high-pitched and angry.

It didn't take speaking the language to know what he was saying, to know he was demanding she put the girl down.

Kira didn't listen, heading to the front of the cabin and out the door, the boy trailing after her, the panic in his voice clear.

The girl clutched at her, fear making her cling harder, her knuckles turning white where she gripped Kira's shirt.

Kira patted her shoulder in wordless sympathy, even as she looked for a way to safety. Jumping onto one of the terraces would be impossible with two children clinging like limpets to her.

"Jin, anything?" she called.

"This engine is dead. There's no saving it. It's not capable of anything but a crash-landing," he said. The chip embedded behind her ear made it seem like he was speaking directly into it.

Kira fought the desire to curse, knowing the children would probably panic more at the sight of her frustration.

Crash-landing the craft on one of the terraces was too risky. It might work, but it also might explode on impact, killing them and innocent bystanders. Their best bet was to jump.

CHAPTER TWO

She looked around, noticing they'd drifted away from the terraces. Far below several platforms stretched, linked to the terraces above by a series of walkways.

They were remnants of the station's past, some of the few that hadn't been deconstructed when the war ended. Fleet ships might have once landed on those same platforms for repair or to offload supplies before taking off through the retractable dome above.

She exhaled heavily. One of them would have to work.

"What about the platform below us at three o'clock?" she asked.

"That jump is nearly fifty yards and at least a twenty-meter drop," he argued.

"You got a better idea?"

A small growl filled her ear. That was a no.

"Give me time to get on the outside. I may be able to nudge this thing's death spiral, so it takes you directly over it," Jin said. "You won't have much time. Drop one of the kids onto it first; otherwise, you'll never make it."

Kira grinned.

"So much for going unnoticed," he muttered as he maneuvered into position.

Kira ignored the comment, knowing he didn't really mean it. Neither one of them were the type to regret saving a pair of children.

She crouched and looked the boy in the eye. "Can you understand me?"

He seemed hesitant, his nod slow, the suspicion in his gaze slightly dimmed.

Kira felt a sense of relief at the fact he could speak her language. Explaining what she needed of him and the girl would have been much more difficult otherwise.

"I have to throw one of you off," she told him.

He started shaking his head before she finished. She set the girl down and kneeled in front of him, making sure he could see her eyes. She needed him to trust her.

"I can't make this jump holding both of you. One of us needs to go first. I'll drop one onto the platform and then jump with the other one."

Timing was crucial. The platform was a good size but it wasn't huge. The sailboat was drifting faster than she'd like while attempting this maneuver. If she missed her window during the second jump, she and the other child would fall to their deaths as the ship opened the distance between it and safety.

He glanced at the platform, his solemn frown out of place in a face so young.

"She goes first." His accent made his words almost lyrical.

Kira hesitated. She'd planned to drop the boy first, then jump with the girl. He was heavier, and his size might slow her.

His stubborn expression told her he wasn't budging on this point. They'd lose valuable time if she continued to press.

She nodded, feeling resigned. In his place, she'd probably do the same.

"Alright, we're moving into position now, Jin," Kira said out loud, holding the boy's gaze as she did so.

Brief curiosity filled his face, but he remained quiet, watching as she took the girl and moved to the edge.

"Commencing maneuver. Brace for impact."

Kira gestured for the boy to take a knee, doing the same and huddling around the girl.

The craft jolted. For a long scary second, Kira wasn't sure Jin's tactic had worked, then they began a slow glide toward the platform.

Adrenaline coursed through Kira. She took the girl's hands and dangled her over the side, watching carefully for her moment. Timing was everything.

For a long second, she worried about what would happen to the girl once she landed. She didn't have the training Kira did. She didn't know how to land properly, and while broken bones were preferable to death, it bothered her to be the cause.

CHAPTER TWO

Briefly, she considered softening the girl's landing, tapping into some of her innate abilities. It wouldn't take much, a simple rearranging of the density of the air molecules between the girl and the platform.

One thing stopped her. She hadn't used that power in all the time since she'd left the service. It was chancy; the power unpredictable. Furthermore, it could take a toll that cost her and the boy their lives. It also might bring Kira to the attention of people she had spent the time since the war avoiding.

The platform loomed closer. Twenty meters. Ten. The boy leaned over the edge, his words frantic as he barked instructions.

Kira ignored it all, waiting, her breathing slowing as she concentrated.

There.

She tossed the girl, aiming carefully. The girl plummeted.

Kira didn't wait to see if she landed. The ship was already picking up momentum as it glided over the platform. Delaying would mean death. She vaulted to her feet as she grabbed the boy up and powered for the opposite side of the sailboat. She hit the edge and leaped, the platform racing by under her.

She dropped. This landing was going to be brutal. She flipped midair, curling around the boy.

Together they hit. Pain from the impact shot through Kira's body. She didn't have time to be grateful before they rolled. The station careened around them. The edge dropped from under them. Kira's hand shot out, grasping at anything in reach, desperation lending her strength.

The sharp edges from the underside of the platform cut into her skin, ripping it open.

She caught a pipe, holding on with all her strength as they came to an abrupt stop. Her shoulder wrenched in protest as the boy slipped out of her grip. She clutched at him desperately, barely catching his shirt.

He stayed quiet as they dangled there, his back to her as he stared at the very long drop beneath them, only the thin fabric of his shirt standing between it and him.

"Don't move," Kira told him. "Don't breathe."

He remained very still, the only sign he'd heard and understood.

Kira looked around, noting their position. The edge of the platform was nearly a meter above them. Looked like swinging him to safety was out.

A small, white-blond head appeared above them, the little girl peering down with eyes of the deepest blue.

Kira gave her a small, reassuring smile—at least one thing had gone right.

"Jin, I could use a little help," Kira said, her voice utterly calm, no hint of stress in it.

"Of course, you can, but I'm a little busy right now," he said. "Someone has to push this thing to where it won't endanger the station or human lives."

"You gonna be done soon?"

"A few minutes." There was a brief crackle of silence. "Are you in immediate danger?"

"Not immediate," Kira said. At least not yet.

She didn't bother explaining her predicament. If Jin had taken it upon himself to redirect the sailboat, it meant it carried the potential to cause significant harm to the station, resulting in a high loss of life. She knew he'd drop what he was doing if he got one whiff of how dire her situation was. To him, their friendship trumped everything else. She couldn't risk so many others paying the price.

She hung there, sifting through different scenarios and discarding them all. Alone, she could have escaped this situation pretty easily. The boy complicated matters. Dropping him wasn't an option either.

She shifted her grip on the boy, bringing him closer and wrapping her legs around him. The pipe creaked above her, giving a small bit.

The boy bobbed, his shirt tearing slightly. Only her legs and luck

CHAPTER TWO

kept him from falling.

Kira's pulse pounded, adrenaline flooding her system. It had been a long time since she felt like this. Like she was balancing on a precarious wire and the one thing keeping her from falling was her peculiar set of skills and dumb luck.

The boy clutched at her thigh but otherwise didn't make a sound. He didn't move. For someone so young, he was incredibly poised.

Shouts and the sound of people running came from above. Kira craned her neck as the girl was jerked away from the edge and several men peered over it.

Relief leaped in her as the pipe in her hand bent a little more.

"Down here," she called.

The men rearranged themselves, two disappearing as the other wormed his way over the edge. Kira caught a glimpse of movement and then hands as the other men lowered their friend.

She was afraid to move as he shifted closer, reaching his hand out to the boy she still clasped between her legs.

The pipe bent a little further.

"Give me your hand," Kira told the boy. "Reach up and back."

He did as she instructed. She strained as she reached for him, her fingers barely touching his. She yanked him up, letting go and catching him before he could fall.

The man above them shouted in the same strange language the boy had used on the craft, the urgency and fear in it unmistakable.

Kira took a breath, the boy's hand secure in hers.

"I'm going to toss you up to him," she told him.

He nodded once, the only sign of his terror his rapid gasps and wide eyes.

She craned her head to see the man. "Ready?"

He stared at her, his gaze narrowed and searching, before he grunted. Kira would take that as a yes.

This would need to be quick. The pipe was seconds and one forceful movement from snapping.

She closed her eyes and breathed out. Now.

Her grip changed as she jackknifed, using every ounce of strength and leverage to swing the boy up to his companion.

The pipe snapped as she completed the swing and let go of the boy. She dropped. The man grabbed the boy, his gaze going from his to hers as she fell.

Well. At least she'd managed to save the boy.

"You selfish, insufferable woman. I can't believe you," Jin snarled.

Kira didn't answer as gravity pulled her down.

"I'm right under you. Brace and don't screw this up," Jin called.

Kira steadied herself as best she could, keeping her body loose.

Jin zipped past and into her hood, the material wrapping around him as he slowed her descent, the pull of the material against her neck and shoulders nearly strangling her.

Somehow the hoodie held as Kira thrashed to find a more comfortable position, one that didn't leave her feeling like she was about to die of asphyxiation.

She didn't get a chance to protest as they started to ascend back toward the platform she'd fallen from, Jin muttering deprecations against her intelligence the entire time.

"Why didn't you tell me how much danger you were in?"

"You had more important things to worry about."

They cleared the edge of the platform. Jin set her down on it, shooting out from her hood to turn a baleful eye on her.

She ignored him, grabbing her hood and pulling it up over her hair. The precaution was probably pointless, but the comforting action helped to quell some of the remaining adrenaline turning her system into a cocktail of chemicals.

Kira ignored Jin's snarl as she took in the rest of those on the platform. Several people had gathered in a circle around the two children, talking furiously. It sounded like they were in the midst of an argument, but she wasn't sure. They broke off mid-sentence at her arrival, their expressions shocked.

CHAPTER TWO

Under the hood, her lips quirked. Somehow, surprising people never got old.

Jin rose to hover near her shoulder as the men assembled themselves protectively in front of the children, facing her with granite-hard expressions.

One of the men barked a command in his language, his tone strident. It was clear he expected compliance.

"You know what he's saying?" Kira asked Jin softly, not taking her attention from the men. The air crackled with danger, the tension thick and cloying.

Three more people ran onto the platform to join the handful who were already there.

"No, but that's synth armor they're wearing."

Jin didn't have to warn her to proceed with caution. There was only one race known for using that type of armor. It had a distinctive appearance and chemical makeup—not the type of thing Jin was likely to mistake.

Tiny ridges ran along the different interlinking plates. The armor molded over their powerful physiques, making their already muscular bodies even more intimidating. They practically screamed threat.

This version was a subdued copper with some type of symbol stamped on the front.

"They're wizards?" she asked, feeling a small curiosity despite the dangerous turn the situation had taken.

"Wizard is the derogatory term," Jin lectured. "They prefer to be called Tuann."

She'd never seen a wizard in person. Few people had.

They were a reclusive bunch and tended to keep to their corner of the galaxy, rarely leaving their territories. Most called them wizards due to persistent rumors comparing them to the myth of old. They were said to be capable of mysterious magic, possessing abilities that defied explanation. Kira didn't know how much she believed in the rumors and thought it was more likely their technology was simply more advanced than humanity's, giving the appearance of magic.

Whether they were capable of magic or not, didn't matter at the moment. Just the fact they were standing on this station meant they were probably on some type of diplomatic mission. Hurting them would be unwise and make staying unnoticed impossible.

"How long until station security gets here?" Kira murmured.

"Minutes."

She sighed. That wasn't good either. She'd prefer to be long gone before they arrived.

A torrent of words came from the man.

She made a tsking sound, irritation getting to her. "You'd think he'd realize I don't speak their language by now."

"They are acting strangely, considering you saved the children," Jin agreed, sounding distracted.

"They're asking what House you serve," a youthful voice sounded nearby. The boy shrugged off his protector when the man tried to hush him, his gaze resolutely glued to Kira.

Kira was silent as she studied him. Now they were getting somewhere.

"I don't know what you're talking about," she finally said.

"We want your affiliation, *aza*." This came from the first man who'd spoken.

Ah. He probably wanted to confirm she wasn't a threat to the children.

"No affiliation. I'm a salvager," Kira said.

She recognized him. He was the one who'd leaned over the platform to rescue the boy. Despite the fact he was the one acting as the group's voice, she doubted he was in charge.

No, that was the man standing next to the boy, his clear gaze on hers. He was older and more experienced than the rest, although Kira couldn't pinpoint what about him made her think that.

All of the people before her appeared around the same age. They were similar looking, taller than the average human, with the same white blondish hair of the boy and girl. The one with dark hair was the man in charge.

Their features were fierce but beautiful, each a work of art in their own way. They were heavily muscled and tall, more so than most humans.

These were warriors of some kind. Guards, Kira thought. Of the little boy and girl? What sort of children required an escort of eight?

The speaker glanced at the one in charge. They exchanged a weighted look.

Kira waited. The men stood between her and her way off this platform. While she didn't think they really meant her any harm, it paid to be careful in her line of work. That same mentality bled into the rest of her life as well.

A gust of wind from a passing craft yanked her hood off. She grimaced but didn't fuss with it, her entire focus locked on the children and their guards.

The speaker stepped up. "It seems we must thank you for the safety of the children."

Kira didn't respond. She didn't need or want thanks. She'd only done what was necessary.

He held his hand out, his expression thawing, so he seemed almost bashfully friendly. "We're sorry for our suspicion. It is a job hazard as humans would say."

Kira could understand that. She faced similar reactions herself, sometimes acting before her brain had caught up with her body, even so many years after the life that had built the muscle memory.

She raised her hand to shake his.

His gaze dropped, the smile on his face freezing. He grabbed her arm and yanked.

She reacted without thought, turning her shoulder into him and kicking out with one leg as she grabbed his shoulder and jerked him to her. She used her hip as leverage to throw him as she twisted her hand out of his grasp.

He stumbled forward with a sharp cry.

"Kira!" Jin warned.

Kira grunted, grabbing the collar of the man's armor before he could pitch over the edge.

The guards who had started rushing her slid to a sharp stop at a shout from their leader.

Kira didn't take her eyes off them as she kept the other man suspended in the air, only his feet touching the platform and her grip keeping him from plunging over the edge.

The moment stretched out as Kira considered the warriors in front of her. They waited, their gazes going from her to their comrade. They seemed torn, wanting to hurt her but also not wanting her to drop their ally.

Every one of them had their hand at their hip and seemed poised to attack. Her eyes narrowed. The station didn't allow projectile weapons on it, but she was willing to bet they had some type of blade style weapon hidden in their armor.

Of course, they did. They wouldn't be very good guards if they couldn't protect their charges.

Another craft raced past them, the force of its passage stirring the air. Kira didn't flinch, her gaze locked on her enemy.

This was quite the stalemate she'd landed in. She couldn't let her attacker fall, else his companions would be on her before she'd taken two steps. She couldn't pull him from the edge either for the same reason.

What to do?

This right here, was why she never liked coming to O'Riley Station. It was always something.

There was a clamor as men and women wearing the distinctive uniforms of station security—blue and black, with their ranks emblazoned on their sleeves in gold—assembled along the platform, laser rifles pointed at all those present.

CHAPTER TWO

"Now they show up," Jin muttered, echoing Kira's thoughts.

"Can we go over the edge?"

"No, my reserves are too low after saving you."

She gave him a sidelong look.

"I didn't say you were heavy," he defended.

No, he'd just insinuated it.

A man in the station's uniform stepped forward, shadowed by his aide, a woman who looked calm and efficient. Recognition flashed across his face at the sight of Kira.

"Captain Forrest, it's been a long time," he said.

CHAPTER THREE

Kira remained motionless as she studied the people in front of her, the rest of the station noise fading into the background. A hand grasped her sleeve and pulled it slowly up. She gave the man she held a no-nonsense stare as he pushed the sleeve up even further to peer at her forearm.

Brave move from someone whose life she quite literally held in her hands.

Then again, maybe he had a reason for his bravery. Kira might have figured out a way to escape his people, but station security? Unlikely. Not when they controlled every feed on the station. There must be hundreds of cameras between her and her ship. Making it back undetected was impossible.

Kira sighed. She yanked the speaker up, dumping him on the ground at her feet. She might as well save her strength, none of them were going anywhere now.

"Spitzy, I'd kind of hoped to never see you again," she said.

His smile was brief and failed to reach his eyes. "I'm sure you did."

He didn't wait for her to respond, his attention shifting to the others. "Commander Liont, what seems to be the problem here?"

The man Kira had pegged as their leader glanced at Spitzy, his face an expressionless mask.

Spitzy waited a long moment. When no answer was forthcoming, he sighed. "Alright, how about all of you accompany us while we get this sorted out?"

It was not a request.

CHAPTER THREE

Liont made a sharp gesture at his men. Their tense postures relaxed as they straightened, the threat they'd presented downgrading from serious to simply alert. They stood down as station security assumed command.

Spitzy lifted his eyebrows at Kira. "You too, Captain."

She had no choice but to comply. Those laser rifles might not puncture the space station's metal hull, but they would do considerable damage to living flesh.

"In and out, my ass," she told Jin as she sidestepped the man she'd dumped at her feet and moved toward Spitzy.

"This isn't my fault. No one told you to perform feats of heroism. You did that all on your own," Jin griped as he trailed her.

Spitzy pulled out a pair of laser cuffs and held them up.

"You're kidding, right?" Kira asked.

His smile was gloating. "Nope."

The woman behind him looked discomforted at the sight of the cuffs, giving Kira an apologetic frown. She was young, younger than Spitzy and had the fresh polish of someone who wasn't more than a few years out of the academy. Her uniform was perfectly pressed with her hair pulled away from her face. She was the poster child for the space force's regulation on personal appearance. Seeing a commander being so petty must have sat ill if her expression was anything to judge by.

"Someone's on a power trip," Jin muttered.

He had that right.

"It's for the safety of my men," Spitzy said, not looking the least bit chagrined at the judgment. No, he was enjoying this—immensely. "You do have a history of violence."

Kira narrowed her eyes and held in what she wanted to say. It would make her situation worse.

The woman came near, saying softly, "Everyone will wear them."

Kira looked over her shoulder. Sure enough, Spitzy's men were putting similar cuffs on the wizards.

"The children too, Spitzy? Really?" Kira shook her head at him in mock disappointment.

His smile disappeared to be replaced by a clenched jaw. "They're wizards. Every one of them is dangerous."

And there was the Spitzy she remembered—the xenophobic asshole convinced anything not human was to be treated with extreme caution and fear.

"I'm sure their people will remember this," Kira said.

Given the dark look on the faces of the children's guards, she had no doubt of that fact. They'd submitted, but the moment Spitzy's men approached the children, every single one of them went on the alert. They looked seconds from violence, especially when the girl started crying again.

"What do you care?" Spitzy said, his words nearly a snarl. "You left, remember?"

Kira gritted her teeth but didn't respond, holding the other man's gaze while burying the sting from his barb.

"She's right," the woman said to him. "Surely restraining the children is unnecessary. Diplomatically speaking, it would be best to treat them as we would any human child."

Spitzy's face darkened at the unvoiced rebuke in her words. Kira was impressed despite herself. Telling your superior he was wrong without actually saying it took skill and guts.

She was either very stupid or had a conscience. The two weren't mutually exclusive. Though they were a rare combination in the military.

"Fine," Spitzy bit out.

The woman released her breath and made a gesture at the man currently trying to coax the little girl to don the cuffs. He retreated with a look of relief. He hadn't been any happier to obey his orders than the woman.

Kira shook her head but held her hands out, letting Spitzy place the cuffs on her.

CHAPTER THREE

"Have J1N power off," he said, stepping back as one of his people took her elbow.

Kira didn't move. "You know I'm not going to do that."

"The unit can either power down voluntarily, or one of my men will shoot J1N with an EMP net," he said with a shark's smile.

Kira didn't move, staring him down. Temptation coursed through her.

"It's fine, Kira," Jin said. "Just get this cleared up so we can be on our way."

Jin floated to the ground, his lights darkening one by one, as he powered himself off. Her friend disappeared, leaving nothing but a hunk of metal in his place.

A woman pointed a device at Jin and nodded. "The drone is off."

"Good," Spitzy said as she picked him up.

"Ensign Waverly, please escort our guests to the containment room."

His aide gave a sharp nod before barking several orders.

"It's good to know you haven't changed a bit in all these years," Kira said sweetly. Her dark smile was anything but nice as she was led off.

* * *

The need for patience had been beaten into Kira at a young age. It was why she didn't particularly mind sitting in a small room on a metal chair, her friend a blind, silent presence on a table behind her.

To the casual observer, she would look like she was sleeping–body slumped, her chin on her arm, her other hand a few inches from the clear forcefield bisecting the room and separating the wizards from her. They'd miss her alert gaze, her eyes hidden by her hood which allowed her to study the people responsible for this whole mess without being seen.

The wizards' leader stared at her from his side of the table, an intent look on his face as if he were trying to figure her out.

What could be seen of her face remained still, even as amusement filtered through her.

These men weren't your average guards. They were soldiers. She'd bet her life on it. She recognized the type from her own years in service to the human space force during the war with the Tsavitee.

They were a unit, anticipating orders not yet voiced. They moved like a well-oiled machine, indicating a long history with one another. She wondered what they were doing posing as guards for children.

Not that it really mattered. Not anymore. She'd left that part of her life far behind her, and she didn't intend to pick it up again.

The door to the room slammed open, drawing the attention of everyone except the leader whose gaze never lifted from hers.

Hm. So they didn't see Spitzy or any of his men as a true threat.

It was understandable, really. While Kira had spent several minutes being patted down, every item on her person confiscated for fear she might use them for some unknown purpose, the station's security had barely touched the wizards, giving them a cursory examination, which failed to uncover the blades Kira was sure were stored in their armor. She suspected they weren't the only weapons these men had.

She had to wonder how many other things security had missed.

Spitzy sauntered toward Kira, his heavy steps making him easy to track despite the fact she couldn't see him with her hood limiting her peripheral vision.

"I want to know what you were doing on that craft."

Kira held her silence.

The man in front of her finally looked away, staring at Spitzy with a glimmer of curiosity. So, the forcefield didn't block sound. That or the man could read lips. Which meant he probably understood at least a little of human standard.

Good to know.

Spitzy nudged her shoulder. "Do you hear me?"

The wizard's leader frowned, the look in his eyes turning turbulent.

"You have the station's feeds," Kira said blandly. "Watch them.

CHAPTER THREE

They'll tell you everything you need to know."

Spitzy was silent a moment, his anger sizzling through the air. "I could do that, but why waste my time?"

Kira's sigh was weary. She longed for the quiet peace of her ship. Dealing with hardheaded idiots had never been her idea of fun. Less so, since she'd spent the past few years around a very small number of people besides Jin. She could count on one hand the number of conversations she'd had outside the *Wanderer*.

"We both know you don't have anything to hold me on."

He snorted. "Who's to say. Maybe the feeds all went haywire during the time in question."

The wizard's forehead wrinkled, a frown crossing his face as thunder gathered in his eyes. The expressions on the rest turned slightly disgusted.

Kira almost felt sorry for Spitzy. If he wasn't on such a power trip, she might be tempted to clue him into the fact he was dangerously close to creating an intergalactic diplomatic incident his superiors wouldn't thank him for. If he continued in this vein, he'd be lucky getting a job as a convoy escort.

The faint sound of running came from outside, then the door slammed open letting in a babble of voices. For a brief second, a tall man with dark hair stood silhouetted in its frame, Spitzy's aide behind him, an expression of relief on her face.

Spitzy snapped to attention. "Sir, what are you doing here?"

The man's gaze had been locked on Kira's bent head, but at that, his focus shifted to Spitzy. There was fire in his eyes as he said in a tight voice, "Commander Spatz, I assume you received the memo passed to every person on this station dictating any incidents involving the Tuann were to be forwarded to my team."

Spitzy didn't move, his expression chilling. "I did."

"Then, is there a reason several of their delegation are sitting in a detention room? Furthermore, why have they been separated from the two children under their care?" The man's voice was excruciatingly polite as he verbally dressed down Spitzy.

Kira couldn't help the smallest bit of amusement.

"Sir, I have a duty to protect those on this station. I felt it best to investigate the incident to ascertain there was no further threat," Spitzy said stiffly.

"And did you bother to review the feeds of what happened?" the man asked, sounding annoyingly reasonable despite the bite in his tone.

Spitzy held quiet, not knowing which answer would damn him more.

"If you had, you would have already cleared everyone of any charges," the man said through clenched teeth.

"Sir," Spitzy started.

"Dismissed."

Spitzy didn't move.

"Was I not clear?" the man said, a snap in his voice. "Dismissed."

"This is my case," Spitzy started.

"Out," the man roared.

Spitzy held in what he had been about to say, giving Kira a fulminating glare before exiting the room.

The door slid shut behind him.

Kira remained still for a moment, studying the newcomer as he did the same to her. She sighed. She'd hoped to avoid this, but it seemed wishes and hopes were not to be. She slowly sat back, pushing her hood away from her face before bracing one elbow on the chair as she made herself comfortable, her body relaxed and pliant as she sprawled in the chair.

"It's true," the man said, his gaze roving over her face.

"It's been a long time, Jace," she said with a smile that was closer to a grimace.

Jace was quiet, his expression blank, his thoughts hidden.

"I see you've been promoted," she said, noting the rear admiral bars on his shoulder and chest. He'd been a captain the last time they'd

CHAPTER THREE

seen each other

He didn't respond for so long that Kira shifted uncomfortably. He touched his hand to the force field. It turned opaque, shielding them from the Tuann's prying gazes.

Kira tapped it. No response.

She assumed the change would block auditory as well as visual. Stupid of Spitzy not to have activated it as soon as he entered.

"That's all you have to say to me after all this time?" he asked in a carefully controlled voice.

Kira held silent, not knowing what response would be best.

"Twelve years and six months since you disappeared on me," he continued. "Not one word to let me know you were alive and not one of the countless casualties from the Falling."

Kira swallowed the lump in her throat, struggling to keep her eyes on his, guilt and regret making her want to slink away.

The Jace she remembered hadn't been capable of such restraint. He would have raged and thrown things, his temper a seething tempest before it inevitably blew itself out.

This man was different. But twelve years had a way of changing people.

"The war has been over for nine years. Where have you been all this time?"

She shrugged. "Here and there."

He nodded, the slight ticking at his jaw revealing his emotions.

He touched the force field again, turning it clear. "O'Riley Station thanks you for your quick and decisive actions. Your intervention undoubtedly saved the lives of those children and countless others."

The words were said by rote, as if part of a formal statement he'd memorized.

He stepped aside and gestured at the door. "We apologize for any inconvenience this experience has caused you."

Kira was slow in lifting herself out of her seat. That was it? She'd expected more.

The Tuann leader straightened, confusion on his and his people's faces.

Kira didn't look back as she made her way to the door.

"Kira."

She paused and turned her head toward him.

He jerked his chin at Jin lying inert on the table. "Aren't you forgetting something?"

Right.

"Come on, Jin."

Jin booted up and lifted from the table, showing no signs of being the worse for wear from being in a device designed to make it impossible for him to power himself on.

Jace didn't seem particularly surprised at the feat. But then again, he wouldn't be, given his history with the two of them.

Kira walked to the door and waited for Jace to open it. There was a long pause where she thought he'd changed his mind about letting them go.

"Don't even think of leaving the station," he said as the door slid open.

Whatever response she'd planned was forestalled as she found her way blocked by a mountain. Her words died in her throat as her head tilted, surprise preventing her from retreating from the dangerous creature in front of her.

A pair of irritated, stormy gray eyes stared at her from a face chiseled from granite. A thin slash of a mouth was the one hint of displeasure in the man's expression.

His dark hair hung loose, complementing his stubborn jaw and the sharp angles of his features. He had an athletic body, long, but built like a tank from what she could see in his synth armor.

His and Kira's gazes locked. She caught her breath at the raw charisma oozing out of every pore. This was a man used to giving orders and having them obeyed. He was a force of nature given form, implacable and demanding.

CHAPTER THREE

He had the same ageless quality as the guard's captain, but in him, it was magnified. He was power and fury, an oppressive weight lingering in his gaze as he frowned down at Kira.

She remained motionless, tempted to back down and clear the way for him. She resisted, something inside refusing to bow.

She waited, her expression unyielding as he lingered in the doorway. She wasn't going to be the first to move.

Finally, something in him relented, and he stepped aside.

She stepped out, brushing past him, her senses heightened like she'd danced along death's dagger and barely escaped with her life.

She almost froze again at the sight of five more like him crowding the hallway. Only Jace calling out to the stranger made her come unstuck.

She marched toward the desk and Ensign Waverly.

"I suppose I have you to thank for the timely interruption," Kira said mildly.

The woman's startle was barely perceptible. "I did as was required by my standing orders."

Kira's lips quirked. "Thank you, nonetheless."

Waverly's chin dipped. "You're welcome, Captain."

* * *

Graydon watched the woman stalk away. He glanced at one of his men. "Follow her."

Baran nodded and stepped away from the wall, Amila following, as they trailed the strange woman.

The rest of his warriors watched him with curiosity, their eyes alive with questions they wouldn't ask in the presence of these humans.

Graydon stepped into the small interrogation room. He grimaced at the space, instantly feeling a sense of claustrophobia. He didn't know how humans could stand such small spaces. It made him feel like he was in a metal box in danger of crushing him.

He put the strange woman and her fierce expression out of his mind. Not an easy task. Something about her warned him she would one day be important to him. At home, you could sometimes feel the coming of a storm when there wasn't a cloud in the sky. He got the same feeling when he looked at her.

Sometimes storms revealed hidden treasures, wiping away the old rot and replacing it with something stronger. Other times they washed everything away, leaving nothing in their wake but devastation.

He couldn't guess which type of storm this woman would bring, but he'd learned to trust his senses. If they indicated she was important, he'd listen.

Not many challenged him so blatantly. Odd to find someone capable of the feat here among the frustrating humans.

He scowled as irritation bit at him for the reminder. He clasped his hands behind him, well aware of how intimidating he would seem to the human and the other Tuann.

"Lord Graydon, I apologize for having to call you in for this matter," the human said, his voice scrupulously polite.

"Why have you?"

Graydon was a busy man. He didn't enjoy having his time wasted on petty matters.

The human grimaced. "I think it's better if I show you."

Graydon said nothing as the human bent to fuss with a device.

He glanced at the other Tuann, his expression severe. A few lowered their chins in unvoiced apology.

Why would they call attention to themselves in this way? While they weren't under his command, Liont had impressed him with his level-headedness, a necessary trait given what he and his people had recently faced.

A holovid started on one of the screens embedded into the walls of the small room. At first, Graydon didn't know what he was supposed to be looking at. The video stream was of the beehive, the small boats

CHAPTER THREE

moving from terrace to terrace.

Suddenly, there was an explosion on one of those sailboats, parts of it catching on fire as it began to lose altitude.

Graydon glanced at the others again.

They shifted. All of them were disciplined, showing few emotions, but Graydon caught the smallest slump of their shoulders indicating shame.

On the screen, the woman with the intense stare appeared. She bounded off her terrace and onto the sailboat. She disappeared into the cabin only to reappear seconds later carrying Ziva, Joule trailing her.

Graydon focused on Liont. "Explain."

The human paused the holovid.

"Ziva wanted to ride on the slow boat," Liont started. "Joule humored her."

Graydon reached for patience, knowing the other man wouldn't have started here if it wasn't important.

"Several of us stayed behind to haggle with the human owner of the slow boat." Liont spoke in human standard for the human's benefit. "Other humans began to act aggressively toward us. We were trying to calm them while Vera accompanied the children onto the slow boat. It exploded minutes later."

Grief touched Liont's face. Vera hadn't made it off.

Graydon bowed his head as a sign of sympathy. Liont and the rest had lost much recently. Any death hurt, but this one would burn given what they'd survived.

"Was it a distraction?" Graydon asked, switching to Tuann.

Liont hesitated. "It is hard to say. You know how these humans are."

Graydon's lips tightened. Yes, he did. They were a brash race intent on challenging those stronger than themselves. It made them difficult to deal with at times. They charged when they should run, and ran when they needed to hold their ground.

The human's expression turned thoughtful. "I'll have my people round up those who interfered with your duties. It's probably nothing, but there has been some anti-Tuann sentiment lately."

Graydon's stare was contemplative as he studied the human. The man was more observant than most of his kind to have picked up on the nuances of Liont's story so easily.

"What is your name?" Graydon asked.

Surprise appeared on the man's face. "Jace. Rear Admiral Jace Skarsdale."

Graydon inclined his head. He'd remember that name.

The holovid began playing again, showing the woman kneeling at the boat's railing, her dropping Ziva over the side, then her grabbing up Joule and sprinting for the other side of the boat before jumping.

Graydon watched the holovid all the way up to the arrest of all those on the platform.

Skarsdale stopped the recording and faced Graydon. "As you can see, the woman acted in good faith. If she hadn't intervened, the two children would have likely died."

Graydon's jaw was clenched tight.

"She is marked," Fari said into the silence.

Graydon regarded him, his bland expression not revealing any of his thoughts as he waited for Liont's second to continue. The man was young, but he showed the potential to be a great warrior one day.

"I saw the glyph on her wrist. She must have thought I was attacking her when I tried to get a closer look." Shame reflected in Fari's eyes. "It wasn't my intent to cause her alarm."

"What House?" Graydon asked.

"Luatha," Fari said.

Graydon and Liont shared a long look.

"Strange Luatha would show up here after the attack on your House," Graydon said.

Liont's House, Maxiim, had been attacked by an unknown enemy,

CHAPTER THREE

the majority of it destroyed. Only a few had survived, including Liont and his men. Joule and Ziva were the sole young left alive, the future of their House if Joule could reach his potential in time.

That someone bearing Luatha's mark appeared, as they stopped in to replenish supplies on their way through the system, was a coincidence that defied belief.

"I apologize for the arrest of your people, Lord Graydon. As you can see, it was a misunderstanding," Skarsdale was saying.

"Your people have violated the treaty," Graydon said, his words having the effect of a bomb.

Skarsdale's expression froze, his gaze turning cool and analytical as he studied Graydon. "I'm not sure I understand."

"The woman who was in here. Tell me everything you know about her," Graydon said, ignoring his statement.

Skarsdale paused, his gaze intent. "I can't do that."

"You will or I will have this station destroyed."

Both men knew the Tuann were capable of it.

To his surprise, Skarsdale didn't immediately submit. "As I said, I can't do that. The Consortium has a policy about sharing information about its citizens, especially when they've served in a military capacity."

Stubborn. Just like the rest of his race.

Graydon flicked his fingers at the rest.

Liont and his people stood, stepping through the barrier easily. En-blades appeared in their hands as they arranged themselves protectively around Graydon.

Skarsdale didn't blink, as if the sight of the Tuann stepping through his security barrier wasn't a concern. Graydon began moving to the door. If Skarsdale wouldn't tell him what he wanted to know, he'd find out the information for himself.

"Lord Graydon, wait."

Skarsdale was interrupted as the door to the interrogation room slid open and humans entered, blades at the ready.

Skarsdale held up a hand, palm facing out. "Don't interfere."

The humans hesitated, backing out slowly, gazes locked on the exposed en-blades.

Skarsdale focused on Graydon. "Why do you want to know about her?"

"She's Tuann," Graydon said, his words short and brusque.

Skarsdale's expression remained fixed and remote, no sign of any reaction to that statement. Graydon couldn't help but be impressed at his composure. It was worthy of a Tuann. Perhaps their race wasn't quite so useless after all.

Not that it mattered. If the humans had broken the alliance, they would pay. Their treaty mapped out what was to be done when one of theirs strayed so far. They were to be returned to their people. The Tuann were protective of their own, and they didn't trust the humans to deal appropriately with their kind.

Not when the humans experimented on their own young, bioengineering unborn children for the purposes of war. They'd have no compunction about doing the same to another race's children. If they got their hands on the Tuann's unique set of abilities, there would be chaos in the galaxy.

The treaty might have put a stop to the practice of bioengineering super soldiers, but humans held the potential and desire to pursue the science. If they were caught mapping a Tuann genome or doing any tinkering with one of his, they would pay dearly.

Skarsdale's forehead furrowed. "I've known Captain Kira Forrest for many years. Long before first contact with the Tuann. She's not one of yours."

"No mistake. She bears our mark. She is Tuann." Graydon wasn't in the habit of having to repeat himself. He wouldn't do so again.

Liont leaned forward. "She did identify herself as a salvager when asked about her affiliations, and she didn't appear to understand our language.

Skarsdale's gaze flickered. Graydon's eyes narrowed, something in

CHAPTER THREE

the man's manner triggering his instincts.

"Why do you react to that?" he asked.

Skarsdale hesitated, before meeting Graydon's gaze stubbornly. "Captain Forrest dropped out of view after the war. I wasn't aware of her current employment."

The words could be true, but something told Graydon there was more to it.

"She is Tuann," Fari insisted. "I saw the glyph. A human couldn't have done what she did."

Recognition flared in Skarsdale's eyes, quickly hidden.

"You know what he's speaking of." The words were a statement.

Skarsdale's mouth tightened. "She's had that mark for as long as I've known her."

The tight feeling in Graydon's chest loosened. The human was telling the truth. If that was the case, it was possible they hadn't knowingly violated the treaty.

He needed to learn everything he could about the woman and her purpose here.

"You may have not known before, but you do now. I want everything you have on her."

Skarsdale straightened, his expression polite but resolute. "As I've told you, it's against our policy to share information about former servicemembers. It's for their protection, as well as that of our space force."

Graydon's smile showed his teeth. There was little warmth in it.

His chuckle filled the air, raspy and containing little humor. It was the sound a dragon made when eyeing its dinner. The prey's struggle for survival might be entertaining, but ultimately it would fail.

"Your rules do not apply here. She is Tuann." Because the other man seemed smarter than many of his race, Graydon offered him some advice. "You should walk gently right now. The treaty hangs on what you do next."

Jace's expression closed as Graydon delivered his threat.

"What would you do with Captain Forrest if, as you say, she is Tuann?" he asked.

"She would be taken home to her people."

"And if she doesn't want to go?"

"She is Tuann. She will go." Graydon's order was definite.

Jace ran a hand through his hair, frustration and a hint of amusement in his expression. "You really don't know her if you think that kind of logic will work on her."

Graydon's eyes narrowed. "Her desires do not matter."

Jace sighed. "I'll let you explain that to her."

Graydon's eyebrows contracted with the faintest signs of confusion.

Skarsdale straightened, drawing himself up as he spoke formally, "You've presented no evidence of her status as Tuann. This glyph could very well be a tattoo."

"It's the mark of a powerful House," Liont argued.

Skarsdale spread his hands. "So you say, but as impossible as it may seem, my statement stands." He turned to Graydon. "Do you have any evidence to support your claim? A blood test perhaps?"

Skarsdale waited with a patient expression. He knew the insult his words had caused.

The door slid open, and a woman appeared.

"What is it, Ensign Waverly?" Skarsdale asked with undisguised irritation.

"There is a message for you from Admiral Himoto," she said, her tone crisp.

He gestured sharply. She handed him a tablet.

He read the message, then shook his head before giving the tablet to the woman.

Skarsdale's gaze was wintry when he met Graydon's eyes. "I've been instructed by my superiors to comply with your demands and arrange for you to speak with Kira."

Graydon's nod was gruff. Finally, someone showed sense.

CHAPTER THREE

"I'll have her picked up," Skarsdale continued.

"Don't bother. My people have been trailing her since she left. They will bring her to me," Graydon dictated.

The man's expression filled with alarm. "That's a bad idea. She's highly paranoid and won't react well to strangers."

Graydon's chuckle held a note of darkness. "My men are elite warriors. I'm sure they can handle one young *azala*."

"That means child, right?" Jace asked. He didn't wait for Graydon's response. "I wouldn't treat Captain Forrest as a child. It'll go badly for you."

Graydon ignored him, already gesturing for his people to prepare to move. "Take us to the children now."

Graydon didn't wait for an answer, already heading for the door, Skarsdale yapping at him the entire time.

His first snapped to attention at the sight of Graydon. "Problems?"

Graydon shook his head. "Tell Baran and Amila to intercept the woman."

His first nodded, sparing a glance for the frustrated rear admiral. Solal spoke subvocally into the auditory implant all his people carried.

Graydon fixed Skarsdale with a long stare. "I will be taken to the children now."

The man sighed, knowing he'd already lost the advantage. "This way."

CHAPTER FOUR

Kira cut through the crowd, her steps unhurried as she ignored the clamor of her surroundings.

"How many do you see?" she asked Jin.

"Besides the two wizards? I count four wearing the station's uniform."

Irritation crossed Kira's face as she stomped along the terrace. Being shadowed by one group was bad enough, but two? She wasn't liking the odds.

The station personnel were at least being subtle about it, not making their presence too obvious. The wizards, on the other hand, didn't bother making an effort to blend in and remain unseen. It was like they were practically daring her to do something about it.

"You sure?"

"Yup. They're keeping their distance, but we've had a tail from the moment we left the detainment sublevel."

His assessment fit with Kira's. She'd made a point of moving aimlessly through the station, meandering in a circuitous route as she debated her next decision.

She hesitated to head toward Vander's until she knew more about why she was being followed and what they intended. It'd be too easy to be ambushed there. At least here, there were a dozen escape routes.

"You head to one of the comm cafes and I'll get what we need," Jin said.

Kira hesitated. She didn't like the idea of splitting up.

CHAPTER FOUR

"It'll be fine," Jin assured her. "You still have to contact your little friend to hand off the data you recovered from the Tsavitee ship."

"We could sit on the data. Wait until a better time presents itself," Kira offered, knowing she hated that idea.

Jin made a rude noise. "Absolutely not. We didn't go through all this just to keep it to ourselves."

Jin didn't wait for her to argue, sinking until he hovered inches off the ground before arrowing away. He wove between the crowd's feet as he headed toward the lift, no one the wiser.

This wasn't the first time they'd used such a tactic. People tended to notice Kira, but they always forgot about Jin. It allowed him to get away with things Kira never could.

Kira gritted her teeth but didn't follow, knowing their tail would be more focused on her. Hopefully, the distraction would give Jin enough time to purchase the part and get it to the ship before anyone realized he was gone.

She wasn't really worried about the wizards taking notice of his absence. They'd assume Jin was a normal AI, smart but ultimately unable to operate without direction. But the humans—Spitzy in particular—would be suspicious. They knew what he was capable of, knew his reputation and history. He was as dangerous as Kira. More so in some ways.

Kira looped around the terrace, walking with no apparent destination in mind. She stopped at small shops along the way, pretending to browse the merchant's wares before moving on. Most of it was junk, the type of thing meant for the souvenir-happy tourists.

A line of children on a tour followed their guide like little ducks as she explained the history of the station, pointing to the different reference points. Kira followed for a short time, smiling at the children's antics before eventually leaving them behind when they stopped to take photos in front of one of the monuments to those soldiers who didn't return.

After that, she flitted from stall to shop and back again, never staying anywhere long, never letting her guard drop.

To most, she would appear to be sightseeing, interested in watching the gondolas and hovercraft as they flitted from terrace to terrace.

In reality, she took the opportunity to keep an eye on her tails, using every small reflection to watch the people watching her.

The humans' motivations were easy to guess, but the wizards' interest was a mystery. One she couldn't yet solve. She had a habit of destroying the things she couldn't understand.

Nothing good ever came of someone with unclear motives stalking her. She itched to be off the station and far from them.

She'd done her time in the trenches. This was her retirement, and she refused to get drawn into whatever this was.

If O'Riley wasn't the only station in this sector with the parts she needed, she never would have stepped foot on it again. The station was like a curse. Every time she visited, it brought nothing but upheaval to her life.

Not this time. This time was going to be different. Even if she had to trample a few obstacles in the shape of people to do it.

She checked her watch. Had enough time passed for Jin to have ordered the part they needed? If she finished her business too early, they risked being stuck on the ship while station security made it impossible to leave.

She waited five more minutes before heading to the lift and taking it two levels down.

She chose one of the cafes with an outdoor space, wanting to sit at a table with a view of the terrace and atrium. The cafe was small, a charming cross between the little eateries of old Europe and the internet cafes of the late twentieth century. A bit of old-world flare mixed with the efficiency and comfort of the modern era.

This time of day in the station, the cafe was mostly empty. A blessing after the chaos of the terraces. A few people dotted the space, their heads bent as they sent or received messages from those off station.

CHAPTER FOUR

A common fixture on any station, the cafes were civilian owned but government sanctioned. They were necessary so the masses could keep in touch with family and friends when traveling.

Most ships weren't equipped to communicate over the distances needed to reach any of the colonies or stations dotted throughout human space. Their reach was limited, a solar system or two in most cases.

It was possible to upload your files to the broadband satellites from the ship when you stopped at any station, but transmission was slow and laborious. It could take a week or more, depending on the data load and whether a bigger fish paid for priority transmission.

That's where the cafes came in. For a fee, you could piggyback off the station's network, one usually kept in much better repair than the civilian side.

Normally, Kira would never pay the exorbitant rates, but the data package she needed to upload was large and it would take forever using the equipment on her ship. The content was also a bit sensitive and she didn't want to chance it being traced to the *Wanderer*. At least here, she had some anonymity.

Kira paused along the edge of the tables where they spilled out onto the terrace. The cafe was nice. Much nicer than some of the dives in the stations she frequented. Each table had a console and the waitstaff were all dressed in freshly pressed uniforms.

Kira took a seat and swiped the microchip embedded in her wrist over the payment scanner. Fifteen minutes ought to work.

The waiter was there as soon as she finished the transaction. "Can I interest you in any beverages or food today?"

"A chai tea would be great," Kira said.

The man gave her a friendly smile and walked away.

Alone again, Kira wasted no time logging into her account. When she first began this little endeavor, she'd learned quickly she was in over her head. Deciphering the Tsavitee's starmaps and ship logs were outside her skill base. She was decent at some hacking, but parsing information as complex as this and breaking the code they wrapped everything in? No. Not even Jin's considerable skills would have been up to the task.

That's where her friend came in—a hacker without equal, a genius among geniuses, someone the human government would kill to get their hands on if they knew of his existence.

Her friend had recognized how dangerous this task was and how committed Kira was to following it to its end. The need for secrecy was high. The starmaps and data logs from a Tsavitee ship were capable of shifting the power dynamic in the Consortium. More so, if they could decipher the Tsavitee's way of coding their information.

Their partnership consisted of each having a set of skills just as important as the other's. Kira salvaged what she could from the Tsavitee ships and when she saw something interesting, she'd find a way to drop the data package into a hidden cache on the galactic web. There, Odin would sift through the information, trying to break the code.

Until now, they'd been getting nowhere fast. Everything she found was fragmented, nearly useless, except as a reference point. The data logs from this last ship had been in near pristine condition. For the first time in a long time, she had hope Odin might actually be able to decipher it and she'd be one step closer to her goal.

The drop point this time, was in a chat room for fans of a little-known game. Most of the users uploaded fan art or fan fiction. Some good. Most not.

Kira wondered if these were real users or if Odin had created them as ghosts to give the site more legitimacy to any who might stumble on it.

She started the upload process and glanced around to see her shadows keeping their distance. Good.

The file was sixty percent uploaded when a chat box popped up.

Allfather: *You're being watched.*

Kira's fingers hovered over the keyboard as she paused.

CHAPTER FOUR

Nixxy: *I know. How do you?*
Allfather: *I know everything.*

Kira snorted. That wasn't arrogant or anything. Still, if Odin knew she was being watched, it meant her friend was close. Perhaps even on the station or taping into their feeds from a ship within the quadrant. The last should have been impossible, but she wouldn't put anything past him.

The file hit one hundred percent.

Allfather: *Oooh, you hit the motherload this time.*
Nixxy: *Can you use it?*
Allfather: *Maybe. This is a lot of data. I don't know if my setup can handle it. Without the proper tools, it could take me years to run the necessary algorithms.*

Kira tensed, frustration skating along her neck. That wasn't what she wanted to hear. The words felt like a blow, stealing Kira's hope.

She dropped her head and shook it before looking up. This had always been a long shot.

Allfather: *Be faster if we had access to Centcom's mainframe.*

Kira shook her head. Odin knew as well as she did that wasn't going to happen, and not just because of her history with Centcom. The moment Centcom got wind of what Kira and Odin had, they'd swoop in and snatch it from them—in the interest of galactic security, of course.

Any chance of finding the Tsavitee homeworlds would be gone. No finding and returning those taken by the tsavitee. Nothing. That information would disappear into a deep dark hole where only the highest levels of the military and government could access it.

She sat back, demoralized, as she looked around the cafe. Kira was one of the few using a console. It made her ridiculously easy to spot, but it also made keeping an eye on the wizards where they waited by a food vendor easier, given they weren't trying to blend in.

The man and woman watched Kira, their focus unwavering. Kira's gaze shifted away from them to where the station security watched them all from across the honeycomb.

She sighed. If she needed proof of why it would be a bad idea to get involved in Centcom affairs again, she only had to look out there.

Allfather: *The wizards' starmaps could speed things up too.*

Odin logged off immediately after, leaving Kira staring at a blank screen. That was unexpected. Her friend often spoke in vague terms, so she couldn't be sure, but it sounded an awful lot like he wanted her to infiltrate the wizards' ship, find their command center and make off with their starmaps.

Not going to happen. She didn't have a death wish, and she wanted to stay as far from the strangers as possible.

A frown on her face, she glanced up at the people in question. They stood in the same spot they'd been since she sat. Unexpectedly, the man's gaze caught hers, an unmistakable challenge there. Neither of them looked away, the rest of the station fading into the background.

Once upon a time, before she took up a solitary life and when she still hung around people, she'd been told her gaze could be disconcerting, that something about the way she locked onto someone challenged them on a primal level, leaving them with the twin urges of fight or flight.

People who met her eyes when she was angry or upset wouldn't do so for long, finding a reason to look away. In extreme cases leaving the room for another.

She'd never understood what they were talking about—until now. Holding the stranger's gaze took physical effort.

It was like trying to stare down a tiger, knowing he was considering how much of a struggle she'd make if he decided to eat her.

Only the slight clink of her drink being set next to her and her waiter's murmured, "Enjoy," forced her to break the wizard's gaze.

She didn't look up, instead choosing to focus on her task, her fingers flying across the holographic keyboard. She sat back. That ought to do it. One job posting on the station's forums and some of her problems would be solved.

CHAPTER FOUR

Task done, she reached for her drink, lifting it and taking a small sip, holding the liquid in her mouth as the flavors burst on her tongue. Something about the combination reminded her of warmth and safety, a comfort she could count on in even the most trying of times.

It was a luxury she didn't often afford herself. One, because the food synthesizer in her ship put out a very poor imitation and she preferred the real thing over a faded impostor. And two, because for her, chai was as decadent as chocolate was for others, something she couldn't even touch because of its bitterness. Same for coffee.

Only after she'd enjoyed several sips did Kira let herself look up again, watching the two wizards where they lurked, careful this time not to challenge either one to a staring contest.

Then she waited.

It wouldn't be long now. Forty minutes had passed since Jin left to secure the part. She figured another five and then she could head to her ship.

The woman gave a sharp nod and nudged her companion. Victory and the joy of the hunt reflected on both faces before their expressions blanked.

Kira stiffened, alert now.

Whatever reason they had for tailing her had come to a head. They'd either leave her in peace or try something.

The man stepped forward, the woman a cool blade at his back.

On her console, the words flashed—job accepted.

She took one final sip of her tea, before setting it down with regret. She didn't like leaving it half finished, but her time was up. She'd have to move or risk a showdown in the cafe with noncombatants all around and limited avenues of retreat.

The wizards started toward her and pulled up short, a group of teens blocking their way as the humans gestured and pointed, excitement on their faces.

A three-tone bell chimed that the station's night had begun. Above, the lights dimmed as the station's dome began to fold back to reveal the deep black of space. A thin, transparent membrane kept the atmosphere inside, allowing those below a glimpse of a star-speckled sky.

Those inside the shops ventured outside as the dome receded, pointing up and gasping in wonder as the lights in the honeycomb winked out one by one.

Even Kira in her urgency stole a second to look up, the sight of the cosmos stealing her breath. Purple and blue dust filled one corner of space, the rest dotted with millions of stars.

It was beautiful and one of many reasons people took pilgrimages to this place, the view unspoiled by a planet's atmosphere or ambient light.

It also served as a perfect secondary distraction.

Kira swiped her arm across the scanner, tipped the waiter and was walking away from her table seconds later.

She didn't look behind her, making her way, quickly but not frantically, along the terrace. She needed to get off this level. The lifts were an obvious choke point and could be used to trap her. She saw a small opening and took it, dropping onto the terrace below. She landed with her knees bent and legs together, then she was up again and moving quickly along the path.

Seconds later a loud thump sounded behind her, accompanied by shouted exclamations from above. She took a chance and glanced over her shoulder. The man straightened from where he landed, cold determination on his face.

A quick look above told her the woman was following from the upper level, moving parallel to Kira's path.

Damn. She'd hoped for more of a head start.

She turned and took off running, sprinting now, no longer caring who saw. People were slow to get out of the way, forcing her to dodge around or over their carts to heated shouts.

A quick glance behind told her the wizard was having no such trouble, people diving out of his way, his bigger form more intimidating

CHAPTER FOUR

than Kira's smaller one.

She turned and picked up a little more speed, reaching deep for reserves she hadn't had to tap in a while. She tried to keep in shape on the ship, but there was only so much you could do on something that was little more than two thousand square feet.

Her endurance wasn't what it had once been, but she'd wager it was better than most peoples'.

Shouts from in front caused her to slide to a stop. Station security poured toward her.

She was trapped. The station's security in front, a wizard in back and a wizard above.

Kira stilled as she examined her options.

The man slowed to a walk when he saw she was cornered. He wasn't even breathing hard.

Satisfaction appeared on his face. He thought he'd won.

Well, when you were trapped on three sides, there was only one choice. Kira walked toward the terrace, hopping up to stand on the railing, her balance precarious. It was sturdier than its thin frame suggested, barely wobbling under her weight.

Alarm appeared on the wizard's face. "Stop. We won't hurt you."

Security approached at a dead run.

The wizard held out his hand, a demand in his expression. "Come," he ordered in accented standard.

Kira gave him a slight smile. She'd never really been one for orders. Probably why she was no longer in the space force.

She leaned back, spreading her arms and letting gravity take her. Her balance passed the point of no return.

The wizard lunged for her, making a desperate grab, his expression incredulous. Kira couldn't help her small chuckle at the sight, before she turned her attention to surviving the fall.

The three linked supply hovercars she'd spotted earlier rushed by under her along their invisible track. She tucked her knees to her chest and flipped, her landing precise.

She stood and grinned.

There was a thud several cars behind her. She turned, the sight wiping the smile off her face. The man straightened, a glare aimed her way.

Kira gritted her teeth. It seemed he didn't plan on being so easily shaken. That was okay. They'd see how long he could keep up out here where the footing was unstable and a single mistake would mean your death.

Kira turned and leaped sideways, grabbing hold of a fast-moving hovercraft as it arrowed in the opposite direction. She pulled herself onto its top and stood, her attention focused behind her as the wizard found his own hovercraft.

"Jin is never going to believe this," she muttered to herself.

Two people crazy enough to play leapfrog with moving pieces. He was going to lose his shit when he found out.

She leaped off her car, letting gravity pull her down as she turned to fall head first in a smooth dive. She flipped, landing on one car to run two steps to the side and leap straight into the air again, vaulting from craft to craft, the wizard in relentless pursuit.

Kira remained focused, knowing he wasn't the only one courting death in this crazy hopscotch involving hovercraft, sailboats and air gondolas. Soon she lost herself in the sheer joy of the challenge, cutting through the air with a dancer's grace. It felt like flying, the gravity of the station less than a normal planet's but more than being out in the great expanse.

The adrenaline and fear of capture, coupled with the feeling of pushing her body as far as it would go, glorying when it rose to the challenge, all combined to make her feel powerful and alive.

She slid to a stop on top of one of the long trams as it glided toward the other side of the station, cutting through the honeycomb halfway through its journey.

She looked up, expecting the Tuann to be far behind her with no hope of catching up. No one had ever stayed with her for this long.

CHAPTER FOUR

Surprise shot through her. His furious face looked down from twenty feet above her and a hundred yards off. She calculated his likely path and grimaced. He'd catch her in the next three jumps.

From here on out, the footing became scarce as they neared the middle of the atrium. Most craft tended to stay close to the terraces, content to move from point to point and avoid the sometimes-tricky air currents in the center. It left her few choices, none of them getting her the distance she needed away from her erstwhile shadow.

She considered her next move. She could always let him catch her, ask him what he wanted and why he was after her. It was what a civilized person would do.

Her smile was dark when it came. No one had ever considered her civilized, not even when she bowed to humanity's will and served on the front lines in the worst war of their long history, a war where more people died than lived.

Her hair flew about her face and she grabbed it with one hand, turning and walking along the tram as it steadily rocked under her.

Far below, there were giant circular openings in the floor. Air intakes and outtakes used to filter air throughout the station. They were massive, necessary given the large open area they were required to service.

Kira peered over the side, what she was contemplating giving her pause. If Jin was here, he'd have a whole bunch of statistics about how unlikely her odds of success. Right before he forbade her from undertaking such a reckless action.

Her smile grew. Good thing he wasn't here.

She straightened, the toes of her boots hanging over the edge of the tram as it rocketed along its path, taking her directly over the pipes.

She stilled, taking several deep breaths and releasing them, reaching for her calm center as every sense she had came online.

She waited, the tram picking up speed. Jump too soon and she would undershoot the pipe, too late and she'd overshoot. She needed to be precise.

In her mind, she was aware of the wizard getting closer, of him landing on her tram and sprinting toward her.

Her vision spiraled to that pipe. Her body tensed. Now.

She stepped out into the air, dropping like a stone. She crossed her arms over her chest and pointed her toes, the air rushing past her, the sound of it roaring in her ear.

Faintly, she heard an angry shout above her.

Down, down she went, until the air pressure under her grew, almost supporting her weight from the force of the air being pushed up. She grinned as her descent slowed, then she was past the opening of the pipe.

Its slant gradually increased until it supported most of her weight. The air pressure rose and she started to move toward the opening. The red light of the emergency hatch flashed and she grabbed for it, using it to anchor her as she twisted the lock and shouldered the hatch open.

She collapsed into a service tunnel, panting. Well, that was fun.

CHAPTER FIVE

Kira jogged past another shipping container, grateful for the sight of the dock numbers as she drew close to where she'd left the *Wanderer*. Finding her way out of the service tunnels had taken longer than she'd anticipated. Her memory of the layout had faded in the past few years and she'd been in a section she'd never visited before.

Still, she was fairly confident she was ahead of pursuit. They would have had to backtrack to the lifts and then make their way to the port side of the station before threading their way through the various ship berths. To say nothing of locating the *Wanderer* in the first place.

Jin would have made sure the registration was disguised so nothing would immediately point to Kira and him. Until now, that had seemed like pointless paranoia on their part, but she was grateful they'd kept up the security protocol, despite never needing it.

"Jin, you there?" Kira murmured.

"Kira, where the hell have you been? I've been trying you forever. The security trees are lit up like the brothel district on Sarat 8," he hissed over their comms.

"I was in the service tunnels. Just got out a few minutes ago."

The service tunnels were built from a material designed to block radio and comms transmission. It was a remnant of the war when protecting the station's self-sustaining systems was paramount.

"What were you doing there?" Jin asked.

"It was the one place I could lose the Tuann," Kira said, glancing around her. Something felt off, but she didn't know what. "I'm almost to the *Wanderer*."

"Me too."

"First one there begins the preflight checklist," Kira ordered. "I want to be off this station as soon as possible."

"You won't get an argument from me. I leave you for a few minutes and you have half the station after you. Unbelievable."

Kira allowed herself a small smile at her friend's frustration before it faded, the same feeling from before drawing her attention to the matter at hand.

She slowed to a stop and looked around. There it was again. A niggling feeling on the back of her neck warning she wasn't alone. Someone was out there, watching. Yet when she looked around, feigning a nonchalance she didn't feel, nothing. No sign of anyone else on the platform, just her and an endless number of shipping crates.

Kira continued forward, slower this time. Her footsteps silent as she advanced, hyperalert as she took in her surroundings.

Briefly she considered turning, disappearing into the service tunnels until all interest had vanished. Unfortunately, it would mean being trapped. Eventually, someone would figure out where she was. If they were persistent enough, they could arrange a thorough search until they flushed her out.

At that point she'd be stuck since her ship would likely be under surveillance and/or locked into the dock.

Given her luck, these people would be that persistent.

No, her only option was to continue on and hope her instincts were wrong. It had been years since they'd seen any action. Maybe they were getting their signals crossed after the earlier excitement.

The bulbous shape of the *Wanderer* appeared out the window port. Relief filled Kira. She was nearly home. Another hundred meters and she'd be there.

Once in the ship, no one would be able to touch her. She hadn't skimped on its security. Not even the best forced boarding specialist

CHAPTER FIVE

in the space force would be able to get on board.

Of course, that left the possibility of aerial attack, but she had a couple of tricks up her sleeve for those too.

She rounded another set of crates, the ship's airlock in sight. She came to an abrupt stop. A man stood in front of a window with a full view of the *Wanderer*, his head tilted as he studied it, his hands clasped behind him. His posture was military straight, as if someone had taken a straight rod and welded it to his spine. It made him seem much taller and more imposing than he already was.

"So, this is what you're calling home these days?" he called.

Kira didn't answer, her gaze moving to the shadows of the bay. Despite appearances, the man wasn't alone. There were others here, watching, waiting. For what, she didn't know.

The station security's interest in her suddenly made sense. She might want nothing to do with Centcom these days, but that didn't mean it didn't want something from her. And this man—he was the personification of Centcom.

"Have to say, it's not where I pictured you," he continued.

"What do you want?" Kira asked, her voice hard, not letting the conversational tone lull her into dropping her guard.

"Many, many things," he said, an ache in his voice.

There was sadness there, something Kira ignored. Himoto might regret having taken certain actions, but that didn't mean he wouldn't do them again if he felt it benefited humanity. No matter who got hurt along the way.

"I'm a full admiral now, did you know?" he asked, his mood shifting with lightning quickness.

Kira took a few steps closer. "I had heard."

"Your congratulations must have gotten lost in the void," he said, giving her a friendly smile. It created a spiderweb of lines around the corners of his eyes. The dark hair she remembered was mostly gray now, making him seem distinguished. The cut of it was familiar, short on the sides and a little longer on top.

"Something like that," Kira murmured, still on the lookout.

"They'll give us time to talk," he said, reading her caution.

She lifted an eyebrow at him. Somehow that wasn't really reassuring. The hidden message being, when they were done talking things would change and her time would have run out.

"You look good," he said, his eyes warm and soft.

"You've gotten old," she said, the words a bit more abrupt than she intended. Her social skills had grown rusty from disuse. To be honest, they'd never been that great in the first place.

Himoto didn't let the comment bother him, throwing his head back on a laugh, his teeth flashing.

His laughter died and his eyes danced with mirth. "I have indeed, despite my best efforts." He studied her. "Not you. You look exactly the same."

Kira didn't show a reaction to that, at least not outwardly. Inside, she fought against a thread of sadness and discomfort. It seemed that was to be her fate, never aging or dying, while the friends around her did both.

It was one of many reasons for her self-imposed isolation. Her oddities were a little easier to take when they weren't thrown in her face on a regular basis. She might look human, but she wasn't. That fact had been made clear to her a long time ago.

"First Spitzy, then Jace, now you; it seems like today is the day for reunions," she observed.

He snorted at the name she'd given Spatz, even as he watched her with fondness.

The shadows stirred and Kira felt a small loosening in her chest. Relief coursed through her. Jin had returned. She wasn't facing Himoto and the entire might of Centcom alone.

"What are you doing here?" she asked Himoto.

O'Riley was an important waypoint, pivotal because of its closeness to both the Tuann and the Haldeel, another alien race humanity had stumbled across in the course of their war. The Haldeel were slightly

CHAPTER FIVE

friendlier than the Tuann, though they were equally convinced humanity was a young race in need of guidance and restrictions.

"Jace and I have been trying to broker an extension of our treaty with the Tuann," he said.

Kira digested that, wariness making her cautious. She didn't like the fact the Tuann had been after her—and here Himoto was, admitting he was trying to curry their favor.

"Kind of you to take time out of your schedule for little old me," Kira said, testing him.

"I looked for you when you left."

She flinched and looked away. She didn't want to dredge up the past. There were too many demons there.

"Get to the point, Himoto," Kira said, forcing steel into her voice. She wasn't the broken mess of before. She wouldn't crumple at the first push by someone she once knew.

"I'd like you to sit down and talk to the Tuann."

"No."

His sigh was long and he shook his head slightly. "You always have to do things the hard way."

"It's the only way I know to be." Kira didn't let herself feel bad about that fact. Maybe once, before she'd rebuilt herself from the ground up, but now, she embraced all her jagged edges.

"If that's it, I have a ship to repair," she said, starting by him.

"Do you want to be responsible for starting another war?" he asked, his words flat and emotionless.

Kira gave him a sharp look, a banked fury burning at her core. "Don't."

He didn't listen, his expression calm. "Because that's what will happen if you don't listen."

Kira hesitated. He was serious.

Seeing something in her face he continued, "Running isn't going to save you this time. Your ship's modifications might protect you from us, but it won't do anything against them."

"What do you know about my ship?" Kira barked.

"Parts from a Tsavitee cruiser in your engine, a new power source none of my engineers can explain and a drive capable of at least three times the speed your ship is classed for. To say nothing of the weapons and defenses it shouldn't have," Himoto said, almost admiringly. "Jin does good work."

"Not just Jin," Kira corrected. She'd done as much on the ship as he had, teaching herself along the way. They'd created something that was much more than it appeared. She was proud of everything they'd done, even if most would never know the full extent of its capabilities.

He gave a small nod of acknowledgment to her words. "Those upgrades won't even give the Tuann pause. All they need is for you to get a little distance from the station and then one well-placed shot would have you dead in the water. They'd be able to board with little effort. Then you won't have any control."

It wouldn't be as easy as that. Himoto had named several of the modifications, but not all. The fact he'd been able to name any was more disturbing than she had words for. It meant someone in Himoto's command had been keeping an eye on them, making a note of their purchases. She thought she'd left all that behind when she left Centcom.

The reason they probably didn't know about the rest was because they weren't kits. They were pieces and parts Kira and Jin had repurposed or adapted from Tsavitee ships. There'd be no other way Himoto would know about their activities unless he had eyes in the ship, something she knew he didn't have.

"What do they want?" Kira asked in frustration. She found it hard to believe the Tuann would go through all this, threaten war, over her saving two kids.

He hesitated, indecisive.

"Himoto," Kira warned, not in the mood for his normal cloak and dagger games.

CHAPTER FIVE

His eyes were piercing when they met hers. "They claim you're Tuann."

Kira's lips parted. Part of her felt frozen, like this was happening to someone else. Another part—the part she thought dead—felt a wild fluttering of hope, the thought of not being alone, of not being the only freak out there, taking wing. She firmly squashed it.

Even if by some odd, unlikely coincidence she did turn out to be Tuann, it didn't mean she was no longer alone. It just meant her freakishness now had a name.

She'd learned many hard lessons about the peril of letting hope run away with you. It was the ultimate liar, an illusion turning smart people into fools, sundering their hearts from their chests when hope inevitably crashed them against the rocky shore.

She didn't know these people, and couldn't even begin to guess their reasons for lying, but she hadn't survived this long by believing everything someone told her.

Jin drifted out of the shadows, his metal exterior gleaming dully. His presence returned her equilibrium, reminding her she was by no means on her own.

"What leads them to that conclusion?" Kira forced herself to ask, trying to be logical about it all.

He pointed to her wrist, before lifting it and turning it so the mark on it was exposed. "Do you know how you got this?"

She frowned at him. "You know the story. You were there when I was discovered."

Their beginning had started with blood and fire. Kira had been near death after doing her utmost to destroy the compound where she'd spent her entire life being tortured and experimented on. Himoto and his team had rescued her from all that, killing the group of scientists who had been trying to train Kira and the others to be the best monsters they could be. Children as young as three taught to fight and then beaten as their caretakers tried to mold them into living weapons.

She and a few others had attempted to escape. The resulting commotion had drawn the notice of the local branch of the military. When they'd investigated, they found Kira and a bunch of dead scientists and guards.

The mark preexisted all that. For as long as she could remember, she'd had it. It didn't match any symbol she'd been able to find. It was tempting to classify it as a birthmark, except the edges were too precise and the shape too detailed.

"Every Tuann I've met has something similar on their body." He drew back her sleeve, and she let him, watching with narrowed eyes, untrusting.

The mark he revealed was in the shape of three crescents over a circle, smaller lines joining some of the crescents.

"From what we can tell, it's a declaration of their House and lineage."

Kira wasn't willing to believe him. "Humans have known about the Tuann for over a decade. How has no one put this together before now?"

He huffed at her. "You've been gone since the war ended. We knew very little about them then."

And they hadn't wanted to lose one of their aces. Kira had been a legend during the war. She had more Tsavitee kills than any other wave runner. Throw in her special abilities and she could see why Centcom kept knowledge of her to themselves.

She pulled her arm from him. "Sorry, Himoto, I have no interest in digging up the past. I like my life right now. Tell them they're about thirty years too late."

She gestured at Jin and stepped past Himoto.

"You know their weapons are more powerful than anything we have," Himoto warned.

"I'll take my chances."

She approached the airlock and the tube leading to her ship, Jin a silent presence next to her. For once, he kept his opinions to himself. A fact she was grateful for.

CHAPTER FIVE

"Rothchild."

Kira froze, her hand half lifted, her insides icing over.

"You manipulative bastard," Jin swore.

"Do this for me, meet with them, and all debts are wiped clean," he bargained.

Kira remained where she was, staring at Himoto. She should have known he'd pull Rothchild out as a means to get her to do what he wanted. Her biggest mistake and her greatest victory.

"You don't have to listen to him, Kira," Jin said. His eye swung toward Himoto and narrowed. She could practically read his mind as he readied some of the nastier upgrades she'd given him—nothing that would kill, but it would hurt. A lot.

Kira's sigh was heavy, indecision weighing on her. "I'll meet with them. I'll hear what they have to say."

It was subtle, but she read the signs of relief in Himoto, a slight loosening of the shoulders, the muscles in his face relaxing.

She dropped into his native language, one from a time when humanity was as divided and fragmented as their loyalties. Standard might be the common language now but many kept the languages and traditions of their origin. Himoto was one of them.

"I do this and you never mention Rothchild to me again," she told him.

He gave her a sharp nod. "Done."

The words should have made her feel better. Somehow, they didn't.

Something shifted in the air, telling Kira they were no longer alone. She tensed, but didn't move as the mountain from the interrogation room stepped into view, the same severe expression as last time on his face. He stared at her as if she was a puzzle he didn't know if he wanted to bother solving.

She stared back, the same challenge in her eyes from their earlier encounter. Only this time he didn't seem inclined to move out of her way.

The men and women he'd had with him earlier appeared, one by one, almost as if they were ghosts, silent and deadly. There was no sound, nothing to precede their appearance. Simply, one moment it looked like the bay was clear of any but the three of them, then the next there were too many bodies taking up space.

Kira could see why people called them wizards.

It was disconcerting to have all their eyes on her, studying her like she was some alien artifact. Her back itched with the need for retreat.

She glanced at Himoto in question. When he'd said he wanted her to talk with them, she'd imagined in a room somewhere, not an ambush in front of her ship.

The corner of his mouth pulled up. "I did say you were unlikely to get far."

So, he had. She'd thought he meant from the station. Now she saw his words were more literal. It would have taken her several seconds to open the airlock and get down the tube to her ship. In that time, the Tuann would have been on her. She would have been forced to fight, which might have meant damage to the *Wanderer*.

It was better to do this here, where such things were unlikely.

A slight scrape of sound from behind alerted her to the fact someone had positioned themselves between her and her ship. It was so polite of them to announce their presence, Kira thought wryly.

Somehow, she wasn't surprised when she looked over her shoulder to see the male Tuann who'd chased her through the station, his female partner behind him.

His frown was fierce as he glowered at her. Guess he hadn't appreciated the exercise or being given the slip.

The woman's eyes danced with mirth as she graced Kira with a tiny smile, the only friendly expression among the Tuann.

Kira didn't react, turning to Himoto and the mountain. "I'm listening."

The admiral faced the Tuann's leader. "Lord Graydon, this is Kira Forrest. She's the woman you met previously and the one you claim is Tuann."

CHAPTER FIVE

Kira noted the lack of her rank in that introduction. She didn't know if it was because of the circumstances behind her leaving Centcom and the military or if he was trying to give her an advantage in her interactions with these strangers. Knowing him, it could be both.

Graydon was silent as he observed Kira with a fierce reserve. His gaze lifted over her shoulder and he nodded at the man behind her.

The small movement was enough warning, allowing Kira to control her reaction, despite the instincts clamoring for her to defend herself, as the man stepped closer and grabbed her forearm. He turned it for all to see.

To Kira the mark didn't seem all that interesting. It had been with her as far back as her memories stretched.

A part of her had always suspected it was a brand her keepers had placed on her. She'd thought about having it removed a couple of times but something always stopped her. What if it was something her parents had given her? And even if it wasn't, it was a tangible symbol of the hell she'd survived.

As long as it remained, the tattoo was a reminder the things behind her were worse than anything she faced in the future. Sometimes, when her thoughts turned down dark paths, that was the only thing keeping her going, the promise of better times ahead.

Graydon said something in his own language, the sound fluid. The man holding her arm responded with a soft word.

Kira's gaze moved suspiciously between the two. It seemed Himoto hadn't been exaggerating when he said the Tuann recognized it. Still, it didn't mean anything.

These people were all considerably taller than her, their ears slightly pointed, with the type of bone structure humans found exceptionally pleasing to the eye. They looked human, but more.

Kira was just Kira. She had freaky eyes and other oddities but that was about it.

There was a sharp pulse of sensation from the man holding her, then her mark responded with warmth, shimmering briefly as it sent up an answering pulse.

She jerked away, the motion sharp and unexpected enough to free her from his implacable grip. Her posture was defensive as she glared at the man.

"What did you do to me?" she asked, a harsh edge to her tone.

He held up his hands and retreated a step. He said something in his lyrical language to Graydon. The two exchanged several words, Kira's suspicions steadily rising, before Graydon released a heavy sigh.

His expression soured. He grimaced before rubbing his face with one hand. The look he fixed on her was unhappy, as if he laid the blame for everything at her feet.

The man beside her let out a small chuckle before saying in his heavily accented standard, "The mark responded. She is Tuann."

Graydon turned toward Himoto, a severe expression on his face. "Your people are in violation of our treaty. We will be taking her and returning to our home. Expect a formal declaration terminating our alliance."

"I said I'd listen, not go anywhere with them," Kira protested.

The man beside her grabbed her shoulders, restraining her as the rest of the Tuann prepared to leave.

Jin floated higher, a high buzz emitting from him, weapons arming as he prepared to act.

She made an aborted attempt to struggle before forcing herself to stop. Not yet. Not while Himoto could talk sense into these people. Attacking now would make the already tense situation worse.

"Wait, Jin," she said softly as Himoto whirled on Graydon.

"Lord Graydon, we need to talk about this," Himoto said, his face calm and his words meticulously polite, despite the alarm Graydon's threat would have caused.

Graydon gave Himoto no more attention than he would a fly, snapping out orders to his people.

CHAPTER FIVE

"Lord Graydon, Kira is a citizen of the Consortium. You may not remove her from our airspace without permission," Himoto said loudly.

"And you don't have it," Kira added—in case that helped.

Graydon spared her a dark look. She smiled, feeling a sense of accomplishment at his severe expression.

"However, as a member of our military, she can be ordered," Himoto said.

That wiped the smile from Kira's face as her gaze turned toward Himoto. "You wouldn't dare."

He sent her a warning glance, one that said he'd dare that and more. "We need this alliance, Kira."

"I'm retired. Your orders have no effect on me anymore."

He knew this. He was there when she told him she was done.

Himoto's eyes were dark pools as he turned to her, his feelings and thoughts carefully hidden. "Rear Admiral Skarsdale, if you please."

Jace stepped out from behind the shipping containers, several humans in the uniform of station security flanking him. He walked toward Kira after a long look at Himoto.

He handed her a thin tablet, the memo already pulled up.

Himoto explained as she read. "You never formalized your retirement. It gave us room to recall you to service. Your orders are included in that packet as well."

Kira felt a dull horror at his words. Jin drifted lower so he could read over her shoulder.

"Is he right?" she asked.

Jin had made a point of studying all the laws and regulations of the Consortium. It was easier to circumvent the system when you knew exactly what loopholes to employ.

"Yes."

The tablet dropped to her side as she glared at the ground. Damn it. What was the use of knowing every law and regulation out there if they got caught in the damn loopholes?

81

Jace's gaze was unsympathetic when she looked up, his face hard and closed. He probably thought she was getting her just desserts. She couldn't really blame him given the manner of their parting, but still, a wild feeling surged in her chest as the sense of being trapped closed in all around her.

It'd been a long time since she got that feeling. It used to be, anytime she stepped foot on a ship or space station she had to beat it back. Now, she was better, except she was struck by the urge to lash out until this nasty feeling in her chest was gone.

Seeing he had her right where he wanted her, Himoto said, "Kira won't be going anywhere without our say so."

The threat was clear. If Graydon continued to push to have the alliance dissolved, then Himoto would make it so his people never got their hands on her. She would feel more comforted by that if she didn't know Centcom would do anything to preserve the alliance.

Where the Haldeel were slightly condescending to the younger humans, they at least were helpful—there when they were most needed and willing to let humanity's best and brightest into their territories where they could study at places of learning and interact on a regular basis.

The Tuann, by contrast, seemed to want nothing to do with humans. They had only interfered under the most extreme circumstances during the war when the threat of casualties on their side were almost nonexistent or when the Tsavitee had strayed too closely to their borders. They didn't have time for humanity, and they made their disdain perfectly clear.

At least that's what Kira had picked up the rare times she was in port.

Unfortunately, the Tuann military were virtually unbeatable, and they were one of the few races to have held the Tsavitee off for longer than humans had been in space.

"You would risk war with the Tuann," Graydon said, a silky threat in his voice.

CHAPTER FIVE

Himoto's smile was humorless. "I guess that depends on you."

Graydon looked at him carefully, as if Himoto had suddenly transformed from a gentle bunny into a spitting snake.

Kira was familiar with the feeling. Himoto possessed the rare gift of getting people to see him as almost harmless, while he manipulated them onto the path he wanted. He'd done it to her enough times in the past she could sometimes see the signs coming. Unfortunately, this wasn't one of them.

Seeing he had Graydon's attention, Himoto said, "Now, let's go somewhere we can all talk and you can tell us exactly what you see in Kira's future and what it will mean for her."

Though the words were polite, his expression indicated he wasn't going to bend on this point.

Graydon inclined his head, just the slightest bit, his gaze flicking to Kira's in a penetrating stare before he turned away, snapping orders at his people.

"Kira," Himoto said expectantly.

Kira hesitated, the inescapable feeling her life was about to be changed irrevocably yet again, swamping her.

She glanced at the *Wanderer*. "If you're really planning to let them take me, I could use some things from my ship."

Himoto watched her, his gaze assessing. "Of course."

Kira turned toward the airlock with a sense of relief.

"I'll accompany you. I would like to see the inside of the place you called home," he said idly.

She glanced at him, noticing she had Graydon's attention again. His head cocked. "I would like to see as well."

"If I said no?" she challenged.

Graydon's smiled at her for the first time. It lacked anything resembling friendliness. It was a challenge, pure and simple. "You're not stepping foot anywhere on this station without one of us by your side."

Something in her rebelled at letting these strangers into her space.

Kira's gaze slid to the *Wanderer* again. Her home. The place where the most dangerous of her secrets resided.

She came to a decision. It wasn't worth the risk. What was inside could wait for her return. She didn't want either man having a look around. Himoto had a way of ferreting out secrets she preferred remain hers, and Graydon unsettled her on some deep level.

She started forward, walking toward the two men and the lift behind them.

"Your ship?" Himoto inquired.

"Never mind. I'm sure I can get my things later."

The sidelong look Himoto slid her way told her he knew why she'd decided against returning to her ship. To her surprise, he dipped his chin in a small nod and didn't push before heading to the lift.

She hesitated, unable to help the slight note of challenge in her expression as she glared up at Graydon. His expression was blank as he stared at her before his lips quirked.

"After you, *coli*," he said.

She didn't respond as she moved on, the Tuann falling in around her until they flanked her, Jace and the rest bringing up the rear.

Her ship had better be in one piece when she returned to it.

CHAPTER SIX

Himoto stepped into a large conference room with floor to ceiling windows looking out into the cosmos. Stars glittered on a black carpet of night, a monochromatic counterpoint to the mostly white room. It left the viewer with the sensation as if they were standing on the very edge of space.

For some, the sight would be disconcerting, given the deceptive fragility the windows implied. Not for Kira, who found the illusion of space mere feet away oddly comforting.

It helped she knew the windows were constructed of material capable of withstanding all but a missile strike and were nearly as durable as the outer hull of the station.

In the middle of the room was a long table capable of seating twenty people. Fruit arranged in the bowls in the center gave the space a bright pop of color.

Himoto gestured for Graydon and Kira to take a seat. The rest of Graydon's people had chosen to wait in the hall, with the exception of the man who'd chased Kira through the honeycomb.

"Now that we're all here and calm," the last was a reminder for Kira. Himoto continued, "Let's see if we can get to the heart of this matter and find a satisfactory compromise for all parties."

Kira contained her snort. Unlikely. Unless any of those compromises involved her on board her ship hightailing it to a less congested part of space. She'd heard the Ghost's Shroud was pretty isolated. No one for billions of miles. Right now, it sounded like exactly what she needed.

Graydon fixed Himoto with a hard stare. "We're taking the child with us. What happens after that is dependent on her."

Kira choked on a laugh. "Is he serious?"

She was many things but a child wasn't one of them. Over thirty years had passed since the mission which had rescued her from hell. She didn't think she could really be classified as a child then either, the circumstances of her upbringing burning any trace of innocence out before it had time to form.

Graydon's head turned toward her. "Yes."

Kira waited. No further answer was forthcoming. Her eyebrows climbed in disbelief. That was it? That was his entire response? Yes?

Himoto gestured for patience. Kira bit her tongue on the many things she wanted to say and forced herself to remain in her seat.

"The Tuann are much more long-lived than us," Himoto said cautiously. "It is possible, in their culture, you might not be considered fully grown."

Kira pointed at her face. "Do I look like a child to you?"

"You certainly act like one sometimes," Jace murmured.

She sent him a fulminating glance. His lips quirked, but otherwise he didn't respond.

"I'm not a child," she stated emphatically.

Jin snickered next to her. So glad someone was finding humor in this.

"Until you pass the *adva ka* and prove yourself, you won't receive the rights of an adult," Graydon stated as if his words were final.

Jace hid his smirk by dipping his head as Kira stared dumbly at Graydon.

"You don't know how old I am," she said. For all he knew she could be hundreds of years old.

She'd stopped growing years ago. There was no way she was still a child, biologically or mentally. Could a child have fought in a war? Become a hero, then a villain because of her successes and failures? Could they have taken a decrepit ship and restored her to perfect

CHAPTER SIX

condition? Or run a business and survived on their own for as long as she had?

No.

This whole conversation was ridiculous.

"I believe this is all a miscommunication," Jace said finally interjecting. "You're ascribing the human definition of child to his words. I think it would be more appropriate to say, Lord Graydon sees you in the same way we see those in their first years of university—a young adult without the responsibilities of one."

Graydon didn't react to that statement, neither confirming or denying it as he stared at her over the table.

Kira settled in. Jace's conclusion made sense, even if it grated. She'd worked too hard, for too long, to let anyone take her accomplishments away from her. Children had few rights, only those adults gave them. They were rudderless kites, bobbing along the wind currents of someone else's ambition and whims. Being seen on the cusp of adulthood was better, but only just.

"What if I don't want to go with you?" she asked.

His gaze was piercing as he gave her his full attention for the first time since he'd sat down. Until now, he'd been focused on Jace and Himoto, as if her presence was an afterthought and she had no real power.

"Your desires don't matter. You are Tuann. Your House and family will have much to answer for when we return, given how they've let you stray so far."

Kira stiffened, her mask slamming down as every muscle in her body tensed at the implication.

Both Himoto and Jace sat forward, knowing Graydon's words for the trigger they were.

"Lord Graydon, I think perhaps you are misunderstanding as well. Kira has no history with your people. She was discovered at a young age—the equivalent of a thirteen-year-old human—in a compound deep in our territory," Himoto said. "She'd been severely mistreated and there were signs of torture. She has no memories of the Tuann. As far as she or anyone knew, she'd been born in that place. Whatever you might think, she did not choose ignorance of your people."

Kira didn't react as her painful history was recited for Graydon's benefit. She didn't often like to think of that place, the memories painful and of a time when she didn't have the power to protect herself.

Himoto left out the experiments and the belief among some of her rescuers that her unique qualities stemmed from those experiments.

Now apparently, her oddities had an explanation. She was from an alien race.

She ignored the look of sympathy on the face of the Tuann behind Graydon, her attention locked on the real threat as she stared him down.

His face remained expressionless as Himoto continued, no sign of a reaction to give her a clue to how this was being received.

"As far as we knew, Kira was human. She grew up human and joined our military during the war. No one knew she was Tuann until today," Himoto said.

Thoughts moved behind Graydon's eyes as he processed Himoto's words. He turned and looked over his shoulder at the other man. His guard nodded and left the room at a fast clip.

"You can prove this, I assume," Graydon said, lifting one eyebrow arrogantly.

"You could take our word for it," Kira drawled.

Graydon's smile was slight, as if her statement amused him. Arrogant, and convinced he would come out the winner in every confrontation, Kira concluded.

"We have documentation, video of her discovery, as well as photos of her growing up," Himoto said. "I'll be happy to provide a copy for you."

"Do that," Graydon said. He lifted himself out of his chair. "This does not change the fact that when I leave here, she will be coming

CHAPTER SIX

with me." He held up a hand when Himoto would have spoken. "I will, however, not advocate for an immediate termination of the alliance at this time. I warn you this matter has reinforced some of our concerns."

Kira shifted in her seat, tensing before relaxing. She didn't like that he was on this whole "Kira must go to the Tuann's territory," nor did she like the way they were using the excuse of her existence as a threat to pull out of an alliance they obviously wanted no part in.

Waiting for a better time to act, when conditions were more favorable to her, was the best option. Fighting her way out of this room with the Tuann standing guard and Jace having no doubt ordered a parking lock put on her ship, meant she had to be patient and wily.

"However she might have come to you, since then, it should have become clear what she was. We should have been informed immediately of her existence," Graydon continued.

"By the time the suspicion was raised, Kira had moved on from her position in our military," Jace said, his head propped on one hand. "For a long time, we had no idea where to look for her. It was thought best to leave this issue alone until the situation changed."

Graydon gave him a cold look. "And that is why we will never trust you. The terms of our treaty were quite clear. That you didn't notify us because it was inconvenient to you shows exactly how far you will go when a fact puts your agenda in jeopardy."

Strangely, Kira found herself in agreement with the Tuann. Admitting guilt once you're caught means nothing. A last-minute apology meant to save face and placate the Tuann made humans look worse. Had Centcom meant to deal honorably with their allies they would have let them know about Kira as soon as the suspicion crossed their minds.

She knew why they didn't. They didn't want to lose control of their leverage. They would have done everything they could to hide her existence.

She would have helped them too. Too bad she had stumbled straight into the Tuann's path, setting them on their present course.

"The past is done, and mistakes were made," Himoto said, his expression grave. "But, we cannot in good conscience let you take her without some assurance of her safety."

Graydon's eyes narrowed slightly. "What is it you want?"

"We'd like to send a team with her," Jace said. "They can make sure she's settled before returning."

Graydon watched the two men and then jerked his head down. "Done. Baran is contacting her House, but I cannot guarantee they will be as accommodating."

Himoto bowed his head. "We understand."

Graydon turned his attention to Kira. "I'll give you time to say goodbye, then our ship will be leaving."

He didn't wait for her to respond, striding out of the room without a backward glance.

Once the door had shut, the room was quiet for several beats as Kira turned to Himoto, murder on her face.

"Explain what just happened."

Not the part about where she was Tuann—she got that—but the part where Himoto had agreed to let them take her like she was a piece of luggage that could be passed around. Not a person with thoughts and opinions of her own.

"As you've seen, our relationship with the Tuann is rather unstable," Jace said. "We have to tread cautiously."

Kira gave him a look of disbelief. "From what I saw, they pretty much dictate to you and you take it."

Himoto rubbed his chin, for the first time seeming tired. "You're not far off."

"Why?" she asked.

"We got off on a bad foot with the Tuann during first contact," Himoto said.

Kira waited.

CHAPTER SIX

"We made certain assumptions about their technological abilities and the strategic value of allying with them," Jace explained.

"Assumptions that are now biting us in the ass." Himoto's voice was frank. "We need them, but we've insulted them during nearly every encounter."

"What assumptions?" Kira asked. Knowing the Consortium, it could be anything.

The two shared a long look.

"In the early days of first contact, the Tuann were careful to appear nonthreatening. Even today, we don't know much about them. They're a secretive race. We do know they've arranged themselves in what they call Houses. People of differing origin work together for a common goal," Himoto instructed.

"Sounds similar to the Consortium," Kira said.

Himoto made an expression of agreement. "In a way."

The Consortium was a collection of Earth's former colonies. When humanity first entered into space and established themselves outside their home planet, they did so to benefit Earth. As a result, much of their resources went to Earth.

However, in the vastness of space, retaining control over territories that were sometimes a year or more of travel away was difficult. War happened and Earth lost control of her colonies.

The individual planets created identities for themselves that endured to present day. Each planet had representatives on the council and was tasked with meeting a quota for military enrollment.

The war with the Tsavitee strengthened the Consortium in some ways, turning it from a collection of planets prone to infighting, to a strong system of governance bound together by the very survival of the human race.

"They place a lot of value on their personal honor and deeds. We don't know much about them, but we do know they seem to have a strong warrior class that seems to share similarities to the samurai of my people's history," Himoto said.

"None of that explains how you went wrong," Kira said.

"Those responsible for first contact were invited to a planet. It was largely agricultural, and those responsible deemed the Tuann as unadvanced, believing they had nothing that would benefit us. The humans involved presented us in a bad light. They broke promises—something the Tuann see as a mortal insult. Furthermore, they strayed where they weren't supposed to go while ignoring numerous warnings."

"The Tuann predate the Haldeel in space travel," Himoto continued. "They are as technologically advanced—perhaps even more so. It has put us in a dangerous position—especially since the Haldeel have let us know they want this tension resolved."

"Admiral Himoto and I have been tasked by Centcom to repair our relationship with the Tuann." Jace's expression was grave.

All interesting points, but Kira suspected there was much more to this.

"That doesn't explain why you're willing to give them anything they want," Kira said.

Himoto sighed. "Show her."

Jace took the tablet from his side and hit a couple of buttons before throwing the screen he'd raised on the hologram at the end of the table.

It was a video of space, the utter black relieved by the bright glitter of stars. Kira didn't know what she was supposed to be looking at.

Jace zoomed in, and suddenly the picture spiraled down, blocking out the stars to show what had both men so serious.

Kira leaned in, a rock settling in her stomach. "That's a Tsavitee ship."

There was a small hum as Jin moved closer. "It looks like a Raven class."

Raven class, named for the small wing-like protrusions on each side and the utter black of its hull, it was a reconnaissance ship. Hard to spot with the naked eye and nearly impossible to track with

CHAPTER SIX

instruments, it had slipped through the lines during the war with ridiculous ease.

"Where did you find it?" she asked.

"Three million clicks from Zepher," Jace said.

"They're back," she said around numb lips. She sat still, suddenly feeling like all thought, all emotion had been drained out of her.

She didn't know how to process the news the Tsavitee might be gearing up for another incursion into human space. It was unthinkable. The last war had cost them so much, in some ways forever changing the course of humanity. Even years after the fact, they were still picking up the pieces.

"We don't know," Himoto admitted. "But the fact it popped up so close to the Tuann's visit to discuss the alliance has a lot of people in power nervous."

She could imagine.

The Tsavitee were here. She couldn't quite bring herself to believe it.

"Why are you telling me this?" Kira asked. This information was classified. Centcom and the government wouldn't want word of this getting out and causing mass panic. That meant they had a reason for revealing it.

"I know you, Kira-chan. I trained you, remember?" Himoto said. "The Tuann might think they have you trapped, but how long will that last? You'll take the first opportunity to disappear. I can guarantee they'll dissolve the treaty in retaliation, leaving us open to possible attack."

Kira lifted her chin but didn't deny his assessment. Why bother? He was right.

"Hopefully, this will convince you against such foolish measures," he said.

She tapped the table as she thought.

"What is it you're hoping to get out of this?" Kira asked quietly.

Jace and Himoto exchanged a glance.

Himoto leaned forward, the lines of his face serious. "The Tuann have some of the most advanced ships of any race. With them, they've held their border since before humanity had flight. We want those ships."

Was that all? He should have asked for planet building technology while he was at it.

"Last I checked, your treaty with the Haldeel meant they would protect you should the Tsavitee attack again," Kira said. The Haldeel would be as advanced.

"Centcom and the government are no longer content to rely on others for our safety. We want the means to protect ourselves," Jace said. "Our own fleet of Tuann ships will be instrumental in our defense. It could advance our technology by fifty years."

To say nothing of no longer having to accede to the demands of the other races.

"Even with those ships, it'll take you years to reverse engineer them." If they even could. They hadn't had a lot of success with the Tsavitee tech the salvagers brought in.

"It'll give us a chance," Himoto said.

"And me?"

Getting the ships for Centcom was all well and good, but Kira would be stuck in the gray area of the treaty. She didn't want to agree only to be told, "Thanks but we need you to stay put and play by someone else's rules."

"We can't help you break the treaty." Himoto clasped his hands on the table in front of him.

They sure expected a lot from her when they had nothing to give in return.

Himoto fixed his stern gaze on Kira. "But I have faith you'll figure something out. Get them to give up their claim to you and your problems will be solved."

Kira's expression could have scorched metal. It was so nice they were leaving everything up to her. She should have known better

CHAPTER SIX

than to hope for anything different.

Himoto stood, his smile slightly wistful. "Good luck, Kira-chan. I'm so glad circumstances arranged to bring us together again."

She bet he did. It sounded like her success meant he was going to get everything he ever wanted.

Jace's face was serious as he waited for Himoto to leave. "Himoto has always had more faith in you than you deserve. Try not to screw this up."

Kira didn't say anything as Jace left the room.

"It seems he's still mad at you," Jin observed.

Kira sighed and pushed herself back in the seat. She rubbed her face, the emotional toll of the unexpected reunions finally sinking in.

"It's not like he doesn't have a reason." She stared out at the stars, her gaze distant and unseeing.

Once, she'd counted both men as her friends, the family she'd never had. That was a long time ago, and last-minute regrets wouldn't reverse time.

Jin didn't argue, his presence comforting as she considered her options. "What do you want to do?"

That was the question. She could continue as she had been, ignoring the rest of the galaxy as she healed and lived her life, or she could do her duty, take up the mantle she'd been saddled with, and figure out a way forward.

"We're going to give them what they want," Kira said.

There was really no question. If the Tsavitee were truly back, humans were going to need every advantage at their disposal.

There was also Odin's message. It looked like she'd have the opportunity to get what he needed after all.

"And if the same thing happens again?" Jin asked.

Kira was silent. She looked up at him. "Then we take more permanent action."

* * *

Kira's steps echoed oddly in the corridor, the two guards the Tuann had left her with almost silent as they guided her to the Tuann's ship. It required much less travel than it had taken to get from hers since it was docked in one of the premium sections.

The station assigned berths based on how much a captain was willing to pay and how powerful those on board were. For someone like her who chose the economy section, it meant cramped shipping lanes and sliding into a narrow berth with a dozen other vessels crammed in next to you. It also meant being further away from everything and having to take sliding walks or trams to get to the more populated parts of the station.

Had Kira been parked in one of the nicer sections she probably could have made it away from the station in plenty of time before being caught. Instead, she'd elected to pinch pennies and wound up in a situation out of her control. There was a moral in there somewhere.

The Tuann, whether due to political preference or a willingness to pay the high docking fees, had a prime spot with the additional benefit of restricting access to all but their own people and select station personnel.

Instead of dodging cargo pallets and a swarm of dock workers, the platform leading to their ship was almost deserted, the only people in sight their own.

Someone had made an effort to make the space welcoming, placing artwork on the walls and rugs on the floors. The corridors lacked the sterile coldness of the economy docks.

The trouble someone had gone to in an effort to make this level luxurious seemed lost on the Tuann guards accompanying Kira. The two who had shadowed her through the station had introduced themselves as Baran and Amila once she exited the conference room. They'd been a silent presence ever since.

Kira didn't know if it was their previous encounter or their normal way of operating, but neither was willing to let her stray more than

CHAPTER SIX

two feet from them. Their intensity had ramped up the moment they walked onto a crowded lift, Amila placing one hand on her shoulder, as Baran took up position in front of them.

When it came to time to exit, he'd cleared the way for them, his intimidating presence sending the shorter humans scurrying out of his way.

Kira didn't say anything about any of this, though she wanted to. Dearly. Instead, she refrained from testing their limits, hoping they would see her as harmless and loosen up their vigilance.

She didn't hold out much hope for that considering her antics on the hovercraft. It's hard to convince someone you're less than you are when they've seen proof of exactly what you're capable of. Still, making things difficult now would mean they watched her more closely later.

The ship came into view, resting gently on the platform. It was a thing of beauty against the backdrop of the interior dock of the space station. None of the other ships docked on the platforms near them came close to comparing.

It looked sleek and fast, its lines fluid and full of curves. Unlike the blocky shapes of human craft, this was a graceful bird, ready and poised to take flight. Its metal shimmered as if a thousand lights were locked inside its body, almost lifelike as it reacted to the environment around it.

Despite its small size, Kira caught sight of unobtrusive protrusions she guessed were its weapons system. It looked like it was loaded for anything. She could see why Himoto and Centcom wanted to get their hands on one of these.

Beyond being a beautiful craft, it looked more maneuverable than anything the Consortium had in its fleet; their warships resembled large barges, easily targeted in battle. This was different, smaller than a human vessel but infinitely more flexible.

Graydon stood near the ship's ramp talking with one of the men who'd come to the rescue of the children, his guards arrayed around him defensively.

Both men looked over as Kira and the others approached. Graydon's expression was one of forced patience as the other man jerked his chin down in a respectful nod.

"You brought her. Good." Graydon's gaze dropped to Kira's empty hands. "Where are her things?"

Kira didn't know why he bothered sticking to standard since he seemed content to talk over her like she wasn't there.

"She didn't want to return to her ship," Baran said, sounding no happier about it than he had the first time she'd said it.

The argument over her refusal to allow them access to her ship had been short but intense. Neither were able to believe there was nothing she wished to bring with her.

Graydon's focus shifted to Kira. "You will not be able to come back."

Kira stared at him, her expression unchanging.

He shook his head. "Suit yourself. Your House will no doubt be happier for it. They'll supply you with everything you need."

Kira didn't respond to that, despite disliking the insinuation these people related to her would want to wipe any trace of human influence from her life. She was sure they'd change their mind once they got to know her. She was told she was one of the most stubborn, hardheaded people anyone had ever met.

Graydon tilted his head, all the while watching her carefully. "The machine will need to stay."

"Jin goes where I go," Kira said flatly.

The corners of his lips tilted up as if she'd confirmed something for him. Kira wanted to kick herself for responding, knowing he was testing her, seeing how far he could push before she'd react. He was learning her limits. Not necessarily a bad thing, until those very same limits were used against you to force your compliance.

She'd exposed a weakness. A big one. She couldn't trust these people wouldn't take advantage of that.

CHAPTER SIX

The other man shifted, making his presence felt. He was familiar, one of the men on the platform when they'd rescued the kids. "I have to thank you for saving the children. Our House is indebted to you. Please, if there's ever anything you need, don't hesitate to ask."

Kira didn't know what to say to that. Somehow her actions with the children seemed so long ago. So much had happened since then, her entire life upturned and reordered. Her very species changed.

Time was passing, each second containing the possibility the man would turn hostile when she didn't give him an appropriate response.

"You don't owe me anything," she finally said.

The man's eyes lightened and he dipped his head again.

The stomp of boots distracted them from their conversation. Graydon's guard slammed up as he looked over Kira's shoulder.

She turned to see what had attracted his attention and stiffened as several humans dressed in the uniform of the space force marched down the corridor.

Clad in dark gray pants and a black top, they moved with military precision, the thud of their boots reverberating in the hall.

Jace led them, his gaze focused on Kira and Graydon. His expression was hard to read as he angled toward them.

Graydon let out a muttered oath before he straightened, his face once again an implacable mask as he watched their approach.

Jace stopped before them. "Lord Graydon, I want to once again extend our thanks for letting us see Kira to her new home."

Kira fought the urge to roll her eyes at that. Jace had grown into an accomplished liar during her absence.

Her gaze wandered to the rest of those with him. Six in all.

She idly noted the star emblazoned over the left side of their chest. Five intersecting lines of various lengths meant to represent a star. Its presence told her these people worked directly under Centcom's command. They had no alliance to any but Centcom.

If they'd been a detachment from one of the colonies, they would have carried its symbol in the place of the star.

Jin made a pained sound.

Kira caught the cause second later. She sucked in a harsh breath at the sight of the patch sewn onto the outer cuff of their right arm. It was in the shape of a dog's paw.

The Curs.

Pain lanced through Kira.

She didn't listen as Graydon and Jace exchanged stilted pleasantries. She was caught up in memories of others wearing that same patch, people she had once known as well as she knew herself. Men and women she would have gladly died for, but who had gone before her.

Kira barely noticed as Graydon took his leave, leaving Kira and Jace standing alone.

"Why would you bring them?" Jin asked into the silence. His voice throbbed with the same pain strangling Kira.

At the sound of it, she drew herself up, taking her emotions and stuffing them deep.

She'd forgotten Jin would have the same reaction. She hadn't been the only one to suffer loss. The thought stabilized her.

Jace's body went stiff and alert, his intelligent gaze picking up some of their emotional turbulence.

"I'm sorry. I forgot you wouldn't have known we reinstated the unit," he said. "Will you be okay?"

Kira was silent for a long moment. "Yes, it's just strange seeing others wearing that patch."

Her patch.

He opened his mouth as a loud exclamation came from the rest.

"Kira, girl, we thought you dead," Tank said as he lumbered over.

Tank hadn't been in her squad, but he'd been a wave runner like her. His unit had supported hers a lot and they'd gotten to know each other as acquaintances. His call sign was oddly fitting. Nearly as tall as the Tuann, Tank had legs the size of tree trunks, with arms to match.

He shouldn't have been as good a hoverboard pilot as he was. She'd

CHAPTER SIX

seen him fly, and he lived up to his name, plowing through enemies like he was a tank.

The woman beside him let out a low gasp, her jaw dropping in surprise. "Is that Phoenix and Tin Man?"

"You know it, Blue," Jin called, sailing over to the woman and circling her once.

Blue put one hand up and let Jin nudge it, a soft, nostalgic smile on her face.

Small and wiry, she'd grown up since Kira had last seen her. Back then, she'd been a scrappy kid who went by her given name of Yuki and had more bravery than sense. Now, it seemed she'd earned a place among the Curs.

Kira was happy for her. She knew being a Cur had been Blue's dream.

Her dark black hair was pulled away from her face, the tips dyed a sapphire blue. Her eyes snapped and crackled with vitality as she looked around with her ever-present curiosity.

The other two faces were entirely new to Kira. They looked at her with wide, impressed eyes.

She glanced away, uncomfortable with the attention.

The last man glared at her with a hatred that seared. He was Blue's opposite, moving with a sleek caution where the other woman bounced through life convinced it would conform to her expectations. He had an athlete's build, long and lean, as he stalked past, not pausing to greet her.

A barely visible scar along his chin from where a Tsavitee had gotten too close taunted her with the past.

Of those present, Raider was the only other from the original Curs. And he wanted nothing to do with her.

"And I thought this couldn't get any worse," Jin muttered, seeing him go.

"It's fine, Jin."

The last woman present stepped up to Jace.

He gave her an awkward smile. "Thank you for accompanying us, Grace. I'll let you return to your duties now."

Grace didn't respond, shooting Kira a seething glare before stepping close and pulling Jace's head to hers. The two shared a long, drawn-out kiss. The seconds ticked by as the rest stared at them.

Kira shifted, uncomfortable. "Have the rules of fraternization changed since I've been gone?"

Blue snickered. "Ignore them. Grace is insecure since she knows Knight had a thing for you."

Kira frowned. "No, he didn't."

Blue rolled her eyes. "It always amazes me how you can be so perceptive, yet blind to the things right in front of you."

Kira's frown didn't lessen. She found it hard to believe Blue. Kira and Jace had always been friends, close friends, but that was as far as it ever went. There had never been anything remotely romantic on either side.

Blue dropped the subject and bumped her with her hip. "Nixxy, where have you been?"

"Don't answer her," Tank said. "She's trying to win the pool."

Kira blinked.

"Don't listen to him," Blue said. "It's not just because I've got a couple hundred credits riding on you answering correctly. I'm genuinely curious."

"There's a betting pool?" Jin asked.

Blue smirked. "Yup. Most of the boardheads think you two are dead. Those who knew you, know better."

Blue looked at her expectantly.

"Here and there," Kira said finally, her throat feeling tight from suppressed emotion.

Jace saved her from having to say anything further as he untangled himself from his paramour and walked toward them. Grace shot Kira another hostile glare before disappearing down the corridor.

"Ask where our quarters are and then stow our things," Jace ordered.

CHAPTER SIX

Blue snapped a salute before bouncing toward the Tuann ship. Tank followed.

Jace paused next to Kira. "You really going to be all right with this?"

Kira shook her head. "I don't really have a choice, do I?"

CHAPTER SEVEN

The trip to Ta Da'an was projected to take over a month. Not exactly ideal for Kira's purposes, but the Tuann were far from the main throughways of space. There were no quick hyperjumps capable of shortening the journey.

In the meantime, Kira was stuck exploring the vessel her former people so coveted.

It didn't take long to see why. The Tuann had an impressive ability to turn their ships into walking pieces of art, designed as much around comfort as function. It made sense in a race who had conquered space travel while humanity was still pulling itself out of the muck and the mud.

There were three observation decks looking out into the darkness of space, each more impressive than the previous. Kira's favorite quickly became the conservatory with a glass ceiling. When the lights were off, it felt like standing planetside after sunset, the starry night sky a familiar and welcome presence above.

The quarters where she'd been settled were also another example of the Tuann's ability to combine luxury with comfort. They were unlike any other ship quarters she'd ever had. Instead of being small and cramped, she'd been given a suite. A room for entertaining should she wish it—she didn't. Another, with the most comfortable bed she'd ever had and a bathroom bigger than her bunk on the *Wanderer*.

Such luxuries would be easy to grow accustomed to—a sentiment Kira resisted. This was temporary, no matter what the Tuann and

CHAPTER SEVEN

humans thought. Soon enough she'd be back on her own ship with its small bunk and smaller bathroom.

Given the size of the rooms, the furnishings built out of real wood, and a closet filled with clothes made from fabrics she'd never seen before, she had to wonder who had been kicked out to make room for her.

Suites this nice didn't go unoccupied, which made her suspicious of who among the crew had a reason to resent Kira moving into their space.

Her days developed a routine. Wake up, grab some food, run on the track, head to her room. Sometimes she varied it by taking a detour to one of the observatories, but for the most part, she kept to herself.

Something easier said than done, on a ship this size.

A week into the voyage, Kira headed toward the Tuann mess hall, grabbing a tray and moving through the short line before stopping at the counter. The cooks knew her, loading up her plate with strange food that managed to be as visually appealing as it was delicious.

She paused as she surveyed the room, noticing the Curs in one corner. Raider and Jace were absent, but the rest of them huddled around a table.

"I think they're talking about you," Jin murmured.

Kira had already picked up on that from the way one of the newbies glanced up and then away, before leaning forward.

"Shall we eavesdrop?" Jin asked slyly as Kira set her tray on an empty table.

Before she could stop him, the Curs' conversation was filtering into her auditory implant.

"That's the Phoenix?" Nova asked.

Since the journey had begun, Kira had managed to get the names of the newbies. William Black was known to the others as Nova. The other man was Luke Rogers or Maverick.

"The person with the highest wave runner kill count in a single battle?" Nova asked skeptically.

"That's her," Tank confirmed.

"I thought she'd be different," Nova said.

"What were you expecting?" Blue asked. "Flames to shoot from her eyes or something?"

"Naw. It's just she doesn't seem like the sort who has done what the rumors say," he said.

The others were quiet.

Nova leaned closer, his voice dropping. "I heard she's the reason Rothchild's moon is in three pieces."

Tank and Blue were conspicuously silent as he continued. Kira absently ate a cube of something white with blue dots flecked inside it.

"You know some people call her a mass murderer for what was done there. She caused nearly ten thousand deaths with that stunt."

Kira paused with her fork halfway to her mouth before setting it down. Suddenly her appetite was gone.

She stood.

"I for one am grateful for what she did," Maverick said, not looking up from his plate. "I'm from Rothchild. I was on the planet during the invasion. If she hadn't set the nuke, we would have lost the entire planet instead of only the moon."

The words cut out as Jin turned off his eavesdropping technology, trailing morosely behind her as she left the mess hall behind.

"Sorry, Kira."

"Don't be. It's good we know what they're saying," she assured him.

Even if the reminder of her past brought to the fore nasty emotions.

She spotted Amila in the corridor, the other woman smiling and waving. "Would you like to visit an observation room with me?"

Kira sighed, somehow unsurprised at the woman's presence. It seemed wherever she went on the ship, she or Baran inevitably joined her within half an hour.

"Sure," Kira said, not quite ready to return to her room.

The observatory would at least present a distraction. Too bad it

CHAPTER SEVEN

couldn't also overwrite her memories.

***

Several days later, Kira hesitated on the threshold to the gym, taking in the many bodies inhabiting it. Normally, at this hour it was empty, affording her the opportunity to exercise without having so many eyes watching her.

Everywhere on the ship, people stared. For someone used to near-constant isolation, it was grating.

Amila and Baran paused next to her, shooting expectant glances her way.

Kira returned them with a bland stare. Somehow, she had a feeling her two tag-a-longs might have something to do with the crowd.

Tattletales.

She sighed and padded forward. It didn't really matter if they did. She was here now, and her body ached to burn off some energy. Might as well make the visit worthwhile. In two hours, this place would be packed as a third of Graydon's crew came off shift.

Then, she'd have to fight for space on the track.

Besides, she wasn't the type to turn tail and run. If they wanted to watch her jog in circles, they were welcome to do so.

Kira found a spot on the mat far from the rest and bent, stretching low as her hamstrings tightened then relaxed, the stretch pulling pleasantly on tired muscles.

It wasn't often she had access to a track and she'd taken advantage, running farther than was perhaps wise.

She kept an eye on the other two groups as she widened her stance and then bent over one leg. Maybe if she took long enough, they'd finish their training and leave.

No such luck.

Kira straightened, pulling one foot up as she balanced on the other. The meaty sound of flesh hitting flesh filled the space. She found it telling, both groups had decided to demonstrate their prowess through hand-to-hand combat.

The Tuann and humans pointedly ignored each other as they sparred on opposite sides of the gym. At least, that was what they wanted you to believe. Kira caught more than one sidelong look from each group as they checked out the other.

Not surprising, given the tense relations between the two.

Graydon stepped onto the mat as Kira finished with her stretching and headed to the track running along the circumference of the room.

A man, slightly shorter, but as well built stepped up to face him. For a long second, they were both motionless, studying each other as they waited for some unseen signal to begin.

They burst into movement, flowing around each other like water as they delivered well-placed hits. The sharp crack of their blocks followed Kira as she started her slow jog, Baran and Amila setting off at a pace a hair slower than hers—enough to stay about ten feet behind her.

She knew from prior experience if her pace slowed, theirs would too. If it sped up, so would theirs. She'd resigned herself to their company and ignored them as much as she could.

Jin peeled off, drifting closer to the ceiling as Kira's body woke up. He liked to tell her, exercise was for those with flesh. He had better things to do with his energy than run around in circles like a damn rodent.

Graydon had chosen a spot easily visible no matter where in the room you were. It made it easy to watch the match. Something Kira shamelessly did.

His opponent was good. Very good. Both men were efficient, no movement wasted. They had power and speed behind every blow. She could see why the Tuann were considered deadly warriors and such important allies.

They were clearly the equal of any Tsavitee Kira had come up against.

CHAPTER SEVEN

Jace and his team would have trouble with them if they fought them one-on-one. It'd be better to overwhelm the Tuann with numbers. In hand-to-hand combat, they wouldn't go down easily.

Something to remember for the future.

Graydon took down his opponent in a movement he made look ridiculously easy but would have probably caused a sprained ankle or broken bone, if someone inexperienced had tried it.

He looked up then, his gaze catching hers. There was a primal energy there, a fierce light in his eyes.

Kira didn't react outwardly, despite the sharp edge of awareness coursing through her. She looked away, feigning disinterest as she returned her attention to her run, letting her mind shut off as she picked up speed.

She sank into the rhythm of her pace as she forgot about her unwelcome fellow gym goers, concentrating on the things of importance, her breathing and running.

She was halfway through her run when the youth she'd rescued on the station caught her attention. His expression was focused and intent as he held a staff taller than him.

Kira's pace slowed slightly as curiosity took hold.

An armored figure, sword in hand, rose from the ground like a ghostly apparition. He was short and squat, his shoulders wider than Tank's. He also had no face, just a blank space where it should be.

A simulation, Kira realized. A lifelike training device used in place of a sparring partner. Instead of a physical blow, you would receive an electric zap whenever you failed to block. Kira had never seen one mimic reality this well. It far surpassed even the most advanced human version available.

Baran and Amila had explained how they worked the first time she'd visited the gym. They'd followed that immediately by asking if she'd like to try it. She'd declined for many reasons, the least of which, she got the feeling the question was a test.

The boy attacked, his movements jerky and clumsy. The armored figure blocked easily and counterattacked. The boy flinched, pain chasing across his face.

Kira passed just as the boy lunged, only to be thrown to the edge of the mat. Bad move. He should have tried to disrupt the simulation's center of gravity, rather than going directly in for a strike.

The girl from the sailboat watched with a pensive expression on her face, a staff similar to the boy's cradled in her arms.

Liont and Fari stood behind her, pained sympathy in their eyes as the boy hit the mat hard.

Kira continued past, keeping one eye on their group as she moved to the opposite side of the gym.

She circled the track two more times as the boy grew more frustrated with each failed attempt, never changing his attack, doing the exact same thing time and again.

Kira slowed as he hit the edge of the simulation. He was going about it the wrong way. He needed to vary his movements up. His form was atrocious and his fighting style utterly unsuited to his small size.

He also demonstrated a distinct lack of thought or even a semblance of strategy, a fact which would bite him in the ass eventually.

Most civilians thought fighting and combat were simple things driven by instinct and decided by strength. This held true at times, but like war, a fight was more than the power behind a punch or the speed of an attack. It took foresight, planning, strategy. Good warriors had brains as well as brawn.

Right now, the boy wasn't demonstrating either quality.

The little girl sitting on the sidelines was the first to notice as Kira stopped on the track and turned toward them, watching as the boy picked himself up to square off against the simulation yet again.

He had guts. She'd give him that.

"Joule," the girl said softly.

Liont and Fari faced her, both men's faces polite as they nodded at her.

CHAPTER SEVEN

The boy looked up, his eyes alert and slightly startled as he noticed Kira for the first time.

He said a word and the simulation froze. He stepped out of the simulation square, his face grave.

Kira watched as he and the girl faced her. They bent in small, identical bows.

Her lips quirked. How adorable.

"Lady, we wanted to thank you for your kindness," the boy said, the words oddly formal. It was a marked difference from the suspicious, fierce thing who had challenged her when she'd pulled them from the burning sailboat.

She watched the two, not knowing how to respond. She hadn't saved them to receive their gratitude. Granted, her actions had consequences she had not foreseen then, but she didn't blame either of them for that.

"What are you doing?" Kira asked, ignoring the thank you.

The two exchanged a look before focusing on Kira. As before, the boy was the first to speak. "I am training."

Kira could see that, but she didn't know the reason why, or why he seemed so desperate. The emotion fueled every move he made.

"Why?" she asked.

The boy's mouth flattened into a stubborn line as he stared up at her. It was an expression she'd seen on other faces, ones who haunted her nightmares. Something about it said he'd had the innocence torn from him, and knew the only person he could count on to protect him from now on, was himself.

That expression kept her rooted in place instead of following her normal routine of retreating to her room as soon as her run was done.

"Joule has to be ready," the girl said.

"For what?"

"To protect us."

Now wasn't that an interesting answer, especially given the phalanx of protection currently circling them.

Baran, seeing the question on her face, stepped forward. "Joule and Ziva are the last of House Maxiim's future. Joule will either demonstrate his fitness as a House overlord or seek to dissolve his House and swear fealty to another House."

"He means give up our name and lineage," Joule said angrily.

That was what was fueling him? A desire not to lose his family name?

Boring. Kira had expected more.

"A name is merely a bunch of letters strung together and given meaning by someone else," Kira said, her eyes never leaving his.

He scoffed. "You are *luijan*, outsider. You don't know what you're talking about."

Perhaps not. Kira had chosen her name from a book, thinking it meant rebirth. Instead, she'd been off by a letter and ended up with a name with a different meaning. She'd taken her surname from the forest where Himoto had discovered her.

"Maybe, but this outsider knows you're doing that move wrong," Kira said.

Insult flashed across Joule's face. "One of the *oshota* taught me this. They're the emperor's best warriors. Undefeatable in battle. What would a *luijan* know about this?"

Kira's mouth quirked up.

Maybe so, but whoever had taught him that move hadn't done him any favors. She doubted they'd intended to help him at all. Not many people could pull off a direct attack on an opponent that size. He was trying to sink all his power into one thrust. Doable, if you were a lot bigger with a strong foundation to work from.

Graydon and his people all could do it. Liont could, Fari too, she suspected. Kira might be able to, if pressed, and if she didn't have to fight afterward.

For someone the size of a child? Impossible. That technique was unsuitable to his small frame and would be for many years. If he was

CHAPTER SEVEN

serious about learning to fight and protect himself now, he needed to adjust his style to one that would work for him instead of against him. If he continued in this vein, the only thing he would walk away with at the end would be a bunch of bruises.

"Suit yourself," she said, giving him a bland smile before turning and heading back to the track. It was his life. She might have saved it, but that didn't give her the right to stick her nose where he didn't want it.

Baran kept pace with her, glancing at her occasionally. He wanted something. She just couldn't be sure what.

"Our names define our loyalties," Baran explained when they were halfway around the track again. "If he loses his, he'll lose the last link to his family and ancestors. Those men and women you've seen protecting him would be cast upon another House's mercy, dependent on their goodwill for survival."

Kira glanced at him but didn't respond. She grabbed the earbuds she'd removed earlier and stuck them into her ears, tuning him out. She didn't want to talk. She wanted to run.

Baran's expression was frustrated as she faced forward and picked up the pace. He fell back several steps when it became clear Kira had no intention of engaging him.

She did another ten minutes at that pace, one a few notches below a sprint. She finally slowed and stepped off the track, ignoring the people around her as she sat and worked through her stretches.

A pair of feet stepped into her view. Kira held the stretch for several more seconds before she sat back and looked up.

Jace stood in front of her, Raider steps behind him.

Nova and Maverick lurked several mats over, one eye on the Tuann as they performed their own stretches.

"Do you need help?" Jace asked as Kira reclined and raised her leg straight up, grabbing her calf and gently pulling it toward her.

"No."

Jace didn't listen, pushing her leg toward her. "Resist," he said, changing his grip and gently pulling it away from her.

With a grunt Kira did.

"I see your social skills haven't gotten any better." Raider glanced at her two guards where they did their own stretching yards away.

Kira didn't respond as she raised her other leg so Jace could help her with it.

"It'll be hard to convince them to relinquish their claim on you if you never talk to them," Jace said.

Kira grunted. He didn't care about that. He cared about the ships and Kira's ability to convince the Tuann to part with them. Beyond that, she was on her own.

"They're not the right people," she said. She'd listened when they spoke. Her House had laid claim to her. The mark on her wrist seemed to declare her origins for her. Until someone from her House said she was free to go, it didn't matter how convincing or persuasive she was.

"Graydon has a powerful voice among his people," Jace said. "It wouldn't hurt to get him on your side."

She fixed him with a dark scowl. She disliked getting close to people because of what they could do for her.

Jace seemed to understand. "Just try to be a little friendlier. Don't antagonize just because you can."

She didn't do that.

"You're wasting your time," Raider said. "She can't help it. She's worse than a territorial porcupine."

"Why are you here, Raider?" Kira asked, abruptly tired of the not-so-veiled hostility.

He shrugged. "No idea. For some reason, Himoto and Jace thought I might have a mitigating influence on you."

"Guess they didn't get the memo that you hate my guts," Kira shot back.

His smile was thin and failed to reach his eyes. "All of us from the old days hate you, even Blue. She's feeling nostalgic right now, but

CHAPTER SEVEN

pretty soon she's going to remember who you are and what you've done. She's going to remember you're the reason all our friends are dead."

Each word was like a blow, merciless as they landed. Kira's mask slammed down as ugly emotions threatened to surge to the surface.

Raider crouched, keeping his words soft, almost gentle-sounding. "Do what you're here to do. It'll make everyone's life much easier."

He let her see inside him, dropping all pretense and masks. He really did hate her. There was loathing in his eyes. She didn't let him see how much that glimpse affected her, locking her feelings away to be examined at another time. If she'd ever thought they might forgive her, that naivety was gone now, washed away by the deep currents of loathing buffeting her.

It was easy to see Jace agreed. He didn't take Raider to task for speaking that way to a commanding officer or warn him to keep his mouth shut. No, he let Raider say his piece, even as he helped Kira stretch, keeping his movements gentle but firm.

She glanced up at him and almost wished she hadn't. His face was blank and emotionless, as if he wasn't even there.

Raider didn't say anything else, standing and walking away. Jace finished with her left leg in the next second.

"Think about it," he said, before following Raider.

Jin's engines hummed as he edged near to where Kira sat for long minutes after they'd left, feeling like they'd gut-punched her instead of simply revealed their true emotions.

"Kira, don't listen to them," he said softly. "They don't know the whole truth."

"And we're going to keep it that way," she said.

Because as hard as it was to admit, both men had a reason to feel the way they did. In their eyes, she was the one responsible for the nuke that killed their entire team when a mission went sideways. She was the one who'd murdered them even if it was to prevent millions of deaths.

To their eyes, it wasn't a fair trade. Most days, she agreed.

She was both hero and villain. It hadn't escaped her the edge of hero worship on the new members of the Curs, or how that worship had faded in the weeks while on the ship. Humans both loved and hated their heroes. They liked nothing better than to watch them fall from grace. Her actions might have been the catalyst that brought about the end to the war, but they'd caused a lot of deaths as well. Not everyone agreed with her methods.

Baran had straightened when Jace and Raider approached. After they left, he looked even less happy. She got the sense he and the rest of the Tuann didn't want the humans anywhere near her.

As Graydon approached, Kira fought a sense of frustration. She wasn't in the mood for another confrontation. Energy licked along her skin, the run not nearly enough to exorcize it from her system.

Her skin itched with the need for a fight. If Graydon pressed her, she was very much afraid she'd give him that fight.

He loomed over her, his size impressive and no less intimidating for the storm taking place behind his eyes. She had to lean back slightly and tilt her head to be able to see his face. The Tuann were tall, all of them. It made her wonder why she was so much shorter.

She wasn't small, especially by human standards. At five-feet-seven with an athletic build, she'd never felt short until now.

"Your run wasn't enough. You have too much energy built up," he said abruptly.

Kira blinked as she remained still. He wasn't wrong, but she was surprised he could tell. Her run had been half the length as normal, and the confrontation with Jace and Raider had ramped up her energy levels even more.

It would only be a matter of time before it boiled over, leaving her with the option to fight or fuck. It'd taken a long time before she could figure out why she sometimes felt like she'd downed a lightning bolt, her energy welling up out of nowhere. To drain it off, she had to exhaust herself unless she could find something or someone to

CHAPTER SEVEN

take it out on.

Given the way he spoke, she had to wonder if this was a trait of the Tuann and not just an oddity of hers.

"We have the simulations for a reason," he said, his expression reserved. "Has no one shown them to you?"

He didn't glance at her guards or look away. He knew the answer. He was waiting for her to admit it.

"I prefer running."

"It is not enough," he said again.

She lifted an eyebrow in lazy amusement. He knew that from the considerable time they'd spent together, did he?

"I disagree."

He bared his teeth in a threatening smile. "Come, you look in need of activity before you wisp away into nothing."

He didn't wait for her agreement, his powerful strides taking him to one of the simulators. Kira glared after him, the audacity of the order rubbing her the wrong way. She didn't have to follow. There was nothing stopping her from turning around and leaving while his back was turned. Somehow, she doubted Graydon was the type to chase her around the ship when thwarted.

"Graydon is not the patient sort," Baran said.

"Yes, the last person came to regret annoying him after Graydon suspended him from the ceiling for three days," Amila added.

Neither guard's expressions changed from the bland mask they typically wore. It was hard to tell if they were joking or not.

Kira leveraged herself up and followed Graydon to one of the simulators, stopping outside the clear boundary marking its territory.

Graydon stood off to the side, swiping through simulations, his forehead creased in thought.

Jin settled in his customary place right over her shoulder. "This should be interesting."

"I'm glad you think so," Kira muttered.

He snickered. "At least there is little chance of you destroying anything this way."

"I don't destroy things," she hissed, feeling off-balance and conspicuous as Graydon's warriors drifted over.

Their interest was clear as they jostled each other and whispered as they looked her over.

"They're like giant kids," Jin observed.

"The kind who can rip your arm off and beat you with it," Kira returned, glaring at the warriors. They seemed to think that was funny. The tallest one smothered a smile as he dipped his head.

It wasn't the reaction Kira was used to. Most humans had heard of her and her reputation. When she glared, they usually ran. Those who didn't, often lacked sufficient brain cells.

"The *Wanderer*," Jin said.

The words came out of nowhere and Kira frowned at him in confusion.

"The *Wanderer*, the latest thing you destroyed. I have other examples, but it looks like the mountain is ready for you," Jin said in a lofty voice.

Sure enough, Graydon had finished and was now regarding the two of them with an interested expression.

Graydon crossed his arms, the muscles in his arms and chest bulging as he gave her a smile full of challenge, the smug conviction he'd already won in his expression. "Perhaps you can demonstrate to Joule just where he's gone wrong."

So, he'd heard that. Their senses were better than she thought. Probably better than hers.

A disquieting thought occurred to her. If he'd heard what she said to Joule, he'd probably heard the exchange between her, Jace and Raider. Not ideal but good to know.

Kira hesitated to step into the simulator, aware of how she was now the center of attention in the gym. Jace and the Curs remained in their corner, but they made no secret of their interest. Even the children had taken a break from their activities.

CHAPTER SEVEN

Kira's shoulders slumped as she fought the urge to bang her head against the nearest hard surface. She'd never particularly enjoyed having all eyes on her, and it was more irritating now, when she wanted to avoid all attention.

Worse, any thought of letting herself get knocked out in the first few seconds went out the window.

She couldn't afford to be seen as entirely weak. The Tuann were much like predators. If they sensed any weakness, they'd run right over her—for her own good of course.

No, if she wanted to meet these people on an even playing field, she needed to be strong enough to protect herself, without becoming a threat or a treasure they wished to acquire.

Just because they weren't from her House didn't mean they lacked the potential to delay her goal. Every Tuann on this ship would carry stories of the lost child home with them. Appear too weak and others might seek to take advantage, appear too strong and any hope of them underestimating her disappeared.

It put her in a tricky spot.

Reluctantly, she moved past Graydon, a shiver of sensation rocking her as her shoulder brushed his. For whatever reason, she was intensely aware of him as a man. Galling, considering he saw her as one step up from a child.

She padded over to the mat marking the edge of the simulator's domain and waited, forgetting the rest of the gym as she focused on the coming fight.

There was a soft thrum, the faintest snap of electricity as the simulation began. From the floor, a being started to form.

Kira tensed. What surprise had Graydon picked out for this little excursion? He had something up his sleeve, there'd been too much arrogance in his expression to assume otherwise.

"Well, shit," she said, her hope this would be easy, disappearing.

She wasn't the only one to have an immediate reaction to the creature. Jin let out a low whistle as alarmed exclamations came from those humans in the room.

Those who'd fought in the war would recognize what she was up against. A Tsavitee war drone, class two, its intelligent eyes locking on her as its cry pierced the air in a sound that chilled her straight to the bone.

CHAPTER EIGHT

That oversized bastard had really gone all out, Kira thought grimly. He couldn't have picked anything simple. No, he'd gone straight for the throat, choosing an opponent he knew would pull a visceral reaction from every human in the room.

She didn't dare turn her attention from the war drone, knowing if she did, it would tear her apart. In a different time, with different people, she might have settled for giving Graydon several choice gestures that perfectly articulated how she felt about this situation.

Since she was supposed to be currying favor, she settled for a soft angry sound as she visualized all the things she'd like to do with the arrogant Tuann if given half the chance. Throttling him featured heavily in her schemes.

The war drone, like some of the Tsavitee lower forms, was digitigrade, meaning it walked on its toes rather than its heels, giving the appearance of knees bending backward.

Taller than Kira by several feet, the war drone was built like a wall. An angry, vicious wall. Its entire purpose lay in its ability to pierce the enemy's lines while the smaller Tsavitee swarmed behind it.

The longer arms made it seem almost ape-like. It lacked fur, its skin a dark blue with smaller rosettes on its arms and shoulders. Horns curled up from its head and it had long lower canines denting the top of its lip.

As much as Kira hated to admit it, Graydon had made a good choice when selecting this opponent. Its larger size meant Kira would be on unequal footing, given she was smaller and physically weaker than her opponent.

Bringing it down would take work. Once it was done, neither Joule or any other would be able to claim she had the advantage of size.

That's if she could bring it down.

She had to wonder what Graydon had been thinking in setting this up. While she could take the drone down—as could every member of the Curs—most wouldn't be able to. He couldn't know for sure her history, which meant this was either a test or he was making a point. To her, or Joule was the question.

"Would you like a *ratan*?" Graydon asked with smug politeness.

Out of the corner of her eye she saw him lift a long staff, much like Joule's. She shook her head. While the staff would increase her reach, she had never liked fighting with one. Its shape had never felt natural to her.

She much preferred the energy edged swords adapted from the katanas of ancient Japan.

Besides, this lesson worked best when no weapon was used at all.

He lowered the *ratan*, a small twist to his lips saying her choice amused him. So glad she could provide entertainment for him and his warriors.

Kira's breath deepened as she watched her opponent. She didn't move as she studied the drone. They'd caught its essence perfectly.

Still, it wasn't real. That intelligence in its eyes was an illusion—a program designed to react to certain preset conditions.

Maybe it was a little more advanced than any simulation she'd ever seen, but it was still a simulation. Fake.

At least Graydon had chosen one of the lower classes. If she'd faced a wraith or lizard, she'd be a little more worried.

The Tsavitee struck, its powerful legs helping it clear the space between them in the blink of an eye. Kira dropped, rolling under it and regaining her feet, her posture defensive.

It was quick, startling so. Kira circled away from it, feeling warier than she had moments before.

CHAPTER EIGHT

The Tsavitee straightened, its back facing her as its head turned toward her, rotating almost ninety degrees.

The sight chilled Kira, the gesture so similar to a real Tsavitee drone. It was like looking through a time machine, everything that had once given her nightmares made suddenly, breathtakingly, real. Abruptly, Kira remembered what it was like to be hunted, to have adrenaline flood your system as every one of your senses revved into overdrive as danger stalked your every move.

The Tsavitee's body turned as it lowered its head, the horns pointed at her like a ram's. It charged. Kira slid to the right, narrowly missing being impaled. If he'd struck her, it would have been like being hit by a car going thirty-five miles an hour. In real life, she would have ended up with broken bones—if she was lucky—and liquefied organs if she wasn't.

She circled the Tsavitee, getting distance. She forgot about the people watching, forgot why she needed to keep her skills under wrap. All she knew was survival and ensuring the enemy didn't live long enough to come after her again.

She hopped back, her head up as the Tsavitee charged again. This time she was ready.

She stepped out of the way, turning with the drone as she reached out and grabbed a horn. She pulled toward her right as she stepped into his charge, using her hip as a fulcrum as she yanked him off his feet. He hit the ground head first.

There was an audible crack as his neck snapped. The Tsavitee went limp, its limbs twitching.

Slowly, he began to dissolve as Kira stared at him with a sinking sense of dread. Crap. She'd meant to drag that out for a lot longer. Maybe let him do a little bit of damage first.

She'd forgotten herself in the incredible realism. It had thrown her back in time to when the stakes in such a battle was your life, and you didn't screw around with fancy moves.

Graydon's eyes met hers, his expression enigmatic and his eyes dark. He gave her a small nod of respect. It was a sentiment reflected on many of his warriors' faces, some slightly disbelieving as they stared at the spot where the drone had been.

Kira controlled her pulse as she made her way to the edge of the simulator. Unease moved through her as she realized every person in the gym had watched the match. Jace and Raider's faces were blank, but the rest of the Curs looked awestruck. Nova seemed shocked. Maverick was a little harder to read as he stared at the empty floor.

She ducked her head and looked away. Joule's mouth was slightly open and there was a stunned look in his eyes. Ziva was the opposite. She stared up at Kira like she was a goddess come to rescue them, hope lighting up her face.

Kira strode away as fast as she could without running. Ziva was going to have to look elsewhere for a role model. She'd gotten out of the business of hope a long time ago.

* * *

The fight with the Tsavitee had quelled some of the restless energy plaguing Kira since boarding the ship, but she still hadn't found her calm by the time she reached her deck.

Instead of returning to her room, she bypassed it in favor of heading toward the conservatory, her two unwelcome guides trailing behind her.

Kira had spent much of her life in the cold ships of space, but she remembered the comforting smells of dirt and growing things. She'd taken the name Forrest not just because Himoto had discovered her in one, but because there was something special about walking among trees hundreds of years older than her. Their presence spoke to her soul.

It was the same feeling she got while walking on the meandering paths in this conservatory. The room itself was as big as the gym, though its exact dimensions were hard to determine given the way

CHAPTER EIGHT

the vegetation blocked the sight lines, giving people the impression it was much larger than it was.

Every plant here was both strange and familiar. She didn't have names for any of them, but they were comforting in a way she couldn't explain.

Kira's pace was fast as she moved along the paths. Several minutes passed before she slowed from a near run to a slow walk, her breathing deepening as the peace of this place invaded her. She found a spot of grass and settled back, looking up at the thick windows and the darkness of space above dotted with its blanket of glitter.

Her hands shook and her stomach had giant balls of snakes in it from the aftermath of the simulation. She thought she was doing better. Perhaps not, if one lackluster battle was enough to engender this reaction.

Jin meandered through the branches, humming softly to himself. He knew she wanted privacy and he was smart enough to give it to her.

She filled her lungs before releasing it slowly. Things could be worse. Yes, she hadn't meant to tip her hand quite so thoroughly, but she'd managed to keep from using the power hiding at her core. That was something at least. Small wins and all that.

There was a soft sound from the path, alerting her to the fact she was no longer alone. She groaned internally, lifting her head.

Graydon's imposing form pushed through the branches. Somehow, she never got used to his size or the almost cruel beauty of his face. The words on her lips died. She sat up, not liking the thought of being in such a vulnerable position with him looming above her.

"You don't have any more Tsavitee simulations waiting to attack, do you?" Kira asked, her voice dry.

A soft snort escaped him as he settled beside her.

"No, I think you've surprised me enough for one day," Graydon said. "I hadn't expected your skills to be quite so impressive."

Kira ran her fingers along a blade of grass, feeling the life and vitality in it as she thought over what he'd said. She didn't know whether she believed him. If he was surprised, it meant he'd set up that test knowing she'd be humiliated and left with several bruises by the end.

The question was why.

"You know I was in the military. Why the shock that I know how to handle myself?" Kira asked.

"I've seen humans fight. They're not that impressive."

Then he hadn't been watching the right humans. It was true most humans couldn't compete one on one with Graydon or any of his men, but given enough training and incentive anything was possible.

Any one of her old team could have set Graydon on his ass. Even Jace and Raider wouldn't go down easily.

"That's not arrogant or anything," Kira said.

He shrugged, not seeming bothered about her words. "I call it like I see it."

Kira shook her head. The more time she spent with this man, the more he irritated her.

Graydon's teeth flashed in a dark smile. He knew he was getting to her, knew it and liked it.

She didn't know what to make of that. Few had ever challenged her in such a way. That he did, someone who wasn't an ally but also couldn't yet be considered an enemy, was unsettling.

"You don't like humans, do you?" Kira asked.

He reclined onto the grass, resting his weight on one elbow as he angled his body to face her. His expression thoughtful as he considered her statement. "Not particularly."

It was truthful enough to startle a small sound from her. Of course, he didn't. The sentiment shouldn't surprise her. More surprising was the fact he'd admitted to it. In her experience, most preferred to lie to themselves. Pretend they were less judgmental and prejudiced than they were.

"You realize my loyalties are with them, right?"

CHAPTER EIGHT

He didn't seem particularly bothered by that statement, his lips curling up for a reason only he could know. "For now."

"Cocky."

He chuckled, the sound whispering across her skin like velvet. She suppressed an involuntary shiver.

There was an awareness in his eyes, one echoed within her. It had been a long time since she'd had such thoughts about another, and definitely never about one who saw her as a duty and a liability.

"I have reason to be," he said. "Becoming the Emperor's Face is difficult. You don't get to my position without understanding things."

Kira gave him a deadpan look. "Please. Regale me with your wisdom. I don't know how I made it this far in life without it."

His teeth flashed again at her sarcasm, the look in his eyes saying he enjoyed their banter. Kira wasn't sure that was a good thing. It was kind of like being the sole focus of a tiger. You didn't know if it wanted to eat you or just maul you a little.

He leaned forward, his eyes half-lidded. "Try as hard as you want, but you'll never be one of them. They'll never fully understand you, not like we would."

This time her smile was dry and humorless. "You assume I want someone who understands me."

The playful seduction in his expression faded, and this time the look he gave her was strangely sympathetic. It made that tight feeling Kira carried around with her all the time worse.

"We all want that," he said simply. "We're not meant to traverse this life alone."

Kira lifted her chin. Maybe not, but that's exactly what she was doing. The time for companions had passed. She'd found a balance in her life. She wasn't sure she wanted to disrupt that for maybes.

"Kira, I found a flower you need to see," Jin shouted, zooming out from the underbrush and breaking the fragile moment. "It looks exactly like cat ears!"

Jin's flight stuttered when he caught sight of Graydon.

Kira was grateful for the distraction and rose. "Let's see this flower."

"I'd be interested in seeing what could so shock your drone," Graydon said, uncoiling as he rose.

Kira hesitated but couldn't think of a way to politely decline. "It's your ship."

He could go where he wanted

"Indeed, it is," Graydon said, with a small smile Kira couldn't decipher.

Graydon followed her as she ducked around trees and under branches as Jin zipped through effortlessly, his smaller size and ability to ignore gravity allowing him to take advantage of passageways they could not.

It didn't take long until they were standing under a canopy of tree branches dotted with thousands of small lilac-colored flowers.

Jin lowered to several flowers growing from dead logs on the ground.

"The *azira aliri*," Graydon murmured when it became clear what had so fascinated Jin. "I'm surprised he found them."

Jin crooned as he flitted from flower to flower like a giant hummingbird. He'd been right. They looked like cat's ears perched on round stamen, if one ignored the fact they were all bright orange and blue.

"They normally hide their faces when strangers near." Graydon's shoulder brushed Kira's as he leaned forward. "They must not sense a threat from your machine."

"Jin has a way of putting people at ease," Kira said.

"You've named it?" Graydon asked.

Kira was silent for a long second as she debated the best response. It wasn't like she hid what Jin was, but she didn't advertise it either. Too many people had tried to call her a liar.

Jin wasn't a typical artificial intelligence. His metal body was more accident than anything else. He'd been a person once; flesh and blood like her. When he'd been hurt beyond healing, his soul had somehow

CHAPTER EIGHT

ended up in that drone. While his outsides were metal, the thing driving him was as human as she was.

"He picked his name," Kira finally said. That was close enough to the truth without bringing up any sticky questions she'd prefer to avoid.

Graydon didn't say anything, turning his attention to Jin.

A small chittering sound from above caught Kira's attention when she would have joined Jin. She jerked as a small creature sailed from the branches to land on her shoulder.

"Easy," Graydon soothed. "It's a *chaterling*. It won't hurt you. It's just saying hi."

The *chaterling* stood on its hind legs and scolded her before settling down. The size of her palm, its fur was a light shade of blue with stripes of darker blue along its back and legs. Two mini horns curled away from its forehead, and long flat ears stuck out from its head.

Two pools of dark brown regarded her as it cocked its head, its tiny wings rising and then settling along its back. Its long tail whipped to circle her neck before it rubbed the side of its face against hers.

Kira held still, not wanting it to bite her. Who knew what sort of diseases it might be carrying.

Finished, it let out a high warble before springing from her shoulder, gliding the small distance to land on one of the *azira aliri*. The stalk containing the round bloom with the cat ears quivered, small bits of fluff burst from the center as the entire flower seemed to perk up.

The *chaterling* curled up on the top, settling its wings over its spine as it let out a high-pitched squeak. From the trees, others appeared, filling the air with small bodies as each found their own flower to perch on.

"There are so many of them," Kira said, impressed.

Graydon's chuckle was warm. "All of our ships carry pieces of home with us. To have a flock of *chaterling*s join your vessel is considered good luck and a sign of an auspicious voyage. Their presence helps keep the garden healthy which in turn keeps those traveling healthy."

It was a complete reversal from the ships Kira had known. Many had hydroponic gardens of some sort but unless you were part of the botany unit, you weren't allowed in. There was too much danger of a careless hand damaging the plants. Since most ships relied on them for oxygen in some small way, contact was kept to a minimum.

Those gardens had nothing on this. They were dim imitations of the real thing. Standing here almost felt like she was planetside again in a strange and old forest, wild but welcoming at the same time.

"We should get one for the *Wanderer*," Jin said enthusiastically, forgetting himself in the excitement of small, living creatures.

"Absolutely not." The *Wanderer* had no plants or garden for these creatures. It would be wrong to subject them to its sterile coldness.

"You never let me have what I want," Jin said sulkily.

Kira rolled her eyes as she bent to peer closer at the plants and their passengers. The wizards were strange. That was for sure.

* * *

Graydon watched the young woman intently. She was different than he expected. Much different.

She held a self-possession startling in one so young. He suspected it had been hard-won on many battlefields, something their own young wouldn't have any experience with. War had a way of changing you and it was almost impossible to escape its grasp unmarked in some way.

Her scars might not be on the surface, but they were there. It made him curious to know what had so shaped her.

What had she been like before all this? Had her smiles come faster? He saw glimpses of the person she'd once been when she engaged with him, but when she thought no one was watching, sadness and loss clung to her like a cloak.

When the humans had told him she'd been part of their military, he

CHAPTER EIGHT

hadn't thought much of it. They preferred a type of warfare the Tuann disliked, shooting their enemy from great distances, the further the better. Unfortunately for them, their weapons were weaker than their enemies' defenses.

However, the way she moved made him doubt his former beliefs. She'd taken down the war drone in less than two minutes. Rarely had he seen someone dispatch one so cleanly. It had been like watching moving art, unbearably beautiful and deliciously lethal. He suspected it only took that long because of her shock at its realism.

Yes, she was not as he believed. He'd do well to remember this lesson. Humans had proved deceptively capable in the past, and for all that she was Tuann, her time with the humans had left its stamp.

"Tell me about these people you claim are my family," Kira said, not lifting her gaze from the *chaterling*.

Graydon tilted his head. It was the first time she'd expressed interest in her people. Baran and Amila had kept him informed of her movements and any conversations she had. They'd said she avoided the subject of the Tuann any time they brought it up.

"They are your family," he said.

"Says you."

He arched an eyebrow. He was not used to such doubt in his word. "You bear their mark. Also, several of their children were taken many years ago."

Her head jerked toward him. "Taken?"

He hesitated, unsure how much of his people's private pain to share with her. It was a dark spot in their history that had affected many. That still affected them.

"Yes, around the time of what we suspect was your birth. We faced great betrayal. The young of many Houses were stolen, you among them. Until we found you, we assumed they'd all been killed." His voice was flat and unemotional as he relayed the information.

She blinked at him, her thoughts hidden and her expression guarded. She held his gaze for several long beats before she turned to the *chaterling*.

"It was a bloody period. Many died. Among them my friends and those I considered as close as family."

There was silence between them as they watched as one *chaterling* tackled another, both crashing off their perches to roll around on the ground as high-pitched squeaks filled the air.

"I'm sorry to hear of your loss," Kira said softly.

He inclined his head. "It was a long time ago."

"You believe I'm one of these children," Kira stated.

"We know you are. The mark on your forearm proclaims your birth House; there are no other marks like it."

"Are my parents alive?"

He hesitated, falling quiet for a moment. "I don't know. We know you are from that House, but your exact lineage is in doubt."

Her eyebrows climbed. "Can't you do a DNA test to find out?"

Graydon gritted his teeth. She didn't know what she was asking. He could forgive her, her ignorance. It wasn't her fault she'd grown up separated from them

"It's more difficult than you assume."

She looked taken aback, her mouth opening before shutting on her questions.

Graydon felt regret as she withdrew. He probably should have found a better way to put that.

"Each House safeguards the secrets locked in the blood of its members. For me to take yours even if it is to confirm your lineage would be considered a grave insult. Wars have been started for less," he said quietly, an apology in his voice. It was the easiest explanation he could think of without revealing too much of their history to her, a Tuann outsider with dangerous ties. "I'm sure your House will make confirming your familial relationship a priority when we arrive."

"Tell me about these Houses. Humans don't have them and I want to understand," she said.

Graydon hesitated, struggling to put into words what most intu-

CHAPTER EIGHT

itively knew. "There are five Great Houses and countless smaller ones. Many small Houses pledge their allegiance and fealty to more powerful Houses in exchange for protection. These are considered branch Houses."

"Is everyone part of a House?" Kira asked.

"For the most part. There are exceptions. A very few elect to become wanderers, their allegiance to themselves. It is a very difficult path. The rest have been exiled from their Houses and are ostracized, deemed too untrustworthy to have dealings with."

Kira made a humming sound as she thought over his words.

"It's a system set in place a long time ago when Houses feuded with one another. Once your loyalty is given, it is nearly impossible to withdraw without your House's permission."

"Sounds restrictive," she observed dryly.

Graydon allowed himself a slight smile. She was not wrong. His people were slaves to tradition and exceptionally slow to change. It could make for a stifling environment at times.

He slid a sidelong look her way. He was curious to see what effect she would have on them. She didn't strike him as the type to bow to tradition for tradition's sake. He'd been named for his ability to see a storm coming before it arrived. Many in their society considered him a danger because of it. But he believed storms were necessary at times.

"Jin, stop playing with your friends. It's time to go," Kira called as the machine swooped and ducked among the *chaterling*, avoiding the young as they fought to land on his housing.

Kira dipped her chin in a nod before the two disappeared through the trees.

Graydon stayed where he was. Solal appeared beside him, his gaze on the flowers that had so fascinated Kira.

"Send Baran and a couple of our warriors into human space to find out everything they can on our Kira," Graydon said, his hands clasped behind him.

Solal turned toward him, a slight surprise on his face. "You would leave her with one guard?"

Graydon flicked an irritated glance at his second. "You know I wouldn't."

Solal's cheeks creased with humor. "Who will you assign to her then? After her demonstration earlier and the way she gave Baran the slip, every one of the *oshota* would volunteer for the honor."

Graydon wasn't surprised. His warriors admired strength, and Kira had demonstrated she had that in spades.

"We need someone whose presence will not be questioned when she is within her House," Graydon said.

Solal's expression turned curious. "That will be difficult. Every one of us falls under the emperor's authority. Our loyalties are owned by him. They will not trust us and it might affect how they treat her."

"Finn will work," Graydon said.

Solal's eyebrows rose. "He's Roake. They won't let him past the front doors."

"His great-grandmother was of Luatha. His line has roots in that House. They'll accept him if only for the chance to bring his bloodline back into alignment with theirs," Graydon said.

"Why him though?"

"I suspect she's not just Luatha but Roake as well," Graydon said.

This time shock crossed Solal's face. "You think she's dual House? You think she's the missing heir for Roake?"

Graydon grunted, giving his second a long look. "Do you know any among the Luatha who could take down a Tsavitee the way she did?"

Solal's expression turned contemplative as he thought over Graydon's statement. "True. They aren't known for their warriors. But you're forgetting, there is no mark indicating Roake and without it you'll have a battle on your hands to get Luatha to share her with those they consider enemy."

"The mark of their House rarely presents before they pass their

CHAPTER EIGHT

adva ka. If she has one, it'll be hidden. Only another Roake elder would be able to reveal it until then," Graydon said.

Solal considered him, his second's gaze contemplative as he calculated the possibilities and their possible outcomes. "Of anyone, you would know given its your birth House. If you're right, House Roake must be informed. This could cause another war if not handled correctly."

Graydon grunted.

"How are you going to get Finn to agree?" Solal asked.

It was a legitimate question, given Finn's tendency to act as a wildcard. After the disaster with his last charge, he'd refused to take another. Convincing him to protect Kira wouldn't be easy.

"I'm going to appeal to his better nature," Graydon said.

Solal sighed. "You mean you're going to threaten him."

Graydon shrugged. Same difference.

CHAPTER NINE

Kira took a deep breath and released it, trying not to let the round blue orb floating outside the star deck intimidate her. They were finally here. Only hours lay between her and meeting people who shared her blood.

No pressure or anything. Just a reunion with a long-lost child everyone assumed dead. Nothing major or anything.

"I thought it would be more impressive," Jin said, moving closer to the window.

"We're still thousands of miles away," Kira said in a distracted voice.

"You know what I mean," he rebuked. "I thought I'd feel different seeing it."

Kira made a wry expression. She'd forgotten. If this was her home, it was Jin's too. When he'd been alive in the traditional sense, he'd been like her, his abilities different but strange. Almost magical.

Her expression turned pensive as she returned to staring at the planet they were fast approaching.

She knew what Jin was trying to say. She felt the same.

There was none of that connection she thought she'd feel upon seeing the planet where she'd been born. She'd felt more nostalgia walking through the conservatory than what she felt for the approaching planet.

She searched her feelings. Still nothing besides a touch more nervousness than normal. That was it.

"Maybe they were wrong about us," she offered.

Jin blew a raspberry. "The chances of that are less than point zero

CHAPTER NINE

five percent."

Kira raised an eyebrow in question before realization dawned. "You sneaky pile of bolts, you've been analyzing them, haven't you?"

Jin's voice was smug. "Of course, why do you think I insisted on playing with the *chaterling* for so long?"

Kira stuffed down her laugh, knowing her friend didn't need any encouragement. "You know Jace told you not to because of the treaty."

The sound Jin made was rude. "Since when do I take orders from him? Besides, the treaty doesn't apply to you because you're Tuann."

Kira was pretty sure it didn't work that way, especially given what Graydon had shared the last time they'd spoken. She'd done some digging courtesy of material they'd given her and found the Tuann were very odd in a universe filled with odd things.

They had an aversion to AIs. She hadn't gotten to the why of it yet, but their laws had seemed pretty definite. Couple that with a slightly feudal society, and they were a walking contradiction, possessing advanced technology with old values.

"Just make sure you're not caught, will you?" Kira said.

He snorted. "I'm not the one who always gets caught."

She shot him a dirty look. He might have had a point, but she didn't have to like it.

"What's that?" Jin asked.

She looked out the viewing screen taking up the entire wall, creating the impression of nothing between her and open space, not even the slim reassurance of triple plated, ballistic glass.

"What?"

Jin emitted a low sound and the viewer zoomed in on a spikey shaped sphere.

"It looks like a porcupine," Kira said. Or an ancient naval mine from humanity's distant past.

"There are hundreds of them," Jin said in fascination.

She stiffened, as she became aware they were no longer alone on the observation deck.

"It's the defense net," Amila said, moving closer and breaking the bubble of space she and Baran normally afforded Kira. "It'll prevent any unapproved ships from approaching the planet."

Kira frowned as she turned her attention to the mine. She'd never seen anything like it. She would have liked to get closer, maybe run tests on it, see what it could do.

"It is nearly time to disembark," Amila politely informed her. "We've been asked to report to the shuttles."

Sounded good to Kira. Whatever it took to get this over and done with.

"Where's Baran?" Kira asked, noticing her second shadow was nowhere present. While Amila and he took turns following her around, she had assumed both would be present for this transfer.

"He's been given another task," Amila said.

Finally. One person watching over her would be a lot easier to shake than two.

Kira and Jin followed Amila as she led them to the shuttle bay which was filled with several small spacecraft. Kira took a moment to admire the many shapes and sizes, noting their differences and wishing she had the chance to fly some of them.

Amila led them to a midsized surface-to-space shuttle. Inside, a dark wood accented the pilot seats, each one slightly different from the next. Graydon and the rest of his *oshota* waited inside.

Kira looked around, noting the lack of any humans. "Where are the Curs?"

Graydon's smile was dangerous, the light in his eyes taunting. "They're taking a different shuttle."

Kira narrowed her eyes. That was not the answer she wanted.

His smile broadened as he sent her a look inviting her to do her worst. He'd better watch out. She might take him up on his offer.

She made a show of looking around. "There seems to be plenty of room on this ship. Inviting them on board would certainly ease my mind."

CHAPTER NINE

His smile widened into a wicked grin. "I didn't think you were so easily unsettled. Perhaps a pacifier might calm your nerves."

Jin made a choking sound next to her at the insinuation she was acting like a baby.

Kira didn't react, her face remaining emotionless as an icy smile formed. It was on. "Perhaps it's not me who needs a security blanket. Are you afraid the extra weight will affect our re-entry?"

One of Graydon's guards smothered a laugh at the insult.

"Not at all. I thought to spare your delicate sensibilities, given your upbringing among the frail humans," he returned easily.

Frail her ass. She'd like to see him break atmo in a wave runner suit with the remains of a dying ship coming down around him while Tsavitee artillery fire targeted him from the planet's surface. They'd see who was frail then.

Her smile became sugary sweet. Jin muttered a curse next to her. "Well, aren't you thoughtful? Too bad you're as dumb as a rock. I suppose intelligence isn't really required of a man in your position."

"Oh god," Jin said, feeling in his voice.

Graydon's expression turned deadly. Before he could say anything, a small form burst onto the shuttle. Ziva wrapped herself around Kira's waist.

"You're here. I've been waiting for days to see you again," Ziva said, tilting her head to look at Kira.

Her expression was cute and designed to pull on a person's heartstrings. Kira couldn't tell if it was a façade or if she was doing it unintentionally.

Joule followed at a more sedate pace, his young face much too mature for his years. His half-bow surprised Kira. He hadn't been nearly as polite by the end of their previous encounter.

"Lady, I hope you are well," he said formally. He was a miniature adult, precious in his solemnity.

Kira fought against showing any amusement, knowing he'd probably see it as an insult.

"The same to you," Kira managed.

Graydon and the rest of his guards watched the interaction with interest, something the boy seemed to realize.

"Would you consider sitting with Ziva and me for the journey?" he asked.

Kira gave him a small nod of agreement.

He pulled his sister away and together they found a seat next to one of the starboard side windows.

Graydon stepped up beside Kira. "The two of them are in a difficult position. It's likely he will ask for your help."

"How so?" She had little to give. She wasn't even in control of her own destiny at the moment.

"Their former House owes allegiance to your House. Having your esteem may strengthen the position of what remains of their House," Graydon said.

Kira tilted her head as she studied Graydon. It sounded an awful lot like he was trying to persuade her.

"Why do you care about this?" she asked, studying him. This meant something to him, but she couldn't tell what.

"Let's just say I was in their position once. Having an ally as powerful as you might become would have been a comfort," he said, not looking at her.

She snorted. "I have a hard time imagining that."

Graydon exuded control and confidence. He gave the impression of being in command of every situation. It was hard to believe there was ever a time when he'd been powerless.

His eyes cut to her, solemn and serious. "I was not always as I am now. Once, my situation was even more precarious than theirs. I was lucky to find a benefactor to take me in and train me. He brought me to the attention of the emperor, which eventually led to my current position. It could very easily have gone the other way. I would not see the children harmed, but our society prevents me from directly interfering."

CHAPTER NINE

Kira could understand what he was saying. When you're weak and powerless, you'll do anything to escape, even if it means endless hours of training so intense your body gives out by the end. Even if it means leaving little pieces of yourself behind.

She looked at the children through new eyes, the direness of their predicament finally registering on her. Liont glanced at her from where he was helping them get situated.

He was the head of the children's honor guard. Until now, she hadn't seen the near desperation on his or his companions' faces. They looked like soldiers about to be sent on a suicide mission. Grim and resigned. They'd do their duty even at considerable cost to themselves.

Graydon saw where she was looking. "The best outcome they can hope for is for Luatha to absorb their entire House. Even then, they will be reduced in standing and rank, while the rest of Luatha looks on them with pity or derision."

"Unless Joule can prove himself worthy of the title of lord of his House in the trials," Kira said slowly, putting together all the pieces.

Graydon inclined his head. "Yes. That is the best option for them. If he were to pass, it means he would be considered strong enough to protect his household and he'd be allowed to hold their fealty. However, such an event is unlikely. There are those who would wish his House to fall into memory. They will make his journey as hard as possible."

"You said best case. What is the worst?"

"Those who aren't accepted will seek shelter with other Houses, their former affiliations dissolved. It is not an easy fate."

And because they'd once been loyal to another, they were unlikely to find another House to take them in, Kira finished for him.

"Why can't Joule wait till he's older to attempt the *adva ka*?" All he needed was a little time to become seasoned and grow into his abilities.

"He could do that," Graydon conceded. "But his path will be twice as difficult. He'd need permission from his new overlord to verify he was ready. Even then, it would likely be too late for the rest. There is no going back in time. They would have been affected by the years apart, and reassembling them would be twice as unlikely and unwise."

What he didn't say was time had a way of changing you despite your best intentions. New experiences shaped you and molded you, forcing you to adapt or perish. Even if you remembered those you left behind with fondness, they might not be the same person when you caught up with them. Their loyalties could have changed, their needs evolved.

This still didn't answer how he thought she could help them. As much as she felt for them, there was little she could do. She was here for a specific goal. Getting distracted wouldn't help her achieve that.

"Don't think I've forgotten about the Curs," Kira challenged, changing the subject.

His teeth flashed, dark amusement on his face. "I wouldn't dream of it, *coli*."

He moved away before she could respond.

"Arrogant ass," she grumbled to herself as she headed toward Joule and Ziva.

"Graydon has excellent hearing," Amila said in a neutral voice.

A wicked smile curved Kira's lips. "I'm counting on it."

Amila blinked at her, the idea someone would purposely pull her commander's tail obviously never occurring to her.

Kira reached Ziva and Joule and took a seat beside them. She ignored the way Ziva's face lit up as soon as Kira arrived, something like hero worship shining from her eyes.

Kira shifted, uncomfortable at the sight. Things never ended well when people looked to her as a hero. She always proved a disappointment, eventually.

Jin zoomed above their heads, completing a circuit of the area before settling in the seat beside Kira. His antics caught both of the children's attention, their gazes fascinated.

CHAPTER NINE

Amila stopped, her expression disconcerted. Jin had taken the last seat. It meant Amila would have to sit in the row behind them with Liont and the others instead of beside her.

"Move. Someone else might want to sit there," Kira ordered Jin.

"They can find another seat," he returned. "I need to be strapped in for re-entry just as much as you do. Do you see any cargo straps around here? Because I certainly don't. I'm not risking my safety if we crash. I plan to be strapped down, nice and proper."

Kira narrowed her eyes at him. "You'll survive."

Probably better than the rest of them, given his ability to magnetically attach himself to anything metal. Nothing would be able to pry him off, not even doing Mach two in a planet's atmosphere. Kira knew, because he'd attached himself to the outside of a hull to test the theory once.

Jin made several rude sounds while flashing his lights at her, letting her know what he thought of that idea.

A frustrated sigh escaped her. She'd forgotten how irrational he got during re-entry. It was probably one of his biggest fears and no matter how much logic you applied, he'd refuse to budge.

Kira sent Amila an apologetic look. There wasn't going to be any reasoning with Jin right now. He'd stick himself to the seat like a barnacle and no amount of arguing or manhandling would be enough to move him. She recognized the signs.

Amila clearly wasn't happy about the events, aiming a glare at Jin before taking a seat in the row behind them.

Kira shook her head at Jin. Sometimes his ridiculousness amazed her.

"Thank you for sitting with us during the return," Joule said.

Kira turned her attention to the two sitting in front of her, facing her.

The two traded a glance, having a whole conversation while Kira watched, with not a word exchanged.

Finally, Joule focused on her. "Where did you learn to fight like that?"

Kira tapped her finger on her leg as she studied him. She should have known that would be his question.

"Many places," Kira finally said.

Her training may have started in the awful compound of her earliest memories, but it continued for long after her rescue. She'd studied every type of martial arts she could find, adapting them into her own style until they'd become something new. The crucible of war had further honed those skills, sharpening and testing them until what emerged was a weapon, dreadful and deadly.

"Can you teach me?" There was an ache to his voice, as if his entire future rested on her answer, the fear of disappointment in his eyes.

Kira shifted in her seat, trying to get comfortable as she tried to find a polite way to tell him no. This was no easy thing he was asking. It would take years to build him into an adequate warrior. Years she didn't plan on devoting to the effort.

"Why do you want to learn?" Jin asked.

Joule stiffened, his chin lifting. "I need to be able to protect us."

"There are other ways of protecting yourself," Jin said, his voice emotionless. "You don't have to become a warrior."

"There aren't," Joule snapped. "This is the best way. We never want to be as weak as we were before. I won't watch anyone else die in front of me while I stand by."

Kira felt an ugly twist inside.

"He's just like you at that age," Jin said wryly.

"Just as stupid too." Kira sat forward and fixed Joule with a dark gaze. "I'm not going to help you down that path, kid. I don't have the time, and honestly, I don't want to."

His mouth formed a stubborn line as he scowled at her.

Ziva sat up tall. "What about the move you used on the Tsavitee?"

Kira flicked a glance at the girl. "Not possible. You need a strong foundation both physically and conceptually to perform that move, which neither of you has. Do it wrong and you could do more damage

CHAPTER NINE

to yourself than your opponent."

Both of their faces fell, leaving Kira feeling like a monster.

"Why me? There seem to be plenty of warriors here," she said. "Ask one of them. Liont and Fari seem willing."

The two traded another glance.

"They tried, but they can only teach us so much. The others won't help," Joule said. "We're not of their House, and we have the potential to grow into an enemy. Even once our name is wiped away and we're added to another House, it's likely neither of us will be trained as warriors since we'll never be considered one of them."

Kira shrugged. "That doesn't sound too bad to me. Find something you like doing and live a life of peace."

"Our families have been warriors for generations. Not following in their footsteps would mean turning our backs on their legacy," Joule said stiffly.

"They're going to split us up and send us to different families," Ziva said, her eyes sad. The look in them slipped through Kira's defenses to prick at her conscience.

Both children stared at her. The boy defiantly—he'd pursue this even without Kira's help. Probably manage to get himself hurt too. Ziva's gaze was more trusting and innocent. She actually believed, down to the bottom of her little soul, Kira had the answers.

Kira rubbed her forehead and looked away, out the window of the shuttle. They'd left the ship and now approached the planet, its warm glow growing bigger with each second, blocking out the black of space.

"Who taught you the move I saw you practicing?" Kira asked.

Joule's face turned guilty. "No one. I watched the other *oshota* practicing and copied them. Fari tried to help, but he couldn't do it either."

That would explain why he was using a technique way more advanced than his current skills.

"You know if you'd been successful, you'd probably have broken your shoulder and given yourself a concussion," Kira said.

His expression turned stubborn.

"We can help you," Ziva said. "I heard them talking. You know nothing about House politics. We can be your guides."

Kira snorted. "You're both children. I somehow doubt you're going to be of that much use."

Arrogance settled on Joule's face. "I might not look it, but I was the heir to our House, and Ziva would have become my first when she got old enough to protect me. Our parents started our education in House matters. Can you say the same? They're extremely difficult to navigate for outsiders, I'm told."

The kid had a point. Tuann five-year-olds probably had a better grasp of the inner workings of a Tuann House than Kira.

She considered their words. Their insight might prove useful. Given Kira knew what they wanted, she could account for their agenda where other Tuann might have hidden motivations for steering her wrong.

She sighed. "I can get you started on the basics and show you things more suited to your current skill level. That's all I'm going to promise right now."

Joule looked cautiously optimistic.

She pointed at him, sinking resolve into her voice. "Just to be clear. I'm not promising to stick around. As soon as I get them to give up their claim, I'm turning right around to head to O'Riley Station and getting my ship."

Kira ignored Amila's stare drilling into the back of her head.

She knew her decision wasn't going to make her popular with Graydon or any of the people he'd set to watch her. She didn't care. She'd spent nearly thirty years establishing a life for herself. It might not be the greatest but it was hers. They could accept it or not. Their choice.

Joule didn't look at his companion as he held Kira's gaze. "We will accept those terms."

CHAPTER NINE

Kira studied him and shook her head slightly. He might say they accepted, but she could see he didn't really mean that. When it came time for her to leave, he'd try to change her mind.

Oh well, she'd done her best to make him understand the facts. At least he couldn't claim she hadn't warned him.

"We're beginning our descent," Amila said quietly from behind her. "You should prepare yourselves."

Kira reached for the seat belt and fastened it around her.

"Kira, do mine too," Jin insisted.

"How do you expect me to do that? You don't have a body I can fasten the belt around." She made it clear how ridiculous she found his request.

He sank down until he was resting on the seat. "You can pull it across me. It'll work."

"I'm not doing that."

"Come on. I'd do it for you," he cajoled.

"Because I have a body it would fit around. Even if I did fasten it around you, the moment we rolled, you'd slip right out," she said.

Jin stared at her. "Kira!"

He was going to be stubborn about this. She knew it.

She growled and reached across him, grabbing the belt and fastening it. Finished, she sat back.

"You look ridiculous," she told him.

The belt clung to the lower third of his sphere, not even giving the illusion of safety. Turning on his gravity booster would lift him right out of the safety strap.

"I'll remember this the next time you need me to save your ass," Jin hissed.

She rolled her eyes, becoming aware of the way the children stared at the two of them with wide eyes.

She didn't say anything, knowing how odd they appeared. For all the processing power of his AI, Jin could be incredibly childish and prone to mood swings as severe as a prepubescent girl's.

Kira ignored them, staring out the window as the planet grew under them, blotting out the darkness of space. The shuttle gave the slightest of shimmies as it slipped into the atmosphere.

It was the easiest transition Kira had ever experienced. Of course, she was normally in a military drop ship, whose primary goal was getting its cargo to the ground as quickly and efficiently as possible. Most times that included staying in one piece, but not always.

They punched through the clouds, trailing ribbons of white behind them. The land spread out below them, an endless forest, mountains stabbing the sky in the distance, the faint sparkle of sun against water hinting at an ocean or lake.

This was it, the place of Kira's birth, if Graydon was to be believed. She might have family down there.

The connection she'd missed upon her first glimpse of Ta Da'an hit her. She wasn't crazy enough to say she was home, but the potential was there. A tantalizing possibility that refused to go away no matter how hard she tried to root it out.

Feelings welled up out of nowhere, a sense of welcome and homecoming, as if the planet itself was glad to have her back. There was a pleasant buzz all around her, as if the very air crackled with energy, licking along her nerves and reaching deep to the core of her.

She shifted as the sensation increased, moving from pleasant to slightly painful.

"What's wrong?" Jin asked.

"Nothing, I'm fine," Kira said.

That turned out to be a lie as the sensation deepened, turning sharp and stabbing. She groaned and bent forward. She would not throw up. She would not throw up. She hadn't done so on a drop, not even the first time. She refused to vomit now when she was set to meet her family. What a first impression that would create. She'd have ruined her reputation before she even really had one.

Cool hands touched her face. She knew without looking it was Amila.

CHAPTER NINE

"She's experiencing overload," she said to someone Kira couldn't see. "She needs to modulate the energy flow."

"What does that mean?" Jin asked from above her.

The energy Kira was coming to associate as the planet surged forward, a tidal wave of power. Impossible to resist or delay.

Kira whimpered as she crumpled forward.

"I was afraid of this," Graydon said in a grim voice.

"Afraid of what?" Jin shouted.

"We could have the pilot take us out," Amila suggested.

Kira fought to stay conscious as the sensations amplified. It felt like something was pouring into her, burning out her nerves as it filled her to bursting.

A large hand landed on her neck, cool and reassuring. She knew without looking it belonged to Graydon. "No, the process has already started. Removing her now would make her next experience that much more painful."

Kira grunted. "I'm fine with never returning to this place again."

Screw any sense of connection she felt. It wasn't worth whatever this was. She wanted out. Her skin damn near felt like it was about to burst.

"Sorry, *coli*. You're not getting off that easily," Graydon said.

Strangely, he didn't sound sorry in the least, Kira noted.

She dug her nails into his wrist in wordless retaliation. His chuckle was warm.

"Steady. I'll help you through this," Graydon said soothingly.

Kira would prefer not to be in this at all, but if he was going to help, he needed to do it soon.

The current running through her was powerful and could turn dangerous. Memories of another time when she'd set that current free swamped her. If that happened, she doubted anybody on the shuttle would be landing safely.

"I've never felt such a strong reaction from the Mea'Ave," Amila said in a hushed voice.

"She's been gone a long time," Graydon said. "It seems the Mea'Ave knows it and is trying to make up for lost time."

"It's too much." Amila's voice sounded strained. "Her mind will break if this continues."

"Let me in, *coli*," Graydon said soothingly, his thumb caressing the side of her throat.

"Someone had better do something, or I'm lighting this place up," Jin snarled. He sounded like he was two seconds from doing exactly that.

"Noor, get him away from us," Graydon rumbled.

There were sounds of a brief struggle and then Graydon's warm presence returned. He scooped her up and suddenly Kira was sitting in his lap. He tucked her head under his chin, making a strange rumbling sound in his chest that sounded like a purr.

"You're holding onto the *ki*. You need to redirect it," Graydon said in her ear.

"I don't know how to do that," Kira panted.

By now, the power was sending painful prickles throughout her skin. She would have given it back if she could.

"Relax, I will help you," Graydon said.

He pressed his cheek against hers. A connection sprung to life between the two of them, strong and radiant. A line snapped taut. Kira fought against it, trying to push it away. No, she didn't want this.

"Stop it," he growled. "You're going to hurt yourself. It's temporary."

Kira stopped pushing, relaxing enough to analyze what was happening.

"Feel what I'm doing," he instructed.

Sure enough, she could feel the push and pull of the energy in his body as it collected the *ki* and then pushed it out, giving as much as taking. There was a limitless well of it inside him, deep and vast, an ocean to rival the one beneath them on the planet.

"Do you understand now?" he asked.

CHAPTER NINE

Kira didn't need to voice her assent, knowing the connection currently binding them meant he would know already.

Her attempts were fumbling at first but gradually she got the hang of it, cycling the planet's energy through her body before returning it. After the first few successes, the line of energy from the planet abruptly abated, as if now that it knew Kira had the capability, it didn't need to push the energy on her anymore.

Her breathing eased as the taut line relaxed, leaving Kira able to process something beyond the incredible energy.

Graydon's presence eased up, the connection between them thinning.

Kira straightened in his lap, her gaze meeting his for one tension-filled moment. Her body shook as she eased her body off of his lap. She collapsed into a chair beside him.

"What the hell was that?" she finally rallied herself enough to ask.

Graydon twitched with amusement. "That was the Mea'Ave, the mother of the planet."

Kira watched him blankly. That told her nothing.

He seemed to understand. "Your people have a name for us, don't they? Wizards, I believe."

Kira didn't confirm or deny. It was unclear whether he found the name insulting or not.

"They're not far off," he admitted. "Our home is capable of filling us with the Mea'Ave. We can manipulate its energy, turn it to other uses to fit our needs. Other societies have often misinterpreted this as magic."

Kira kept her reaction to that under control.

"What you experienced was the planet feeling your plight and offering itself up to heal you."

"I'm not injured," Kira pointed out.

Graydon rubbed his neck. "You've been separated from her for decades. All Tuann exist off her energy in part; it's what renews us. The Mea'Ave must have interpreted your low reserves as dangerous and tried to adjust them for you."

And Kira's body would have viewed that as an attack after what amounted to years of starvation and tried to hold onto what it had gathered.

"I see." She did, but only in part. "You said you were afraid of this. Why wasn't I warned beforehand?"

"It shouldn't have been this severe," Graydon said, his expression contemplative. A hint of trouble pulled at his mouth. "It reacted like you were near death's door. Why is that?"

Kira didn't like the question. "It's your crazy planet, you tell me."

Graydon's head tilted as he studied her. "You're keeping secrets, *coli*."

She snorted, not letting his seriousness intimidate her. "Who isn't?"

The smile that took over his face took Kira by surprise. It was the first unguarded expression she'd seen on him. It spoke of a joy edged with ruthlessness, breathtaking while hinting at the brutality inside.

There was a slight hum and then the smallest of jolts.

Graydon looked up, his expression turning serious, but not before she caught a glimpse of a fierce anticipation. "We've landed. It's time."

CHAPTER TEN

Kira stood on the edge of the field, nerves churning in her stomach and the shuttle a comforting presence behind her. She visualized walking inside it, commandeering the pilot chair and flying away from this place.

She sighed. Tempting as that would be, running away now would only create problems down the road. Besides, if she truly wanted to disappear, her best option was light years away, waiting for her at O'Riley.

Men and women dressed in synth armor of the darkest green, gold detailing on their crests, marched out of the woods. As they neared, Kira saw the symbol on their armor was remarkably similar to the one on her forearm.

Guess Graydon hadn't been lying when he said she bore their mark. Not that she really doubted him at this point. The encounter with the planet's energy had cleared up any reservations she had.

The men and women approached, their gazes dark and flinty, grim masks meant to intimate and cow.

Strangely enough, the sight steadied Kira. She'd always been the rebellious type. Give her an ounce of disapproval and she'd do everything in her power to prove you right. It was a flaw, but one that came in handy right about now.

The leader of these new guards strode toward Graydon, a gold cape flapping in the wind. He looked like a holo actor from a period drama of a time in Earth's history when they fought battles with swords and arrows, a hero come to rescue the princess from the dragon.

He was a handsome man, secure in his position with just a trace of arrogance and superiority stamped on his features. His blond hair shone in the sun, furthering the impression he was some unattainable prince.

Kira disliked him on sight.

A short but intense conversation took place between the two men as their people faced each other, each group filled with the same imperturbable resolve as they looked over the other.

"It's like watching lawmen and cowboys square off for the gunfight at the O.K. Corral," Jin said in fascination.

Kira snickered. "Which is which do you think?"

Jin was silent as he studied the two groups. "Graydon and his people are the lawmen, obviously. They'd be the ones to win."

Kira tilted her head. She had to agree. There was something in the way he and his people held themselves, loose but ready. If anything happened, they were prepared to meet it head-on.

She was surprised by how tense each group was. They were all Tuann, Graydon a representative of their emperor. Why the stare-off?

"When in another House's territory, it's customary to negotiate the terms of your stay before proceeding," Amila said softly, guessing the direction of Kira's thoughts.

"You're the emperor's people," Kira said. "Why would you need to ask permission?"

Amila looked at Kira, her gaze warm. "Would your leaders step foot in your home without permission?"

Jin snorted. "If they could guarantee she wouldn't kill them? Yes."

Amila's forehead wrinkled as if she was trying to judge the truth of Jin's statement. Kira could have saved her the trouble and told her Jin wasn't joking. The Consortium was ruled by families who had been in power for decades. Yes, representatives were picked by voters, but somehow only the rich ever managed to get elected.

Oh, they'd have some reason for the intrusion, like a threat to

CHAPTER TEN

galactic security or something like that, but the result would be the same—her rights trampled in the interests of others.

Amila continued her instruction, ignoring Jin's comment. "Each House is a power in its own right. Forcing our way in is possible, but unwise, and will only lead to strife down the road. Graydon prefers to save such measures for when they are absolutely necessary."

Jin snickered. "Perhaps you could learn a thing or two from them, Kira."

She swatted at her friend, unsurprised when he dodged.

The antics drew the notice of the Luatha. The man talking to Graydon paused, looking Kira up and down, his thoughts impenetrable.

"This her, then?" he asked.

"It is," Graydon said.

"Are you sure she's Luatha? She looks nothing like us."

There was some truth in that statement. Every person in green synth armor was tall with varying shades of honey-blond hair, where Kira was short with hair the deep burgundy color of red wine. Theirs was stick-straight, falling in smooth sheets down their backs, while hers was an out of control tentacle monster that hadn't seen a comb in days.

The speaker was tall and thin, his build lanky. Tiny braids held his hair from his face, exposing sharply pointed ears and highlighting his sharp features.

About the only thing Kira had in common with these people were her eyes. Almost every person in green had eyes of varying shades of lilac, some light and faded, others so intense a purple it was hard to believe they were real.

The weird eyes, at least, seemed to be a House trait.

There was suspicion and a faint touch of hostility in the pinched features of the speaker. The same tightness was reflected in the faces of those arranged behind them.

It made Kira want to revisit her fantasy of stealing the shuttle and making a great escape. The nerves from earlier disappeared, leaving her ready for a fight.

Her face carefully blank, she studied them as carefully as they studied her. Somehow, she didn't think these were people overjoyed to have found their lost child. No, they looked more like they'd like to show her to the nearest ship and blast her off planet.

Her lips curved up the slightest bit. This might be even easier than she'd assumed.

"She wears your mark," Graydon said in a ruthlessly polite voice.

Kira shifted slightly as she detected the faintest edge of frustration in Graydon. It was unexpected, given their short acquaintance. Graydon wasn't the type to show his emotions easily.

Maybe it was a lingering result of the bond they'd briefly shared? It couldn't be because she'd developed a habit of studying him as closely as he studied her.

"You said she was raised by humans," the stranger said, the slightest sneer in his voice. "Perhaps they've found a new way to mimic us."

Kira stiffened at the insult. The obvious scorn told her exactly how he felt about her adopted species.

Graydon's soldiers stilled, the air turning icy. Before, they'd been tense but not on edge. Violence now simmered just below the surface. They hadn't liked the implied insult to their leader or Kira.

Amila stepped forward, placing herself between Kira and the strangers as she stared down a man who'd ventured too close.

"Careful, Roderick. You're not just insulting them when you question me," Graydon said, his voice a silky rumble.

"This should be interesting," Jin said.

Roderick's gaze shifted to him and a look of distaste filled his expression. "Bring her, but the human toy stays here."

"Not happening. He goes where I go." She gave him a friendly smile. Those who knew her would have warned him to be careful. Kira rarely smiled like that unless she was planning something—usually something painful and embarrassing for someone else.

"Children aren't to speak unless invited," Roderick instructed

CHAPTER TEN

haughtily.

Anger coiled in Kira's gut. This guy was beginning to irritate her.

"Remember the mission," Jin murmured in Japanese. He took a chance in assuming the Tuann present didn't know the language.

"I never forget," Kira said through gritted teeth.

It was tempting to lash out. Oh, so tempting. She could practically taste the satisfaction it would bring, to teach these people the error of underestimating her. However, to do so would be foolhardy and shortsighted.

Instead, she gave him her sweetest smile. Graydon's lips twitched before he quelled his amusement, hiding it as if it had never been. She wasn't the only one beginning to recognize the subtle hints in the other's expressions.

"I'm far from everything I've ever known. Surely, you wouldn't deprive me of my companions. They give me such comfort," Kira said. It was a shameless play for sympathy, meant to force them to think "poor, little, lost child."

Graydon, ironically, had been the one to give her this idea with his pacifier comment.

Her ploy worked as Roderick dismissed her, turning to Graydon. Amila and another of Graydon's soldiers exchanged glances, a small trace of humor glinting in their eyes. They knew what she'd done and approved.

"We'll take her from here," Roderick stated brusquely. "You may report to the emperor we've done our duty."

Kira was a little impressed with the man's balls. Graydon wasn't the sort you dismissed. He did the dismissing, not the other way around. Roderick had stomped all over that. He was either secure in his abilities or just plain stupid. Jury was out on which it was.

"I'm afraid we won't be departing yet," Graydon said with a smile devoid of warmth or humor. It was raw, holding all the savagery of a warrior. It said he'd be happy to do this dance with Roderick because he knew beyond a shadow of a doubt, he'd come out the winner in the end. "Until Kira is formally claimed, she remains under the emperor's protection."

Roderick straightened, his frown fierce.

A shuttle roared into sight above. It hovered over the wide field they stood on before lowering and touching down softly.

"How many of your *oshota* are you expecting us to House?" Roderick asked, his eyebrows lowered in displeasure.

"Only those present. However, several humans traveled with us," Graydon said before Roderick could relax. "They wanted to ensure their friend was settled and to provide a reminder of home in this difficult time."

Kira fought her smile as Graydon made the same argument Kira had moments before, insinuating the child would be extremely troubled so far from the comforts and people of home. It seemed she wasn't the only one who found Roderick obnoxious.

She never would have guessed how irritated Graydon had been with the Curs' presence if she hadn't seen his expression when they first came on board.

The lines on Roderick's face deepened, ire showing as he spat several sentences in his native language. Graydon responded in kind.

Kira wished she knew what was being said.

"You getting anything interesting?" Kira asked Jin, still in Japanese.

On her end, she was catching every other word. She'd made an effort to study the Tuann language during the journey from O'Riley to Ta Da'an. She'd made some progress given she was a quick learner with a knack for languages. To date, she could speak four and read six if you counted binary code.

Jin was even better than Kira at picking up new languages. A fact she attributed to his processing power and people ignoring him because they thought he was only a machine.

"Something about how the humans shouldn't be here. He had no right to bring them into their House," Jin said. He paused for a moment. "He's now saying the Luatha will hold Graydon responsible

CHAPTER TEN

if anything should happen."

"I'd like to know why they hate humans so much," Kira said, not taking her eyes from the two men.

Himoto had explained some of the reasons for the strained relations, but that couldn't be all of it. There had to be more to the story.

Another question she should have asked Himoto before accepting this assignment.

Kira fell silent, becoming aware of the Luatha looking her over, their thoughts and conclusions hard to read on their inexpressive faces.

"Fine, you win. I don't care what you do with the humans as long as they don't get in our way," Roderick spat. He stabbed a finger at Kira. "She will stay with us. The humans stay with you."

Graydon spared Kira a glance before giving Roderick an abrupt nod.

Roderick grimaced, looking no happier about winning the skirmish before barking several abrupt words at his people. He stalked away.

Graydon waited until Kira stopped next to him, keeping an eye on their not so thrilled escort. His expression remained carefully neutral, though if Kira had to hazard a guess, he wasn't entirely happy with the turn of events.

"Charming bunch you're saddling me with," she said.

Graydon made a small sound of agreement. "They're the *oshota* for Luatha House. The safety of their House and all those who fall under it are their first priority. You and your friends challenge their purpose."

"Me? A child? I am a threat?" Kira touched her chest in feigned shock. She dropped the pretenses, turning serious. "How insecure."

"Even a child can kill, given the right circumstances," Graydon said mildly.

The emotion left Kira's face. "Yes, yes they can."

She had firsthand experience with that fact. She was just surprised

Graydon understood.

His gaze was sharp and piercing, a question lingering in his eyes. Like the smart man he was, he stayed silent, not voicing it. Now wasn't the time or place.

"And as you made so clear from our first meeting, you're not exactly a child," Graydon said wryly.

Kira's sidelong look was sly.

"You would be smart to let them think what they will," Graydon said, raising both eyebrows.

Kira's paused, understanding the warning.

"That's a mighty fine cape he had. Very spiffy," she said, changing the subject. She gave Graydon a once over, taking in the defined muscles even his armor couldn't fully hide. "Why don't you have one like that?"

Graydon's lip curled. "His cape is ridiculous. An opponent can grab it and strangle him with it. No other weapons necessary."

Kira tried to choke back the laugh trying to escape. She was fighting a losing battle, his incredulous expression at her comment too funny to resist.

Graydon watched her with a frown, his jaw ticking.

Kira managed to compose herself, saying with a semi-straight face, "But you would look so dashing."

"All the girls would worship at your feet," Jin assured him.

Graydon's face turned slightly disgusted as he shook his head. He strode off, saying over his shoulder, "Come. Roderick won't be patient long."

"I would like to see him in a cape as well," Amila murmured in an undertone to Kira.

Kira sputtered, losing the battle against her mirth.

A woman took the opportunity to approach. She wore a simple dress and her hair was bound in an unadorned tail down her back. She was the only one on the field besides Kira not wearing synth armor.

CHAPTER TEN

"Lady, my name is Ayela. I've been assigned to carry your things," she said in accented standard. Her smile was polite as she bowed her head diffidently.

"You're off the hook then," Jin said, sounding bored.

Confusion shown on Ayela's face.

"I'm sorry, but I don't have anything for you to carry," Kira explained.

Ayela's mouth opened in a small O. "How could your people send you so far with nothing? That is barbarous."

Kira's smile grew forced at the accusation implied there. "I chose to come like this."

Ayela blinked, aware she'd slipped somewhere. "I'm sorry, lady. I meant no offense."

Kira buried her emotions. "None taken. If you'll excuse me, I don't want to fall behind."

"Oh, but—I'm supposed to escort you." Ayela's protest fell on deaf ears as Kira strode away.

"Will all of your people think of humans as barbarians?" Kira asked Amila as they followed the path Graydon had taken.

Amila hesitated. Her silence confirmed Kira's suspicion.

Kira frowned. If they thought of humans as less than themselves, the same sentiment would filter to Kira since she had spent considerable time among them.

"Not many will be so bold as to do so to your face," Amila admitted. "Strange, that one of her station would be so rude."

Kira didn't comment as she caught up to Graydon and the others.

At the edge of the clearing, she paused, giving the second shuttle a long look where it waited, not having disgorged its passengers yet.

"Leave them," Graydon ordered, instantly setting Kira's back up again.

She sent him a hard look. Not this again.

He rolled his eyes. "You need to do this without them. Meeting the Overlord of House Luatha is an important opportunity, one best accomplished without their polarizing presence."

Kira hesitated, part of her wanting to cling to the familiarity of Jace and the others' presence. The rest of her understood what Graydon was saying. Until she understood more of what fueled the dislike in the Tuann toward humans, she would be best served perceived as a neutral party. Staying on the Luathan's good side would increase the chance of her attaining her twin goals.

Still, something bothered her about the request. It was like being asked to forget the things and people who defined her—to put them aside because they no longer served her purpose. He was asking her to bury the pieces of her history that had shaped who she'd become.

Humans, whatever they might mean to the Tuann, had saved her. At her lowest moments, they'd found her, given her warmth and companionship. Not just once, but many times. She'd sacrificed more than Graydon would ever know for humanity's cause, for their very survival.

She might have distanced herself from them, but it didn't mean she'd forgotten. Nor did she plan to leave them behind because it was convenient.

Graydon waited patiently as she worked through her possible responses, making no move to hurry her along. He gave her the time to come to her own conclusion even when the Luatha stirred, impatient.

His understanding was what decided her.

She inclined her head. For now, she'd follow his lead.

It was a trust she didn't bestow easily or lightly.

Approval moved across Graydon's face before he looked away, already issuing orders. Two of his people stepped aside to wait as the Curs disembarked, while the rest of the *oshota* flanked Graydon and Kira as they followed Roderick.

The Luathan warriors fell in behind Graydon's people, unobtrusively surrounding them. For their protection or the Luathan's, was hard to tell.

CHAPTER TEN

The green synth armor did a good job of blending into the trees as they moved through the forest. Only the cape Graydon had called ridiculous, stood out like a sore thumb.

They stepped onto a dirt road filled with several odd-looking vehicles. They appeared to have been lifted from a mad scientist's fantasy-filled dreams, wheel-less and attached to a creature that was a cross between a woolly mammoth and a bison—its fur shaggy and long. Only its ears, snout, and horns peeked out from under the furry length.

"Whoa, that's not something you see every day," Jin said, making a circuit of the beast.

"Jin," Kira cautioned when several of the Luatha looked over, their gazes ranging from mildly suspicious to hostile.

"What? I call it like I see it."

Kira shook her head in dismay, even if privately she agreed.

One of the beasts gave a low coughing sound as it dipped its head and lipped at some grass at its feet. Its partner rubbed one horn against a foreleg before stamping the leg down again.

"They're *ooros*," Graydon said. "They're mostly harmless."

"Mostly?" Kira asked.

She'd have preferred entirely. The creature outweighed her by several hundred pounds, dwarfing her in size. It looked like some prehistoric grazing animal, only more dangerous. If it decided to take a sudden dislike to her, it would be difficult bringing it down without a weapon.

"They were once used for warfare," Graydon continued with a faint smile. "Don't disturb it during feeding time or mess with its young, and you'll be fine."

Well, that should be easy. Kira didn't plan on ever being around them again if she could help it.

"What are those?" Kira asked, nodding toward where a creature nearly as tall as the *ooros* stood. Several Luathans were fiddling with saddles as they prepared to mount.

The horse creatures had long, slender limbs similar to a horse's, but their manes and tails were much thicker and coarser, similar to a Friesian, a breed of horse from old Earth. These creatures were more primal and rugged looking than any horse Kira had ever seen—something that might have evolved in an alternate primeval version of Earth in an environment ten times more dangerous.

Around its chest and below the knee, its coat was thick, coarse and hairy like the *ooros*. A set of four white horns jutted from its head, two pointing straight up while the other two curved forward.

Along the edge of its mane, white symbols appeared, almost glowing, even in bright daylight.

The horse creature pranced in place, dangerous and beautiful. Kira itched to touch, to stroke, and pet it. She would have given anything for a ride on one of these proud, terrifying creatures.

A snort above Kira's head sent her stomach flopping as she froze in place. Jin's ominous silence warned her of the danger she was in. Somehow, one of the alien horses had gotten close without her knowledge.

She didn't move as a soft muzzle pushed aside her hair, the creature snuffling along her neck. She remained still despite the ticklish sensation, her face calm while inside hyper-alertness beat at her.

Graydon had tensed beside her, his face expressionless even as his tightly coiled body warned of how precarious her situation was.

Adrenaline surged through Kira.

"What do I do?" Kira mouthed at Graydon.

"Don't move," he mouthed back.

She had visions of being impaled by the creature's massive horns or being stomped to death under the lethal-looking hooves. How ironic would it be for her to come through a war, only to be killed because an alien horse decided it didn't like her scent.

One of the Luathan warriors advanced cautiously as his gaze moved from Kira to the giant monster standing over her.

He said several soft words in his own language, a loving croon in

CHAPTER TEN

his voice.

The alien horse snorted and dipped its head, dropping its muzzle over Kira's shoulder. His head was heavy, the lethal horns inches from her face.

"Sarath is asking to be petted," the Luathan warrior said.

Kira gave him a dark glower. She didn't care what the damn creature wanted. He could ask for affection from his own people and leave her alone.

"He likes when you scratch his neck and jaw," the warrior offered.

Kira sighed. She really didn't want this. Given the monster showed no sign of moving away, she was left with no choice. Kira reached up and gave a small scratch along the jaw.

The monster made a happy sound and moved closer, jostling Kira. She tensed again but settled when the creature did nothing more.

"Just like that," the man said.

With nothing else to do but satisfy the horse's wishes, Kira continued petting him, making sure her movements were slow and nonthreatening. To her surprise, the alien horse's jaw was soft under her hand, like warm velvet.

The horse lifted its head and then sneezed all over the side of her face and hand.

There was a strangled noise from the warrior as Kira remained motionless as the big monster trotted away, its horse-like tail partially raised in satisfaction. Her glare could have lit the damn thing on fire. For a long moment, she fantasized about going after the horse, teaching it a thing or two about manners.

"You'd better run," she muttered at him. If that creature came near her again, she wasn't going to be responsible for what she did.

"I'm so sorry. Sarath does that to the people he likes," the warrior said, not sounding apologetic enough, given the laughter she could hear in his voice.

He handed her a handkerchief before moving off to corral his wayward mount.

"Thanks for the help," Kira told Graydon as she wiped at the snot on her face and hand. She grimaced as she pulled a hunk of hair forward. She'd need a shower to get it all off.

"I'm not stupid enough to get between an *etair* and something it finds interesting," Graydon said, looking entirely too amused at the disgust on Kira's face. "You should be honored. The *etair* are fickle beasts. That he let you pet him, a stranger to his House, confirms your lineage."

Kira paused in what she was doing, her forehead wrinkling. "How?"

Graydon gestured to the carriage. After a long moment of hesitation, Kira reluctantly moved toward it and settled herself carefully in the seat, not trusting the *ooros* pulling the carriage.

Graydon folded in beside her, his large shoulders taking up the majority of the space.

Jin hovered outside while the rest of Graydon's people took up positions around the carriage.

Graydon leaned over and conferred with Liont. "I think it'd be best if your people stay here or on the ship until I've had a chance to talk to the Luathan Overlord."

Liont's face got tight, but his nod was resigned. He reached up and shook Graydon's hand. "We'll await your instructions."

He and the rest stepped away. Liont knelt in front of Joule whose expression and posture hinted at nerves. Joule's shoulders were stiff, but the boy's nod was firm. "I won't let you or the rest down."

Joule took Ziva's hand and walked her to the carriage, helping her into the seat behind Kira before climbing up himself, his face an expressionless mask. His eyes were pools of despair as they met Kira's.

She didn't know what to say to him. In the end, she said nothing.

Graydon settled back, returning to their conversation of before. "The *etair* were bred to act as mounts for their House's soldiers. They're fiercely loyal and are trained from birth to recognize those of the House's bloodline. If Sarath had seen you as a threat, the

CHAPTER TEN

encounter would have gone very differently. That he didn't will reinforce your claim to this House and raise your esteem," Graydon explained.

Kira looked around with a frown, noticing the truth in his statement. There was a noticeable lessening in the hostile glances being aimed her way. Several of the Luatha were more willing to meet her gaze, giving her a respectful nod before looking away.

There was a reserve there, but not as deep as before.

Strange people to allow such a small thing to affect their actions, Kira thought.

Graydon stretched out beside her, his powerful body taking up a large amount of space as he relaxed. Kira frowned at him as she moved to accommodate his sprawl. It was on the tip of her tongue to tease him given how he resembled a redolent lord, come to survey his holdings. She bit the comment back. She was already getting too comfortable with him. Best to keep her distance.

Their road wound through the forest, the trees around them ancient and tall as they stood sentinel over the travelers. Their branches interlocked, twining together to create a canopy where no sunlight could pass, leaving the ground underneath cool and shaded.

Earth no longer had forests like these anymore. What humans hadn't destroyed in the centuries before spaceflight, had been ravaged during the war with the Tsavitee. Some of the planets settled by humans possessed vegetation resembling forest, but nothing that came close to what they currently traveled under.

This was something else. The world smelled clean and fresh, a welcome change from the processed stuff on her ship. She could smell dirt and growing things. The air tasted sweet on her tongue.

She closed her eyes, ignoring those around her and let herself feel. The everpresent knot in the pit of her stomach loosened as the peace of this place soaked into her soul.

A humming filled her ears, vibrating through her bones. The

sensation was similar to when the Mea'Ave offered itself up, only gentler, these voices patient and wise.

Kira's eyes popped open as she looked around. Her lips parted in surprise and wonder.

"Do you hear that?" she asked Jin in a hushed voice.

"Hear what?"

She didn't answer, busy pinpointing the origin of the sound. She thought it was coming from the trees.

The sensation was indescribable, soothing her and leaving her feeling more herself than she had in years.

Graydon's gaze was contemplative when she looked up at him. He didn't say anything as he closed his eyes and leaned back, a soft smile on his face. That smile made Kira pause. It turned him from the autocratic ass she was used to into someone real.

She settled in and enjoyed the ride. There was plenty of time for her questions later.

They came out of the trees on a hill overlooking the land below. The scenery was beautiful and fierce, a patchwork quilt of farmland—tame, but with a hint of the wild too. In the distance, a large collection of towers stood, sprawling out in a dizzying array of lines as their walls glimmered in the afternoon sun.

Kira found herself leaning forward, curious, despite her reservations.

Three spires reached up to the sky from within, smaller towers and buildings framing them. It looked nothing like a human city, delicate and impossibly fragile while still managing to project a sense of strength. Momentous and wondrous in a way that made you feel small inside.

"The Citadel of Light, said to be the most beautiful gem of the Houses. It's been the seat of House Luatha's power for over five thousand years," Graydon said, watching the sparkling monument through veiled eyes.

Kira sat back. "It doesn't look very defensible."

CHAPTER TEN

Graydon's gaze shifted to Kira, a hint of wry humor on his face. "Don't let the Luathan's obsession with beauty fool you. They've managed to hold their position of dominance for many years. Just because something is pretty doesn't mean it won't bite."

Kira watched him, carefully dissecting his words. "Consider me warned."

The rest of the journey passed quietly and soon they were pulling up into a gravel courtyard.

The Citadel was no less impressive close up. If anything, it seemed like something straight out of a fairytale, complete with singing animals and dangerous beasts.

Its walls defied gravity, the swooping lines seemingly impossible as they held up the weight of the structure. Arches seemed to be a main theme, each as delicate and intricate as a snowflake.

If light and air had a physical embodiment, the Citadel would meet the requirements.

The place was meant to intimidate and impress, its history written in every line, stamped on every stained glass and lovingly crafted carving. It shouted "This is us. Our history spans thousands of years. You have no hope of competing with our greatness."

It wasn't just a building, it was a work of art, carved over centuries, perhaps millennia, by the hands of hundreds of master craftsmen. Pride shone in every detail.

Despite its beauty, it left Kira feeling chilled, with the undeniable impression she didn't belong. That much was obvious. She didn't think it would be any different for the rest of the Curs either.

Judging by the forbidding expressions on the group awaiting them on the stairs in front of the Citadel's doors, they thought so, too.

The Luathans stood straight and proud, their bearing regal as they watched Kira and the rest approach. There was no sign of friendliness. Nothing to indicate they were looking forward to recovering a lost member of the flock. No. They wanted to throw Kira out and bar her from ever returning.

Her lips curved up in a private smile. That was fine with her.

Graydon disembarked first before holding out a hand to Kira. He arched an eyebrow at her when she didn't immediately take it, as if daring her to reject it. "If you want them to underestimate you, you need to play the part."

Kira didn't react outwardly to the statement. She shouldn't be surprised he'd guessed her plan. She liked it less that he was right.

Her instincts told her to present a strong front, to give these people no reason to think her weak. Reason, and years of experience warned it was better to keep them guessing about her true strength. If they saw her as someone weak and in need of protection, it would make manipulating them easier.

Still, it galled to accept Graydon's help. More so, since he was the one to land her in this mess in the first place.

His expression said he knew exactly what she was thinking. He arched an eyebrow as if saying, "Turn down my help. I dare you."

Never one to back down, Kira took his hand, alighting from the carriage as she looked up at the group on the stairs.

All of a sudden, she was grateful for Graydon's support in the presence of so many cold gazes being aimed her way.

His hand squeezed hers as he turned and presented her to the rest.

"Overlord of the Luatha, your hospitality is appreciated," Graydon said with the slightest of head inclines.

The woman in the middle didn't speak for several interminable seconds. She was younger than Kira had imagined. Not much older than Kira and beautiful in the way of all Tuann. Her skin was creamy and pale, her hair long and golden like the rest. It was bound in a long, complicated braid down her back.

Unlike the building behind her, she was a vivid palette of colors, her lips red and her eyes a vivid lilac, clad in the green synth armor of her House, an ornate long cape draping around her. It looked like someone had distilled the color of golden sunlight into the fabric as it stretched behind her, pooling on the stairs.

CHAPTER TEN

It was even more impractical for battle than Roderick's. Kira could think of a dozen different ways to use that cape against the woman. Not to mention, although the armor itself looked delicate, Kira knew it would be difficult to move in.

Despite that, it was clear she was the one in charge. Authority was stamped on her young face.

She and Kira stared at each other for several silent seconds. The woman's face was expressionless, her thoughts hidden.

Kira waited, holding her breath. Now that she was standing here, she couldn't exactly define what she was feeling—excitement, nervousness, and a host of other emotions. Despite not wanting to be dragged all the way here, she couldn't lie. She was curious about these people whose blood ran through her veins. All the half-forgotten wishes of her childhood pressed to the forefront.

A small movement in the windows above caught her attention. She was unsurprised to find several curious faces peering at her.

The sight grounded her, chasing away some of the nerves, allowing her to focus. She took in the rest of those assembled behind their Overlord. Among them was an older man and woman with the slightest signs of age in their faces and hair, the first indicators of aging Kira had seen among the Luatha. Arrayed below them on either side of the steps were a dozen warriors.

It finally dawned on Kira what she was seeing. This was a show of force. A position of strength meant to impress upon her, her place within the house. It said "Don't even think of fucking with us. Step out of line and we will end you."

The barely sprouted hope she'd been nursing died. She stuffed it deep inside. This wasn't some storybook reunion.

Whoever these people might have once been to her, they were no longer. You couldn't change the past. Wishing and dreaming wouldn't rewrite history. Her fate had been written with blood and pain long ago. Her path no longer lay with these people.

She straightened her shoulders. Easy acceptance was cheap anyway.

This was better.

She studied them as Roderick mounted the stairs. She did have to wonder why they'd felt the need to go through all the trouble of such posturing for little old her—especially when they assumed her weak, ignorant, and helpless.

She glanced at Graydon out of the corner of her eye. Maybe this display of force wasn't for her after all.

Roderick stopped next to the woman, leaning near to murmur in her ear. Her expression didn't flicker, remaining hard and closed off as she stared at Kira and the rest.

"Let's see this mark," the leader said, her voice carrying.

With her peripheral vision, Kira saw the Curs arrive, the *ooros* slow as they lumbered forward.

She didn't turn to acknowledge them, knowing this moment was important.

Beside her, Graydon had tensed, his face tight, the faintest trace of fury deepening the furrows on his forehead. Kira shot him a questioning look. He hesitated before his chin dipped in a small nod.

Kira sighed. Might as well get this over with. They'd already come all this way because of this damn thing, all she had to do was play the game a little longer.

The courtyard was silent as Kira made her way toward the three at the top.

Kira stopped two steps below the Overlord and rolled up her sleeve. She hesitated before turning her arm for them all to see.

The woman held her gaze for several seconds before her eyes flicked downward. They widened slightly at the sight of the mark but otherwise remained expressionless.

There was a small tsking sound from the older woman.

Kira remained with her arm outstretched for several long seconds, giving them more than enough time to look their fill. When she'd judged they'd had long enough, she let her sleeve drop to cover the mark and waited.

CHAPTER TEN

"She bears the mark of the Luatha," the older woman grudgingly admitted.

She and the man beside her looked like they'd bitten into something sour.

"A branch House?" Came from one of the people arranged behind them.

The leader finally stirred. "No, she is from the main family."

"Liara," the older woman cautioned.

Liara's head moved a fraction at the unmistakable chiding in the woman's tone but didn't react otherwise.

There was tension in their ranks, it seemed. Kira made note of it in case she had need of the information later.

Liara may have been the leader, but it wasn't a position she held without challenge. The older woman must have felt secure in her station to risk chastising the head of Luatha's house in front of strangers.

Kira contained her own tsking sound.

It was one thing to air such grievances in private, but another to do so in front of potential enemies. Unwise.

It was the first breach in their façade, offering Kira insight into their inner dynamics.

"The tests will reveal the truth soon enough, Alma," Liara said.

"Wait until then," Alma urged. "There is a possibility we're wrong. As the seneschal, it's my duty to protect our interests."

"Say the word and I can be on my way. You'll never see me again," Kira assured them with a small smile.

Alma opened her mouth, falling silent when Liara lifted a hand, an unmistakable gesture for quiet.

"That's not possible. You're clearly of Luathan descent. I will not dishonor my House by turning away one of its blood," Liara said, her expression serene and composed, yet her lilac eyes were piercing, as she met Kira's gaze. "Especially not for one who is cousin."

CHAPTER ELEVEN

A hushed shock filled the air.

After several surprised seconds while Kira blinked dumbly at Liara, she asked, "What sort of cousin?"

"Cousin" was a broad term. It didn't necessarily mean they were closely related.

Liara's mask cracked for the first time, the smallest glimmer of an emotion Kira couldn't place, flickering before it was hidden again. "You're the daughter of my mother's sister."

"Ah, that sort of cousin," Kira said blandly.

For some reason, Kira had assumed these people were loosely related to her in a distant sort of way—not people who shared a direct bloodline with her. Not individuals who may have actually known her parents at some point.

It should have occurred to her. It was an obvious conclusion, but she felt completely taken off guard.

Questions brewed in her mind, but Kira hesitated to voice them. It felt like she'd be giving too much power to these people, here, in this moment, to ask anything. She'd wait for a better opportunity, one where she didn't feel like a poor relation begging for crumbs.

Liara didn't address Kira's ridiculous statement, instead turning her attention to Graydon. "You've delivered a child we thought lost to us. We thank you; it's a debt we can never repay. You may be assured she and those of our branch House will be looked after. We won't keep you any longer. I'm sure the emperor will appreciate your presence once again."

CHAPTER ELEVEN

It was a clear dismissal.

"Thank you, Overlord. However, I'm afraid we won't be on our way just yet."

"Oh?" she said sharply.

Graydon's smile was aggressive, daring those assembled to try to thwart him.

"The children's futures are not set. Until they and their household are pledged to you, or the oldest has won the mantle of Overlord, I have an obligation to them. I will see it carried out," Graydon said, the pleasantness of his voice at odds with the steely resolve in his face.

"Of course, they will be absorbed into one of our branch Houses," Alma argued.

"No, we won't. Joule's going to take the *adva ka* and become the head of our House!" Ziva shouted.

The woman's eyes got wide as she sputtered.

The man looked at Graydon. "What have you been filling their heads with?"

Graydon started to answer.

Ziva got there first. "We're not going to let you take our House. We're House Maxiim. We'll always be Maxiim. Kira's going to help train Joule."

Kira choked in surprise as all eyes turned her way. That wasn't exactly what she'd said.

Graydon seemed amused at the predicament she found herself in. Alma's mouth snapped shut and her spine straightened as she stared at the three. That was easy for him. He was no longer on the firing line.

"You'll see. Joule will become Overlord and we'll stay House Maxiim," Ziva proclaimed.

"Quiet, child," Alma snapped. "You should be grateful we're taking you in at all."

"Seneschal," Liara said in soft rebuke.

175

Alma bit her tongue, but her narrowed eyes gave away her thoughts. If she'd had her way, she would have had plenty more to say on that subject.

Liara turned on her heel and strode off, the rest of those on the steps following. Roderick and a squad of his men were left behind.

"We will show you to your quarters," Roderick said with a dour expression.

Kira waited for the rest to catch up with her on the stairs. Graydon was the first to reach her.

"Your attempt to procure your release was nice and subtle. I commend you," he said.

"It wasn't good enough," Kira said as they walked up the stairs together into the Citadel.

"The House won't give up their claim so easily," he told her. "If you want freedom from their influence, you'll have to take it."

She gave him a dark look. It was good advice, but it left the question of why he'd offered it. He'd made it clear where he thought she belonged, and it wasn't with humans.

Kira turned slightly to make sure Jace and the rest of his team were following. They brought up the rear, not bothering to hide their gawking as they looked around at their surroundings.

She saw Blue subtly aiming a small device at the carvings near her. A camera probably. It confirmed one of her suspicions. Jace and the rest weren't here just for her and the ships Himoto wanted. They were here to gather intelligence.

The Consortium might desperately want the ships, but Kira suspected they were just the start. Their primary goal lay in a different direction—to learn all they could about the Tuann and what they were capable of.

Oh, Himoto would gladly accept any ships she could negotiate for on his behalf, but he was also desperate to understand what made the Tuann's technology so superior.

"They're certainly not the most welcoming of hosts." Jin aimed his

CHAPTER ELEVEN

eye at Kira. "I'm beginning to see a resemblance."

Kira stuck her tongue out at him as Graydon made a sound of agreement. "The first meeting could have gone better."

"Oh, I don't know. It's not the worst greeting Kira's ever gotten," Jace drawled from behind her.

He'd caught up sometime in the past few minutes.

"True. There was no bloodshed, and everyone is still breathing," Jin added.

The Luathans around them paused, peering at Kira with suspicion. She smiled sweetly at them. They didn't seem to know how to interpret her expression, eventually returning to treating her and the rest with disinterest.

She found it interesting none of Graydon's warriors reacted to the statement beyond signs of amusement.

"Thanks, you two. It means a lot to know your opinion of me," Kira said, watching Graydon's warriors.

Sneaky. They used the fact most saw them as part of the furniture, to watch and listen. No doubt they understood more of the hidden undercurrents and saw more secrets than most visitors to a House. She'd have to keep that in mind. They'd make excellent sources of intelligence and gossip.

"You're welcome," the two said in tandem.

Kira shook her head. She'd forgotten how those two tended to gang up on her, given half the chance.

The amusement fell from Jace's face as he gave her a sidelong look, his expression grave. "I thought we agreed you were going to get to know these people."

It was a thinly veiled criticism, meant to say, "Don't go getting any bright ideas until you complete your side of the bargain."

She gave him a sharp smile. "Why would I want to spend time with people who make it clear they don't wish to know me?"

His expression tightened as he read between the lines. Why would she bother with getting Himoto what he wanted when she could just as easily gain her freedom?

"I forgot. You always have to be the first to leave." The words held a snap to them.

Kira fought her flinch, her mouth already opening to fire another salvo.

"Children, enough," Graydon rumbled.

The look on Jace's face startled a bark of laughter out of Kira before she stifled it.

"That word suddenly doesn't seem quite so funny now, I'm betting," Kira murmured to Jace.

"I'm not a child," he responded.

"To me, you are," Graydon said. "You're what? Fifty? I'm nearly two hundred of your years."

"I'm thirty-nine," he snapped.

Graydon made a less than impressed face.

"Somehow I don't think you're helping your case." Kira leaned toward Jace.

He shot her a dirty look. "In the eyes of humans, I'm considered a mature adult."

"Try middle-aged," Kira said with a wicked smile, touching on the phrase he'd carefully avoided using.

Jace snarled. "I'm not middle-aged. I have years to go before I'm considered that. I haven't even had kids yet."

Kira blinked, surprised. Jace had grown up an only child of only children and had lost both parents in the early part of the war. He'd always talked about the family he'd have one day when the war was over.

"Better get on that," Kira told him, keeping her voice light. "You don't want to be chasing them around when you're an old man."

Amila leaned forward, her gaze curious as she stared at Jace. "You're really forty years old?"

"Thirty-nine."

"It's one year, Jace. Just get over it," Kira told him.

CHAPTER ELEVEN

"It's an important year," he said stubbornly, trying for dignity and failing.

"That's right, boss man," Nova called. "You hold onto your thirties as long as you can. Once you hit forty, it's all downhill from there."

Kira bit her lip to keep from laughing as Jace's shoulders bowed, the man's words hitting him where it hurt.

As much shit as they were giving Jace, he was right. He wasn't quite middle-aged. With health advances from the last century of space travel, humans now lived to be close to a hundred and fifty years—longer if they could afford the anti-age boosters. Jace was at least four decades from retirement and considered to be in the prime of his life.

"How old are you?" Pare, one of Graydon's *oshota* warriors, asked Blue.

"Twenty-six."

Pare choked as several of Graydon's people stared at Blue with wide eyes.

"What?" she asked.

"You're a child," Amila said in a hushed voice. She turned to Jace. "How can you let a child serve in such a dangerous position?"

He started to defend himself before giving up and shaking his head.

Kira took pity on him. "Blue's not a child. She's considered a full adult."

She might be considered an adult now, but when she'd attached herself to Kira's team fourteen years ago, she had been a child in truth.

Blue had learned the hard way—war spared no one. Not even children. The only way Kira had known how to protect her was to show her how to fight and keep her close.

It'd worked out for Blue. The tactic wasn't as successful for others.

"None of us have anything on the Grandma over there," Raider said with a curl of his lip.

Kira didn't react to the statement or the barely veiled dislike there.

"You're what, sixty-five?" he asked.

"She's ninety-two," Graydon said, not pausing as he strode down the hallway, leaving the rest of them staring after him in surprise.

Kira hurried after him. "How do you know? I thought you didn't know who my parents were."

"I didn't. Not until Liara confirmed you were a first cousin. She only has one—a girl, stolen days after her birth. If you're her cousin, as Liara believes you are, it would make you ninety-two," he explained.

"Damn Phoenix, you're so old," Blue said.

Kira didn't respond, her expression pensive as she followed Graydon. If he was right, it meant she had lost more decades than she wanted to think about in that awful place from her childhood.

Roderick stepped to the side and gestured inside a room. "This is your wing, Lord Graydon. The Overlord felt it would be best to keep your people together."

Most of Graydon's *oshota* filed inside, leaving Graydon and Amila outside waiting with her. The Curs followed, Raider pausing beside Jace as he shot him a questioning look.

"I'll be there," Jace said.

Roderick frowned at Kira. "You're this way."

He led her away from the others, the twisting halls and stairs confusing. He gestured at a door.

Kira stepped inside.

"The Overlord hopes this meets with your approval," Roderick said tersely. He didn't wait for a response, stalking off without another word.

Graydon watched him go with a frown. "If you need anything, call for Amila. She'll stay out here for now."

Kira grunted, wandering around the large sitting room. It was roomy. At least ten times the size of her ship's entire living space.

High ceilings overhead contributed to the airiness of the room. It was decorated in shades of white and subdued neutrals, as if the

CHAPTER ELEVEN

Luathans were afraid colors would destroy their calming palette.

A wide bank of windows led out onto a stone terrace.

The warm tones of wood furniture saved the space from being stark. It was a welcome relief from the whites and faded blues.

Jace peered around, his eyebrows climbing. "It's a lot of room for just you."

Kira glanced back, noting Amila standing sentry outside the door as she and Jace drifted through the room, exploring.

Kira headed further into the suite, moving toward an intricately carved wooden door. She opened it and ventured inside to a bedroom out if a dream. A large wooden sleigh bed dominated one end of the room, framed on cither side by tall rectangular windows. The bathroom was easily half the size of the bedroom with a large tub that could have fit ten people.

She'd certainly say this for her cousin's people—they sure knew how to live comfortably.

If this was how they treated unwanted guests, what must their normal quarters be like?

"Nice room," Jace said from the archway.

Kira glanced at him but didn't respond beyond a nod.

"If you ever told me I'd be standing in a place like this back then, I would have checked you for drugs," Jace said, glancing around. "It's unbelievable. Hard to believe first contact ever mistook them for unadvanced."

Kira hummed in agreement.

"I'm sure you want to get settled. I'll send someone by in a bit to check on you," he said, moving toward the door.

Kira fought to keep her silence, but in the end, she couldn't let him leave without a warning.

"Jace, be careful," she called. Her face was grave as he looked at her in question. "This place is beautiful, but I have the feeling its also deceptive."

Jace arched an eyebrow at her. "You know something?"

"Not for sure," she said. "But if I was you, I'd watch what you discuss with your squad."

Awareness filled his eyes as he caught onto her meaning. He glanced around, suspicion creasing his forehead. "Did Jin pick something up?"

"Nothing definitive, but their technology is way more advanced than ours," Jin said. "Just because I can't find it doesn't mean it isn't there."

Jace studied the two of them with a somber face. "You don't think you're being a bit paranoid?"

"If the situation were reversed and our people thought they could get away with it, they'd have this place wired from one end to the other. You know they would."

Jace grimaced. He couldn't argue with that. Kira would be surprised if Himoto or he hadn't put something in the common areas the Tuann frequented while on the station. She knew from conversations with Amila and Baran the Tuann had elected to sleep on their ship during their visit.

He nodded and pushed off the doorway.

"Jace, whatever you're up to, make sure you're smart about it," Kira said.

He gave her a wry smile. "I could say the same about you. I'm not the one chaos follows."

Fair enough.

He left without a backward glance, leaving Kira to get acquainted with her new surroundings.

***

Kira jolted awake from a restless sleep. The cobwebs of her nightmare still clinging to her—madness and death all around, the dying screams of her closest friends ringing in her ears.

For several moments, Kira stared up at the ceiling, disoriented.

CHAPTER ELEVEN

This wasn't her bunk on the *Wanderer*. The bed was too comfortable and there was no soft gleam of the emergency lights.

Memories from over a decade ago filled her head. The dreams disjointed and illogical, as they recounted events out of order and gave her glimpses of scenes she'd never actually witnessed.

Failure tasted like ash on her tongue. The feeling in her chest tightened until it was an almost physical ache.

Kira lay still, letting her heart rate slow and her breathing steady.

It'd been a while since those dreams haunted her. She hadn't missed them or the havoc they played on her mind. She blinked up at the ceiling, struggling not to feel crushed under the mountain of guilt she didn't know how to let go of.

Jace had a reason for his anger as did Raider. She couldn't even blame them for the harsh words. She'd abandoned them before the war even ended, disappeared without a word unable to live with all the things she'd done. For her own good—and theirs—she'd needed space and time to heal the wounds both inside and out.

Of the original Curs, the three of them were the last. Sad, that they felt more apart than ever.

She'd finish this mission, get them an "in" with the Tuann and make sure her departure didn't affect their treaty. Then she was gone. This time she would make sure she stayed gone.

Feeling calmer, she lifted her head and looked around the shadowy bedroom, the moon's silvery light turning it dreamlike.

She wasn't surprised when she saw no sign of Jin. He was probably off getting the layout of the place and sticking his metal in places the Luatha would dismantle him for, if they caught him.

Kira sat up and swung her feet out of the bed, feeling restless. Staying put and trying to sleep after one of those dreams was pointless. She'd just end up crabby and irritable in the morning. Better to get up and get moving, maybe tire herself out so she could try for sleep again later.

If nothing else, it would give her some quality alone time, a precious commodity since O'Riley.

The night air felt chilly against her skin as she stepped out onto the terrace, but not enough to send her inside. The stone under her bare feet was cool as she made her way to the railing. Steps to her right led down into a small garden, the start of the forest a few feet beyond its edge.

The night felt alive around her, making her forget the dream as she relaxed into its song. The sound of the wind moving through the trees, the rustle of branches, the calls of alien animals and insects, all making their own music.

It was totally different than what she was used to. Ships were by no means quiet places. There was always air hissing through the vents, the grumble of the engine, the creak of metal as the ship flexed around you.

She tilted her head and looked up. At least one thing hadn't changed. The stars still shone. Perhaps not as brightly or vividly, given the three moons dominating the sky, but they were there.

The sight eased the tight spot inside her chest. This was here. This was now. Some things might have changed, but others remained the same.

She was still Kira. A long-lost cousin and the people of her birth weren't going to change that. She needed to remember that.

She pulled out the communicator Jin had procured for her when she'd told him what she wanted. She powered it on.

I'm here. Stand by for next phase.

She sent the message and waited. She didn't have long before a message popped up.

Allfather - *I'll be waiting.*

Kira released the breath she'd been holding. That was it. The first part was done. This wasn't what she'd planned when he first suggested it, but fate had conspired and now she was standing at a precipice. The only thing to do was jump.

She couldn't decide if this was a good idea or not. In some ways,

CHAPTER ELEVEN

hacking Centcom would have been easier and less dangerous. They, at least, were a known entity.

The Tuann? Who knew what they were capable of, or if it could even be done?

This plan was insane; that's what it was. Unfortunately, desperate people did desperate things, and Kira had been desperate for a long time.

It was the reason she was contemplating such an action.

If worse came to worse, she could always abandon her plans. She wouldn't risk her life needlessly. She'd remember her promises. That's all she could do for now.

She exhaled slowly. Things would work out. Somehow.

Something tore through her senses, a hint of metallic ice accompanied by acidic rain.

She dove to the side. The railing in front of her exploded, chips of stone slicing her arm and leg.

She was up and moving in the next second. Metal projectiles and energy bolts flying hard and fast.

She sprinted, barely avoiding the blast of energy or the throwing knives concealed in its wake.

There. To her right. The attack was coming from those trees.

She didn't hesitate, leaping over the edge of the railing, snagging a few of the blades sticking out of the stone, before sprinting across the ground.

Twenty feet. Ten. Almost there.

Yellow light tore from the dark. She lunged sideways, then sideways again, when more blasts streamed toward her.

Bastards.

Shouts filled the air behind her, the chaos of the fight drawing the attention of those in the Citadel.

Kira didn't let that distract her, finding cover as another barrage streaked from the trees.

The lights tore the small tree she'd dodged behind to bits, bark and branches raining down on her.

Two could play that game.

She leaned to the side, throwing the knives in quick, sharp movements, aiming in a split-second before diving behind cover.

She had no idea if any of the knives hit their target.

She waited several seconds before standing. Whoever the attacker had been was long gone now. Probably a result of those she sensed approaching from the Citadel.

She moved closer to where her attackers had lain in wait, her body tense and poised for action.

There was no sign of her assailants when she got there, the spot empty and silent. Kira frowned at the area, a frustrated sigh escaping her.

She'd missed her chance. The dark hid any signs of her assailants' passage. Following would be out of the question until daylight. By then, they would no doubt be far from here or hidden among those inside the Citadel.

She closed her eyes and inhaled. The same faint trace of metallic ice and acidic rain filtered to her again. Her eyes popped open.

A Tsavitee had been here, standing in this exact spot.

A dim form appeared out of the darkness, reaching for her arm. Kira reacted, grabbing the person's wrist, yanking them forward as she stepped into them.

It was a classic judo throw. There was a soft sound of surprise and then the man flipped, landing agilely on his feet as he used her grip on him to jerk her forward into a throw of his own.

She landed hard on her back, blinking up at the man. Much of his face was in shadow, but she registered the dark hair and piercing eyes.

She didn't recognize him, and he definitely wasn't Graydon's man. Likely not Luatha either, given the dark hair.

It was all the analysis she had time for before he was on her again, reaching down and grabbing her shirt.

CHAPTER ELEVEN

She jackknifed up, trapping his arm against her as she got one leg around it.

He growled as she started putting pressure on the joint. He picked her up and slammed her down. Then again, when her grip didn't loosen.

Pain ran up her spine as her grip broke. She kicked him in the face in retaliation.

There was a wordless shout from their right.

Kira didn't hesitate, kicking at his knee, savagely happy when her foot connected with a crunching sound.

It didn't stop him. He roared, tackling her as she made it to her feet.

She landed back on the ground with an oomph as he fought to pin her arms and legs. She headbutted him, pain blazing from her forehead.

He didn't rear back as she expected, though he did curse, the sound vicious.

She smiled.

Kira wiggled for better leverage, punching up with her hips, while simultaneously grabbing one of his wrists and throwing her weight against that arm. His grip broke as he crashed onto the ground next to her.

She rolled on top, punching down with everything she had.

He didn't make it easy for her, protecting his face and neck.

A force hit her from the side, carrying her off her attacker.

Kira exploded into a frenzied rage, losing herself as she fought for her life.

"Enough, I'm not your enemy," Graydon roared.

She threw one more punch, gratified when it landed just below his eye. He barely turned with the force of the blow, his eyes narrowing.

"You done?" he asked.

She shrugged. "For now."

He bared his teeth at her. She bared hers right back.

The sight made him chuckle as his hands slid from her shoulders and he stood. He didn't help her up, which was probably a good thing, since she might have savaged his arm given the way she was feeling.

The strange man said something in their language.

"She doesn't understand Tuann. Stick to human standard," Graydon said as he looked around them.

She noticed with a start Graydon wore a pair of pants and nothing else. His shoulders and chest were wide and developed, tapering into a narrow waist. Every muscle was rigidly defined, making it hard to take her eyes off him. He had the sort of body the barbarian romance holos liked to feature. Women everywhere would pay a fortune for any scrap containing a picture of his chest and waist.

"Where did you get the hellcat?" the stranger asked, nodding at Kira.

"It's a long story," Graydon said, sparing a glance at her. "It's good to see you again, Finn."

"Can't say the same," Finn said sourly.

Kira smirked when he reached up to touch the gash on his forehead. It matched hers and made the headache quickly forming behind her eyes almost worth it.

"What are you doing here?" Graydon asked.

"I heard the fight. Got here and found her," Finn said, jerking his chin at Kira.

Kira stared at the two men as they focused on her. "I was out for a stroll and thought I'd investigate."

Neither man looked like they believed her.

"She was their target. She sprinted straight at them after the first salvo. Didn't even hesitate," Finn said, not taking his eyes off Kira.

Graydon growled as he glared at Kira. "Usually one doesn't run at the people trying to kill them."

"Does it happen to you often?" Kira asked politely.

His face got even grumpier.

CHAPTER ELEVEN

"Will you do it?" he asked, not looking anywhere besides Kira.

She frowned, not understanding.

Finn's sigh was heavy and depressed. "Yeah. There's not much choice. She has too much of him in her."

Satisfaction flashed across Graydon's face and he slapped Finn on the shoulder. "Good, that'll make things easier."

"For you, maybe," Finn said as the sounds of others approaching reached them.

Roderick and several of his people slipped through the trees, taking in the sight of them with varying degrees of dismay and caution.

Roderick's gaze lingered on Finn before he focused on Graydon. "What is going on here?"

"I'd like to ask you the same thing," Graydon said in a painfully polite voice. "A child of your House was attacked. Where were your men during this?"

Roderick's attention shot from Graydon to Kira. "We cannot protect you if you leave the safety of the Citadel without notifying anyone."

Kira lifted an eyebrow, unimpressed with the way he'd tried to shift the blame for this to her shoulders.

She held her silence, waiting to see how far he would go.

"Kira was on the terrace when she was attacked. Your men should have been guarding her," Graydon said, a dangerous undercurrent to his voice.

"My men have more important things to worry about," Roderick snapped.

"Someone just penetrated your House defenses and attacked someone under your Overlord's protection. What is more important than that?" Graydon demanded silkily.

Roderick fell silent, glaring at Graydon for several seconds before switching his scowl to Kira. She gave him a polite expression. Graydon had raised excellent points. She was interested in hearing the answer.

"You've made it clear she's under your protection," Roderick shot back. "Until she is declared part of our House, her safety isn't my responsibility."

That response seemed to infuriate both Graydon and Finn. Both men straightened, seeming to grow larger for a brief moment. Graydon's eyes were bright and furious. For a moment, Kira thought he might grab the shorter man by the throat.

Roderick broke the standoff by spinning and stalking away. He barked an order over his shoulder.

"Incompetent fool," Graydon snarled quietly.

"I'd like to say I'm surprised, but I'm really not," Finn drawled. "Luatha has gotten fat and lazy."

That was one word for it.

Roderick hadn't even taken the time to investigate. He hadn't sent his men to sweep the perimeter or make sure there were no other points of insertion. For all he knew, the attack on Kira was a decoy used to gain access to the House for some other agenda.

Was his lack of concern because this was an attack on her? Or was this their normal operating procedure?

Either way, it pointed to a dangerous lack of foresight.

Had the safety of the Citadel and those inside been Kira's responsibility, she would have made sure to hunt the perpetrators no matter who their target. It said bad things about your leadership if someone under your protection could be hurt with impunity. It was only a matter of time before others attacked too.

The same thoughts seemed to have occurred to Graydon, his expression darkening further.

There was a small sound behind them as Amila ghosted out of the woods.

"They got away," she told Graydon.

Impressive. Kira knew exactly how quick Amila and the other *oshota* were.

The assailants would have had to be reasonably versed in the area

CHAPTER ELEVEN

for them to have pulled off their escape. Kira just didn't see a stranger being able to evade the *oshota* otherwise.

A disturbing thought, considering she thought she detected a Tsavitee presence. Her frown grew pensive. She could be imagining things that weren't there, her nightmare influencing her.

"Did you see how many of them there were?" Graydon asked Kira.

"At least two. Other than that, I'm not sure. I didn't get a look at them."

"How do you know there were two?" Finn asked.

"Two weapons," she said. "The energy arrows and these."

She tossed one of the throwing knives at Finn. He caught it easily, lifting it as he examined it closely.

"These are of Luathan design," he confirmed.

"Are you sure?" Graydon asked.

"Very. They're the only ones who bother with the filigree along the sides," he said, tilting it for a better look.

"Form and function. It's practically their motto," Amila agreed.

"Why go after me?" Kira asked. "I haven't been here nearly long enough to make enemies."

"You're of the bloodline. Not just a distant relation but a direct descendant. If you wanted to, you could challenge Liara for her position as Luatha Overlord," Graydon said grimly.

Politics. Great. The last thing Kira liked dealing with.

"Where's your little friend?" Graydon asked, focusing on Kira. "I would have thought he'd be the first one out once the action started."

Kira met his gaze with a cool one of her own. "He's resting."

She didn't let her expression shift, keeping it calm and confident. She didn't want Graydon or the others to know about Jin's extracurricular activities, not now that his spying had become more important than ever.

The look in Graydon's eyes said he didn't quite believe her. She tensed, expecting him to force her to prove it. If they checked her room, they'd know instantly she was lying.

Graydon turned, saying over his shoulder, "Come."

"Where are we going?" Kira asked.

"We need to report this to the Overlord," he said.

"Haven't we already established the Luatha don't care at best, and at worst she was the one to order the assassination," Kira said, following as he headed toward the manor.

"Yes, but seeing how she reacts to this information will tell us a lot," Graydon said with forced patience.

Kira let herself smile, liking the fact she was getting to him. It was obvious Graydon was used to being obeyed without question.

He turned and caught sight of the smile. He paused before fixing her with a look that indicated he knew what she was doing, knew it and would relish his revenge.

Fair enough, but he'd find she wasn't the easiest of opponents.

His smile deepened. No, he looked forward to that.

CHAPTER TWELVE

"Where's your Overlord?" Graydon barked at the two *oshota* standing guard in front of a great door.

If Kira had thought her quarters were needlessly fancy, they had nothing on this. It looked like the entryway to a palace, ornate with finely carved details into the wood panels. Whoever had made these doors had taken their time, poured all their soul into them. They would have taken years to create.

Just like everything else in the place, they were works of art modified to fulfill a purpose.

"She's sleeping," the woman to their right said. "She's not to be disturbed."

Her partner took in the sight of them, his gaze lingering on Kira, noting her dirty bare feet, the slight dishevelment of her clothes. Rolling around on the ground while fighting a full-grown Tuann wasn't easy on the clothes or appearance. Her hair was a mess of snarls and her face had blood on it.

"Get her," Graydon ordered.

The man didn't wait for permission, turning and disappearing into the room as the woman barred their entry.

They waited in silence. Kira shifted, exhaustion pulling at her as the adrenaline from the fight faded. The close brush with death and the ensuing aftermath had wiped the last bits of her nightmare from her, leaving her ready for sleep.

The door opened again as the woman's partner returned.

"She will see you," he said.

Graydon brushed past him, his face a grim mask. The woman remained at her post as the rest of them filed in after Graydon.

Their footsteps echoed in the large cavernous space, the ceiling high above supported by ornate columns. They reminded Kira of some of the ancient buildings on Earth. There weren't many left, not since the war. The Tsavitee didn't seem to care whether something was a cultural treasure before they set out to destroy it.

Liara waited on the other end of the room. She was attired in slightly less formal clothes than the last time Kira had seen her and wore a soft looking, gauzy gown in white, her hair loose.

Like Kira and Graydon, she wasn't wearing synth armor. It made her seem slightly vulnerable, transforming her from the untouchable Overlord into something real and tangible.

Kira's attention was caught by the large painting behind her that took up a sizable chunk of the wall. It was easily twice the height of a person and featured a woman with hair similar to Liara's, loose and unbound, with waves cascading down her back.

It would be easy to assume the woman was Liara's mother or grandmother given the resemblance. Except those eyes. They were a copy of Kira's eyes, though their expression wasn't one Kira had ever been capable of—warm and gentle with a hint of playfulness

Kira's lips parted in surprise and yearning. Before she could say anything Liara spoke. "What is your reason for disturbing me?"

Her gaze flickered when she noticed Kira's state.

Liara stayed focused. "As the Emperor's Face, you are given a lot of leeway, but you are quickly wearing out your welcome."

"Tell me, Overlord. Do you often condone assassination plots against those in your House?" Graydon asked in a reasonable tone.

Insult moved across Liara's face as her guard tensed, his hand dropping to the sword at his side. He stepped forward, stopping when Liara held up a hand.

The two exchanged a glance and his face softened. He relaxed, folding his arms across his chest as he stared at the rest of them.

CHAPTER TWELVE

"What are you accusing me of?" Liara asked with forced calmness.

Graydon looked from her guard to her, his movements precise, a coiled danger waiting for the right opportunity.

He was testing her, Kira realized with a start. Prodding and manipulating to see what lay under that glossy exterior. Smart and sneaky. He played the big dumb brute, but underneath that muscled façade was a man who knew exactly what he was doing, a puppet master making the rest of them dance to his whims.

"Your cousin was attacked in your own home. Had Finn not happened by in time, she would likely have died," he said.

Well, that was an overstatement. Finn hadn't played any role in saving her.

"Look at her face," Graydon thundered. "Someone got close enough to bleed her."

Liara's face grew troubled, her guard's expression equally upset as both focused on Kira. She did her best to seem like the night had been an ordeal, like she was weak and frail, moments from collapse, after the trauma of it all.

"I am beginning to think Luatha does not care about the preservation of its own," Graydon challenged.

"That's not true," Liara argued.

"If you cannot keep a child of your House safe in your own territory, then perhaps that child should be removed," he said as if she hadn't spoken.

"That's not necessary," Liara said, her voice overly loud. "The oversight in her protection was mine. Her re-appearance has thrown us off balance. She should be assigned her own guards. I will make sure it happens and have someone I trust investigate this incident."

She looked at Kira, reassurance on her face. "This won't happen again. I promise."

Graydon's smile was cruel. "I know it won't. You don't have to worry about assigning her an *oshota*. I've already corrected your mistake."

195

Liara's forehead wrinkled in a frown.

Graydon gestured at Finn. "He has agreed to act as Kira's shield. He should be a powerful deterrent against any further assassination attempts. She'll also be moved into our wing so my personal *oshota* can assist in her protection."

Kira's head whipped toward him, her previous admiration of his tactics turning to fury. He'd been waiting for this.

He met her eyes and smiled, knowing he'd trapped her. Yup, he'd definitely been waiting for this opportunity. He'd probably had Finn already picked out, long before they'd stumbled across each other.

The two were obviously acquainted. She wouldn't be surprised if they were friends. Finn's appointment as her guard meant Graydon would be able to keep an eye on her even if he was forced to leave for any reason.

Had he planned the attack for this possibility? She considered the question thoughtfully. No, she was forced to conclude. The assailants had been trying to kill her.

That first shot would have taken out her head and the daggers would have pierced her chest. Only dumb luck and instinct had saved her.

Which meant Graydon was simply taking advantage of the situation presented to him.

She mentally added several notches to the level of danger he represented.

"I would prefer people I trust to serve in the role of her *oshota*," Liara said, her gaze lingering on Finn where he slouched against the wall. He didn't look away from Liara's guard, studying him with a hawk-like intensity. It was a look the other man returned, both men's faces locked in blank masks as they regarded each other.

"I don't care. You lost your right to decide when an assassin took aim," Graydon said. "Finn has Luathan lineage. He is acceptable."

"He's also Roake and has already failed once as a shield. We allowed him entrance into our House because we remember the sacrifice his

CHAPTER TWELVE

mother's mother's mother made for us and wanted to bring his line back to ours," the guard returned. "He's can't be fully trusted with the protection of someone as important as the child."

"I trust him," Graydon said. "That's enough."

"He wants someone who knows what they're doing with a weapon," Finn said, tilting his head at the sword the guard had grasped. "Draw it and I'll demonstrate my meaning."

Kira stirred. "That's enough. I've had enough violence for the evening. If we're done here, I'm going to bed."

Somehow, she didn't think Finn beating up Liara's guard would endear her to her cousin. She didn't need anything else working against her.

Liara stood. "Please. Stay. These quarters are meant for the direct family. I can protect you better here."

Kira paused. Her cousin's face reflected the first glimpse of real emotion since she'd arrived. There was pleading there.

Kira hesitated, her glance going back to the painting above Liara.

The Overlord noticed where she was looking. "She was your mother."

Kira absorbed those words, unable to take her eyes off the woman who'd given birth to her. She'd half-convinced herself she'd been wrong about those eyes.

"What was her name?" Kira asked softly.

"Liliana." Liara watched her carefully, looking for some break in Kira's mask, an indication she cared.

Kira did care—more than she wanted to admit—but she didn't allow any evidence of the turmoil filling her to touch her expression. Kira refused to give her cousin any leverage against her.

"She was a special existence to me. There was no one else like her," Liara said, glancing up at the painting, a soft expression on her face. "My mother was the Overlord and didn't always have time for me. My aunt filled in for that role. At least before she left us to marry your father."

Kira's expression was blank as she listened. It was so odd to be staring at this stranger who was not a stranger at all.

Over the years, she'd had so many conflicting emotions toward the people who were her parents. They'd run the gamut between hatred for allowing her to fall into the hands of monsters and longing for the love that could have been hers.

"She was so happy when you were born," Liara said. "She called you her gift. You became her whole world."

"And my father?"

There was a pause. "His name was Harding. I did not know him well."

Kira looked away from the painting, pinning her cousin with a look. "What happened to them?"

How had they let Kira be taken was her real question.

Liara hesitated, pain flickering across her face. "They both died during the Sorrowing." Seeing the question on Kira's face, Liara offered, "It's what we call the night when many of our Houses were attacked and our children stolen. It was a devastating time for many of us."

Kira concealed her flinch, looking away instead.

"Your mother was killed trying to protect you," Liara offered.

Kira turned away from the painting. She rubbed the ache behind her breastbone. It burned, creeping its way up toward her throat. She didn't want to hear any more about this.

She glanced at Graydon. His expression was neutral, no sign of his thoughts on what Liara had revealed. Kira supposed this was old news to him. He'd indicated he knew her parentage after Liara revealed their relationship as cousins.

Kira shook off the dark thoughts, forcing herself to consider Liara's previous offer. Going down the dark roads of the past wouldn't help her now. It would only lead to distraction and heartache, neither of which she had time to indulge.

Stay on mission. It was the only way to survive.

CHAPTER TWELVE

Liara's offer to stay with her tonight would give Kira an easy way to thwart Graydon's plans, enabling her to get rid of the spy he'd assigned her.

The problem was she'd just be trading one spy for another. She had no doubt any guards her cousin assigned would be loyal to her cousin first, second and last. Not exactly a healthy situation when there were assassins on your tail.

That led to another issue. She didn't quite trust Liara. She wanted to, if only because she was supposedly family. Liara seemed sincere, especially when talking about Kira's mother. However, the instincts of a lifetime were telling her to be careful of the other woman.

Better to keep to the devil she knew for now.

"Thank you for sharing about my parents. I appreciate it more than you know, but I think it best I stay with Graydon for now." Kira's voice was quiet as she tried to soften the rejection.

Liara's expression shuttered, the brief flash of emotion gone as she withdrew into herself. She inclined her head, once more the proper Overlord. "Sleep well, cousin."

"You too," Kira said.

Their group was quiet as they headed to their section of the Citadel, accompanied by the escort Liara had sent with them. Kira had a feeling a perimeter would be set up around the guest wing as soon as they arrived.

They reached Graydon's wing easily. He led her inside, ushering her through the sitting room where Jace and Raider were talking.

Their heads lifted, alarm and curiosity in their gazes as Graydon opened a door and gestured inside.

"You'll stay here for tonight," he said.

He didn't wait for her response, giving her a curt nod before striding off without a backward glance. Guess he had better things to do than answer her questions.

She was tempted to hurry after him anyway and badger him with requests.

"He's focused on determining how the attackers got so close without detection," Finn said. "It's doubtful he'd welcome any distractions."

In other words, stay put or risk angering her only ally.

She sighed and shook her head, turning to her new bedroom. Might as well get some sleep while she could. This would all still be here in the morning.

She took several steps toward her bed but stopped when she realized Finn was shadowing her. "Do you mind?"

"Not at all," he said.

She took another step and shook her head when he moved with her. "Are you planning to watch me sleep?"

"Yes."

She frowned at him. "No."

"It is not your decision," he told her politely. Or that's what it should have been. Instead, it came off as sounding more like "Fuck you."

Kira should know. She'd pulled the same trick on more than one commanding officer. Strange to have it turned around on her.

Jace and Raider barreled into the room.

Finn's en-blade cleared its scabbard as he crouched. He sprang at them seconds later, clearing the distance with two steps.

"Wait," she shouted, dashing after him.

Jace drew his side pistol in a smooth movement.

Finn knocked the barrel away with the edge of his sword, grabbing Jace with the other hand and pinning him against the wall.

The room hovered on the edge of calamity.

"Holster your weapons," Kira ordered.

She approached Finn and set her hand on his shoulder. "You too."

He shot her a hard glance, his reluctance to listen clear.

"Let him go and put away your sword." Kira enunciated each word, sinking her will into them.

They stared at each other for several seconds. Neither one willing to back down.

CHAPTER TWELVE

For a moment, she thought he was going to refuse. She tensed, prepared to act if he became a threat. They'd already tangled once. He'd be difficult to neutralize, but it was doable.

If he pushed her, she'd show him exactly how she earned the name Phoenix so many years ago.

With a grunt, he loosened his hold on Jace, not moving away from the other man, but no longer strangling him.

"Who's this?" Jace asked, rubbing his throat.

Since Finn wouldn't move, Jace was forced to slide around him until he could back away, unwilling to turn his back on the warrior.

"A new fuck buddy?" Jace asked.

Raider choked and stepped away

Finn snarled, rage descending as his muscles locked.

"No," Kira shouted, moving between the two men.

"He's a little touchier than your normal sort," Jace observed.

"Shut up and stop talking out of your ass," Kira snapped. Jace's pride was insulted and he was lashing out at her. She didn't have time for this stupid posturing.

He shrugged at her. "What are we supposed to think when you show up with him this late at night while looking like you've been rolling around on the ground?"

She narrowed her eyes, grinding her teeth as she said slowly, "Someone tried to kill me tonight. I don't have the patience for your games. Say what you need to say then get out."

Jace stiffened. "What are you talking about?"

Kira sighed, already resigned to not sleeping anytime soon.

"Earlier tonight someone tried to kill me. He is the Tuann's response," Kira said, gesturing at Finn.

Raider let out a low whistle. "They've assigned you your own personal protection? Guess it pays to be related to the overlord."

Jace folded his arms over his chest as his face creased in thought. He didn't look happy at the news. "Is the assassination attempt where you got that?" he asked, pointing at her forehead.

"Not exactly," Kira said sourly, unable to help her glance at Finn. His expression didn't shift, no sign of regret or discomfort there.

Jace studied the two of them. His intelligent eyes noted the cut on Finn's forehead and the presence of dried blood.

"You've gotten rusty if he scored a hit like that," Jace said in Japanese. "How long were you on that ship for?"

Kira looked away.

He made a hmphing sound. "Must have been a lot longer than we thought to degrade your skills this much. It's not like riding a bike. The longer you avoid training, the worse off you'll be, especially if there are now assassins after you."

"I'm fine," Kira said, shame making the words come out harsher than she intended. The skin around Jace's eyes tightened slightly but he didn't lash out.

"What are you guys doing here anyway?" she asked in standard.

There was a long pause as the other two conferred silently, their interactions having the same ease and familiarity of people who'd spent countless hours together, risking their lives for one another in impossible situations.

Kira had been a part of that once. Seeing it now reinforced how much of an outsider she'd become since.

"We came to check on you since I thought you were staying in a different wing," Jace said. "Also, there was some action earlier, but no one will tell us anything."

He sounded accusing.

In other words, he thought she was the reason for the commotion, and he wanted to ensure she hadn't done anything to derail the mission.

"You came to make sure I hadn't done something stupid," she said flatly.

"You do have a history," Raider quipped.

Kira gritted her teeth. "As you can see, I'm fine. You can leave now."

"Wait, we're not going to talk about this?" Jace asked.

CHAPTER TWELVE

"What's there to talk about? Someone tried to kill me. They failed. It won't be the first time, and now it looks like it won't be the last," Kira said.

Jace shook his head at her, his frustration clear.

Kira relented. "Don't worry too much, the guard they saddled me with seems to be halfway competent, as you just saw."

Jace wasn't convinced. "I want one of us watching you tonight. Two are better than one."

"I'll be fine, Jace. I don't need another babysitter," Kira said. If she could have banned Finn, she would have.

Amila and Baran had been bad enough on the ship, but at least they had had the decency to stay outside her private quarters.

"I'm not giving you a choice, Kira. This is my mission and you're my primary. It's my job to make sure you survive," Jace said.

At least until they got what they wanted, Kira finished for him.

"Don't try to lie to me," Kira said, leaning forward, a threat in her face. "We both know I might be the excuse you used to get a foothold here, but there's way more to it than that."

He made a strangled sound like he was trying to dredge up patience. Unfortunately, it didn't look like he was successful. That was more like the Jace she knew.

He shot a glance at Finn and switched to Japanese. "You're being difficult. Again. I'm the mission commander on this trip. Not you. You gave up that right when you left."

"Careful who you're talking to," Kira warned.

"Or what?" Jace challenged. "We're not your faithful mutts anymore. You might be able to take one of us. But all? Not likely. Looks to me you spent a little too long on your ship and a little less time remaining combat ready."

Kira's teeth clicked closed as anger tightened in her throat, strangling her voice.

Jin flew through the window, whistling a jaunty tune.

Finn fell into an attack stance, his sword clearing its scabbard as his focus locked on Jin.

"No, not him either," Kira yelled.

Jin beelined for the ceiling, staying out of reach of the overprotective *oshota*.

"What is that?" Finn hissed, not relaxing his stance.

"It's Jin. He's with me," Kira said.

That didn't seem to comfort Finn at all.

Jace took advantage, saying over his shoulder as he moved toward the door. "I'll send Tank in. He can take the first watch and the rest of us will rotate in."

Kira watched him go, Raider following, as words burned her tongue. There was a lot she wanted to say, so much, it all got tangled up and refused to come out.

Jin slowly lowered from the ceiling, keeping a careful eye on Finn.

"That thing's unnatural," Finn said, pointing at Jin.

"Maybe, but you touch him and you're dead."

Finn didn't look particularly impressed with the threat. That was okay. It wasn't a threat. It was fact. If anyone hurt Jin, Kira would ensure it was the last thing they ever did.

"Where did he come from?" Finn asked.

Kira didn't answer.

"If the Luatha Overlord or her guards figure out he was roaming around, they would order your death."

"Seems like a bit of a harsh reaction," Jin muttered.

"Jin sleep flies," Kira said, trying not to wince at the ridiculousness of her statement. It was the first thing she could think of.

"Sleep flies," Finn repeated in a flat voice.

Jin rotated to see her better.

"Yup, like sleep-walking but with flying," Kira said, doubling down on her lie.

Finn didn't seem convinced, but he didn't argue with her. "Well, keep him in here. The Overlord's warriors will dismantle him if they catch him out of the room."

CHAPTER TWELVE

Kira didn't argue as Jin flew by her.

"That was pathetic," he muttered in a low voice meant only for her ears.

She growled at him as she slumped on the bed. The confrontation with Jace and the rest, coupled with everything else had left her feeling drained of energy.

Finn was quiet for a long time as he watched her.

"Your supposed friends don't seem to like you very much."

"Nope." She didn't see much point in lying. Five minutes with all of them together and it was obvious there was history between her and the Curs.

Why had Himoto sent them?

"Why?"

Kira sighed and flopped back, staring up at the ceiling as she debated how to answer.

Some strange urge prompted her to share the truth.

"Jace blames me for abandoning them and breaking up our dysfunctional little family," she said finally.

"He's the one who thinks he's in charge," Finn guessed.

Kira made a small sound of amusement that ended up sounding sadder than she intended.

"And the *tijit*?" he asked.

"What does that mean?"

"It's a rodent. Small, but filled with anger and unexpectedly vicious," Finn said.

Hmph. That was actually a good description of Raider.

Kira turned onto her side giving him her back. "He holds me responsible for the death of the woman he loved."

"Were you?"

Kira closed her eyes. "Yes."

Quiet fell between them. One Kira was grateful for, since she didn't feel like talking anymore. She was done answering questions for the night. She'd already shared more than she should have.

There was a noise behind her, and she lifted her head to see Tank lumber through the door, carrying a M340 Bravo. It was a long-barreled rifle capable of spitting out 600 rounds per minute.

"That's a bit of overkill, don't you think?" Kira asked.

"No such thing," he assured her.

She snorted and jerked the blanket over her. Sleep wasn't likely to come again tonight, but she didn't plan to spend the rest of the night staring at those two.

CHAPTER THIRTEEN

Her feet propped up on the same terrace railing she'd stood next to last night, Kira slouched in her chair. She'd made it a point of hunting down the spot where she'd been ambushed, curious to see what she could learn in the bright light of day.

Kira dug into a small bowl of neon blue fruit. So far, she had concluded she was extremely lucky to still be breathing. The singe marks from the attack stood out in stark contrast against the white stone, their color black and angry.

Knives sprouted from the railing like porcupine quills, not quite as numerous but still impressive. She flicked one with her foot, still surprised at how deeply they were buried. What sort of metal cut stone?

It was a wonder she'd survived. In the fury and chaos, she hadn't registered how many shots she'd dodged. If she'd been even a second later in reacting, she would have lost her life.

Her muscles ached pleasantly as they reminded her she still wasn't quite used to the difference in gravity from the *Wanderer*.

During her exploration earlier, she'd found the terrace wrapped around the entire exterior on this side of the building, connecting Graydon's wing with her former one. She'd walked the entirety of its length twice before settling down for breakfast.

She took another bite of her fruit and hummed as the tart sweetness burst on her tongue. Finn loomed behind her like an angry cloud. He hadn't liked her insistence of eating out on the terrace—especially on this section of it.

Too bad. She didn't like hiding, and time in the sun while enjoying the outdoors was a precious commodity she'd denied herself too long.

Even the dark glower he directed at her every time he glanced her way wasn't enough to ruin her enjoyment of the sun bathing her in its warmth.

Raider plopped in the seat next to her and tilted one of the many bowls toward him. She didn't know what half of them were and none of the servers seemed to speak enough standard to explain.

The small bowls with their bright foods offered a plethora of choices. She wondered if someone had included the variety so she could try several things at once to determine what she liked or if this was their normal breakfast set up.

Raider made a face at the bright pink ribbons in the bowl and sat back.

"You should try it. Tastes like fish," Kira said.

"No thanks. We have rations in the room," he replied.

She paused in her chewing and looked over at him. "Not afraid you're going to insult your hosts?"

Many human cultures had guesting customs. If you were to refuse the food or drink they offered, it could be considered a grave insult. There was a chance the Tuann were similar.

He shrugged, bracing one wrist on the chair next to him as he slouched in his seat. He was Tank's replacement, but he didn't seem particularly inclined to act like a guard.

"I don't care about the wizards or their damn feelings," he said.

That much was obvious in the disdain behind his eyes and the suspicion in his face when he looked around the terrace.

Kira took another bite of her fruit, chewing slowly.

"Why did Himoto send the Curs?" Kira asked. "Why not a squad with less baggage?"

She could have asked Jace, but Raider, oddly enough, was the

CHAPTER THIRTEEN

one most likely to give her the truth. He'd never been particularly interested in diplomacy or couching hard truths behind kind words.

"You'd have to ask the old battleship," Raider said. "You know how he likes his schemes."

Kira did know, knew and hated it. She'd been caught up in them one too many times.

"If I had to guess, it's not so any of us can get anything as sappy as closure," he said, scratching his neck. "Or even to protect you. We both know you're more than capable of protecting yourself—especially at the expense of others."

Kira lifted her spoon in a salute at the jab, not letting it bother her. "Good to see you haven't changed."

Raider bared his teeth at her, his eyes dead as he fixed her with a dangerous stare. "Let's be clear. If I'd had my way, I would have thrown you in the brig while you waited for the day we spaced you. I don't like being here begging for scraps from the damn wizards, but I'll do my duty and put my personal feelings on hold. Unlike some, I know what honor is."

"You keep telling yourself that, Raider," Kira said as he stood.

He turned to her, thunder on his face. "What's that supposed to mean?"

She gave him a nasty smile. "It means you have just as much blood on your hands as me. The difference is you're human and I'm not."

He leaned over, rage on his face. Kira pushed back from the table, giving herself space in case she needed to act.

Jin flew out of the trees making a beeline straight for Kira. The distraction served to remind Raider of where they were.

He straightened. "One day we're going to finish this, Kira."

"I'll look forward to that. Until then, why don't you run along and be the good little soldier boy? Blue can act as the human guard."

"Oh no, cupcake. You aren't calling the shots. You're stuck with me until the end of my rotation," Raider said.

"I can't do what I need to do with someone who so obviously hates the Tuann at my side," Kira said through gritted teeth.

He shrugged. "Not my problem."

Kira tapped the spoon against her bowl trying to resist the urge to punch him in the face.

Jin arrived, twisting to take in both of them. "What's wrong?"

"Nothing," Kira said, putting her bowl on the table. She suddenly wasn't hungry anymore.

"Oookay," Jin said, drawing out the word.

"What do you want, tin can?" Raider asked.

"You know that's not my name, meat sack."

"You seem to think I care about your feelings. I don't."

Jin's sigh was gusty. "I forgot how much of an annoyance you were."

"Happy I could remind you," Raider said.

Kira shook her head. Just like old times. It was amazing how she ever thought she'd missed this.

She picked up another bowl and forced herself to eat several bites. She was going to need the fuel later.

She glanced at Jin in question. A small light flashed twice. He'd found something but didn't want to talk about it where the other two could hear.

She grimaced. Finding a time without any listening ears was going to be difficult, especially since both groups seemed hellbent on keeping as close an eye on her as possible.

When she finally couldn't eat another bite, Kira rose. "Let's explore, Jin."

"The Overlord will want to speak to you today," Finn said.

Kira gave him a sideways glance. "When?"

"She'll send for you when she's ready."

Kira walked away. "I'm sure whoever she sends can find us if need be."

She didn't plan to stay cooped up in a room until these people figured out what they wanted to do with her. She'd found being proactive worked a whole heck of a lot better than waiting for others

CHAPTER THIRTEEN

to make the decisions for you.

They passed Blue tinkering with the innards of some electronics, the purpose of which was a mystery. Kira couldn't tell what it was after Blue had done such a thorough job disassembling it.

Blue looked up, her eyes magnified by the goggles on her head. "Where are you two going?"

"The princess wants to explore." Raider jabbed a thumb at Kira.

She shook her head at him and kept walking. If she let him, he'd keep picking at her until she found herself retreating to her room to escape. There'd be no wandering the Citadel then.

There was a clatter behind her and then Blue hustled after them.

"I'll come with," Blue said with a happy smile.

Kira glanced behind them at Raider. He folded his arms and looked away but didn't comment.

Kira returned Blue's smile. "Sounds good."

"I'll lead," Finn said with a sigh.

Blue kept up a running chatter as they left Graydon and the *oshota*'s suite. Kira nodded and pretended to pay attention as they turned right, heading deeper into the Citadel.

It wasn't long before they entered the more populated section, passing Luathans who peered at Kira with interest.

None wore synth armor. Kira assumed that meant they weren't warriors.

Instead, the Luathans they passed were clad in garments that at first glance appeared almost simple. When Kira looked closer, she saw details she'd missed the first time. Some wore dresses with intricately braided material. Others were pieced together, panels creating a subtle three-dimensional pattern.

The style the men wore was similar, buttons with some type of intricate detail to draw the eye. The longer you looked, the more you noticed, as if only by studying each person could you take in the full effect of them.

Kira looked at those they passed with the same interest aimed her way. The Luathans, she noticed, were more individualized than she'd first assumed. There was more variation in hair and eye color, though blond hair and purple eyes seemed to dominate.

"It's like some scene out of a holovid," Raider said. "It's creepy."

Blue rolled her eyes. "You're always so grumpy. I think it's nice. They seem happy."

"You think everything is nice."

Blue wasn't listening. She darted to a doorway that led into a sun-drenched room. She paused on the threshold, not entering, as she examined the pattern etched into the doorframe.

"See something?" Kira asked.

Blue hummed.

Kira waited, drifting closer to see what had so fascinated Blue.

"I was right," Blue said, bouncing up and down, nearly vibrating with excitement.

"About what?" Kira asked.

"See these." Blue pointed to several points on the pattern. "They bear a startling resemblance to Elder Futhark runes dating from the second to eighth centuries in parts of old Europe."

Kira's forehead wrinkled in thought.

"And here. These look like they derive from the Phoenician alphabet which would have originated somewhere around the Mediterranean."

Blue stepped back, peering up at the doorway with something approaching awe.

Kira and Raider watched her, Finn a disinterested presence behind them.

"I've seen similar runes all over the parts of the Citadel I've seen," Blue said. "Admittedly I haven't seen much."

Raider scratched his neck. "So? Why is that important?"

Blue's gaze darted to Finn before she stepped closer to the two of them and lowered her voice. "Because it means at some point in Earth's past the Tuann visited, saw the runes, and then etched them

CHAPTER THIRTEEN

into this place."

Kira drew back.

Blue gestured to the runes again. "These are old. This whole place is ancient as far as I can tell."

"Graydon did say it was nearly five thousand years old," Kira admitted.

"These weren't put here recently," Blue said. "Do you know how momentous it would be if they visited Earth at some point? I mean, this places their advance to space flight thousands of years before our own. No wonder we can't understand their technology."

By now Blue was babbling, her brain working overtime as she worked through all the possibilities. Kira could see the scientist inside taking hold.

Blue was the technician's specialist for the Curs, but she was also more than that. Jin had pulled her records—all their records—while still near O'Reilly's orbit. Blue had several degrees and PhDs in fields Kira had never even heard of before. The level of her intelligence was awe-inspiring, more so since she had elected to take a position in the military—a path not many with her capabilities would have embarked upon.

Raider stared at the doorway, one side of his mouth pulling in skepticism. "Couldn't it be coincidence? There are only so many ways you can make a squiggle. Maybe it seems similar, but they aren't related."

Blue fixed him with a glower. "Do you know the odds of that?"

"No, but I bet you do," he muttered.

"That's right. The odds of it being coincidence are so infinitesimally small it's not worth calculating. If one symbol was similar, maybe, but I've seen at least ten." Blue stared at both of them before slapping the doorframe. "These originated on Earth."

Or they originated with the Tuann, and Earth's ancient people appropriated the runes for their own use, Kira thought.

She kept her speculation to herself as Raider shook his head and walked away, saying over his shoulder. "Let's move on. I don't care about a bunch of lines."

Blue's gaze went to Kira, pleading in them. Kira shrugged at her. "There's a lot to see. We can come back later."

Blue sighed and then trudged after Finn.

Jin took up his spot over Kira's shoulder. "It could explain their seemingly deep-seated dislike of humans."

Kira nodded as they shared a glance. Each of them sank into their own thoughts as they followed Finn.

After several minutes of awkward silence, Kira quickened her footsteps until she was walking by the terse *oshota*. "Since you're the resident expert, tell us about this place."

Finn stirred, shooting a veiled look her way.

She shrugged. "If these people really are my family, I should probably know something about them."

And if it would distract Blue from her pouting, even better.

Finn sighed. "The Citadel is ruled by House Luatha."

"Is everyone in it Luathan?" Blue asked.

"Most, but not all. Some smaller Houses have settled here. Others have sent their most talented to study under Luatha's masters."

Blue's mouth opened on another question.

Finn answered before she could voice it. "Luatha is known for its artisans and inventors."

Kira hid a smile as Blue settled in with a frown.

"How much of the planet belongs to Luatha?" Kira asked.

"All of it."

She frowned at him. "What do you mean?"

"This is the Luathan home planet. Everything you see here is under their protection."

Blue leaned forward, her expression intense. "How many worlds do the Tuann claim?"

Finn was quiet as he considered Blue. His gaze shifted to Kira. She lifted her eyebrows. She was curious as well.

CHAPTER THIRTEEN

Raider had stopped short, his interest in the topic obvious.

Finn appeared uncomfortable for the first time. "Many."

Kira blinked.

How was that possible? Himoto was going to be very upset, when he learned how badly first contact had erred.

Kira could see Blue doing the math. There were five powerful Houses, each likely to have at least one world if not more. Add in an untold number of branch Houses and the less powerful unaffiliated Houses and there was no telling how many worlds were claimed by the Tuann.

They might even rival the Haldeel's empire for size.

"Ta Da'an is one among many territories Luatha claims. They also have a considerable presence on the emperor's world," he said.

Raider and Blue's shocked expressions mirrored hers.

"This is among the oldest of our worlds. The structure of the Citadel is nearly five thousand years old in some parts and has always rested in Luathan hands," Finn continued as they walked.

"This next section is called the hall of ancestors," he said, gesturing.

Still reeling from his revelation, Kira looked where he indicated. A long hallway stretched before her, arches meeting at the ceiling high above, the walls surprisingly blank given the decorative features on every surface they'd passed previously.

A deep green light bathed its length.

She paused on the edge. "You sure have an odd decorating scheme."

Finn ignored her comment and stepped into the green light, Jace and Blue following as they glanced around in curiosity.

Kira's progress was slower as she examined the hallway. Despite its name, she didn't see any presence of her ancestors. There were no paintings or sculptures, no symbols on the walls. Nothing.

"Why do you call it the hall of ancestors?" Kira asked, her head tilted up as she took in the ceiling high above.

Silence answered her.

Kira looked up.

Her normally imperturbable *oshota* appeared shocked, his gaze disbelieving.

There was a panicked squeak as Blue stumbled, fear filling her face. She cowered away from Kira as she fumbled for a device at her side.

Raider cursed. His pistol was out and pointed at her in the next second. "Turn it off, Kira."

Kira stilled, blinking in dumb surprise at the weapon aimed her way. She expected a lot from Raider, but not this.

"What are you doing? You know you're not going to shoot me," she said in exasperation. If this was another game of his, she wasn't in the mood. "Stop pointing that at me."

He shook his head. Unlike Blue, there wasn't fear in him, just an angry defensiveness.

It forced her to pause.

"Kira, your arms," Jin said softly.

She looked down hesitantly, blinking in blank surprise at the translucent lines and symbols etched on every inch of exposed skin.

How? What?

Fear grabbed hold of her throat. She panted in near panic at the first marker of her shift, fearing she'd somehow lost control of the monster inside.

This wasn't the first time she'd seen such marks, but it was the first time they'd displayed themselves when not called.

She suddenly understood Raider's fear. "It's not me. I'm not doing this."

He shook his head but didn't drop the weapon.

Blue pressed herself against the wall behind him, trying to get as far from Kira as she could.

Hopelessness choked Kira. This, this right here was why she left. It didn't matter how many people she saved or how many times she risked her life. Most humans would only see the monster.

His finger tightened on the trigger, and Kira steeled herself to act. Before she could move, Finn was there, his hand on the gun. He

CHAPTER THIRTEEN

shoved it away, before grabbing Raider and tossing him back as if he was no heavier than a bag of feathers.

Raider landed with a thud, rolling and regaining his feet seconds later. He didn't take his eyes off Kira. He knew who the real threat was in this situation. His legs remained flexed, his posture defensive as he waited.

Kira touched the lines on her skin. It hadn't escaped her Finn lacked similar lines, his skin as smooth and unblemished as Raider's. It seemed even among her people she was a freak.

She turned from them and made her way to the other end of the hall.

"Kira," Jin called.

"Make sure Finn doesn't kill Raider," she told Jin, her voice flat.

Then she was gone, running as fast as she could for outside. The walls seemed to close in on her as she flew past startled faces. No one bothered her as she raced by.

Soon she found herself outside, the sun shining on her as her breathing slowed and calm gradually replaced the frantic need to escape.

She touched her arms, relieved to see no trace of the symbols. They were a part of her, but it was a part she feared.

For a brief moment in the hall of ancestors, she'd remembered what it meant to be the Phoenix, to be the person feared, even as people worshiped her as a hero. She'd spent the past several years burying that person, only to have her resurrected by a green light and a few lines.

She sighed. Sometimes it felt like no matter how hard she tried, the past kept dragging her back.

Her arm dropped to her side and she lifted her head to the sun. It didn't have to. She'd proven that. She was more than a weapon of war.

Her life might be small and meager to some, but it was hers.

Whatever the humans thought, whatever the Tuann believed, she knew who she was, and she wasn't going to let anyone take that away from her.

With that decision, it felt like a weight released from her and Kira began moving again, paying more attention to her surroundings.

The gradual sounds of laser fire coupled with laughter drew her notice and she walked toward the noise, the need for a distraction riding her.

The shouting got louder even as the high-pitched buzzing sound grew. Kira moved through the trees into a clearing as she followed a narrow dirt path to a fence that reached several handspans above her head and stretched on either side as far as she could see until it disappeared into the trees.

It was made from a material she'd never seen. Translucent and see-through, but impenetrable, as Kira found when she tried to stick her hand through it. Pillars were embedded deep in the ground at a set distance all along the fence, supporting it.

Beyond it, she saw the endless stretch of a shallow lake, with trees and rocks sticking out of the water, creating uncertain footholds for those brave enough to attempt crossing it.

Kira joined the crowd watching the event as she tried to make sense of what she was seeing. All around her the crowd cheered and jeered, black synth armor mixing with green, Graydon's soldiers mingling among the Luatha.

Kira pushed her way to the front for a better view.

Inside the fenced-off arena, two people raced along the most extreme version of an obstacle course Kira had ever seen. Some of it looked natural—rocks and stumps showing just above the surface of the water the participants could use to cross—other parts were Luathan-made. Raised platforms dotted the arena, joined together by perilous bridges—the kind where the wood planks were attached to each other by rope but lacked handholds. You'd have to be both fast and precise as you ran across its surface or risk a dunking in the water.

CHAPTER THIRTEEN

Vertical walls and mud pits designed to slow a competitor's speed further complicated the dangerous course. And if that wasn't enough, they'd also created drones capable of shooting laser fire to make competitors' lives as difficult as possible.

As Kira watched, the course suddenly shifted, the water beginning to thrash and grow turbulent as foot paths rose from its depths. The entire course's difficulty and obstacles could be controlled, Kira realized. It was basically a physical simulation, using the natural world as its base.

Graydon's lithe form appeared, springing from rock to rock as he dodged beams of laser fire. He made the difficult task look ridiculously easy as he twisted and flipped, never pausing or missing a step. Several drones similar in shape to Jin but bulkier and slower chased him from foothold to foothold, trying to pin him down as he leaped and ducked, deftly avoiding their fire.

On the other side of the course, another crowd cheered the combatants on as they raced across the watery obstacle course toward the finish line, avoiding the streams of laser fire.

"What's going on?" she asked a woman in green standing next to her.

The woman was tall, her hair short. She had a dusting of freckles on her cheeks and nose, and pretty amber-colored eyes.

"The Emperor's Face accepted a challenge from the overlord's marshal," she said excitedly.

"What does that mean?" Kira asked over the crowd's roar as Graydon leaped, catching hold of one of the ropes dangling from an overhanging branch, before using its momentum to swing his body in an arc before releasing it. He landed on top of a drone. He hammered a vicious punch into its metal body, puncturing it. He withdrew his fist, wires clasped in it. He leapt from the crashing drone, landing on one of the bridges before racing across it and swinging down.

The woman finally shifted her attention from the arena, and glanced up. Her eyes widened at the sight of Kira. "You're the person everyone's been talking about. The lost child raised by the humans."

Kira frowned, not exactly surprised the woman knew of her, but wishing her circumstances weren't known by quite so many strangers.

"I'm Eta," she said happily. "I'm so glad I'm getting to meet you. The rest of my squad will be so jealous."

"Why?" Kira asked.

"Because you're a mystery, and your survival gives hope for others who lost their children during the Sorrowing," the woman stuttered.

Kira fell silent, fiddling with the cuffs of her sleeves.

Eta visibly shook off her awe, returning to the previous topic. "They'll compete to see who reaches the other side the fastest while doing the most destruction to the drones."

Kira turned to see Graydon make an impossible leap, snatching one of the drones out of the air and hurling it at another. The two crashed with a harsh crunch and dropped into the water.

Eta sighed, the sound happy and admiring. "The commander is winning. Not that I'm surprised. He's one of the best. Roderick just challenged him because he's an ass."

Kira made a noncommittal sound, not wanting to distract the chatty woman.

As they watched, Graydon swarmed up a wall and across one of the bridges, while Roderick struggled to evade the three drones locked on him.

For defense, Roderick carried a long wooden staff, using it to deflect their fire.

Not very well, she noted when several beams hit his leg and torso.

Pain reflected on his face even as he pressed forward.

Graydon reached the final platform easily, crossing the line amid groans of dismay from those in green and cheers of victory from those wearing black.

Graydon raised one arm in response, looking around the arena. His gray, stormy eyes found Kira's and then moved beyond her. When

CHAPTER THIRTEEN

he realized she was alone, the smile faded from his face, leaving the hunter staring back at her.

"Ah, crap," Kira muttered.

She thought about retreating, fading into the trees and making her escape before he could reach her. She'd been on the opposite side of enough dressing-downs to know this wouldn't be pretty.

She sighed and stiffened her spine. Running would only prolong things and make them worse. Besides, the last time she'd run from one of the Tuann hadn't exactly worked out for her.

"He's coming this way," her new friend muttered, sounding torn between two extremes—excitement and nervousness.

"Unfortunately," Kira muttered.

"You don't understand. To be considered for his detail would be the greatest of honors," Eta said.

Kira was sure it would be. If the prowess he'd demonstrated was anything to go by, she should assume his warriors were as well-trained as he was.

He stalked around the obstacle course as another group prepared to enter. He stopped in front of her, his expression carefully controlled.

"Is there a reason your *oshota* is not with you?" he asked in a tone that made it clear he thought her an idiot.

"Perhaps because I did not want him with me, and so he is not," Kira returned politely.

Eta drew in a sharp breath, before pressing her lips together, hard, as her gaze darted between the two.

Kira ignored her, too focused on winning the battle of wills with the commander.

Graydon visibly struggled with patience. "I don't care what you want. Finn's job is to keep you alive. Let him do it."

"Somehow, I've managed to survive all these years without your or anyone else's protection."

"That was around humans," he scoffed. "The Tuann would eat you alive."

Kira's eyes narrowed. Oh, would they now? She was half-tempted to show him the error of his thinking.

"I didn't know your kind were cannibals," Kira said, retaining her polite façade. "Thank you for warning me."

Graydon made a sound like a growl. "You're deliberately misunderstanding."

"Only because you are being so damned condescending."

There was a muffled snort from Isla behind Graydon. Another of Graydon's *oshota*, she looked fierce in her synth armor. Noor, beside her, was better at controlling his amusement, though Kira caught the glint of humor in his eyes.

"What's the holdup?" Roderick asked from Graydon's side. He frowned when he spotted Kira. "Where is your guard?"

Kira glanced at Graydon. "It's like you guys only know how to ask one thing."

His lips twitched, showing a brief spot of humor before he squashed it again. "The *azala* was telling me how guards were unnecessary for someone of her ability level."

That hadn't exactly been what she'd said, but close enough. She didn't react to the statement beyond a slight narrowing of the eyes.

Roderick's guffaw made it clear how ridiculous he found the notion. When he finally sobered, he jerked his chin at Eta. "Escort her to the Citadel."

Eta snapped to attention, stepping forward and reaching for Kira's arm. Kira let her take it, conscious of Graydon's regard as she said lightly, "I wasn't aware I was to be a prisoner."

"You're not," Roderick said. "This is for your own protection. My Overlord has impressed upon me how important your safety is. We don't want anything to happen to you while you're wandering around. Your protection should never have been assigned to the half-blood in the first place. One of my soldiers would be a better choice."

Kira recognized the insult implicit in a term like half-blood. She wondered if Roderick realized that when he insulted Finn, he was

CHAPTER THIRTEEN

also implying an insult against her lineage too.

"He's very arrogant," she told Graydon.

"Indeed."

Especially for someone who had allowed an incursion into his security perimeter.

"I'm enjoying my walk," she informed Roderick. "I'll return once I'm done."

One thing she'd learned from interacting with Finn was that when she was direct and firm with her wishes, he was hesitant to force her to do otherwise. She was curious to see if the same held true for others among the Luatha.

Roderick's face darkened.

"Between your people and mine, I'm sure the Overlord would agree Kira has adequate protection here," Graydon said in a neutral voice.

Roderick's expression soured before a shout from the obstacle course distracted him. "Since you've decided to stay, perhaps you can demonstrate your prowess in battle."

Kira should have seen that coming. From the carefully guarded look on the other *oshota*'s faces, she sensed a trap.

Unfortunately, she didn't see a graceful way to refuse. Even then, she hesitated to accept the challenge. Jace hadn't been entirely wrong last night when he accused her of being out of shape. Her body ached with the demands she'd already placed on it.

"Sounds fun," Kira said, feeling like it would be anything but.

"Excellent. I'll inform them you're next," Roderick said.

The carefully neutral expression on Graydon's face remained in place as Roderick stalked off. After a respectful nod, Eta trotted after him.

"That was unwise," Graydon murmured.

"I didn't have a lot of choice. If I'd refused, he would have used it an excuse to send me to my room like a child."

"Instead, he's going to use this experience to humiliate you and damage your credibility with Luatha," Graydon said. "They may be more known for their craftsmen and master artists than their warriors, but they are Tuann. They respect strength."

"Thanks, I hadn't figured any of that out for myself," Kira said tartly.

She watched the current group on the course as they fought for each foot of progress. They worked as a team, their wooden staffs spinning as they defended themselves. Each covering the other as the next person surged forward.

It wasn't until the midsection that they got into trouble, the drones pinning them down with laser fire.

A flash of translucent white settled around them in a cone-like shape, anchored by one man as he spun his staff around him. Seconds later another man burst forward, his sword cutting through the air as a thin ribbon of light sliced from it, cutting a drone in half.

Kira jolted forward. "What was that?"

"The reason this isn't going to be as easy as you think," Graydon said. "We call it the *ki*. Roughly translated, it means soul's breath. The en-blades help them manifest their *ki* to manipulate. Until you learn to use it, you will be at a serious disadvantage should you be challenged to personal combat."

Kira didn't comment, staring across the water as one of the combatants used their *ki* to create a hole in the drones' defenses.

"Tell me about this soul's breath," she said. "Could you teach me?"

"I could teach you the basic concepts given enough time, but to truly learn you would need to study what your people have to teach you," he said.

"Why?"

"While the ability to manipulate the *ki* is common to every Tuann, its manifestation varies greatly. Each House has spent generations perfecting its techniques and then passing them down. I couldn't teach you the Luathan's techniques simply because I don't know them," Graydon said.

Kira looked from the obstacle course up at him, her forehead furrowed in thought.

CHAPTER THIRTEEN

"What about other techniques?" she asked.

"Each House guards their techniques zealously for their own safety. Giving them to outsiders is tantamount to treason," he said. "Even if I did, it would do you little good. Most of the higher-level techniques are bred into your blood. If you don't hold the talent, then it doesn't matter how much you study, you won't be able to use them."

"And all Tuann have this ability?" Kira asked.

Graydon hesitated. "To a degree."

"He means there are some things we can't tell you until we're more confident of your loyalty," Liara said in a strong voice from behind Kira.

CHAPTER FOURTEEN

Liara stood, her hands behind her back and her expression serene.

"Overlord," Graydon said in greeting.

Liara's attention shifted to him, her gaze lacking warmth. "Lord Graydon, you're here at our sufferance. Sharing Tuann secrets with outsiders is forbidden. I believe the emperor is the one who suggested the policy of keeping the existence of the soul's breath from the humans."

Graydon inclined his head. "Your rebuke is wise."

Kira snorted, not buying his humble routine. He'd known exactly what he was doing.

"Here I was thinking you welcomed me with open arms," Kira said lightly, wishing the other woman had come a little later.

Frustration at the interruption ran through her. In response, Kira shifted and fought to keep her emotions in check.

She'd been so close to learning something real, something of vital importance to her.

Because she suspected she knew what the *ki* was and had used it before. Only her use tended toward more widescale destruction—not a simple shield or pretty blade of light. Helpful during war, but a danger out of it.

When she used this *ki*, soul's breath, or whatever it was, she wielded it with none of the grace or subtlety exhibited by the Luatha below. Instead, it was like a volcano, scalding hot and destructive.

Her former team hadn't called her the Phoenix for nothing.

CHAPTER FOURTEEN

Liara gave Kira a soft look. "As much as I wish to share all of our secrets with you, our people have not stood against our enemies for so long without taking certain precautions. There are some things not in our interest to reveal."

Especially when she suspected Kira would turn around and give the information to the Consortium.

Fair enough. Kira had secrets of her own—such as the fact their soul's breath wasn't the secret it should have been. Kira blew that one wide open. Himoto and several highly placed military officials were aware of her capabilities. Had even made use of them on more than one occasion.

"I fear, cousin, there are some things I will never learn then," Kira said with fake disappointment. Her expression sobered. "You may not like them, but the humans are my choice. They will always have my loyalty. If you can't accept that, I suggest ending this now."

Movement from the forest caught Kira's attention. Raider and Finn moved through the trees at a fast clip.

As they neared, Kira saw Raider's furious expression, his face sporting fresh bruises and a cut on his cheek. Finn stalked at his side looking no happier. Unlike Raider, he showed few signs of their disagreement anywhere on him.

The slight tightening of the skin around Liara's eyes and mouth said she saw them too and didn't approve. Her bright eyes came back to Kira's. "We do welcome you, but I have a duty to all those I've pledged to protect. I can't afford to place my trust wrong."

To her credit, she seemed apologetic about that.

Kira gave a shrug. "You'd be an idiot if you didn't have some reservations."

Liara inclined her head, the corners of her lips tilting up.

"Just like I'd be an idiot to place my trust in you," Kira continued, wiping off the ease that had been forming on Liara's face.

"You're family. We don't intend you any harm," Liara said, the words stilted.

A rusty laugh escaped Kira, her expression sympathetic but firm. "We're not family. You're several decades too late for that. We're strangers who happen to share blood. Maybe we can be more, maybe we can't. Only time will tell."

Kira paused, her expression hardening. "Our relationship would be much easier if you drop this ridiculous claim and stop treating me like I'm a child."

Liara's expression remained set, her eyes stricken. "That isn't an option. My station requires I ensure your protection and those who've pledged loyalty to our House."

Kira sighed. She hadn't thought it would work, but she'd needed to give it a try.

The Tuann seemed obsessed with the concept of protection and duty, dedicating their entire society to its altar. They'd turned their values into a noose and wrapped it so tight around their necks they were going to eventually strangle themselves.

It was like a giant, never-ending circle. The overlord protected her people and was protected in turn.

Oaths and honor defined their lives. Break one or step out of their pattern and you were thrown away.

In a way, it reminded Kira of the code of bushido, the way of the samurai from feudal Japan. The samurai had understood being a warrior was about more than your prowess on the battlefield or how skilled you were with your sword. The measure of your worth was in the people you protected, and how you treated them and they you.

They believed in honor, respect, courageous heroism, righteousness, benevolence; all markers she saw in the Tuann to some degree. A few things were different, but the underlying principles remained the same.

It didn't give Kira a lot of hope for herself of ever fitting in. She was a tiger among wolves. A survivor, ready and willing to do what was necessary. It didn't always leave a lot of room for such luxurious notions as honor. Their way of thinking and acting weren't hers. She

CHAPTER FOURTEEN

doubted they'd ever be.

If Liara knew the real Kira, she'd waste little time in kicking her off the planet. If she didn't finish what the assassin started first.

That left Kira trying to win her freedom without showing too much of her more ruthless self.

"What if I was too weak to ever be an asset to the House?" Kira challenged

Liara shook her head. "Everyone has a purpose, whether it be big or small. Either way, we would protect you, even onto death."

"And if I was so strong, I could fend off a hundred enemies?" Kira tested.

"We would use your skills to protect others," Liara said simply.

So, she was damned if she revealed the depth of what she was capable of, and damned if she didn't.

"Doesn't give me much incentive to trust you either way," Kira concluded.

Liara inclined her head. "I can see how it might seem that way. Unfortunately, the House test will reveal the depths of your soul one way or another."

"House test?" Kira asked.

"The *ruma ah*. It's a series of tests all Tuann seeking to join a House undergo. When you reach the point where you can pledge your loyalty, you experience this as well," Graydon supplied. "I wouldn't waste time trying to fool it into thinking you're weaker than you are. The test will figure out your potential no matter how you fight it."

Kira didn't like the sound of that. Her expression was pensive as her thoughts turned inward. She wished she knew more about what was expected of her. There were things she'd like to keep hidden, partly because of her past, partly because she didn't want to face the questions their revelation would inevitably bring.

While the Tuann seemed to have many things in common with her, there was the ever-present worry her time in the compound had changed or damaged her in some way. The experiments they'd performed on her and others had been brutal. It wasn't outside the realm of possibility she'd been changed as a result.

The Tuann, for all their stiff-necked insistence on family, weren't likely to be accepting of too many oddities.

She released the breath she was holding. It was pointless to agonize. If she couldn't figure out a way to rig the test, Jin would.

Graydon turned his attention to Finn. "Would you like to explain how you let your charge wander around without you?"

A threat threaded through Graydon's voice as he fixed Finn with a hard stare.

Finn opened his mouth.

"No," Kira said.

She shook her head at him. She didn't want him explaining. She didn't want the cause of the incident brought up, discussed, and dissected.

There was a chance those symbols had been normal. There was also a chance they weren't.

Finn's mouth clicked shut and his expression went neutral.

His silence surprised Kira. She hadn't expected him to listen to her, his friendship with Graydon trumping her wishes

Graydon arched an eyebrow at her. "No?"

Kira lifted her chin, not letting him intimidate her. "That's right. This is between me and him."

Liara's mouth made a soft O. Even the two guards at her rear seemed impressed at Kira's stubbornness. Both looked away after a second of shock, struggling to contain their amusement at the sight of her standing her ground against a man she was beginning to realize wasn't often challenged.

Graydon's eyes darkened as he studied her. "You're being ridiculously stubborn."

"Good. It's my life to be stubborn with," she said.

He chuckled. "That statement shows me how little you understand. If you die, he will be the one to face consequences. He's already lost

CHAPTER FOURTEEN

one charge. To lose a second would result in no others accepting him as their *oshota*. This means he could no longer contribute to the wellbeing of the House."

And dead weight was the first to be eliminated in times of strife, Kira supplied mentally, seeing where Graydon was going with this.

He leaned closer, saying for her ears, "Think carefully upon your actions. While his duty is to ensure your wellbeing, you have a responsibility to him as well. It's a two-way street as the humans would say."

Kira gritted her teeth and glared as he straightened. "Perhaps you should have tried to explain all this last night." She hadn't realized quite how serious Finn being assigned to her was until that moment. "I would never have accepted his protection otherwise."

"Exactly why I didn't bother explaining."

She held in her growl at his amusement. This was all fun and games for him, but what was she supposed to do with a man who by all accounts was now her permanent watchdog?

Roderick chose that moment to approach, distracting them. "The final team has finished their run. You're next."

"Next for what?" Liara asked.

Roderick's eyes widened slightly as he finally noticed her standing in the cluster. "Overlord, I didn't expect you today."

"Obviously," she said, her voice dry. The two guards in attendance twitched slightly, their eyes dancing with a hidden mirth. "What is she next for?"

"The *odiri* course," he said diffidently.

He was trying for humble and conciliatory but not quite succeeding, frustration and arrogance still present in his expression.

"That's bold," Liara said, surprise wiping the haughtiness from her face for a second. "Who is she running it with?"

Roderick's face grew even more remote. "She did not say."

"She cannot run the course by herself," Liara said. "It's meant to be tackled with a team of at least four."

"She made it clear she didn't want help," Roderick said stiffly.

None of those present bothered to correct him; Noor and Isla behind Graydon exchanged disgusted glances while Kira's jaw clenched.

Roderick hadn't bothered to explain the course was impossible to run solo. Protesting now would make her look even stupider than she already did.

"She doesn't know better, you do," Liara said, the rebuke fierce.

Roderick shifted, his expression turning dark.

"Send the human in with her," Roderick said, flicking a glance at Raider. "They can perhaps educate us in their battle tactics. Many are interested in how they managed to survive the Tsavitee considering their vastly inferior technology." He looked Raider up and down. "And their less than impressive physical abilities."

Roderick gave the two of them a look filled with arrogant challenge as he waited expectantly. He thought he'd won this round.

Worse—he was probably right.

It was a legitimate solution, even if it was intended to put Kira and Raider in a tight spot. There were two of them. With the rest of the Curs scattered around the Citadel, it was likely to remain that way.

If they wanted another member, they'd have to ask the Tuann. The chances of one agreeing were unlikely given the stiff reserve they'd made obvious since Kira and the Curs arrival.

Still, if the two of them refused to participate, the Tuann would assume they were weak or afraid. Kira didn't really care what others thought of her and could have twisted that assumption to her benefit, but Raider and the rest would care.

From the pinched expression on Raider's face, he'd come to the same conclusion she had.

Roderick waited, knowing they'd have little choice in forfeiting. His mouth pulled up on one side as he anticipated winning this little skirmish.

"Since they'll be down two, I will compete as well," Graydon said.

CHAPTER FOURTEEN

Roderic looked like he wanted to argue but couldn't think of a polite response.

"Me too," Liara said.

Surprised appreciation shot through Kira. Until now, she'd assumed Liara would come down on Roderick's side in this situation. She might regret it, but he was one of her people. It would make sense if she placed her loyalty with him, over a long-lost cousin she'd known less than forty-eight hours.

"You can't, Overlord," Roderick protested. "You are our shield. If you were to be injured, it would affect our standing."

Liara's expression fell, disappointment filling it as she conceded his point.

"I'll do it," Finn said, his expression stony.

Roderick grunted in agreement. "Fine, I'll inform the rest."

He stalked off before anyone could speak.

Kira and the rest followed slowly as Liara escorted them to the beginning of the course, keeping pace easily. "I apologize for my marshal. Our people have always been resistant to change. Please don't judge them too harshly."

Kira held up a hand. "Don't bother. Just give me an idea of what I'm about to face."

She didn't care about apologies or justifications. They were already past that. This was the current state of things. She had to concentrate on getting through this next part before bothering with the messy emotional side of things.

"It's called the *odiri* pattern. It's meant to test your teamwork."

Kira let out a soft huff. That wasn't the news she wanted to hear, given one member of their team hated her, another would be focused on trying to protect her, and the last had joined for reasons only he understood.

Excited chatter from those gathered accompanied them as they approached the entrance to the training field. Kira ignored the onlookers and focused on ferreting out all the information she could before they were thrown into the arena.

"Avoid getting hit by the drones' laser fire. Their weapons are meant to simulate actual wounds. It can be quite shocking to the system. Some freeze up as their bodies struggle to reconcile the pain with reality," Liara explained.

"Good to know," Kira murmured.

Raider snorted.

"You get points for every drone you take down and every salvo you successfully repel. Points are deducted for every hit you take. The time until completion also factors into your overall score."

Kira nodded. Seemed simple enough.

"Good luck," Liara offered. "If you can, stay behind Graydon and Finn. Both men have run this course before. If you're wounded and can't continue, raise your hand to forfeit."

Liara stopped at the edge of the fence, her expression grave as Kira moved past her.

Jin settled right over Kira's shoulder. "I'm going with you."

"Much as I appreciate that, I want you to stay out here," Kira said. "Keep an eye on things while we're competing."

He sighed before rising, gaining altitude so he could watch the scene from above.

Graydon handed her and Raider two wooden swords. "Try not to hit yourselves in the face with these."

Kira took the sword, aiming a dark glare his way. He chuckled to himself as she tested the swing of it in her hands. It was light and flexible. Not quite as well balanced as her old energy sword, but not bad.

Raider's expression was dissatisfied as he took his.

Kira sighed, wishing any of the others were here. Blue, for instance, would have been a good choice. The other woman preferred using her brain and would probably have rigged up some type of trap in the space of five minutes, incapacitating the drones and allowing them to stroll unmolested to the other side.

CHAPTER FOURTEEN

Raider was too much like Kira. He relied on brute strength and speed to dominate the field. She didn't know if either skill would be enough today.

Finn was an unknown quantity. Her only experience was the brief tussle they had last night. She assumed he had some level of skill given his status as warrior and guard, but how that would mesh with the rest of the team Kira had no clue.

"Think you can handle this?" Graydon asked Kira with a taunting smirk.

"We're about to see."

"If you get too scared, you can always hide behind me." His smirk deepened into a wicked smile and he leaned closer. "Don't worry, I can protect your weak self."

"I'll keep that in mind," she said dryly.

She'd do nothing of the sort.

"Have to make sure you don't damage your frail body," he continued. "You and the human can hang back, let us do the heavy lifting."

"Ah-ha," Kira said, her voice sounding slightly strangled.

Raider scoffed next to her. "Is he serious right now?"

"Hard to tell," Kira responded. She sure hoped not.

Graydon's chuckle was husky.

Kira's eyes narrowed. He knew exactly what he was doing, throwing down a gauntlet Kira and Raider would have no choice but to pick up. Raider, because of injured pride—Kira so Raider didn't get himself hurt.

Jace would never forgive her if Raider got himself killed trying to prove a point.

"Let me get this clear," Raider started. "You think you and the pain in the ass can take on this entire course by yourselves?"

Graydon's expression turned smug. "I know we can."

Raider and Kira exchanged a glance.

"Prove it," Raider challenged.

"Wait," Kira started. The whole point of the other three's inclusion was so they could work together.

"Alright, how about a bet?" Graydon asked.

"No. Don't do it," Kira tried, already shaking her head.

"What sort of bet?" Raider asked.

Kira made a frustrated sound. He was playing right into the Tuann's hands.

"If either of you make it to the finish line before us, I'll make sure you're not saddled with any more guards besides Finn," Graydon said, capturing Kira's interest. He fixed Raider with a dark look as the playfulness dropped from Graydon's expression. "And I won't mention to our hosts the human ship sitting about five hundred units outside this system."

Raider's face drained of emotion, leaving only the predator behind. This was the man who had faced the Tsavitee down, never flinching. Death was in his eyes as he watched Graydon.

Kira tipped her head back and groaned. "I should have known."

"Shut up, Kira," Raider said.

"Make me," she snarled.

Raider didn't move, though he wanted to. She could tell.

She scrubbed one hand down her face, calling herself an idiot. She should have known Himoto would have something up his sleeve. A ship hidden out of sight would be just like him.

He was probably waiting for some sort of signal from Jace and the Curs. Not a bad idea, and normally she would have been thrilled at the prospect of possible backup, except the Consortium had agreed not to trespass on Tuann territory unless invited.

"They're holding just outside our territory," Graydon said pleasantly. "But the Luatha would be very displeased if they discovered your fellow humans knew the location of this planet."

Translation—if they found out, they'd likely kill the Curs and maybe even Kira, since she had technically agreed to bring them here.

Her shoulders bowed.

Graydon stepped forward, bending so only she could hear. "I

CHAPTER FOURTEEN

suggest you make it across the finish line first."

"You're an asshole," she said without heat.

He grinned, not taking the insult. "I'm an asshole looking forward to seeing what you're capable of."

"Wasn't the whole point of this to work as a team?" Kira asked plaintively.

"It would never work," Graydon said, his gaze piercing. "None of us trust each other, and we don't have time to build that trust. The only way through is brute force and hoping the others are strong enough to survive on their own."

He was assuming a lot, even if he made several excellent points Kira had already considered.

There was a loud chime and then the gates before them opened, revealing the starting platform that transitioned to the course several feet below.

Finn was the first through, taking off at a smooth run. He leaped onto the uneven boulders peeking up above the water line in a broken, crooked path of stepping stones.

He made it halfway across before the first drone came online. It surged up from beneath the water like a great sea monster, fire flying from its mouth as it and its brethren darted after Finn.

Graydon gave Kira a roguish smile and then stepped backward off the platform, disappearing from sight. He appeared seconds later, running about a foot above the water as if on some invisible surface.

"Guess that's why they call them wizards," Kira muttered to herself.

"How do you want to do this?" Raider asked.

She turned to find him next to her, frowning out at the course. While they hesitated, the drones had swarmed. Countless numbers of them converged on the two men. She saw now why Liara said there had to be four. This would have been impossible odds if faced alone. At least with four, the focus of the drones was somewhat split.

"You're willing to work with me now?" Kira raised an eyebrow. "Thought you hated me and couldn't trust me."

The words were an echo of what he'd once said to her. She hadn't realized she'd been carrying them around all this time until this moment.

"I do. You're a wild card, unpredictable—as likely to get your own people killed as the enemy."

Kira's jaw locked.

"But we can't let him tell these people about the ship, and you're my best bet for success."

"Enemy of my enemy," Kira said.

He made a frustrated sound. "Something like that."

Kira was tempted to tease him a little longer, make him beg a bit. His need for success was far more pressing than hers. She'd survive being stuck with additional guards. He and the others might not survive the Tuann's displeasure.

"Fine. Do you remember the old days?" Kira asked, giving in. It wasn't in her to tease about something this important.

"We still use those patterns. Although we've modified them a bit," Raider said.

"Good, we'll use Sierra Sierra," she told him.

Like sports teams, the military scripted certain maneuvers. The patterns were usually preset and evolved as the changing circumstances did. This one was really meant to be used while wearing a Hadron battlesuit while riding a waveboard.

The Curs original directive had been as a space to ground combat unit, similar to the paratroopers of the twentieth and twenty-first centuries. Only the Curs began their insertion from orbit and had much more control of their breakneck descent. The waveboards were lightweight and highly maneuverable, allowing the user to turn on a dime while also coming in handy for ground warfare.

They were soldiers of space, air, and land, easily adaptable to any condition. What had begun as an entertaining pastime for teens racing waveboards in tournaments became humanity's answer to their greatest tactical weakness.

CHAPTER FOURTEEN

Sierra Sierra wasn't the best tactic given the circumstances—they could have used at least one more person—but it was the one with the greatest odds of success.

"I'll act as decoy and draw their fire," Kira said. "You run through the opening I create."

Raider grunted in acknowledgment.

Kira was happy when he didn't try to argue. She stepped up to the edge of the platform and studied the field. She'd chosen Sierra Sierra based on her observations of Finn and Graydon.

Neither had been attacked until they were halfway across the water. Even now, the drones hovered beyond that invisible marker.

She hoped the other part of her hypothesis held true and the drones were attracted to those who actively fought them. Otherwise, they were in a bit of trouble.

Kira hopped to the stones below, noting the way they wobbled under her feet. Raider would need to watch his step. If his landing was off by even a little, the stone would tip, dropping its burden into the water. She had no doubt the drones would key onto that person in a second.

She made her way slowly, not bothering to hurry, conscious of Raider dropping to trail her. Since no sound of a splash reached her, she chose not to worry about him.

The drones hovered overhead as she picked her way across. This close, they looked like much larger, sleeker versions of Jin. Where he was small and dark, these shimmered with the color of their surroundings, almost blending in except for when they moved too fast or were seen from above.

They managed to seem organic rather than mechanical, their shapes not uniform and their movements closer to that of a hummingbird or bee.

They were double the size of a basketball and as quick as any strigmor eel Kira had ever come across.

As she watched, one of the drones crackled with lightning. Its blast

239

darted at Graydon, snaking through the air much like a strigmor eel. He leaped out of the way, raising his hand and pushing out. A force sailed from him, striking the drone. It dropped, plunging into the water as if a hand had swatted it out of the sky.

Finn wove among the obstacles, never pausing his sure-footed passage as the drones pummeled him with laser fire.

Kira adjusted her grip on her sword. It was about time they got started. If they waited much longer, there would be no hope of catching Graydon or Finn before they passed the finish line.

"You ready?" Kira asked.

"I'm not the one who's been sitting on her ass in retirement."

Kira's smile flashed. Guess that answered that.

She hopped to the next foothold. It was farther than the others had been. From here on out, the footholds got scarcer and scarcer. The one she'd landed on looked like a large wooden pillar sticking out of the water, thin and narrow, forcing her to balance on one foot.

A drone burst out of the water beside the pillar. A bolt of light flashed from it. Kira shifted slightly, letting it glance off her arm.

Pain screeched up the limb. She hissed, but didn't move.

"How bad is it?" Raider asked.

"They weren't lying," Kira said, her voice tight with pain as she glanced at her arm. Vague surprise moved through her at the sight of unmarred flesh. "It feels like getting shot. I'd advise avoiding getting hit at all costs."

"Understood," Raider said.

"I'm going. Count to ten and then begin." Kira bent her leg, focusing on the other end of the water. This was going to be fun.

Between one second and the next, she burst forward, going from a standstill to a full-out sprint in the blink of an eye, the unevenly spaced footing not giving her more than a second's pause.

The drones reacted—her fast movements pulling them away from Raider—just like she wanted.

She grinned. Time to see how they reacted to a little friendly tap.

CHAPTER FOURTEEN

Up ahead, the broken path diverged, three paths emerging. Kira approached at a run, dragging her sword in the water as the drones sped toward her. She ran a thin line of her power—what she suspected Graydon called *ki*—to the very tip of the wood. Careful, careful, she cautioned herself. She didn't want to break the wood.

Her soul's breath was incredibly destructive. The last thing she wanted, was to explode something right now.

She judged the tactic a small risk, but one worth taking.

She poured the smallest amount of herself into the blade, gathering small droplets of water behind it until a sword of water extended nearly five feet behind her.

The pull of the blade began to grow heavier, resisting as more water gathered, increasing the friction of its passage. She tightened her grip and waited, her eyes on the drones as they lined up their shot. Almost there, almost there.

Now.

She swung the sword through the water, cutting it as she might a blade of glass. The water followed the path of her blade, creating a perfect arc around her. The screen of liquid restricted the drones' sight for a split second.

It was all she needed.

She dashed forward, taking the middle path as Raider darted for the one on the far right. Her water diversion worked, distracting the drones from Raider and focusing all their attention on her.

Droplets of water rained down on her, making the path slick as she sprinted forward. She'd chosen the shortest one, but she was betting it was also the most difficult. The Tuann seemed like the type to turn a simple exercise into one of deceit. No doubt she'd chosen the most treacherous.

As if to confirm her assumption, she spotted Graydon ahead, Finn on the path to her left.

Kira flipped in midair, barely managing to avoid twin bolts. She came out of her flip, landing on one foot and immediately leaping sideways to avoid another blue bolt.

For several long minutes, she lost herself in the difficulty of avoiding being turned into swiss cheese, ducking and swerving as she pushed her body to the limits.

Exhilaration fed into her movements as she listened to her instincts, leaping and twisting whenever danger threatened.

For the most part, her wooden sword hung forgotten at her side. She preferred to evade and dodge instead of attack. She used the sword when absolutely necessary, which was to say never.

She landed on a tree branch, taking a second to get the lay of the land.

Graydon roared as he challenged twenty drones, his movements full of restrained fury as he snatched one out of the air and threw it at another. At that moment, he was the warrior, fierce and powerful, and full of a heated need to destroy.

She'd never seen anything like it. The sight tempted her to challenge him, to test her skills against his to see who came out the victor.

She shook off the thought. She couldn't afford such things right now. She had a match to win.

She turned and looked for Finn.

She muttered a faint curse when she finally spotted him, way too close to the finish line for comfort.

He just needed to clear a twenty-foot wall, walk across a log on a see-saw, and then find a way across a ten-foot chasm.

Raider, by contrast, had over half of the course to go.

They were going to lose.

Kira whirled, catching the drone behind her with the flat of her sword. It reeled away, crashing into the tree where she perched.

Seconds later, its broken pieces began to reassemble. It rose, turning to Kira as a light pulsed deep inside.

"Calling your friends, huh? Bring it on," she told it.

She didn't wait, turning and leaping onto the obstacle course again. Something drastic needed to happen to turn the tide.

CHAPTER FOURTEEN

The obstacle course had been built into a long lake and had seen much use over the years. The ruined remnants of previous paths lay barely visible beneath the water. Some pieces broke its surface, but not many.

Taking it would be a risk but worth it if she could delay Finn.

Kira arrowed over the water toward her guard.

She leaped and whirled, evading the drones, her feet flying over the unsteady footing as if they'd been given wings.

This was what freedom felt like. For one timeless second, she remembered what it felt like to fly, defying both the odds and gravity as she used every ounce of strength and willpower to reach for a bit more speed, to add a little more height to each jump.

Her footholds changed from the smooth wood and polished surfaces of the obstacles, to barely submerged rock or broken tree branches.

The drones raced after her, turning an already difficult route more perilous. One swooped close, and only her quick reflexes kept it from hitting her in the head.

Halfway to Finn's side. Not far now.

She leaped, catching the edge of one of the drones as it veered too close. She grabbed it and swung her body, using the momentum to vault into the air, completing the arc to land on another drone.

The slightest tingle ran under her, like a storm gathering power. The warning came microseconds before lightning crackled beneath her feet. She catapulted off the drone, flipping in midair.

She landed on a half-submerged tree trunk, checking Finn's progress. As far as she'd come, it wasn't going to be enough. He was too close to the finish line, and her path forward too broken.

Damn. Not good.

Raider had a third of the course left. She could abandon the plan, make for the finish line. Maybe she'd beat Finn. It was unlikely.

Graydon wasn't far away, battling it out with the drones, his face almost feral as he took down one after another. His very success meaning more and more drones swarmed him, giving the rest of them a breather.

She glanced at the water. There was one way to pull Finn's attention away from winning. It was a bit drastic.

She thought the chances of success were good anyway.

He was her protector. What would he do if she put her life in danger? Would he give up the fight to save her ass?

There was really one way to find out.

Two drones rose behind her, their camouflage nearly perfect. Just the slightest wavering in the air alerting her to their existence.

Kira took a deep breath. This was going to hurt, but there was nothing for it.

Graydon looked over from where he was fighting. His eyes widened, his mouth opening on a warning.

Satisfaction filled Kira. He'd been so sure he'd win. Guess he'd thought wrong.

Several things happened at once.

A powerful mind brushed hers, tainting it with the feeling of metallic ice and acidic rain. She jerked, everything in her stilling,

A large force hit her. A powerful jaw clamped around her accompanied by the familiar pain of being shot in the back.

She had no time to process before lethal teeth bore down.

Desperate, Kira reached for the broken bits of power nestled inside her.

The jagged, damaged pieces of her soul fought to answer. They were a thorny, tangle of vines as they uncurled. She coughed blood as they ripped through her.

A small, barely functional bubble sprang into existence around her, protecting her as the creature tried to crush her.

She caught a terrifying glimpse down the creature's throat.

In response, Kira rammed the wooden sword into its mouth, aiming for the back of its throat. It spit her out.

She sailed through the air, strong arms catching her moments later.

CHAPTER FOURTEEN

"You're definitely a source of trouble. I regret our bet," Graydon said into her ear.

"Not my fault," Kira managed to get out. Her ribs protested each movement, every word reminding her she'd almost been eaten. Her insides felt like a razor blade had been taken to them, a consequence of the small amount of power she'd used.

Graydon lowered her to her feet until water licked at her boots.

"What is that?" Kira asked, peering up at the creature.

It looked like the ancient ancestor of a Chinese dragon crossed with its avian cousin. It had a serpentine body which lay half-submerged in the water. Horns curled from its head, and feathers rose in a crest behind its head and jaw. Long whiskers trailed from its snout, adding to the beard-like whiskers under its chin.

Edged in blue with a red mane, it was a thing of beauty. Sleek and lethal, it rose above them, bugling a challenge at the sky. It had powerful forelegs tipped with deadly talons, and fins meant to cut through water along its side.

"It's a *lu-ong*," Graydon said grimly, not taking his eyes off the creature. "Barely more than a baby."

"You consider that a baby?" Kira asked in disbelief. No wonder they insisted on seeing her as a child if they counted that giant creature an infant. Their definition of what constituted a baby was seriously off.

"A full-grown *lu-ong* can grow up to three times its size. This one is nowhere close to that."

Kira's mouth clicked closed. That put things in perspective.

The *lu-ong* lowered its head, snorting at them. Its lips curled, exposing the terrifyingly sharp teeth of a carnivore.

Kira swallowed hard, the thought of where she'd been minutes before making her slightly queasy. She wasn't afraid of death, but the thought of being some creature's snack was terrifying.

Graydon let out a low curse. "We're going to have to kill it."

"Wait," Kira started.

Graydon didn't listen, his powerful stride taking him close to the *lu-ong* before she could do more than form a token protest.

Kira screamed in frustration.

The insufferable man was going to get himself killed. What did he think he was going to do? Punch it to death?

Kira darted after him.

The *lu-ong* tossed its head, biting at the air as it reared, springing even further out of the water, its movements frantic and mindless.

"Stop," Kira shouted, kicking the back of Graydon's knee and sending him stumbling forward. "You can't kill it."

"What do you suggest I do? Let him eat you?" Graydon asked sarcastically.

"Perhaps you can take a moment away from needless posturing and actually analyze the situation," Kira spat.

Graydon showed her his teeth, displeasure pouring off him in waves. "What's there to analyze? Once it's dead, you can talk about your feelings about its tragic end all you want."

He did not just say that.

Kira glared at him and pointed. "Look at the side of its neck. That's a Tsavitee control collar. The moment it senses its host's heart stop beating, it will attach itself to the next closest source."

Where Kira pointed, there was a large lump. On closer inspection, it resembled an alien tick, tentacles plunging deep into the *lu-ong*'s skin.

"But if you'd like to be used as a Tsavitee puppet, go ahead, kill the *lu-ong*," Kira said, her words dripping with acid.

Graydon's eyes spat fire as Kira raised her eyebrows at him, unmoved by his temper tantrum. She was right and he knew it.

"What do you suggest?" Graydon said, the words sounding like they were forced out of him.

"Thank you for asking," Kira said, unable to resist prodding at him. His ire deepened until his eyes looked like storm clouds. "It'll be easier if we destroy the collar first. After that, the *lu-ong* will either

CHAPTER FOURTEEN

run off or you can kill it."

She'd prefer the *lu-ong* escape with its life intact. Something that beautiful didn't deserve to be destroyed because of a Tsavitee's poisonous interference.

"Fine," Graydon said, his voice rigidly controlled. "How do you suggest I do that?"

"Destroy the collar's brain first. One hard blow to the body should do it," she said. "Just be careful. If it senses its mission is compromised, it might try to attach itself to you."

She spoke from experience. The alien tick was a pain in the ass to kill. You had to be quick and precise or risk falling under a Tsavitee's control.

"Think you can handle that?" Kira challenged.

Graydon curled his lip at her. "The day I can't handle something like this is the day I admit a human is better than me."

Kira rolled her eyes at him, exasperation making it hard to keep her retort to herself. "I'll act as decoy. You take care of the collar."

"No, just stand where it's safe."

"That's not happening," Kira told him. "Accept it or get out of my way."

He growled at her, but she didn't move, just folded her arms and stared him down.

The *lu-ong* chose that second to strike, its head snaking forward with the speed of a cobra.

Kira dove into the water. It closed around her, cold and wet, as panic beat at her. It had been instinct to seek the water's protection, but now it worked against her.

The *lu-ong* was aquatic, at home in its depths much like an alligator. She needed to escape before she ended up as lunch.

She kicked her legs, propelling herself for the surface. Her first gasp of air tasted like razorblades.

A dark shape loomed over her. The *lu-ong*'s slightly mad eyes watched her, pain and fury deep in their depths.

Kira froze. Its fear choked her as it mentally thrashed under the collar's control.

I'm here, she thought at it.

There was a brief hesitation as all that deadly focus zeroed in on her. The *lu-ong* was intelligent, she realized with a start. A fierce intellect burned inside, the likes of which threatened to break Kira's brain under the pressure.

As it stared at her, she was conscious of Graydon, absurdly small next to the great beast as he worked his way up the *lu-ong*'s neck.

Kira shouted when she felt the dragon's attention slipping away. *Here.*

The *lu-ong*'s head snaked forward, hovering over Kira, its teeth on display.

Graydon reached the collar as that head began to descend. Kira held still, knowing if she lost the *lu-ong*'s focus, Graydon likely wouldn't survive.

Hurry, she urged him silently as her death closed in.

He drew his arm back and hammered at the tick, cracking its shell in a single strike.

Kira dove to the right as the *lu-ong* plunged. Finn hit the *lu-ong*'s side, his face a mask of fury, his arms and hands glowing with a faint red light as he struck. The *lu-ong*'s teeth scored a bright line of pain along Kira's arm and torso as it dove, barely missing her.

It kept going, disappearing into the water.

Blood stained the water around her red.

She clapped a hand onto the wound on her arm as coldness invaded her limbs. "Shit. Where'd it go?"

She tried to staunch the blood, even as she struggled to find the shape of its body under her, convinced it was about to swim up from beneath and gulp her down.

The thrashing sent waves of pain coursing through her body. Graydon appeared next to her, reaching down and scooping her out.

CHAPTER FOURTEEN

"I don't see it," she said, trying to fight through the pain. She needed to stay awake and aware for when it returned.

"It's gone," Graydon said soothingly, clutching her to his wide chest. "You were right about the collar."

"Of course, I was. I'm always right," she said through stiff lips as relief rushed through her. She'd survived. Yippee for her.

His chuckle was rusty even as concern pinched his face.

"The *lu-ong* has its own power. As soon as I broke the control collar, it wasted no time in escaping," he said, trying to distract her.

"That's nice," she said, barely able to keep her eyes open. She'd lost a lot of blood, she realized.

"Is she all right?" Finn yelled as he raced toward them.

Graydon didn't answer, worry in his face as he started to jog toward the end of the course. "Hang on, Kira. We're going to get you some help."

"I didn't want to be eaten by a *lu-ong*," she told Graydon as she lost her battle with consciousness.

CHAPTER FIFTEEN

Kira blinked at the white ceiling. Her body ached in ways she didn't know it could. Everything hurt. Even her fingernails. Her left side felt like one giant bruise, while her shoulder felt like someone had ripped it open and then tried to staple it together with metal tacks.

The worst thing by far, was the scratchy, dry feeling in her throat, like someone had stuck a sandblaster in there and turned it on high.

If she hurt this much, it probably meant she wasn't dead. A good sign, given death had to be less painful than this.

She chanced looking at her arm. The drape of the white sheath she wore was undisturbed by bandages or the remnants of blood.

She touched the slightly raised scar where it ran nearly the length of her arm. That was new.

"The healers did the best they could, but you'll likely have a scar as a reminder of your close call," Finn said from the corner of the room. "Few survive a *lu-ong*'s bite. You're lucky."

That was one word for it. She couldn't help but feel it would have been better to never have ended up in the *lu-ong*'s mouth at all.

Kira glanced at Finn, noting his tense posture. His muscles were coiled so tightly it looked like his tendons might snap.

His face was haggard, the skin wan and pale. He held himself in a way that indicated he was at the end of his rope.

The look in his eyes—haunted and bruised like he'd seen and done too much—kept her mouth closed against any smart comments.

Kira hated to admit it, but she tended to have that effect on

CHAPTER FIFTEEN

people—usually it took several years to get to this point, but hang around her long enough and you were bound to get some bumps and bruises along the way.

Only this time, she suspected she wasn't the entire reason for the defeat she saw around his edges.

"You look worse than I feel," Kira said. She grimaced at the sound of her voice. It sounded like a frog had set up shop in her throat.

Finn opened his mouth but was interrupted when Jin shot up from the spot he'd claimed at her feet. Kira hadn't noticed him until then.

"Kira! You're an idiot," Jin shouted, his voice overly loud in the small room.

"Did we win?" Kira asked, blinking groggily at him. Her thoughts didn't feel quite right, like she was rising from a centuries-long nap. They were slow to start and discombobulated as she got her bearings.

"Who cares about that?" he snapped. "You damn near died."

"I care. I went to quite a lot of trouble to ensure our win. I'd like to know it was worth it," she said.

"Idiot."

She made a face, but didn't disagree. Right now, she felt like an idiot; *lu-ong* mouths and human bodies didn't agree.

"So, did we?" she asked, looking at Finn.

"No one won," Graydon said from the doorway.

"That's a pity. I feel like the win should be mine by default," Kira said. She made one aborted movement to rise, before letting herself ease back. The wave of dizziness that preceded the attempt wasn't worth the possible humiliation.

"That's a bold statement, considering you needed both of us to save you," Graydon said, arching an eyebrow.

Gone was the concerned and slightly distraught man who'd whisked her out of the water. The untouchable commander was firmly in control.

Kira gave him a lazy smile. "All part of my master plan."

"You planned to nearly die?" Graydon asked skeptically.

"Yup."

Kira's thoughts felt floaty and far away as Jin groaned. "She doesn't know what she's saying. Ignore her."

"I do, too," Kira said, glaring at her friend. She turned to Graydon. "I planned to get shot by the drones and fake drown. Finn would have come to save me. Wasn't sure about you, but either way Raider would have been the first across the finish line."

She smiled at them as she outlined her brilliant plan. Her head listed to the side and she let it fall onto the pillow.

"How devious," Graydon said, not sounding as impressed as he should.

She nodded into the pillow. It was so soft and snugly. "I know."

"Too bad you didn't tell your friend that. He came running when you were attacked. From reports, he took down several drones before they managed to overwhelm him. The Luatha are quite impressed," Graydon said.

Kira groaned. Of all the times for Raider to express concern for her wellbeing. "He knows better than that."

"Evidently not," Raider said dryly from the doorway.

Kira's head popped up, her hair a tangled nest around her face as she glared at him. "We should have won."

"Instead, no one won," Graydon said smoothly.

Kira's head sank and she curled around her pillow.

"What's wrong with her?" Raider asked.

"She's under the influence of the sedative they gave her. One of the side effects is lowered inhibitions and a susceptibility to suggestion," Graydon said.

Raider's gaze was speculative as he glanced at Kira.

"Where did the *lu-ong* come from?" Raider asked.

"That is the question everyone is after, and one I've already set my people to answering," Graydon said. "The *lu-ong* are sacred animals to the Tuann, but they're not normally aggressive unless provoked."

"I know a secret," Kira said in a sing-song voice. She paused

CHAPTER FIFTEEN

afterward and frowned. This sedative was powerful if it could make her sing. She hadn't so much as whistled a note since—her head tilted as she considered. She didn't want to think about that.

She tuned into the conversation to find all three men staring at her. She blinked at them. "What?"

"The secret," Raider said, exasperation in his voice. "What is it?"

"The Tsavitee did it," Kira said grumpily. Hadn't she already told them this? It was fairly obvious.

Raider scoffed. "Not this again. You're tilting at windmills. The Tsavitee are gone. They have been for nine years."

Graydon folded his arms over his chest, contemplation on his face. "It's true, I did remove one of their collars from the *lu-ong*, but it could be a trick to throw us off. The person responsible could have procured it from the black market. I doubt a Tsavitee was involved. Our defenses are impenetrable. We haven't had a sizable incursion in over a thousand years."

Kira made a choked laughing sound. "That's what you think."

Raider's sigh was heavy and frustrated. "I thought you gave up this line of thinking when you left the Curs. The Tsavitee were beaten. They're gone. Get that through your head."

The look she gave him was full of sympathy. "They're not. They never left. They're hiding in plain sight. Just like they always have been."

She got distracted by the room. The lack of color was beginning to bother her. "This place is too white."

"Focus, Kira. Why do you think the Tsavitee are here?" Graydon asked.

Perhaps yellow or blue would be better for the space. Those colors were supposed to be soothing.

"Kira," Raider snapped.

It was a struggle to get her thoughts to take shape. "Because I felt them before the *lu-ong* attacked and before the assassination attempt last night."

"What?" both men shouted.

Kira blinked at them and yawned. "Pretty sure it was them. They've tried to capture or kill us a lot since we took over the *Wanderer*. But we always get away because we're sneaky ninjas."

"Hell yeah, we are," Jin said.

"Don't egg her on," Raider told Jin. His gaze was intent as he focused on Kira. "What are you saying?"

"About what?" she asked.

"The Tsavitee. You didn't tell anyone you thought you saw one last night," he said.

"Didn't see it. Felt it. Just like I did in Idra and Rothchild," she told him. "You wouldn't have believed me. You guys never do."

"Do you have any proof?" Raider asked with skepticism.

Kira snorted. Of course, he wanted proof. He never could trust her word.

He scowled at her and she realized she'd said that out loud.

"Ask Jace. They caught images of a Tsavitee Raven class buzzing Zepher."

A growl escaped Graydon, and he seemed to expand, waves of energy pouring from him. Kira leaned closer cooing at them. How interesting.

She lifted her arm to see if she had the same and frowned. No pretty waves for her.

"Oh brother," Jin muttered. "You probably shouldn't have said that."

Raider looked frozen in place as Graydon's expression darkened.

"This is why they've been pushing to expand the treaty," Graydon muttered. "The humans should have told us."

"We're tired of dancing to your and the Haldeel's tune. You've placed so many restrictions on us that our science and technology are unable to advance," Jace said from the doorway.

"Hi, Jace," Kira waved.

He sent her a quelling look. "I'll deal with you later."

"Did I do something wrong?" Kira asked Jin.

CHAPTER FIFTEEN

"I don't think you were supposed to tell them that."

"Oops." Kira thought a moment. "Do you think they'll blame me?"

"When don't they blame you?"

Good point. Kira decided not to worry about it, concentrating on the pleasant floating sensation instead as the two began arguing.

"There is a good reason we have closed certain avenues to you," Graydon said. "You want to play with things you don't understand. If it was only your own species' extinction, we would let you be, but your hubris would pose a danger to all of us."

Kira yawned, too drowsy to pay attention. She drifted on a cloud of bliss as the argument flowed around her.

She started when Amila appeared at the end of her bed.

"Commander, they're here."

Kira didn't hear his response, losing her battle with sleep.

* * *

Her rest was fitful as she dozed on and off before returning to awareness in spurts.

She opened her eyes to find Raider standing guard. "Where's Finn?"

"The big guy was dead on his feet. Told him to get some sleep," Raider said.

"Surprised he agreed to that," Kira said, adjusting her position in the bed as she tried to find a comfortable spot.

"I may have pointed out he'd be no good to you if he fell over from exhaustion," Raider admitted.

"You always were surprisingly good at persuasion, considering you're the equivalent to a battering ram in most situations," Kira said, watching him through slitted eyelids.

"Someone had to be. You were always like an elephant in high heels in any diplomatic situation," he said.

Kira made a rusty sound that resembled a halfhearted chuckle. He was right. She had been exactly like that.

"They said it'd be a few more hours before that stuff wears off," Raider said.

"Hmm." Kira made a lazy sound.

"Why did you leave?" he asked.

"Didn't mean to," Kira muttered burrowing deeper into her covers. "By the time I realized, it was too late. Had to protect you and Jace. Himoto said this was the best way."

"Protect us? From what?"

"The next phase," Kira mumbled.

Sleep closed its jaws around her, stopping any further conversation.

The next time she woke, her head felt clear and the cobwebs were gone. The sound of whispers next to her bed made it impossible to sleep.

"What are you guys plotting?" Kira asked, without opening her eyes.

"Go to sleep," Raider told her.

"I'd love to, but a couple of someones decided to use my bedside as a location to have an intense conversation." By the end, Kira had shifted so she was half-reclining.

Her body ached, but nowhere near as bad as it had the first time she'd woken. At least she thought she'd been awake. Everything since the *lu-ong* was kind of hazy and disjointed, like a series of waking dreams.

She felt slightly weak and off balance, the very small use of the *ki* draining her. That was better than she'd expected. The last time she'd tried using it had left her in a much worse state.

Raider reached out and pulled the pillows into place behind her to support her weight.

Once she'd finished adjusting the sheets, she fixed the two men with a hard stare. "Now, spill."

Jace looked like he was on the verge of arguing. Raider was the one to meet her eyes calmly.

"The Tuann want to confine us to our quarters," he said.

CHAPTER FIFTEEN

Kira's mouth dropped open. "What did you guys do?"

"That's ironic coming from you," Jace said bitterly.

Kira looked between the two men, noting the anger in Jace's face and the neutrality in Raider's. "What're you talking about?"

"Evidently the sedative they dosed you with has some side effects," Raider said. "It makes you quite talkative."

Surprise and dismay ran across Kira's face as she got a sinking feeling. She vaguely remembered some of the conversation with Graydon.

"Oh no." Kira's head sank into her palms. This was not good. She definitely remembered revealing things that were supposed to stay secret. "How bad was it?"

Raider arched an eyebrow, amusement tugging at his lips. "We now know you find the Luatha's use of the color white concerning and see it as an indication of a lack of soul."

Kira groaned, not bothering to lift her head.

"You also seem worried over Jace's childlessness and that I'm going to die a lonely, grouchy old man," Raider continued mercilessly.

If Kira could have sunk through the bed, she would have.

"At least we finally know what you'd be like if you were able to get drunk," Jace said with a sigh.

"Yes, very, very chatty—and emotional," Raider responded, not bothering to hide his gloating at Kira's predicament.

"The Tuann also now know about the Tsavitee Ravens we picked up on our scanners. They're unhappy we kept their existence from them," Jace said, each word bit off.

Kira looked away. Of all the secrets she'd spilled, she'd given away one that wasn't really hers to tell.

Maybe she disagreed with the Consortium keeping the Tsavitee's return from their allies, but it hadn't been her decision to make.

"Confining you to the brig is a bit of a severe reaction, don't you think? What else am I missing?" Kira asked.

"Someone managed to infect them with your paranoia. They now think the Tsavitee have infiltrated the Consortium and want to expel all humans from this planet. There is also talking about dissolving the alliance." Jace said, acid dripping from his voice.

"Ah, that," Kira said lamely.

Damn, she wished she'd kept her mouth shut. The Tuann suspecting the Tsavitee had adapted enough to hide among humans would spell the end of the alliance.

"Luckily, they need the emperor's approval for that, so we have some time to warn our people to prepare," Raider said.

"Why would you tell them that?" Jace snapped. It was hard to separate the emotions in that question. They were all tangled together. Anger primarily, with a side of hurt and fury. "Especially when you know it's not true."

Except it was true. The humans didn't want to accept it, but their determined blindness didn't change the facts.

Kira had no words to explain so she kept silent, as she always did.

"I know you hate us, but do you really want us dead?" Jace asked.

She flinched inside.

"She's not lying," Jin said, drifting down from his spot near the ceiling.

"Jin, enough," Kira said tiredly.

"The cat's out of the bag now. Might as well paint them the full picture," Jin said stubbornly.

"Stop trying to dredge up ancient history," Kira said. "Just leave it alone."

"Not this time," he told her. He turned to the other two. "We've known for a long time there were Tsavitee sleeper agents among the Consortium. It's partially why we left."

"Bullshit," Jace said, his denial instantaneous and complete.

It didn't surprise Kira. She knew how hard it was to accept a betrayal of that magnitude. She'd done her own battle with denial when the truth had been shoved in her face.

Jin didn't respond in words. He knew as well as she did that without

CHAPTER FIFTEEN

tangible proof there was little chance of Jace believing them. He'd live in the land of denial, just as he always had.

Jin projected a small stream of light onto Kira's bed. Over her legs, a small hologram took shape. A tiny Kira stood on the real Kira's knee, the faded outline of a space station taking shape around her. Her face was covered in blood from a cut on her forehead, and her eyes glittered with rage.

Crouched in front of her was a Tsavitee drudge, class one. Small and agile, it was the perfect agent when it came to fitting into small spaces—making them the ideal candidate for infiltrating space stations.

They spawned at an alarming rate. A single class one could create enough offspring to overrun a station in a window of ten days or less.

The recorded scene had taken place not long ago on New Neptune, a space station in the no man's land between systems. It wasn't quite under Consortium control, but it was operated primarily by humans.

Until this encounter, the station had been her preferred offloading point for the junk she salvaged. After the attack, she made sure to avoid it and any other stations in that quadrant.

The Kira on the hologram turned into a whirling, dancing dervish, her edge blade flashing as she carved up the Tsavitee as they attacked in mass.

The hologram ended with her standing over the bodies, panting with exhaustion before she jerked in response to something off camera.

"That happened three months ago on a human-controlled station," Jin said.

The two men had grown quiet as they watched Kira battle for her life.

Jace looked sick as he scrubbed a hand over his face. "All this proves is the Tsavitee are up to their old tricks."

"They were waiting for us," Kira said, finally speaking. "A human contact of mine told them where we'd be and when. That person was the only one who knew I frequented the station."

"We've known they had a line into the Consortium for a while," Jin said. "We first suspected after Idra. Too many things went wrong on that planet. We launched an investigation, kept things quiet."

Jace shook his head, not wanting to believe it.

"Think, Knight. You're too smart to have not suspected something was wrong. Battles where they knew where we would be long before we did," Jin pressed. "Ambushes, where we lost so many. The only way they would have had that information is if someone fed it to them."

Raider nodded. "I agree. What he says makes sense."

"If you knew this, why didn't you tell anyone," Jace burst out. "Why didn't you warn us?"

Kira withdrew. She should have expected the question and the underlying blame, the betrayal that throbbed in his voice. She deserved it for not having seen the writing on the wall sooner. It hurt, nonetheless.

"We did," Jin said simply.

Both men looked at him, surprise and disbelief in their eyes. Kira held herself stiff and expressionless.

"We told Himoto. By then you already had the alliance with the Tuann. He said if it got out there were traitors among the humans, it would end any hope of keeping that alliance," Jin said.

"Why didn't you say something to us?" Jace asked.

Kira stirred. "By the time I put everything together and had proof, it was too late. The war was long over."

"You couldn't have said something before?" Jace asked.

"Kira was hurt during the Falling," Jin said, referencing one of the biggest battles of the war, the one that had turned the tide. "She was in a coma for the last three years of the war. She only woke up about seven years ago. That's when all this came out."

Both men stared at her in shock. This, more than anything else

CHAPTER FIFTEEN

had surprised them.

Kira fidgeted in the bed, trying to avoid their eyes. Their pity cut deeper than any wound, to a place she'd done her best to spackle over and call healed.

"A coma?" Jace's voice was soft.

She jerked her shoulders up in assent.

"Why didn't any of us know?" he asked.

"Himoto didn't want the Tsavitee learning the ignition weapon and the Phoenix were the same thing," Kira said softly. "When I woke up, the worlds had moved on."

Her friends had also moved on. Each one happy or at least thriving, since her disappearance.

By then, Kira's legacy as a hero had faded, tarnished by the misinformation and her disappearance.

Her friends were convinced she was a coward for abandoning them on the cusp of victory. Many of her former peers noted her absence in the past three years of the war and blamed her for not being there.

"It's fine. Being a salvager suits me. No politics to dance around." Her smile was strained.

Himoto had been the one who made that possible. He'd gotten her a bonus for her contributions to the war effort. It'd been enough to buy her home and business.

Jace didn't look particularly comforted by her words. He looked shocked, his expression blank as he stared into the distance.

Raider's expression was more reserved, his thoughts harder to guess.

To be honest, she hadn't thought either of them felt enough anymore to care. It was all water under the bridge at this point. They'd all survived. It was enough.

"He let us think you'd betrayed us," Jace said, emotion throbbing in his voice. His eyes were glassy as he shook his head, walking out of the room without another word, his expression lost and confused.

Raider remained behind.

"You should go with him. See if you can find a place in the Citadel to lay low," Kira told him. "If the Tsavitee are here, we need to be prepared."

Before he could respond, there was the sound of boots in the hallway.

"I have a feeling it's too late for that," Raider said, turning to face the door.

Green armored warriors filled the room, led by Roderick. A dark-haired woman in a long dress that clung to her upper body before falling in a graceful drape to the floor kept pace with them, her expression furious.

As was the case with all Tuann, her face was beautiful, something belonging on a painting rather than out in the world. The braids in her hair pulled her brown hair from her face, exposing sharply pointed ears.

"You're coming with us," Roderick informed Raider without delay.

Raider cocked an eyebrow but didn't move. "Am I, now?"

Roderick didn't look amused by Raider's question, gesturing sharply to his men.

"What are you doing?" Kira asked, as Roderick's men surrounded Raider.

"He and the rest of the humans are being taken into custody," Roderick said in a crisp voice.

Kira struggled out of bed. She was less than graceful as she fought free of the covers.

"Nope, not happening. Stay in bed," the dark-haired woman snapped, one hand landing on Kira's shoulder as she put pressure on it, forcing her into the bed. "You're barely healed."

Kira tried shrugging the woman off. Unfortunately, the stranger wasn't inclined to let her. It resulted in an odd tussle where every touch or shove was gentle but firm. The woman's face had turned murderous by the time she finally trapped Kira in the bed by wrapping the blanket around her torso and tugging it tight before

CHAPTER FIFTEEN

sitting on the ends.

Every person in the room regarded the show with disbelief and no small amount of amusement.

"As I was saying before someone so rudely decided to interrupt," Kira huffed, jerking an arm free and glaring at the woman.

"Oh hush, you shouldn't even be awake. You still have another twelve hours before I would even think of letting you out of this bed," the woman snapped. "I don't know what it is about warriors. You're all idiots. You don't know when to stay down. You'd think being nearly eaten would knock some sense into you."

Jin cackled. "I like her. She's feisty."

The woman started to glare up at Jin where he hovered by the ceiling. Her eyes widened in fascination. "I've never seen a human AI up close before. I thought their technology hadn't advanced to the point of make thinking sentients."

"The abomination should be used for target practice and destroyed," Roderick muttered, eyeing Jin with distaste.

"Jin is one of a kind," Kira said, diverting the attention back to herself. "He's a test model."

She allowed the stranger to keep her misconceptions. Somehow, she didn't think she could say the soul of a long-dead friend had taken over Jin's body. That would probably cause all sorts of questions, and given how touchy the Tuann felt about some things, she didn't want to give them a reason to decide Jin constituted more of a threat than he already was.

"Enough of this," Roderick said. He lifted his hand and beckoned his men impatiently. "We're taking the human into custody."

"Who authorized this?" Kira asked.

"The Overlord," he answered. "And you're lucky you're not being taken, too. It's only because our House would never overcome the scandal, that you've been spared."

He jerked his chin at the rest before striding out of the room without a backward glance.

Raider gave her a slight head shake when she sucked in a breath. She bit her lip as he gave her a wink before walking out of the room flanked on either side by the Luathan warriors.

"They won't hurt your friends," the woman said, standing. She watched Kira for signs of rebellion, relaxing when Kira stayed put. "I'm Shandry. I'm the one responsible for putting you back together. Try to show a little gratitude."

Kira didn't move, waiting as the woman bustled around the room, straightening things.

"Where is Liara now?" Kira asked.

Shandry cocked her head. "She's likely in the Nexus. I heard House Roake sent a delegation. She'll want to receive those brutes from a position of strength."

"The Nexus?" Kira asked.

Shandry nodded. "It's the heart and brain of the Citadel."

Kira nodded as if any of that explanation made sense. She flicked a glance up at Jin. He moved up and down in a yes. Good, he knew where this Nexus was. That would help.

All she had to do was wait until the healer was reassured enough to chance leaving her alone.

It wasn't lost on Kira that Roderick had taken her guard and left her with none to replace him. Given she'd survived two assassination attempts, she had to wonder if that was purposeful and if Graydon or Finn knew.

She was guessing not.

There was a knock at the door as Joule stuck his head in, looking around in confusion when he found only the two of them present.

"Please, just come on in. It's not like this is a place of healing, or anything," Shandry grumbled.

"Pardon me, master healer. I'd hoped to visit my friend and reassure myself of her safety and good health," Joule said gravely, dipping his chin at the woman.

Shandry waved her hand, dismissing his words. "Never mind. Do

CHAPTER FIFTEEN

as you wish."

Joule nodded at her again before looking at Kira. "Where is your guard?"

"That's something I'd like to know as well," she told him.

"You shouldn't be alone," he said seriously.

Shandry huffed and threw away the cloth she'd been folding. "This is a sanctuary for those who need it. No one is going to try to kill her here."

Joule suddenly seemed much older and wiser than his age would suggest. "She's already survived two attempts on her life since she landed. Do you intend to endanger the rest of your patients on the belief her enemies will respect a healer's sanctuary?"

Shandry frowned, suddenly seeming unsure. "The *lu-ong* wasn't an attempt. That was an accident."

"Would a *lu-ong* normally nest so close to your home?" Joule asked politely. "The waters near the Citadel are too shallow for them to hunt, especially as they grow to majority."

His words seemed to resonate with Shandry, her face turning pensive as she bit her lip in uncertainty.

"The Emperor's Face would no doubt like to be informed of the change in her status," Joule said.

Shandry nodded slowly. "Fine, I'll send someone to let him know, but she's not to leave this room."

Joule gave her a polite bow as she swept out of the room.

Kira waited several seconds before untangling her feet and swinging her feet out of the bed.

"Good job. Perhaps you can be of some use after all," Kira told Joule.

"Where are you going?" he asked with a frown.

"I need to find Liara and ask her what the fuck she thinks she's doing taking my friends into custody," Kira said.

Her feet touched the ground, the white sheath slithering until the hem touched her ankles. She plucked at the material. It was light and airy but had a silky sheen to it.

The dress fit well enough, and she didn't think she'd have to worry about modesty since it wasn't see-through. It would do for now until she could find something better.

"The healer said to stay here. I promised her you wouldn't leave," Joule protested, hurrying after Kira as she left the room, her bare feet slapping against the stone.

"First thing to know, if you're going to hang around Kira for any length of time—she rarely does what she's told," Jin said, bringing up the rear.

Joule nodded, his face pensive.

He was probably wondering what exactly he had gotten himself into. She should have felt some sympathy for him, but she didn't. These were the kind of things you vetted before you made someone your mentor.

CHAPTER SIXTEEN

In theory, Kira knew the general location of the Nexus from her tour with Finn where he'd referred to a certain direction of the Citadel as its heart. In reality, it was more difficult than she'd anticipated, to locate the Nexus.

The home of her mother's people was an insanely complicated jigsaw puzzle, almost impossible for strangers to navigate. Unlike human cities, where buildings were joined by streets and alleys, each one their own separate structure, the Citadel was one jumbled mass, lacking easily navigable pathways.

Each building wove in and around the next, making the concept of a first, second, and third floor obsolete. Instead, it had been constructed over many centuries, each building or tower added to the whole as it was needed, the trends and styles of the time influencing its design.

It forced Kira to tramp up and down, over and under, through doorways that doubled as windows, and hallways leading nowhere.

Its layout defied logic and reason, giving her a glimpse into the genius behind its construction. What she had at first assumed was indefensible was actually their greatest asset. The very confusion of the chaos that was the Citadel would make it impossible to corner its inhabitants as they flowed around their enemy using any one of the jumbled paths.

Unfortunately, it was almost impossible for a stranger to find their way. You were as likely to wind up on top of a roof as you were your intended destination.

Jin couldn't help her with Joule watching. It would have given away how much of the Citadel he'd mapped in his free time, an advantage that might come in handy, now that the Curs had been taken into custody.

It left Kira to find her way on her own. A frustrating exercise in futility.

About the third time she ventured past the same set of statues—Tuann clad in synth armor holding en-blades and staffs as they impassively stared out—Kira gave up.

She beckoned Joule from where he'd been following. "Where do we go?"

To his credit, he didn't gloat or point out how she should have listened to him in the first place. For that, Kira found herself liking him a little bit more.

"The Nexus is considered the seat of power for the House," he told her, his young face serious. "For that reason, they've designed the surroundings to disguise its location from enemies. In theory, this would allow time to evacuate the Overlord and her council if they ever felt the Citadel was lost."

It was a nice history lesson, but didn't tell her what she needed to know

"Does this mean you don't know?" she asked.

She was already turning to ask Jin to take over leading when Joule spoke up, his voice irritated. "I know. I was just explaining its significance, so you understand what you're up against. You won't succeed like this."

"How about you leave the method of entry to me and just get us there," Kira suggested.

His sigh was heavy. At that moment he seemed like any other teen she'd encountered, the weight of the world on his shoulders as he dealt with stubborn adults.

Joule took the lead and soon they were in a section of the Citadel Kira didn't recognize.

CHAPTER SIXTEEN

The walk did Kira good, calming some of the desperation and worry that had sent her scrambling from the healer's room. It also gave her time to think. The Luatha weren't likely to execute Jace and the others. They wouldn't want to risk a diplomatic incident over a possible miscommunication.

Kira needed to get to Liara before anything else happened.

"Do you have a plan?" Jin asked as he hurried to keep up with her.

"I'm working on it."

"Good. Just remember to think before you do anything drastic," he cautioned. "We don't need to be thrown into whatever place these people call a brig along with Jace and the others. We'll do them no good if we're locked up too."

"I'm aware of that," Kira told him calmly. "I won't give them a reason to act against me."

Jin seemed to find that sufficient reassurance, falling quiet. Just in time too, as they came into view of an ornate set of doors with intricate carvings.

Kira made a small snort. They might as well have posted a sign that said "important thing behind this door." It practically shouted its strategic significance. If the Luatha hoped to fool an enemy combatant, they hadn't done a very good job.

Four guards watched them approach with curiosity, confirming Kira's belief they didn't yet see her as a threat. She released a breath. That was one piece of good news.

"*Aza*, you should still be in bed," the one in front said, greeting her with a warm expression and sympathy in his eyes.

Kira paused, at a loss to reconcile the guard's friendliness with Roderick's earlier disdain.

"I had hoped to speak to my cousin," Kira said. "It seems my friends are being detained."

The friendly one nodded. "Yes, this is true. They were determined to present a potential threat. I can personally assure you we mean them no harm. This is for everyone's safety until we fully investigate."

Kira relaxed slightly at that. His assurance rang with truth.

"I'd like to see and talk with them," she said, not giving up.

He shook his head regretfully. "I'm afraid that won't be possible. The seneschal and marshal wish to question them to make sure they had nothing to do with the repeated attacks on you."

Frustration moved through Kira. There was a difference between being told someone was fine and seeing it with your own two eyes.

"Then I'd like to talk to Liara," Kira tried.

"Now is not a good time, *aza*," the man said.

"We're not trying to keep you from airing your grievances," a female guard said, reading her frustration correctly. "She is greeting visitors. It would not be an appropriate time to interrupt."

Kira sighed. She couldn't argue with that. She was about to tell them she'd wait, when the doors behind them opened and the men and woman guarding them snapped to attention.

Graydon's gaze was searing as he stopped short. His eyes locked on her before growing suspicious. He recovered quickly, turning to check her surroundings and reaching the conclusion she was once again without protection.

Kira stopped paying attention to Graydon as her gaze snagged on two figures behind him, each as mountainous as Graydon, their armor and faces hidden by the cloaks they wore.

"What are you doing here?" Graydon asked, striding forward.

"I have business with Liara," she said. Her attention went past him to a large room with cathedral ceilings above it. Liara stood in the center of a glowing circle, her body slightly out of focus as stars hovered all around her.

A starmap, Kira realized, fascination compelling her forward. It was a three-dimensional map of the galaxy, incredibly detailed and surprisingly realistic.

Thoughts and plans raced through her head. What she couldn't do with an invaluable tool like that. Himoto would go crazy if he knew the Tuann were sitting on maps as comprehensive as what was in

CHAPTER SIXTEEN

front of her.

Graydon snagged her arm and drew her several steps away before she could get any closer. With effort, Kira managed to drag her attention from the many pinpricks of light to focus on the male nuisance at her side.

"What is your problem now?" she asked.

"Besides the fact you have already survived two attempts on your life, yet you stand here with no protection? Again," he finished with a bite in his voice.

"I'm plenty protected," she said, waving her hand at the four guards. The one woman ducked her head trying to cover her smile.

Graydon growled, the sound raising the hair on Kira's neck. She blinked at him. Was he really growling at her?

The sound continued.

Yes, yes, he was.

She gave him an exasperated look.

"Their first priority is their Overlord," he said in a precise voice as if he was having to explain something to a flighty child. "They will not make the first move to help you if it turns out she is the one who wants you dead."

That wiped the looks of amusement off the Luathan guards' faces.

It seemed Kira wasn't the only one capable of burning bridges.

"Isn't that what you're here for? To make sure everyone plays nice with each other?" Kira asked sweetly. "I sincerely doubt whoever keeps trying to kill me would do so in such an obvious way."

One of the cloaked figures made an aborted movement, drawing Kira's attention.

"Who're your friends?" she asked.

Graydon shifted to block her view of them as he spat out several sentences in Tuann. There was a rumbled response before the two figures moved away, down the hallway in the direction Kira had come.

She watched them go with narrowed eyes. There was something

familiar about their energy. She just couldn't place her finger on what.

"What are you doing here?" A strident voice came from the doorway.

Kira forgot about the strangers as the seneschal approached. Alma's expression was haughty as she looked Kira over.

"I'm here to speak to the Overlord about the people she had taken into custody," Kira said, stepping forward and speaking before Graydon could interfere.

The seneschal's mouth tightened and she looked down her nose at Kira. "The Overlord doesn't have time for your problems. She's a busy person. You'll be informed when a decision has been reached."

"A decision," Kira said, fighting dismay. "I won't take up much of her time, but I'd like to understand why they were placed under guard."

And convince Liara why that wasn't necessary.

A ladylike sound of derision escaped Alma. "They're human with inferior morals and a penchant for deceit, that's why."

"What a Tsavitee-like thing to say," Kira said, her eyes narrowing as anger warmed her belly.

The Tsavitee had called humans inferior and tried to wipe them out. To hear the same thing from her mother's people was disquieting.

Alma sneered. "We found evidence they were poking where they didn't belong. I suspect it's only a matter of time before we tie the attacks to them as well."

"What do you mean?" Kira asked.

"One of them was caught in our solarium. She had no business being there," Alma said.

Blue—it had to be. Her scientific mind was curious and bright. If she'd seen something of interest, she would have pursued it. She wouldn't have been able to help it.

Although Kira didn't understand why a location like a solarium would be considered off-limits.

CHAPTER SIXTEEN

"The Overlord would be in her right to have them all executed," Alma continued. "It's what she should do, and as her seneschal, it's my duty to guide her onto the right path."

She didn't wait for any further comment, flicking her fingers at the guards before turning and striding back into the room.

With a look of regret at Kira, they closed the door behind her before arranging themselves in front of it. Their message was clear; Kira wasn't getting by them without a fight.

"Come on," Graydon murmured, taking her arm and drawing her away. "Arguing with them right now will cause trouble for you later."

"I can't let them stay locked up," Kira said.

"Yes, you can. I have my men standing guard with Roderick's. They'll protect them from harm. Your Curs will be fine for now."

Kira hurried to keep up as he propelled her down the hallway. She shot a look over her shoulder at Jin, mouthing "Find them."

He shot up to the ceiling and followed it until he found a hallway, disappearing within seconds. Joule watched him go with wide eyes, his gaze dropping to Kira. She gave him a wink before turning to face forward again.

"Why is it that every time I see you, your *oshota* is nowhere around?" Graydon asked conversationally.

"Because Roderick came and detained his replacement," Kira said in as pleasant voice as she could manage.

Graydon frowned in frustration. "I'd like to say I'm surprised, but the level of incompetence here has become a theme."

Kira's attention snapped to Graydon as she considered his words. She wasn't the only one who suspected betrayal and deceit.

"What would happen if I died while under Liara's care?" Kira asked.

Graydon steered her out of the maze of hallways and into the sunshine. They walked through a courtyard, towers surrounding them on all sides as it overlooked a small section of the forest.

They turned down a small path, well-trodden and narrow as it meandered through the many bushes and trees inhabiting the lush space.

She looked around in unconcealed pleasure, appreciating the hidden oasis, one of many throughout the Citadel.

Kira let Graydon lead, knowing that for this conversation it would be best if they were away from any potential listeners.

"It would weaken her politically and could have very real consequences for her and Luatha in general. Her House is a strong one, but it suffered during the Sorrowing," Graydon said. "Liara is a relatively new overlord. She's fifteen years older than you and her rule is considered unstable."

"How am I considered a child and she adult enough to rule?" Kira asked, sidetracked momentarily.

"She has survived the highest form of the *adva ka* and earned her name," Graydon said.

"So, I have to survive this *adva ka* and I'll be considered an adult?" Kira asked.

"Yes."

"That is a ridiculous way of determining someone's maturity," Kira complained.

Graydon shook his head at her and walked up to a statue. He set his hand against it. His forehead furrowed. There was an explosive crack as power flashed around Graydon's hands. The statue remained standing for several beats before it slowly folded in on itself, collapsing into finger-sized bits of rubble.

"Attend, Kira. The stage you now stand on is dangerous. Many wait in the wings looking to topple you. This was a tiny drop of my power. Until you can defend yourself from this and other powers like it, you will always be considered under the protection of another, your wishes superseded by theirs," Graydon stated, his seriousness giving his words weight. "Some never reach this stage."

Kira studied the statue, considering his words carefully.

Himoto and the rest of the military lacked some very crucial pieces of information when it came to understanding the Tuann.

CHAPTER SIXTEEN

This wasn't a simple feudal society with clear lines. Hidden subtleties shaded everything.

Children were protected. They were the fragile future of the race. Kira could see why she was lumped in with them. A child couldn't be challenged to personal combat by an adult, nor could they carry out any of the many duties of an adult Tuann. They weren't responsible for their mistakes as an adult would be—all necessary factors to consider when you were entering their society as an adult with none of their training.

Without proving her control over the soul's breath, she would always be relegated to a supporting role, her desires overridden by those more powerful than she.

Fear kept her silent. She did not want to be trapped here forever.

Revealing she had inherited more from them than they assumed, might do just that. Her control was elusive at best. If she'd tried Graydon's trick, she'd have reduced the statue to dust—along with everything else within twenty feet.

"Just because someone doesn't possess the ability to harness the soul's breath doesn't mean they should be considered a second-class citizen," Kira said softly.

People could have other skills, ones as important as manipulating energy.

Graydon inclined his head. "I agree with you, but there are things you aren't considering. Just as much duty rests on the shoulders who pass the *adva ka* as those who do not."

Kira knew Graydon meant what he said. There was a purity when he spoke about the obligations each had to the other. Unfortunately, the Tuann were entirely too much like humans, their emotions complex and their motivations just as likely to be selfish.

Graydon might believe what he was saying, but she'd seen too much to think it could be anywhere near that simple. People in power inevitably took advantage of those weaker than them. Just as those who could never rise, would eventually become resentful of those they envied.

She sighed, the issue was more morally complex than it seemed.

As an outsider she saw things differently, but it didn't mean she was right. For that reason, she left the subject alone. She couldn't argue against something she was only beginning to understand.

"Why would my death impact her at all?" Kira asked. "Besides the fact the Consortium would strongly object."

Unless they were offered a dozen ships and an ironclad alliance. Then they might overlook the fact Kira had once been one of theirs.

"There are several parties besides those you've seen who've taken an interest in your existence," Graydon said, seeming to choose his words carefully. "The emperor is one. He would be upset if you were murdered by your own House."

"It's about perception," Joule said, interjecting.

He caught their attention.

"If the Luatha were behind the death of a child who hadn't passed their *adva ka*, it would be a serious breach of their most sacred duties. The Houses were created to shelter those too weak to protect themselves. A betrayal of that magnitude would call their entire existence into question."

"He is correct," Graydon said with a faint smile.

Joule straightened, pride in his expression.

"If we take all that into account, we can assume someone is deliberately trying to weaken Luatha. Probably so they can create a chink in their defenses," Kira supplied.

When you followed that reasoning, it would be understandable to assume Roderick was a part of the conspiracy. Since her arrival, he'd been deliberately obtuse regarding his duty. Not just incompetent but almost maliciously so.

Kira hesitated to point all the blame at him, knowing there might be other explanations. It could be he was simply untrained and in over his head, allowing his emotions to cloud his judgment.

"Roderick was appointed by Alma and Rayan, the seneschal and

CHAPTER SIXTEEN

majordomo who served as Liara's regents until she came of age," Joule supplied. "The gossip is she wishes to replace him, but she doesn't want to go against the other two."

"How do you know that?" Kira asked.

He shrugged. "They consider me harmless because of my age. It makes them less guarded in their words. I listen."

"Smart."

He gave her a grin, the expression bright and open. The stress and worry he seemed to carry with him everywhere lifted for a brief moment.

Kira gave Graydon a sidelong look, several things beginning to make sense now. "You knew about the rot in this House. You're using Joule's and my presence to work on behalf of the emperor's interests."

It wasn't a question. It was the only answer that made sense. Graydon's duty should have been over as soon as he delivered them to Luatha. That he hadn't abandoned them immediately, but chose to stay and insert himself into events, said he had an ulterior motive.

She suspected he'd been looking for a reason to remain once he delivered Joule and Ziva. Her discovery had given him the opening he needed.

"You must have been counting your lucky stars when you found me," she said.

Graydon didn't look away from her, his carefully neutral expression confirmation enough.

"I don't like being used," she told him softly.

Shrewd amusement tinged his expression. "But you are perfectly willing to use others. Or are you not here to negotiate on behalf of the humans—I believe they want several ships?"

He stepped closer, his shoulder brushing hers as he leaned closer and murmured. "Face it, *coli*, we're in a position to use each other. Might as well take advantage of that."

He didn't take his gaze from hers as he moved back, giving her the slightest bit of space.

Her lips curved in a sly smile. She couldn't argue with that. "What are you suggesting?"

"We help each other where we can," he said with a small shrug.

She considered him. It was tempting, even as her instincts warned he was playing a deep game, one with potentially devastating consequences.

Still, did she have many options?

"Alright, you're on," she said, agreeing to the alliance.

Joule shifted beside her, drawing her attention.

"On one condition, you or one of your minions help train Joule," she said.

Joule's eyes were wide as he looked between the two of them, a painful hope on his face.

"There are reasons we leave the training of the young for their House. My interference might make it harder for him to find his place later," Graydon said.

Kira shrugged. "He can make the decision of whether to take the risk or not."

"I would," Joule burst out. "I definitely would. My parents started me on an *oshota's* training."

"Perfect. It's settled. I won't say anything about your real purpose for being here. You don't say anything about mine, and we both carry on like nothing happened," Kira said.

Graydon gave her a veiled look, his expression turning slightly smug. "Very well. You have a deal."

He started along the path again, turning the corner as they stepped down several weather-beaten stone stairs into an orchard of carefully manicured trees.

It was pretty, but tame. Kira preferred the wildness of the forest outside the Citadel.

"Why go so far for them?" Graydon asked.

Kira fell into step beside him, brushing one hand against the trees they passed. She didn't have to ask what he meant. "One of my first

CHAPTER SIXTEEN

memories is watching a boy have the flesh whipped from his back."

That boy had been Jin. He had committed some infraction neither of them remembered anymore. Their keepers had punished him severely for it. It hadn't been the first time, nor had it been the last.

Kira ignored Graydon as he stopped, his expression severe. Dark emotion rolled off him.

"My next memory is having the same done to me," Kira said. "Say what you want about the humans and their motives, but they saved me from that fate."

And for that they would have her undying gratitude. If Himoto hadn't arrived when he did, it was likely Kira would be dead. Or worse, turned into a merciless weapon with no concept of morals or ethics. Just a tool someone pointed and fired at the enemy.

She could never repay Himoto for saving her from that fate, though it hadn't stopped her from spending half her life trying, even when it broke her to do so.

Liara and Graydon hadn't asked many questions about her childhood in the camp. Partly because it hadn't been Graydon's place, and Liara hadn't had enough time with Kira to broach the subject.

She knew both half-suspected humans had been involved. It had taken her a while to get to that conclusion, but now that she had, it made sense. It explained their dislike of humans if nothing else.

How would they react if they found out their suspicions were only half of the puzzle? The question haunted Kira and was one reason she refused to let herself get too invested in the Tuann.

Because humans hadn't overseen that camp or the countless others she'd tracked down in secret through the years. Tsavitee had.

Graydon's body became a tightly coiled spring with no outlet for the tempest of emotions she could see moving across his face. He didn't speak for a long moment, his gaze growing distant as if he wrestled with some great inner turmoil.

He drew her to a stop, his expression inscrutable as she stared up at him, waiting patiently. She raised her chin.

She didn't often share her past with others. She hated the looks of pity and sympathy, or worse, the judgment that came when they found out about what she'd done in the name of survival.

She wasn't ashamed of her history. She'd survived it and wore its scars like the badge of honor they were.

She'd decided giving Graydon a piece of what she'd endured was necessary for him to understand how deep her loyalty to the Fleet and the Consortium went. She wasn't a child clinging to the familiar. She had history with them, the sort not easily untangled to make room for something new.

He touched a sore spot on her cheek where a bruise must have formed. His fingertips were almost unbearably gentle as his eyes became soft and searching.

Lyrical words came from him, the promise in them almost tangible.

There was a slight gasp of surprise from Joule behind her, hinting more was happening than a simple expression of sympathy for her beginnings.

Kira stiffened, her expression becoming guarded and watchful.

The moment was broken by rustling in the branches next to them. Both of them froze, realization they were being watched sinking in.

Kira flicked her eyes to the right and down, asking if he was ready.

He gave her a careful nod, his hand dropping, so his thumb could skate across her collarbone in a delicious caress. Shivers skated over her skin despite the tense moment.

He grinned wickedly at her, his eyes dancing as she returned the fierce expression.

Together they moved, Graydon blocking the person's escape on one side as Kira reached in and snagged an arm, yanking the watcher out of their hiding spot.

Snarled hair and a dirty face were the first things to register. Kira realized she held a young child, her face scraped and bruised, blood dotting her shirt.

"Ziva," Joule exclaimed in horror.

CHAPTER SIXTEEN

"Didn't your mother tell you it's rude to spy on others?" Kira asked, setting Ziva gently down, mindful of the bruises that covered the child.

Ziva looked like she'd been on the losing end of a fight. Her left eye was beginning to turn purple and swell while her expression remained rebellious and truculent.

"My parents told me a smart first watched friends and enemy alike to make sure they weren't plotting against them," Ziva said defiantly.

"It sounds like your parents would have gotten along nicely with Jin," Kira observed.

The response was odd enough for Ziva to lose some of the defensiveness, her natural curiosity serving to make her more receptive to questions.

"What happened?" Kira asked.

Ziva's shoulders rounded as she stubbed a toe into the ground. She kept quiet, her head bowed as she made a concentrated effort to avoid meeting Kira and Graydon's eyes.

"She probably picked a fight," Joule accused.

The way Ziva hunched in on herself, like a turtle seeking the safety of its shell, told Kira he'd guessed right.

Kira glanced up at Graydon, expecting him to take the lead since both children were under his care. He arched an eyebrow at her, signaling with a supercilious expression she could deal with this problem.

Kira shook her head.

Why her?

She glanced to where the defiant child watched her carefully.

Kira sighed. She remembered what it was like to be that age and mad at the world. She'd had so much rage at the injustices dumped at her feet that sometimes it felt like her skin was a balloon. One wrong word could make it pop, causing all that rage and pain to come pouring out, oftentimes in violent and destructive ways.

She saw too much of herself in Ziva. More so, even than she did

Joule. Ziva was a survivor, scrappy and stubborn. Her family had been taken from her in a manner Kira suspected had been bloody and violent. She'd been uprooted from all she knew and thrust into a House that didn't seem to want or need her.

Demands and angry recriminations were more likely to make her retreat further.

Kira waited patiently, crouching so she was eye level with Ziva.

"Stop stalling," Joule said impatiently.

Kira held up a hand, motioning for silence. She waited until Ziva looked up at her, the expression in her clear blue eyes trying to tug at Kira's heart.

Kira lips curled in a small smile. Ziva would have to work harder than that to get the sympathy vote from her.

Kira lifted her eyebrow's expectantly. "Well?"

"They said we were mutts," Ziva muttered. "And that we should be grateful for what we were given and not get uppity."

"And?" Kira asked.

Ziva shrugged. "And I challenged them to a duel."

Kira glanced up at Graydon, asking silently if this was normal protocol for children.

"As long as no one is injured permanently and there is no danger of death, an adult will not step in. We believe children should learn from their own experiences rather than being told what to do."

Kira tried not to let her surprised consternation show. She turned to Ziva. "What happened then?"

"I lost." Ziva's eyes flashed up to meet Kira's.

Kira nodded, considering and discarding several responses. "Well, that was dumb."

Mutiny flashed across Ziva's face, her tiny body bunching as if she would leap for Kira's face. "It was not," she shouted. "I defended my family's honor."

"Did you?" Kira asked. "Seems to me like you took exception with what someone said and then lost a challenge you issued. You look

CHAPTER SIXTEEN

twice as stupid now."

Kira straightened, dusting imaginary dirt off her pants.

"I am not," Ziva shouted, her eyes pooling with tears and her lower lip beginning to tremble. "I was winning but then his friend threw a rock."

"The weak tend to travel in packs," Kira agreed. "But you showed stupidity too. Picking the time and place for a fight is as important as training for it. You chose a time where he was at his strongest, surrounded by allies. Now he knows your weaknesses and he will come for you again."

Bullies always did. They couldn't help themselves. They now knew what set Ziva off and they'd use the leverage whenever they wanted a boost for their confidence.

Graydon crossed his massive arms and looked at the child. "Better yet, you should have avoided fighting someone stronger than yourself."

"She didn't," Ziva said, pointing at Kira and her assortment of bruises.

"I'm a horrible role model," Kira said lightly. "You shouldn't base any of your actions off me."

She cocked her head. She needed to give the kid something to hold onto. "I'll tell you this much. I didn't go looking for the fight that gave me these. Also, if it'd been my family he insulted, I wouldn't have attacked him. I would have waited until he was alone and vulnerable, and then crushed him so utterly he would never have dared show his face in front of me again."

Ziva looked up at her, her eyes wide as she dipped her chin in grave understanding.

A small sound from the door leading into the Citadel drew their notice. Ayela stood there, her expression slightly incredulous after listening to Kira's advice. Her honey-colored hair was bound in an undone braid that showed her pointed ears.

"Excuse me," Ayela said diffidently, her eyes darting nervously to

Graydon. "I'm here for the young ones."

Ziva stiffened, moving closer to Kira's legs, one small hand reaching out to clutch at her pants.

"You were at the airfield when I arrived," Kira said, remembering. She also thought she'd seen her in the audience at the obstacle course.

"Yes, since I am not a warrior or artisan and possess no specialized skill set, my duties vary depending on need," Ayela said.

Kira nodded slowly. "I'll take responsibility for them and see them to the nursery when we're done."

Ziva's hand relaxed slightly.

"Pardon me, but I would be in trouble for letting them wander off," Ayela said. Her tone diffident even as her words challenged.

Graydon shifted next to her, his expression remote. "You may trust they will not come to harm in our care."

Ayela opened her mouth again then closed it, finally bowing and backing away, but not before Kira noted the small flash of anger.

"There is something off about that woman," Kira said once she was gone, staring at the door she'd disappeared through.

"There is something off about a lot of this place," Graydon said seriously. "It's becoming hard to distinguish between what is truth and paranoia."

Kira made a small sound of agreement.

She turned to the two she'd saddled herself with. Someday she'd learn not to take on more responsibility. Today was not that day.

"I guess you two will get your way. I'll show you a few moves before dinner time," she said.

The two let out twin cheers.

Kira glanced at Graydon. "Call your minions from their hiding spots. They can be useful and act as punching dummies."

Graydon's expression was inscrutable as he held her gaze. After a long moment, he gave a nod.

Two of his soldiers materialized in the middle of the courtyard as if stepping out of thin air. One second she and Graydon were alone

CHAPTER SIXTEEN

with the children, and then suddenly they weren't.

Handy trick that. She'd give her left arm to learn it.

Kira watched them, not particularly surprised at their presence. Given Graydon's insistence she be accompanied by Finn at all times, she'd assumed they'd be around somewhere, hidden but close, in case of need.

"I thought so," she said. They were good. She'd barely detected their presence and she knew the woman hadn't.

Nor had the children, if their wide eyes and exclamations of surprise were anything to go by.

Kira clapped her hands. "Alright, let's get started."

CHAPTER SEVENTEEN

The afternoon was surprisingly pleasant as Kira ran the two through a set of drills to discover what they already knew and what they thought they knew but had applied incorrectly.

Their base was good. Much better than Kira would have assumed given their ages.

She straightened from where she'd been showing Joule how to set his feet, as Finn strode out of one of the alcoves leading to the Citadel, his expression thunderous.

"Where have you been?" he spat.

She cocked her head. "Around."

"I left to sleep for two hours and you were gone when I returned," he ground out. If he'd been a dog, his ears would have been pinned against his skull and his teeth bared.

"You've found me now," Kira said.

"Several hours later. Do you know what could happen to you?" he said.

"No, but I have a feeling you're going to tell me," she said.

"You could have been kidnapped. Not to mention killed ten times over in the time you've been wandering around unprotected," he spat. "How would you feel if someone tortured you for that length of time? I promise you a minute can feel like hours if the right technique is applied."

"Sounds awful," Kira observed. "Perhaps you could demonstrate one of these methods. For educational purposes, of course."

CHAPTER SEVENTEEN

Finn blinked at her, obviously wrestling with a desire to strangle her that was in direct contrast to his duty. He slowly started shaking his head and then kept shaking it, physically taking two steps back as he looked around the impromptu training yard.

Graydon's minions looked sympathetic to his plight, their lips twitching.

"You're a menace," Finn told her.

Kira nodded. "So I've been told."

She'd never let that stop her before. She didn't see why she'd change now.

Finn cast a look at Graydon who shrugged his massive shoulders and smirked, as if to say what did you expect.

Finn noticed the children as they performed their drills at a pace three times slower than normal. Their movements were simple, the kind of thing even beginners could do. Both had protested they were past this stage, but Kira had insisted.

The complicated maneuvers had their place, but without a firm foundation in the basics, they would face problems later. Kira was a firm believer that sometimes the simplest methods were the most effective. The rest was improvisation and adapting to the changing dynamics of the situation.

"What are they doing?" he asked with a scowl.

"Practicing," Kira said succinctly.

"Practicing for what?"

"The shitstorm that is life."

He narrowed his eyes and sent an expectant look Graydon's way. "You approved this?"

Graydon nodded, giving Kira a sidelong look filled with speculation. "She presented a very good case."

"You going to help or not?" she challenged.

He shook his head, his expression inscrutable as he moved toward the two children. He stopped Ziva and corrected her form before prowling toward Joule to do the same. Both children brightened at his presence, their faces turning worshipful as they hadn't when Kira had done the same.

"That's a surprise," Graydon murmured.

"What is?"

"He approves." Graydon turned to face her, a glimmer of admiration in his intelligent eyes. "As do I."

There was a sharp stab of pleasure at his words, surprising Kira. Such a simple statement shouldn't have been enough to unbalance her to this extent, even as she found herself craving more.

She shook off the feelings. She wasn't here to care what Graydon thought of her or her actions. She had more important things to consider, a long overdue mission deserving completion.

She couldn't afford to be tempted by emotion, even if the seriously sexy packaging made her want to spend hours exploring the hard planes and grooves of his body.

He didn't say anything else, moving past her to help Finn as they both worked to guide the kids through the moves, showing them easy modifications when Ziva and Joule struggled.

The children were like flowers in their care, blossoming under the men's instruction.

Kira stayed in the background, her smile dying as loneliness surged up to grab hold. As much fun as flirting with Graydon was or watching the kids come into their own, this was temporary, she reminded herself.

Soon she'd return to her ship and its isolation. Once she might have welcomed the reprieve it offered; now she found herself hesitating as Graydon, Finn, and the Curs made her crave things she hadn't allowed herself to think about in many years.

"There's to be a formal welcome ceremony tomorrow evening," Finn announced, glancing her way. "All of your attendance is mandatory."

The tangent was enough to pull Kira from her melancholy thoughts. Joule and Ziva paused, looking at each other with guarded expres-

CHAPTER SEVENTEEN

sions, their earlier levity disappearing.

"How big a ceremony are we talking?" Kira asked.

"All of the Overlord's council and most of the Citadel will be there," Finn said. "The three of you will be given the first test of the House and then they will hold a celebration."

Kira nodded. A big party where most of the populace of the Citadel would be distracted. Good. She could work with that.

"I assume you're bringing this up for a reason." Kira arched an eyebrow in expectation.

Graydon answered for him. "You need to learn proper etiquette. Luatha is an old House, and for this occasion they will be scrupulous in making sure the niceties are observed. Creating a good impression will only serve to help you."

Kira pulled a face. The prospect didn't thrill her but she understood his reasoning. "Fine, what do I need to know?"

His smile was slow in dawning. "So very much."

* * *

Kira contained a wince as sore muscles protested. Evidently practicing bows and other forms of greetings used unexpected muscles, and they were not happy.

Graydon had proved a surprisingly effective, though merciless, teacher. He seemed to take a sick pleasure in snapping out instruction after instruction and then pointing out all the ways she'd gone wrong.

Tuann society was filled with nuances wrapped in nuances, and then tied with a bow of more nuances. It was enough to give Kira a headache.

Governed by tradition and rules, their restrictions were meant to clearly outline expectations of personal conduct. Since duels and personal combat were an accepted form of settling grievances, she'd learned it was important to guard your interactions to prevent inadvertent offense.

No, when they planned to kill each other, they wanted it to be because they were good and infuriated with their opponent.

All this served to make Kira's head hurt by the end. She barely understood human social behavior. She had no idea how she was going to make it through this ceremony without offending everyone present.

Kira groaned just thinking about it.

"Cheer up, Nixxy," Jin said. "At least Graydon said you couldn't be challenged until after the *adva ka.*"

"No, he said I couldn't be challenged by another adult. Other children or those who haven't passed the *adva ka* are fine," Kira corrected.

Jin made an amused sound, knowing Kira would have difficulty if someone Joule's age tried to challenge her.

"You haven't called me Nixxy in a long time," Kira said, looking up at him.

She stood on the terrace off the suite Graydon and his people had procured. In the dark, Jin nearly blended in with the night, only the odd flicker of light reflecting off his metal body.

"You left Phoenix behind when you made the *Wanderer* your home," he said.

She had. She'd tried to bury the parts of her that had made the Phoenix such an effective weapon.

"You sound like you miss her," Kira said, feeling vulnerable. When she'd chosen not to return to the Curs, she'd never considered how Jin might feel, taking his presence for granted. He was the one constant in her life.

Perhaps she should have made more of an effort to figure out what he wanted.

"I do sometimes," he admitted. Seeing her expression fall, he rushed to add, "I know why you left her behind. You had to keep your promise to Elise. You had to."

She nodded. Yes, she had, but perhaps she could have found a better

CHAPTER SEVENTEEN

way.

"That life was killing you, slowly but surely. Everyone could see it," he told her. "They might not have wanted to admit it, even to themselves, but they did."

By the end of the war, she was a walking shell of her former self. Her light and humor gone, leaving nothing behind but a vicious animal—dangerous to everyone, including herself.

Elise had been a Cur, her best friend, her sister, and the woman Raider loved more than life itself. Before she'd gone, she'd made Kira promise to survive, to live for all those who hadn't.

So, Kira had, even when some days it felt like she was abrading her skin with volcanic ash as she struggled through one hour after another.

Eventually, it got easier. She started to feel again. She reclaimed the tiny bits of herself she'd lost. It hadn't been easy, but she'd never stopped pushing forward.

Being around Raider and Jace and the new Curs, she found herself asking if she'd done the right thing. Maybe there had been a way for both sides of her to survive.

She didn't know.

The Phoenix had been glaringly bright, a shining beacon whose light attracted everyone to her until it flickered and went out.

Kira knew the Phoenix was her, but some days she couldn't even remember what it felt like to be that person.

"She's not dead, you know," Jin said. "I've seen echoes of her through the years. Here, I've seen more of her than I have in a long time."

Kira didn't move, turning his words over before tucking them away for consideration at another time.

"Tell me what you found," she said.

"The Curs are safe. Angry, but unharmed," he said. "Raider was talking about staging a breakout. Jace talked him out of it."

"Where does he think he'll go?" Kira asked. "It's not like the Tuann will let them take one of their ships."

"It seems your commander was right. There is a ship waiting outside Tuann space. I suppose Raider thinks a drop ship might be capable of slipping through the defense net."

Not unless the Consortium had extremely advanced technology Kira didn't know about. A waveboard might work, but you could only carry one person at a time on those and there'd be no way to get enough waveboards to the surface of the planet without risking detection.

"Anything else?" Kira asked, knowing there was more.

"The Nexus is the one place in the Citadel with the starmaps."

"Can we get in?"

"It'll be difficult."

"But not impossible?"

He hesitated. "I'm not sure the risk would be worth the reward."

Kira nodded. She understood his reservations. If she were caught trying to infiltrate that area, or worse, stealing the data inside, she would likely be treated as a traitor. Any protection that came from being one of their lost children would disappear. They'd take it as evidence of human subterfuge and likely kill the rest before ending the alliance.

No pressure or anything.

Her head tilted as she squeezed the railing in front of her. She'd waited too long to give up now. Those starmaps could be the answer to everything.

"I'll be careful," she promised.

Jin was quiet, his silence carrying weight to it. "Perhaps it's time to let this go. It's been long enough."

"No, I won't do that," Kira said forcefully. "I can't. You know why."

Jin's sigh was sad. "You know they wouldn't want this. They'd want you to move on with your life."

"Maybe, but I can't give up," Kira said. "Just like you wouldn't if the situation was reversed."

Jin made a soft sound.

CHAPTER SEVENTEEN

"What about Tsavitee presence?" Kira asked.

His silence this time was filled with stubbornness, but eventually he gave in. He'd try again at a more opportune time, Kira knew. Her friend had her best interests at heart. It was too bad she couldn't listen.

"You were right. Signs of their influence are all over the place if you know where to look."

"Anything to be concerned about?"

"From your description of your attack and my own readings, I'd say there's at least one telepath among their number," Jin said.

Not good. That spoke to a concentrated effort on their part, a big mission.

"Any generals?"

The generals were a highly dangerous form of Tsavitee Kira would do almost anything to avoid running into again. If one was here, the whole planet was at risk.

"Not that I've detected yet," he said.

"So much for no Tsavitee incursion," Kira muttered.

"Yes, our hosts have been quite arrogant."

"They have to be working with someone." Exactly the way they had during the war.

"I agree, but I doubt you'll be able to convince the Tuann of that unless someone stood up and waved their hand to admit they were the mole," Jin said. "They're even more arrogant about their incorruptibility than humans."

Kira sighed. "Good work, Jin. I couldn't do this without you."

The sound he made was rude. "I know. You'd be running around in a circle like a chicken with its head cut off going 'whatever shall I do?'"

Kira snickered at his impression of her as he headed inside.

"Lord Graydon," Jin said in greeting.

Kira's mirth cut off as she looked up to find Graydon standing silhouetted against the lights of the suite. He gave Jin a respectful nod as he passed, leaving the two of them alone out on the terrace.

"I'm surprised to find you out here given what happened last night," Graydon said in a light voice.

"I've never been one to live my life according to what's safe," Kira said as she turned to stare into the soft shadows.

Graydon came up to stand beside her, his warm presence wrapping around her like a soft blanket. She was painfully aware of him beside her, like he was a magnet exerting an almost physical pull.

"I didn't see your friend for most of today," Graydon observed.

"He was tired and needed to charge."

"Strange he would need another energy boost so soon after last night. I had thought human technology more advanced than that," Graydon said, his jab as subtle as a knife thrust. She got the sense, despite the shadows, he could read every thought and emotion to cross her face.

"What can I say? He likes his downtime," Kira said.

"Hmm." Graydon's shoulder brushed hers as he shifted. "I'm tempted to ask if he found what he was looking for, but I suspect you wouldn't tell me the truth."

Kira's lips curved at the thread of lazy amusement in his voice.

"I have no idea what you're talking about. I'm a fount of information. Ask anyone," Kira said.

Graydon let out a masculine rumble of amusement, the gravelly sound brushing against her senses. He moved closer, one hand going around her to rest on the railing. He was careful not to let any part of him touch as he caged her in. Not that it mattered given the almost painful awareness she had of him.

She stiffened for a moment and then relaxed. She could easily escape his hold if needed. She suspected he knew as much, which made the game all the more fun.

"Dancing," he said unexpectedly.

"What about it?"

"I didn't run through any with you today," he said.

CHAPTER SEVENTEEN

"And you're not going to do so now." Her muscles ached and she'd crammed all the knowledge into her head she planned to.

"Tired?" he said with a teasing lilt.

Kira snorted. "I'd say nearly getting eaten by a dragon's primordial piscine cousin after surviving an assassination attempt is enough excitement for me."

His expression sobered. "My *oshota* are working on finding who lured the *lu-ong* so close to the Citadel."

There was a dark promise in his voice. Those responsible would beg for a mercy he didn't have.

In that moment, he was the embodiment of a predator, dark and dangerous. Easily able to conquer his enemies so he could crush them beneath his boot so they might never rise again.

It should have scared Kira. He could very easily turn that dark intent her way. Probably would if he ever learned all her secrets.

It failed to do any of that. She understood him. The person who had put the Tsavitee control collar on the *lu-ong* and led it to the obstacle course had endangered not only her life but the lives of everyone there.

The protector in Graydon wouldn't allow such an action to stand. He'd hunt down and punish them with all the rage and fury he was capable of.

Kira would do the same. In that, they were alike.

"What brings you out here?" Kira asked, changing the subject.

He settled closer, the heat of his body wrapping around her, warming her against the cooler night. "What? Do you have a monopoly on this terrace? I'll have to inform the Overlord."

Kira looked at him. "You don't strike me as the type to enjoy a quiet night under the stars."

No, he was more apt to find a warm companion to tantalize and tease in bed, driving them mad with passion before leaving them in the morning.

Kira had seen the force of his presence on those around him. Even the Luathan women eyed him with desire when they thought no one was watching.

He was handsome and seductive, likely growing bored almost as fast as he fell into lust. But for a night or a week, he would be insatiable.

He leaned closer, his breath whispering across her face. "I am full of surprises. I'd be happy to show you."

He leaned back and waited.

"Why do I get the feeling your surprises might be more than I can handle?" she asked.

His smile was slow and wicked. "You can handle me, *coli*. I promise."

Kira ignored the innuendo in that statement, though it was hard. Part of her wanted to take him up on the offer, if only to see if they'd burn as hot and bright as she suspected.

"You were good with the children today," she said instead.

He made a sound of amusement, guessing exactly what she was doing. "I understand what they're going through. I was in much the same situation when I was their age."

"Did your parents die in the Sorrowing?"

There was a strained silence, Graydon's gaze growing distant as painful memories surfaced. "No, they died much earlier."

"What were they like?" Kira asked.

A sad smile touched his mouth. "My mother was soft-spoken, quiet. She let my father lead, unless something threatened me, then she was a fierce foe."

"They were both warriors?" Kira asked. This was a different side of Graydon, softer, more inviting.

"Yes. They were *oshota*, the overlord's personal warriors," he said, his voice wistful. He reached up and tugged on a lock of Kira's hair, straightening the wavy piece only to release it and watch with fascination as it sprang back.

"They died protecting their overlord during an assassination attempt. The overlord and many others survived. They did not,"

CHAPTER SEVENTEEN

Graydon said, an ache in his voice.

Kira's lips parted. She held in what she wanted to say, unsure what words were fitting in the face of his very real pain, even after all this time.

She didn't know what that was like. She'd never had parents to miss. In the compound where she'd been held, such things didn't exist. By the time she was rescued by Himoto, the concept of parents and family seemed more fairy tale than anything else.

Still, she'd seen other families since, had friends who filled that spot in her heart. She knew what it was to lose those you cared about.

"I was luckier than Joule and Ziva, the overlord's brother was a friend of my father. He took me in, trained me as my father would have," Graydon said.

"Why didn't you remain with him?" Kira asked.

A grin flashed. "I wasn't born to follow."

"That's obvious," Kira said. Graydon would always be the biggest, baddest thing in the room. She hesitated on this next question. "Did you know my parents?"

As the Emperor's Face, he would probably have had contact with them at some point—unless his position was a more recent development. Two hundred might seem old to her, but for his people he was probably still considered young.

His thumb brushed the edge of her hand. Quiet stretched between them. "I was more of a passing acquaintance of them," he finally said. "Your father is more familiar to me than your mother."

"What was he like?"

Graydon paused as he considered the right words. "Kinder than you'd expect. He was an overlord, but he didn't let that turn him cruel. He was playful, but when he was mad, he was scarier than even a *lu-ong* mother protecting her unhatched eggs."

That sounded like more than passing familiarity with her father. There was nostalgia in his voice, almost as if he missed him. Had Graydon been her father's friend?

Sensing her eyes on him, he straightened and cleared his throat. "Anyway, the emperor noticed me during my *adva ka* and gave me a new path. It is a good one."

Kira let him change the subject. She knew how painful it could be to speak about the people you've lost.

"They call you the Emperor's Face. Why is that?"

He was quiet as he thought over her question. She didn't take offense, knowing he was struggling to put into words something their people intuitively knew.

"The emperor cannot be everywhere at once. This is especially true after the Sorrowing because his travel now carries an element of risk to it. And yet, being fully absent would invite strife."

"I take it that's where you come in," Kira said.

He inclined his head as one corner of his lips tilted up. "Indeed. There are several Faces. I'm just one of them. A Face acts in the emperor's stead. They forsake their birth House in favor of the emperor's. For all intents and purposes, they are his face and if needed, they can guide or punish with the full authority of his name and might. They are both generals and mediators. Diplomats and warriors."

His words stole Kira's next question as she stared at him in shock.

"That's a lot of power," she finally got out.

"Yes, it's why it's rare for him to bestow that responsibility on another," Graydon said. "I'm one of five current Faces."

"Why accept a position as dangerous as that?" Kira asked.

"Our people have begun to let House loyalties divide them. It might one day lead to our downfall."

"And you want to fix all that?" she asked.

He made a rumbling sound of assent.

"How noble."

"What is your end goal?" he asked.

"Survival."

He made a soft sound of skepticism. "Somehow I don't see you

CHAPTER SEVENTEEN

being a salvager for long."

She raised an eyebrow. "And you know this from all the time you've spent with me?"

"I don't need to spend a century to learn all I need to know."

Kira crossed her arms, her spine pressing against his arm. "Enlighten me, oh knowledgeable one."

He took the touch as an invitation, brushing her cheek with his fingers.

"Your loyalty, once earned isn't easily lost. It's the bedrock of your foundation. I also know you wouldn't have left your humans for so long if there wasn't a damn good reason. You're lonely, but you've given up on ever finding your place. Sorrow clings to you like a shroud, but you haven't let it turn you bitter."

His eyes roved over her face, searching, seeing. Kira held her breath as his words reached deep inside, leaving her feeling vulnerable and exposed.

"You need purpose or else you will eventually wither and die. I don't know what drove you into exile, but you've begun to heal. When you do, you will be ready to take risks again," he said.

Kira wanted to look away, but knew if she did, he'd take it as a sign he was right. There'd be no escaping him then.

"That's a lot of guesswork," she said, pulling back from his touch and turning to where the moonlight bathed the forest.

"I'm right," he said, not an ounce of humbleness in his tone.

Kira kept quiet, her expression turning pensive as she stared out at the splendor around them.

"I forgot how beautiful nighttime is," she said.

The moons were high overhead, full and round as they dominated the sky. They looked close enough to touch.

Kira made a small sound of interest as a small furry face peered out of the branches of a tree, green stripes glowing on its fur as it wound its way through the canopy, searching out blooms Kira realized were now unfolding.

"Moon's glove," Graydon said. "It only blooms at night. The *ooril* is drawn to their scent."

"They're beautiful," Kira said, turning her head slightly to find his face startling close, his breath mingling with hers.

Bathed in silver moonlight, with the harsh planes softened, Graydon seemed like some prince of the night, intimidating and forbidden.

For a split second, she was tempted to close the distance between them, touch her lips to his and see what happened. She saw the same need in his eyes as he waited with the patience of a hunter for her to make her decision.

She hesitated, on the brink of withdrawing, all the reasons why this wouldn't work beating at her. He was too demanding. Too autocratic. Her path lay elsewhere.

"Fuck it," Graydon murmured, closing the distance.

His lips touched hers, barely there as they brushed against hers in question. In answer, she rose to her toes, fitting herself against the hard length of him.

He made a guttural sound but remained still, not closing his arms around her. He was letting her take the lead.

That decided her, making her bold as she explored his mouth, the warm pressure sending tingles quaking through her.

It was sweet and gentle, until suddenly it wasn't. Desire engulfed them as they crashed together, fury and need rising.

There was a burst of sound, laughter from inside the suite as the door opened. It broke the spell they'd fallen under. Kira jerked back.

Graydon's eyes blazed at her as he struggled not to reach for her again. For a moment she thought he would, and she knew it would put them past the point of no return.

She waited, not knowing what she'd do if he did.

He shook himself, his face calming as his expression turned inscrutable.

"This was a mistake," she said. For so many reasons that she couldn't

CHAPTER SEVENTEEN

afford to name.

"One I fully intend to repeat again and again."

She had no answer for that, choosing to stage a tactical retreat instead. She headed for the safety of the suite, knowing the presence of others would keep her from doing anything unwise.

In future, she'd need to avoid moonlit terraces. They seemed to bring out the incautious side of her.

Her steps faltered when she caught sight of Finn and Solal waiting.

"Did you enjoy the show?" Kira asked.

"It was certainly an interesting one," Finn said.

Kira shook her head and moved toward the door.

"I don't think I recall the commander ever being so obvious when making his interest in a woman known," Finn said. "Do you, Solal?"

His voice was neutral, but Kira suspected he was laughing at her.

"Never. He usually lets them pursue him," Solal said. "He is very particular."

Kira didn't respond, prowling toward the door.

"And I've never heard him share even the barest details of his past with any of them," Finn murmured.

Kira's head turned toward him slightly. Her mouth firmed. No, she wasn't going to get drawn into this, even if curiosity was a bitch.

She stepped into the bright lights of the common room of the suite, the source of what had interrupted their moment immediately obvious.

Graydon's minions were arranged in various poses of relaxation around the room. Two were in the center playing some type of game involving daggers and juggling.

They flung the weapons at each other almost faster than the eye could see, each one catching a dagger before flinging it back at the other.

Kira counted. There were five daggers in play.

Dangerous game. It was impressive there was no blood or holes in the furniture.

As she watched, someone standing to the side tossed a dagger to one of them. Isla caught it, sending it spinning toward her opponent in one smooth movement.

There were shouts of encouragement and jibes as those watching tried to break the players' concentration.

"They'll go until one of them dodges or draws blood," Graydon murmured, coming up behind her.

Kira didn't jump, having sensed him seconds before he spoke.

"Whoever lasts the longest wins. The more daggers you can keep in the air, the more impressive," he continued.

"That seems like a good way to put someone out of commission," Kira said blandly.

Graydon shrugged. "They need the danger to burn off their excess energy. Better this than pointless duels because everyone is irritable."

Kira turned to look at him.

He arched an eyebrow. "There are consequences to our gifts. I suspect you already know what I'm talking about."

Kira's expression remained neutral.

Jin lowered from the ceiling where he'd been watching the proceedings. "That would explain so much about you."

Kira glared at her friend.

"If we'd known that, maybe you wouldn't have decided to tangle with the strigmor eels and razor ash and we'd still have a working ship," he said, ignoring the signals she was giving him to shut up.

"I'm beginning to see why you keep leaving your drone behind," Graydon said dryly.

From over his shoulder, Finn scowled at her. "You know Tsavitee toys are very dangerous, right?"

"Somehow I managed to figure that out."

"You should avoid them," he pushed, ignoring her.

"I'm a salvager. They're a hazard of the job."

"How much energy does she need to burn to be a reasonable person?" Jin asked, ignoring the exchange.

CHAPTER SEVENTEEN

Kira picked up one of the small items on the table next to her, an intricately cut figurine. She spared a moment to regret its likely fate before chucking it at Jin.

It stopped an inch from him, hovering in the air.

"Oh, I didn't realize you wanted to play," Jin said cheerily. "All you had to do was say."

Kira's eyes widened as he threw the figurine at her. He pulsed once, then three of the daggers the *oshota* had been flinging about, turned and darted for Kira, one after another.

"Damn it, Jin," she spit out.

She caught one and flung it at him, doing the same with the other two. The figurine nearly beaned her in the head. She managed to stop it before sending it winging at him.

He chortled, having fun. The daggers she'd flung reversed direction as he added another, this one zipping from the belt at Graydon's side.

"Bet you can't beat me," he taunted.

"You're on, Tin Man," she returned, forgetting where they were for a moment.

The daggers flew back and forth, the movement a dance. Soon other objects entered the game as they both added whatever they could reach.

Kira caught a rock and chucked it back at him. The uneven shapes made the task more difficult.

Kira was conscious of the others giving them room, the cheers and boos as Graydon's soldiers urged them on.

Soon Kira was laughing as the items got more and more ridiculous. It didn't take long before it was impossible to keep up and she was forced to rely as much on instinct and blind luck to protect herself.

"Is that all you've got, Nixxy?"

"Some of us don't have the luxury of antigravs."

He blew a raspberry at her, no sign of stress in his voice. "Excuses, excuses."

She missed a grab, the item sailing past her.

"Score," Jin crowed.

The rest of the items dropped to the ground as he did a victory lap. Kira bent over, slightly winded.

"I don't think I've ever seen such a lively game," Graydon said mildly, looking around at the mess they'd made.

"Whoever is responsible for this place is going to be upset when they see this," Kira observed uneasily.

While a few items were broken, most of the rest were scratched.

She winced when Amila reached into the wreckage, pulling out one of her daggers.

"Sorry, Amila. We may have gotten a little overenthusiastic." It was habit. Neither one of them liked to let the other win.

Amila aimed a happy expression her way. "Don't be. That was fun to watch. I didn't know some of those human insults before. Flibberjibit was my favorite."

Kira snorted. "You probably won't hear them again. We tend to make things up when the mood strikes us."

A yawn cracked Kira's jaw.

"You're tired," Finn said. "The healing you received would have strained your normal resources. You should retire. They will clean up."

Kira didn't argue. The encounter with Graydon on the terrace, followed by the contest with Jin had left her feeling pleasantly drained for once. Exhaustion made his order more palatable than it would be otherwise. She had a feeling that soon it would be less of a decision and more of her falling unconscious at their feet.

CHAPTER EIGHTEEN

"This way," Ayela said, bowing her head diffidently as she led Kira along the hall. "We're late. Preparing you took longer than I anticipated."

Kira smiled at the subtle jab, meant to imply Kira's lack of attractiveness as the cause, given how hard the girl had to work to make her appealing.

Ayela had claws, delicate but sharp, nonetheless. Good for her.

Kira didn't move any faster, continuing at the same pace, despite the look of irritation the other woman shot her.

She didn't care. They'd get there soon enough. For now, she concentrated on not tripping over the long fabric of her dress.

The wave in her hair had been magnified and then woven with strings of precious metals.

The dress she'd been given to wear was fitted on top and through the waist, before falling in a graceful train behind her. It was diaphanous and floaty, except for the metal woven into the bodice and waist.

Excluding its length, it was surprisingly easy to move in since it was short in front, long in back. If she didn't turn too quickly or forget about the excess she was dragging, she'd be fine.

Secretly, Kira adored the way it drifted around her legs.

Ayela slowed her pace to accommodate Kira, her expression wiped clear of any irritation.

Jin rotated his eye to Kira and blinked once, as if to ask if she was picking up on their guide's impatience too.

She nodded.

"You helped with the children yesterday?"

Ayela nodded.

"And today you're helping me with my dress. You must be very talented," Kira said.

"I don't contain enough soul's breath to have a specialty, lady." Ayela's voice was soft and unassuming. "I go where there is need. Since I am one of the few who speak human standard, it was thought I would be of more assistance."

"You hear that, Jin? She goes where she's needed," Kira said, an edge to her tone. "You should learn from her example."

"Then who would save you from your stupidity?"

Ayela glanced up, her mouth opening on a surprised oh as she noticed Jin for the first time. She bowed her head. "Hello again, Mr. Jin."

Jin was silent for a long moment. "Hear that, Kira? She knows a thing or two about respect and manners."

Kira rolled her eyes as they approached an intersection in the hallways. She slowed as she noticed Graydon and several of his warriors waiting for them.

Graydon looked up. He froze, his expression arrested at the sight of her. Kira felt a feminine thrill of satisfaction at seeing the impact she had on him.

"Someone likes the way you look," Jin teased.

"Hush."

He made kissing sounds.

Ayela looked between the two of them, confusion on her face. "The Commander has expressed an interest?"

"Yes." "No." Kira and Jin said at the same time.

Ayela seemed thoughtful. "I've never heard his name paired with another's. All the women gossip about him."

"See, told you that you were special," Jin muttered.

"Be careful," Ayela said suddenly. "He is a dangerous man. If he

CHAPTER EIGHTEEN

turns on you, there'll be little anyone can do."

Kira's eyes narrowed. Was Ayela trying to warn her because she was honestly concerned or because she wanted to mislead her? It was hard to say.

Graydon hadn't taken his eyes from them during the exchange, his body tight and coiled as Kira neared. Amila and Solal exchanged amused glances. It seemed the servant wasn't the only one who'd picked up on his interest. His guards had too, and they approved.

"You didn't have to wait," Kira told him.

"And yet, I have." He turned with her as she approached, the look in his eyes appreciative. "Are you ready for this?"

"I've faced a horde of Tsavitee. A little gathering of Tuann is nothing compared to that," Kira said.

"Hold onto that thought," Graydon advised. "Soon, you're going to wish for a foe you can kill."

On those reassuring words he escorted her into a wide-open room, the ceiling a glass dome high overhead, tinged orange by the fading light of the sun.

Staircases led up to balconies overlooking the floor below. The House had gathered throughout the large space, more people than Kira could have imagined, rimming the many balconies.

Most were dressed in outfits similar to her own, their dresses long and flowing. The warriors were the exception, in distinctive synth armor as they moved throughout the space.

Noticing them, Kira glanced around, noting people in armor at all the exits and placed in other strategic places in the room.

"Are they expecting trouble?"

"It's standard protocol when dignitaries of another House are present," Graydon said.

"Sounds tense."

"Coups are not as commonplace as they once were, but they're still a threat. The Houses are always one minor offense away from war with each other," he said, keeping a pleasant expression on his face as he nodded to someone in the crowd.

Kira was beginning to understand why the Tuann had not had a bigger presence in the fight against the Tsavitee. If tensions between the Houses were as bad as Graydon insinuated, it would be difficult to bring to bear the focus and cohesion necessary to beat a powerful enemy like the Tsavitee.

From what Kira had seen of the Tuann so far, they relied on their technology and reputation as superior fighters to safeguard their borders. That arrogance would eventually bite them in the ass.

"Every day I find myself more and more glad you disrupted my normal, safe existence to drag me into this nest of vipers," Kira said dryly.

Graydon snagged two glasses of a peach-colored liquid and handed one to her. "You're Tuann. We need certain things in our lives. Boredom would eventually cause you to do something unwise."

"Like take over a station just because someone looked at you wrong," Jin chimed in.

Graydon lifted his glass in acknowledgment. "We weren't created for peace. We were created for war."

"What do you mean by that?" Kira asked, sensing a deeper undercurrent in his words.

He took a sip from his glass. "You'll have to stick around to find out."

"You know I'm leaving as soon as I can arrange it?" Kira said.

He gave her an enigmatic smile. "We'll see. I have faith I can change your mind."

Kira felt a spurt of alarm. Graydon was the type of man who felt the need to conquer any obstacle in his path. She was the ultimate challenge, a woman unimpressed with his station and utterly consumed with running as far from him as possible.

She should have let things run their course last night. He'd have lost interest and she could go about her business without distraction.

She sighed. Too late now.

CHAPTER EIGHTEEN

Kira turned to the gathering, people watching for several minutes. Those around her seemed curious, peeking at her before looking away when they noticed her attention. They giggled and gossiped with their neighbors.

None approached, leaving a ten-foot bubble around Kira, Graydon, and his three minions.

"I can't tell if they see me as some exotic zoo animal or if there's another reason for their avoidance," Kira said, holding her glass up to her mouth but not drinking as she studied the other Tuann.

"They're not certain of your standing. My presence and my warriors probably don't help," Graydon said. "People are often intimidated by those who've joined the ranks of the *oshota*."

Kira took a sip of the liquid and closed her eyes as a tart, sweet flavor coated her tongue. She'd never tasted anything like it. If nothing else, she could say there was one aspect of Tuann society she enjoyed. They knew what they were doing when it came to food and drink.

"Because you're likely to kill them?"

"They rely on us for protection but prefer our presence from a safe distance," Graydon said.

There was no bitterness in his voice, just a statement of facts.

Kira looked around at their guards, their expressions neutral masks as if the topic had no relevance to them.

She looked at her glass, feeling empathy for them. She knew what it was to be sought after but held at a distance because of what you could do.

The potential for violence didn't automatically equate to the likelihood.

Being revered didn't make the nights and days any less lonely if those you'd lay down your life to protect wouldn't let you close enough to have a conversation.

"Yet you protect them anyways," Kira said in a soft voice.

"That is our purpose, lady," Solal said with a slight smile.

Her lips quirked in response, though her eyes remained remote and sad. She'd thought the same once, until she'd found that purpose was not a replacement for the warmth of skin against hers or a conversation after a long shift.

"The seneschal approaches," Amila murmured in a voice pitched for their ears.

Any levity or softness vanished from the expressions of Graydon's guards. They tensed, their focus laser-sharp as they turned their attention to the approaching woman.

Alma's hair was bound up in a complicated, undone knot that exposed the tips of her ears. She looked like a regal noble, come to bestow her blessing on the peasants. The arrogance and haughtiness of her expression would have made lesser people feel self-conscious.

Kira took another sip of her drink and waited expectantly.

Alma's eyes went to Jin and she made a moue of distaste. "Couldn't you have left the toy behind for one night?"

Kira didn't answer, just stared Alma down. Graydon and the others were equally silent beside her. For just a moment, they were a united front against the interloper. It didn't matter that the Citadel was Alma's home. Kira had people willing to stand at her back.

Alma sighed in frustration. "I suppose we can't expect much, given you were raised by humans."

Kira's expression didn't waver at the insult, if anything it became even more polite.

Graydon's *oshota* stiffened as they took umbrage at the slight. Their expressions didn't shift from their normal remoteness, but the air crackled with intensity. The pressure felt like the sky before a thunderstorm, the potential for destruction there.

It surprised Kira. She hadn't thought they felt such empathy for her.

"Is there a reason you're here?" Kira could do icy disdain too.

Alma's eyes narrowed. "Don't get lippy with me, child. I won't be as gentle as the commander. I'm the seneschal for House Luatha and I'm due respect."

CHAPTER EIGHTEEN

Respect was earned, not given. So far Alma had proven she was capable of pointless posturing against a supposed weaker member of her House. Kira wasn't known for respecting those who abused those under them.

Her cheek twitched with all the emotion she was suppressing. She couldn't say any of that. To do so would betray the façade she was trying to keep up. Graydon and his warriors might suspect Kira's true colors, but these others did not.

The utter wrongness of the woman's assumptions turned Kira's annoyance into a game. She couldn't upset Kira because she had no idea of who she was dealing with, and Kira wasn't yet ready to educate her.

"Of course, seneschal," Kira said, giving her a humble nod. Graydon choked on a laugh beside her. Kira ignored him as she beamed sweetly at Alma. "I assume your time is precious. What is it you came over here for?"

"The ceremony will begin soon," Alma said. "Prove a credit to your bloodline and your life will be very easy going forward."

And if she didn't? Would they cast her out or sentence her to a life of drudgery?

Kira kept those questions contained as Alma swept off.

"It is such fun watching you toy with them," Graydon murmured next to her.

She twitched a shoulder.

"I'm interested to see how your game will end," he said.

"Or when they'll realize the mouse is actually a *lu-ong*," Finn said acerbically.

She gave him a sidelong look but didn't confirm his guess. She didn't feel too bad Graydon and his *oshota* had seen past the mask she'd crafted for the Luatha. If she'd wanted them to underestimate her, she would have needed to handle their first encounter better.

"What is it I can expect from this ceremony?" Kira asked.

"They'll test your affinities to the soul's breath. They'll use knowledge of your strengths to determine what position within the House you would be best suited for," he said.

He steered her across the room toward a raised dais in the middle of the floor, a carved stone table on it. The balconies above all had a perfect view of the spot.

Ziva and Joule waited near the dais, their faces grumpy despite their finery.

Joule wore a high-necked vest, his arms bare except for a metal cuff around his thin biceps. He hadn't quite filled in yet, but his arms contained a hint of the man he might be one day.

Ziva's outfit was a more feminine version of his, a silky overdress over a pair of pantaloons. Her hair had been slicked back and a diadem affixed on her head, a single pearl hanging on her brow.

Neither looked thrilled to be there. Their frowns became even more pronounced at the sight of Kira.

She arched an eyebrow at them. "What is it now? You were perfectly happy when I left you yesterday."

The two traded a look. "They're not going to offer the rest of our House a position here."

Kira was quiet, blinking at them. She could see how that news would be upsetting—especially since she knew how desperately Joule and Ziva wanted to ascend so they could ensure the safety of those they had left on the ship.

She and Graydon exchanged a look, each understanding what a blow this would be for the children. "Can they refuse Luatha's claim on them?"

Graydon shook his head. "No, not without another House putting forth an offer to take them. He'd need to pass the highest level of the *adva ka* to be able to form his own House."

"That's not likely to happen if she gets her way," Ziva said sulkily, glancing at Alma.

Kira was silent as she took in the situation. Ziva was likely correct. Alma had already proved she liked the status quo and she wasn't

CHAPTER EIGHTEEN

likely to make the lives of two orphans easier when there were full blood Luathan children needing the same resources and guidance.

"It wouldn't matter anyway. Not after we take the tests," Joule said quietly.

"Why not?" Kira asked.

"You're afraid your affinity will prevent you from pursuing your goal of ascending to the position of Overlord for House Maxiim," Graydon said from beside her.

Joule's nod was reluctant.

Kira looked up, surprised. "Why would it?"

You could be a warrior and be good at other things. Take Blue. She had a near genius level intelligence, could dismantle any machine and reassemble it better than new. She was also one of the best shooters Kira had ever worked with, and handy to have around in a pinch.

"In our House, the affinity didn't matter as much, since we were so small. You could do several things as long as you proved willing and strong enough," Joule explained.

"Here, everyone has a place and a task to fulfill," Ziva said sulkily.

Kira didn't respond for a long moment. "You're right."

The two's faces grew more morose.

She leaned forward. "But sometimes you need to make your own path despite what anyone else tells you."

Their expressions brightened.

Kira straightened. "One test does not decide your fate."

No, you had to work toward your goal day in, day out, even when times got hard or things seemed impossible.

"I'm not sure you should have told them that," Graydon said when they drifted off, distracted by one of the floating lights.

"Why not?"

"Because they're right. Everyone has a place in our society. It's not so easy to buck tradition."

"Hmm," Kira said, glancing around at the splendor around her. "You're right if a talent is so rare no one else could take their place, but one less artisan won't destroy your civilization."

"People should play to their strengths," he said.

"Yes, but they should also decide for themselves what those strengths are," Kira returned. "Take Jin. He is one of the most advanced pieces of technology humans have ever created. He can analyze a million different problems at once, track hundreds of data streams while problem-solving. His purpose should have been to serve as the AI of one of the space stations."

Graydon gave her friend a skeptical look.

"He's also responsible for saving nearly three million souls," Kira stated. "If he'd performed the function he'd been designed for, those people would be dead, as would I. He didn't and because of that, the universe is a better place."

"That's an intriguing perspective," a low, soothing voice said from behind her.

Graydon's body stiffened, his expression going blank. It was enough to put Kira on edge.

She turned to find a man looking at her, the faintest trace of crow's feet around his eyes as they smiled at her. His expression was pleasant. He wore a cloak which covered his body from neck to feet.

"You know the rules, Silas," Graydon rumbled in warning.

Silas waved his statement away. "Relax, old friend. I don't intend more than this. I just wanted to see the lost gem you were so kind to see returned to Luatha."

Kira watched the stranger, not trusting his easy manner or his words of friendship. Whatever threat he presented wasn't physical. The *oshota* next to her didn't seem threatened. They remained guarded but not tense. There was a difference.

The man focused on Kira, his eyes soft as they roved her features. Unlike many of the Luathans she'd encountered, she didn't see a trace of judgment there.

"You look like your mother," he said.

Another man, attired similarly with a cloak covering him, joined

CHAPTER EIGHTEEN

them. His expression was interested and watchful as he took in Kira and Graydon.

"I wouldn't know," Kira said politely, meaning it this time. This man had obviously felt something for a long-dead woman. "I don't remember her."

"At all?" he asked.

She shook her head. She didn't think he'd like to know what her first memory was, but it wasn't the gentleness of a mother's touch.

He nodded. "Welcome back to your people, little one."

She inclined her head.

He switched his attention to Graydon. "I will see you after the ceremony."

Graydon waved him and the other man away, a trace of resignation on his face.

"Interesting man," Kira said once they were gone. "Friend of yours?"

"You could say that. He was one of my teachers when I was younger," he said. "He was a pain in the ass, even then."

Liara stepped onto the dais, a hush falling over the gathering as she paused until she held everyone's attention.

Her hair was bound into an undone tail and wrapped in various tiny chains. Her face had been painted, the eyes dramatic. Her dress was stiff from metals and sang as she moved.

That wasn't what caught Kira's attention and held it. No, it was the power that roiled around her, a tidal wave battering her senses. It surged and frolicked around the Overlord like a well-trained dog.

Liara smiled. It was the type of expression poets would have once written sonnets about. "Friends, family, thank you for your attendance. We gather today to welcome back into the fold one who was lost for much too long."

Kira felt the focus move to her. She kept her face placid and unchanging.

Liara turned her attention to the other two. "And to bring into the House two who have lost much. We can never replace your House, but know you are welcome here always. Let something good come out of all the tragedy. It would be our pleasure to guard and guide you in your family's stead."

A cry of agreement rose from those assembled.

Liara gestured at the dais. "Step forth those who seek to join our House."

"I wonder what would happen if you didn't step forward," Jin muttered.

"Let's not find out," Kira said. She had a feeling the Luathans would see her refusal as a grievous insult. She didn't want them taking their anger out on the Curs.

She mounted the steps to the dais behind Joule and Ziva.

Alma and Rayan stood well behind Liara as she smiled at the children.

Joule and Ziva bent forward in polite bows.

"The first of the tests is simple. It will determine your affinities," Liara said. "Do not fear, all affinities are welcome."

She gestured at the table, which Kira could now see held a bunch of perfectly formed spheres on them. They represented every color imaginable, polished until they gleamed. The air above the table had the faintest haze over it, like heat coming off pavement.

Kira looked closer and felt a deep sense of peace emanating from the table. This was like the planet's consciousness on an immeasurably smaller scale. It lacked sapience but held an impossible depth of emotion. Right now, those rocks were happy and content in their place.

"You first, little one," Liara said with a welcoming smile at Ziva.

Ziva screwed up her face and reached over the table, her hand shaking as the strain showed in her pursed mouth. When it looked like she could move her hand no further, she plucked one of the spheres up. It lit up at her touch, glowing a light bluish green.

"A melder. A fine affinity," Liara said.

Ziva didn't respond, her face stony as she stepped back, cradling

CHAPTER EIGHTEEN

the stone to her chest.

Joule was next, moving without prompting. Sweat beading on his forehead as he reached for the far edge, struggling against a force Kira couldn't see.

With a gasp, his hand descended as if he'd lost the will to keep it up any longer. He picked a sphere that blazed white hot in his hands.

"Well chosen, young Joule. A shield is always welcome in our ranks. Our master architects will be happy for an apprentice with an affinity for earth," Liara said.

Kira saw what the children were saying now and why neither had wanted to participate in this ceremony. Liara, and no doubt the rest of the Luathans, assumed the children would fall into line with the House's needs and wants, not even considering whether the children might have a different plan for their lives.

It was like saying, you're welcome here, but only if you play by our rules and toe our line.

Having been on the receiving side of such a mindset, Kira could understand the need to run as far and as fast as you could, lest you be trapped in an endless loop of duty and sacrifice.

Joule stepped back.

It was Kira's turn.

She looked over the board with its multi-colored spheres before glancing up at Liara. Her cousin's expression was calm but Kira thought she detected a trace of expectation.

What affinity was her cousin hoping she'd have? And how did she hope to use Kira once she knew?

Kira's hand hovered over the table. The stones gave a slight pulse of welcome, their presence warm and tingly under her fingers. None drew her, however. They felt the same, alive but she didn't feel any of the compulsion Ziva or Joule had displayed.

Her hand reached the far side of the board. Still nothing, Kira's hand dropped to her side as she looked at Liara.

Liara's mouth was slightly parted as she stared at the board like it had betrayed her. The murmurs around them grew in volume.

Kira chanced a quick glance at Graydon. His forehead was furrowed as he crossed his arms over his wide chest. A thoughtful frown creased his face.

"Something wrong?" Kira asked.

Liara's smile was strained and obviously false. "No, of course not. There are several tests to conduct tonight."

When Liara turned to face the crowd, all trace of uncertainty was wiped clean from her expression, leaving it serene. "The first test has ended."

Liara swept off without speaking to the three of them, her expression troubled.

Jin floated to join her on the platform. "Is it just me or was that weird?"

Kira didn't respond, still bothered by Liara's reaction.

"I've never seen anyone not receive an affinity before," Joule said. Both he and Ziva looked at Kira like she was a stranger.

"Is it that concerning?" Kira asked.

Joule was silent for a long moment as he thought over her question. "There are two reasons for you not to show an affinity."

Kira waited as Ziva and Joule conferred silently.

"You're either so weak that no affinity presented, which is impossible given your lineage," Joule started.

"Or you're a primus strain," Ziva said, her eyes almost feverish with excitement.

"I've never heard that term before," Kira said. "What does it mean?"

"Most Great Houses have at least one primus," Joule started. "They're usually the overlord. They're the most powerful weapon at the House's disposal. Right now, there are two Great Houses without one. Luatha and Roake. Both of the previous overlords were killed during the Sorrowing and neither overlord who ascended has that power."

"Not that Roake needs a primus," Ziva said, her voice that of a

CHAPTER EIGHTEEN

teacher. "They have some of the best warriors among the Houses."

"So Liara's not a primus," Kira said.

Joule shrugged. "No one knows. She's young. Sometimes the ability doesn't show up for years after maturation."

"If you're a primus, they'll never let you go," Ziva said gravely, getting to the heart of the matter.

"What does a primus do?" Kira asked.

Both shrugged and shook their head. "We don't know. Our House didn't have one either and they just said each great House's primus was different. All we know is they're capable of bringing down a Tsavitee fleet by themselves."

Kira withdrew, almost physically recoiling. She gave the two a strained smile of thanks. She needed to digest this.

Out of the corner of her eye, Kira saw Graydon approaching. She cut right, away from him, placing several of the gathered Luathans as a screen between her and him. She wasn't quite ready to talk to him yet.

She needed to consider what this meant and how this affected her. More, she needed to figure out what the next test was and how to beat it. There was no way she was going to let herself be identified as a primus.

The Luathans she passed stared but didn't try to engage her.

Jin trailed behind her, quiet for once, keeping his thoughts and opinions to himself. Kira was grateful for the reprieve.

She waited until Graydon's sight of her was obscured by another group before ducking into an alcove.

Kira waited, pressing herself against the wall. Graydon was smart, but she was hoping he wouldn't check her hiding spot.

She glanced around, realizing her alcove was connected to several others, creating a maze of smaller passageways for those wanting a secret assignation. She ducked past two lovers, moving deeper into the space, and hoping they didn't notice her passage.

Voices in a room off the small hall drew her notice. She caught the sound of her name, and crept closer.

She hesitated on the threshold to the next room, listening as those inside spoke Tuann.

She waved at Jin and then pointed to her ear. The translation of what they were saying filtered into her implant.

"She has no affinity for House Luatha's abilities. She's either a dud or she takes after his line. She'll be of no use to us," Alma said.

"We don't know that. There's a chance she's of the primus strain," Liara argued.

At the sound of Liara's voice, Kira moved closer.

"Even worse. She'll take your position, child," Alma said urgently. "Think. Expel her while there's still a choice."

"We should consider the Roake proposal," Rayan said. "Let them deal with her. If she's a dud, better she drain their resources than ours."

"I won't do that. We are not Tsavitee to kill any who aren't of use. Luatha does not abandon our own, even when they prove less talented than previously hoped for," Liara said in a strong voice. "My mother wouldn't have condoned it, and neither will I."

"Don't deceive yourself. Your mother would have done what was necessary," Alma said. "Just like she did when she sent your aunt to those brutes."

"That was at the emperor's behest as part of an alliance. She could do no differently," Liara argued. "This is different."

There was a tense silence between the three in the room.

"There is the possibility she is primus," Rayan conceded.

"You will regret it if she is. If she takes our House, she'll kill us all trying to protect them," Alma said scornfully.

"We don't know that," Liara protested. "From what I've seen, all she wants is an alliance for the humans, and for us to rescind our claim to her."

"All we have is her word on that," Alma said, exhaustion in her voice. "What kind of person would walk away from the power of the

CHAPTER EIGHTEEN

overlord? Our House is among the wealthiest. She would be insane to leave. No, if we want to protect ourselves, we need to act now before it's too late."

"We can't do anything while the Emperor's Face or the envoy is here. It would create an incident," Rayan cautioned.

"Let it," Alma said. "We have no reason to fear them or the emperor."

Jin bobbed beside Kira, drawing her notice. He flashed his lights, twice quick and once for slow.

She nodded. Every second they lingered, they risked discovery, and this wasn't the type of conversation she wanted to be caught eavesdropping on.

"I won't hear any more of this," Liara said. "I've already made my decision."

Jin started reversing seconds later. Kira followed as he led her into a small alcove off the hallway. They hid there as Liara swept past, Rayan trotting after her.

Kira released her breath once her cousin had disappeared from sight. That had been entirely too close.

She started to relax and then tensed as she realized Alma hadn't followed Liara. She looked up at Jin and mimed a question about whether there was another exit.

He moved back and forth and then dipped to say he had no clue.

She gave him a wry look. After all his exploring he hadn't discovered this area? He was getting rusty. Time was he never would have allowed any nook or cranny to go unexplored.

He read her expression and flashed several lights on and off rapidly, flicking her off.

They waited several tense seconds as the quiet murmur of voices reached her. Kira peeked out of their hiding spot.

"Kira," Jin hissed.

She held up a hand and moved forward on silent feet.

Jin made a frustrated sound before following.

"What are we going to do?" Alma asked in a hushed voice.

"If the Overlord won't protect herself, it is our duty to act in her best interests," a woman said. "Her fall would leave all of Luatha vulnerable."

"There's no way we could act without placing ourselves in danger," Alma said.

"There's a way," the woman said. "But it would require the defense codes—something I don't have access to."

"Why would you need those?" Alma asked.

"Our common enemy waits outside the defense net. We let them through to deal with the humans and the lost heir, and our hands will be clean. No one would ever know what we'd done," the strange woman said.

They were talking about the Tsavitee, Kira realized with a dull horror. They had to be.

She shifted closer for a better look at the speakers. Of the two, she recognized Alma's voice.

"You're talking treason. I should have you arrested and executed just for thinking it," Alma said sharply.

"But you won't. You know as well as I do Luatha has no chance if the mongrel takes control. We need to protect our House from outside influences, even if the means to do so wouldn't be condoned under other circumstances."

There was a long silence as Alma considered her words.

"There would be Luathan casualties," Alma said, her words slow.

"That would be regretful, but if it means a stronger Luatha overall, I feel the loss worth it," the woman said.

Kira strained her senses, trying to pick up on anything from the second speaker. The voice was familiar, but the hushed murmur made it hard to place. She caught no trace of Tsavitee, which meant both speakers were Tuann. She wondered which of them had already made the deal with the Tsavitee.

"And they would kill the mongrel and her Curs?" Alma asked.

"They might take care of the commander and the envoy for us as

CHAPTER EIGHTEEN

well," the woman said in amusement.

"Alright, I'll get the codes. You do the rest," Alma said, sounding resolute. "I want the half-blood dead before the night is through."

CHAPTER NINETEEN

Kira's muscles tensed in anticipation as she wavered on the cusp of attack. Her entire being begged her to rip out this threat at the root and crush it before it could do harm.

Two things stopped her. The first—while she was nearly positive she could deal with both women, there was always the possibility she'd fail before she succeeded in neutralizing them. Her death here would leave the rest in danger with no one to warn them.

It was an unlikely scenario, but chance and luck played as much of a role in battle as skill and training. She'd seen elite soldiers lose to weaker opponents simply because of a stray shot.

The second was the possibility these two weren't the only Tuann involved in this plot. She could kill them only to find herself ambushed from behind by their co-conspirators.

If she acted now, she might lose any chance to ferret out all of her enemies at once. Reveal what she knew without a full proof plan, and they'd disappear into the woodwork faster than she could hunt them.

She refused to allow any to escape.

No, her best option was to secure the Curs—get them off-planet and to safety.

She just needed to convince Liara or Graydon of the conspiracy she'd overheard. Jin would have recorded the two as soon as he realized the significance of what they were hearing, but she didn't know if it would be enough given the Tuann's aversion to most human technology.

CHAPTER NINETEEN

She flicked her hand at Jin, telling him to follow before she turned and headed down the hallway. She moved quickly and silently, not wanting to draw attention—now, more than ever. Jin glided after her without question.

Their path took them into one of the numerous carefully tended rooftop gardens. Only then did Kira judge it safe enough to speak.

"Tell me you located the Curs this afternoon," she said.

"Of course, I did. Who do you think you're talking to?"

"A drone with more attitude than sense."

He blew a raspberry before taking the lead. "Just follow me."

They moved swiftly through the Citadel, Jin signaling her to hide whenever his sensors picked up evidence of other Tuann.

Their journey ended not far from the suite they shared with Graydon and his *oshota*.

"Last time there were two guards on the door," Jin said.

"What about the window?" The room had an exterior wall. Chances were there was a window.

"Guarded too," he said.

"Damn." Of all times for Roderick to actually display an aptitude for his job, it had to be now.

She could take out the guards, but it would alert the rest to danger as soon as the shift changed. That could be five minutes from now or five hours.

If she had the time, she would have chosen a spot from which observe the guards, pick up their habits, their comings and goings, their communications, whether they used a challenge and response, or if they were laxer with security.

Time was one thing she didn't have. The two co-conspirators could come for the Curs at any moment.

"There's an extensive network of small passageways in the ceiling. They're like the furnace ducts humans put in their homes except they're made of stone, are considerably less dusty, and would fit a full-grown person," Jin offered.

Kira curled her lip at him. Small spaces. She hated them with an undying passion. Left to her preferences, she'd avoid them. However, circumstances dictated going outside her comfort zone.

"Or you can ask someone to pull rank and order them away," Finn said from behind them.

Kira froze, giving Jin big eyes that asked, "What the hell?"

He made a strangled sound. "I didn't sense him. I swear."

Kira turned slowly to find Finn glaring at both of them, his mouth a thin line of disapproval.

"One of the first techniques an *oshota* learns is how to disguise their passage from any and all," Finn said. "That includes inferior human technology."

Jin bristled. "There's nothing inferior about me, meat sack."

"You're welcome to test yourself against me," Finn offered coldly. "I would be happy to teach you the error of your ways."

"No, you're not doing this now," Kira hissed when Jin started toward Finn.

Sometimes her friend had all the impulse control of a toddler.

"Would you like to explain why you're standing outside this room?" Finn asked, his expression deadly. "I know the commander has already forbidden you from contact."

Kira studied him, mentally calculating her options. She'd seen him on the obstacle course. Taking him down silently and unnoticed would be difficult.

Trusting him didn't feel like an appealing option either. He was part of the House actively trying to kill her. He could well be part of the conspiracy.

"Jin, play the recording for him," Kira said.

Trust needed to start somewhere and there was no way he was going to unbend enough to let her go on her merry way. Not without a fight guaranteed to attract any Citadel guards in the vicinity.

She watched him carefully as Alma and the other woman's voice came through. His face went blank, his head tilting as he listened.

CHAPTER NINETEEN

Fury grew in his expression as he realized what the two women planned.

By the time the recording had finished, his normal impenetrable mask had dropped, and a predator stared at her.

Kira's stomach tightened, the primal fear people experienced when facing the thing in the dark sinking deep.

It answered the question of whose side he was on.

"You're here to get the humans out," he guessed, his voice flat.

"They're vulnerable here," Kira said. "I have to get them to safety before I can consider doing anything else."

He fell silent, staring off into the distance. Finally, he shook his head as a gruff sound escaped him. "Where do you think they'll go? Luatha controls the airspace. There's no way to get them off-planet. The defensive net would rip them to shreds."

"We send them into the forest. They only need to hide long enough for us to expose the conspiracy," Kira argued.

"We should inform Graydon," Finn argued. "The defense network affects more than just the Luathans. Bringing it down would leave all of our worlds vulnerable."

Kira understood his loyalty. Graydon held an authority Finn recognized and trusted. Kira was tempted to agree, the idea the commander was part of this too terrible to contemplate.

She shook her head. No. She couldn't take the chance. They didn't know how far this conspiracy went.

"Can you guarantee beyond any shadow of a doubt Graydon has no part in this?" Kira asked.

He couldn't. No one could. Right now, the only person she trusted completely and utterly was Jin. They'd gone through too much to do anything else. The Curs she trusted to a lesser extent, but only because she knew their motives.

"He is the Emperor's Face," Finn said as if that explained everything.

"Empires have been brought down before by those in trusted seats of power," Jin pointed out.

Finn's lips tightened. "Not the Tuann. Not Graydon. I would trust him with my life—and yours."

Conviction thrummed in his words. His expression said he wouldn't give in on this point. Kira didn't know the players well enough to judge. It was obvious his history with Graydon went deep—perhaps as deep as hers did with Jin and the Curs.

"At least let me get the Curs out," Kira bargained, sensing she was losing him. If he really decided Graydon needed to be informed first, there would be little she could do.

"Alma and her people could come for them while we're wasting time finding Graydon," Kira argued. She needed him to agree. "My people have no weapons and stand little chance against warriors in synth armor."

Finn looked torn, her argument swaying him. He scowled.

"We're already here," Jin added. "We'd waste valuable time backtracking, assuming Graydon's where we left him."

"Which is unlikely given someone's disappearance," Finn said, shooting a meaningful look Kira's way.

She shrugged, unconcerned. "If I hadn't needed some time to myself, I never would have overheard their scheme."

Not entirely true, but close enough.

"Fine, we'll do it your way," Finn said, his dark eyes piercingly intense.

Kira breathed a sigh of relief.

"But at the first sign of danger, I want you out of there," he said, pointing a finger at her.

She nodded. If an empty promise made him feel better, she'd give him all the empty promises he needed.

"I must have done something to anger the commander for him to suggest you to me," Finn said with a sigh.

"Why did you accept?" Kira asked as they moved toward the guards.

"Because my choices were limited. It was either act as your guard or sit around for another hundred years feeling invisible," Finn said.

CHAPTER NINETEEN

"*Oshota* are meant to protect their Houses. To be of no use to them is like living a life with no color."

"Empty and meaningless," Kira said in a soft voice.

Finn looked at her, understanding in his expression. "No one to care if you disappear or not. No one to care for or take comfort from."

Kira nodded. That's exactly what it felt like to exile yourself. Finn was an outcast in Luatha. It was more painful in its own way, to look at what you'd lost every day and know you were no longer part of it.

Kira had gotten off easy in that sense. When she'd left the Curs and her life with Centcom, she hadn't looked back or allowed herself to remember what had been. She focused everything on the salvaging business and told herself she didn't miss what she'd given up.

It was a lie, but she'd believed it enough to survive, never realizing that surviving was only the first step to living.

Being here, seeing her cousin and the Curs had reminded her of what it was like to live again, to laugh and cry, to feel sorrow and pain. It wasn't always pretty but she felt like she'd been wrapped in cotton and was only now experiencing things again. She didn't know how she was going to return to the isolation of the *Wanderer* when it came time.

They rounded the corner to find four guards standing sentry in front of the room—two wearing black, the other two in green.

Finn called a greeting in Tuann.

They looked from him to where Kira stood behind him, Jin hovering over her shoulder. Boredom and disinterest showed on the faces of Roderick's men. Those in black remained wary, their expressions cautious as they frowned at them.

"Why is she here?" the Luathan soldier asked in Tuann.

Jin's translation program was running, allowing her to understand most of what was being said.

"She needs to see the humans," Finn said crisply.

"She doesn't have permission," the same soldier from before replied.

Noor and Isla exchanged a glance, something in Finn's posture or presence alerting them.

They shifted to the side, keeping the other two guards in sight. Their hands lowering toward the en-blades at their sides.

Neither Luathan guard noticed the movement, but Jin and Kira did.

Jin rose a little so he'd have a better vantage point and room to maneuver. Kira edged back, not wanting to be in the line of fire.

"She doesn't need Roderick's permission. The Emperor's Face will allow the visit," Finn said smoothly.

The man and woman exchanged a glance, then turned to Finn, hostility peeking through.

"He is not Luathan," the woman said in a flat voice. "He does not command us."

Jin bobbed overhead, drawing her attention as he asked silently if she wanted him to take care of them.

Kira hesitated. She'd like to avoid violence if possible. There was no reason to assume these two were part of the conspiracy. Once they used force, there was no going back.

She held up two fingers at her side. It was a signal to wait and see.

Finn sighed and shook his head. "As long as I've been here, you'd think I'd learn. You lot always do things the hard way."

The two frowned in confusion. Finn lashed out, grabbing one and jerking him forward. The other drew her blade, a startled cry escaping. Isla kicked it out of her hand, following up with a brutal punch to the throat. The woman dropped to the ground choking.

Isla leaned over, lifting her, then slamming her head into the ground. The guard sagged unconscious in her grip.

Finn straightened from where he'd already rendered his opponent unconscious.

Kira glared at the bodies. Guess Finn hadn't gotten the message they were hoping to avoid unnecessary violence.

"This was your grand plan?" Kira asked, spreading her hands to

CHAPTER NINETEEN

indicate the two unconscious guards. "Knock them out?"

"It worked," Finn said.

Kira gave him a disgusted look.

"Good god, it's like stumbling into a planet of Kira clones," Jin murmured.

"If I wanted to knock them out, I could have done it myself," Kira said. "Now I can't ask them questions to determine if they're part of this."

"Would either of you like to explain why we just assaulted these guards, possibly signing our own death warrants and starting a war between Luatha and the emperor?" Noor asked in an irritated drawl.

"Play him the recording," Finn ordered as Kira moved to the door and swung it open.

She stepped into the other room as Jin brought the two up to date. There was a tight feeling in her chest, that loosened when Jace glanced up.

None of the relief she expected to see was in his expression—only denial and anger.

"Please tell me you aren't this stupid," he said.

She stopped in the doorway and cocked her head. "Not really the greeting I was expecting."

"We were fine," Jace snapped. "They hadn't hurt us and weren't going to. You've destroyed any chances of the alliance withstanding this debacle."

Kira raised her eyebrow at him as she sauntered into the room, taking in the rest. All the Curs were here. Nova sat up from where he had stretched out on a couch, and Maverick turned from the window he'd been staring out, hands in his pocket.

Next to him, Blue straightened from her bench, hastily trying to disguise the odds and ends beside her.

The faint glow on some rods told her Blue had used her time to take apart a few pieces of Tuann technology to examine.

Tank and Raider walked in from the other room, their expressions hard to read.

"That's some thank you you're working up to," Kira observed.

Jace let out a frustrated sigh. "At least tell me you didn't kill them."

Kira raised her hands. "I didn't lay so much as a finger on them."

Finn and Noor dragged the two unconscious Luathans into the room.

Jace stared pointedly at them and then raised his eyebrows, silently asking if she'd like to try that lie again.

"I didn't. I swear," Kira said, feeling a touch of amusement at the situation. She wasn't the cause this time. Jace and the rest would be able to claim ignorance of any offense.

Jin zoomed in. "Strange as it seems, she's telling the truth. Finn and the two giants in black did all the heavy lifting. All she did was stand there."

Jin's assurance seemed to reassure him. Jace relaxed slightly, although worry set in quickly.

He wasn't dumb. He might half-believe Kira would wreck a chance for alliance by attacking Luathan guards in the misguided notion she was helping him—she really wasn't that foolhardy or brash—but there was no way Finn or the other Tuann would have helped her.

Which meant there were only a few reasons for her presence here. None of which were the sort you wanted to consider.

"We need to go," she said. "Right now."

Jace didn't argue, picking up on some of her urgency. He looked at his people. "Let's move."

Finn backed into the room quickly. "This way is no longer an option."

"All the windows are guarded," Blue said quickly.

Kira gave the three Tuann a considering look. They'd been so handy in disposing of the first two guards. No reason they couldn't do the same to the ones outside the window.

Finn shook his head, already guessing where her thoughts were going. "I'd like to avoid harming any more Luathans than we already

CHAPTER NINETEEN

have."

"Perhaps now is a good time for you to break down the situation for us," Jace said.

"Maybe later. Suffice it to say, the Tsavitee are here, they're working with the Tuann and all of us are first on their to-do list."

"We knew that," Jace said.

"Not the last part," Blue corrected.

"They're also planning to bring down the defense grid. Tonight," Kira finished.

Jace nodded, his lips tightening. "Good enough. Blue, show them our exit strategy."

"Roger that," Blue said, grabbing several of the items she'd tucked under her leg before scrambling over to a decorative table.

"What are you doing?" Isla asked.

"She's going through the vents," Jin said, sounding impressed.

Blue shot him a crooked smile. "Right you are, Tin Man. They go on for miles and are big enough even Tank can fit through if he doesn't mind crawling."

"The escape tunnels," Finn said thoughtfully. "They're a defensive feature of the Citadel."

"Are they safe to travel through?" Kira asked.

He nodded slowly, his mouth set in a thoughtful frown. "Yes, as long as we don't linger. They're an escape route if the Citadel is overwhelmed and its people need a hidden way out. They've never been used."

"Stupid of Roderick not to have placed someone up there to make sure his prisoners didn't use them," Kira said.

"I doubt he remembers they're there. Most Luathans don't. They've fallen out of fashion."

Isla and Noor traded glances, a faint trace of scorn in their expressions. Kira agreed. A good head of security would have made it his business to search out any potential security threats and neutralize the danger they presented. That he hadn't was good news for them, bad news for the Luathans.

Blue finished fiddling with her device. There was a hissing sound and then the red glowing outline of a square appeared on the ceiling.

Seconds later a giant chunk of it fell to the ground with a crash.

"Let's move, people. They would have heard that," Jace ordered.

Outside Kira could hear the sound of running footsteps as voices shouted in Tuann. The door rattled against the furniture Finn and the other Tuann had secured against it.

Tank and Raider went first followed by Blue and Jace.

"You're next," Finn told her.

"Let the rest through first. I'll bring up the rear."

He gave her a sharp smile. "I don't think so."

Before she could protest, he grabbed her and lifted her easily up to the ceiling. Not willing to argue when they lacked time and because she was already up there, Kira grabbed hold and pulled herself up.

Jin tucked himself in after her, his running lights illuminating the shadowy space.

Jace and the others had already started moving, giving those following room. Kira crawled after them.

Blue and Jin had misled them about the size of the escape tunnels. They were little more than a narrow crawl space, setting off every claustrophobic instinct Kira had.

Her head didn't quite brush the ceiling as she moved forward, but it was close. She couldn't imagine how much worse it was for Tank or the Tuann behind her who both dwarfed her.

"You would think they could have made these a little bigger given how tall they are," Kira muttered as she neared Jace's feet.

"Only children and those who can't fight would have used these," Finn said.

Kira glanced to see if everyone had made it into the ceiling tunnel, but couldn't see past Finn's bulk.

Kira faced ahead again and wiggled forward. They wouldn't be able to stay in these long. Crawling this way took effort and stamina.

CHAPTER NINETEEN

She made it less than the length of one hallway before she had to rest again.

She reached behind her and wrestled with her dress, pulling its length out of the way. Again.

She'd loved the way it had looked when she'd been going to a party. Now, while crawling through a small tunnel, tripping on it every other second, not so much.

There was a loud rip as she tore the bottom off near her knees. That should make moving a little easier.

"Phoenix is getting naked," Raider taunted from up ahead.

"You try crawling around this place lugging a bunch of extra fabric," Kira whisper-hissed back.

There were a couple of chuckles as they all rested. Soft panting filled the air.

"You can see why these fell into disuse," Finn said in a strained voice.

Kira nodded, trying not to feel like the walls were caving in around her. She hated tight spaces. She'd deal, but her stomach would be a tight mass of nerves until she was out.

"We need to get out of these tunnels," Kira said. "They're going to know we're using them. It won't be long before they send people up here to search us out."

They'd traveled several branches already in the short period they'd been up here so it might take a while for Roderick's people to find them. Still, Roderick might get lucky.

"Find us an exit point, Tank," Jace said in a low voice.

There was a low grunt from ahead.

After a few more minutes of crawling, Tank signaled he'd found something. With Finn calling out instructions on how to find the access panel, they didn't have to resort to burning their way out.

Kira lowered herself into a deserted room, the Curs having already secured it. She dropped to the floor and straightened, looking around in curiosity. Beakers and oddly shaped items were strewn throughout.

Raider folded his arms and leaned against a table, crossing his ankles. "What's the game plan? Do you have one?"

All eyes turned toward Kira, identical questions in their expressions.

She rubbed her hands on the remnants of her dress, thinking.

"Step one was making sure you weren't a stationary target," she said. "I'm working on step two."

"We could steal a ship. Fly it out of here," Raider suggested.

Noor snorted. "This isn't one of those human holovids. Stealing a Tuann ship isn't that easy or else your kind would have dozens of them by now."

"The ships are coded to us," Finn said quietly. "You won't be able to even open the doors let alone get one off the ground."

"Not to mention the defense grid would shoot any unauthorized ship that took off from the planet," Noor said.

"What about this defense grid you say these people plan to bring down?" Blue said, tilting her head.

"There's an idea," Jace said.

The Tuann frowned in confusion.

"What is?" Isla asked.

"We wait until it falls and then we fly ourselves out of here," he said, folding his arms over his chest.

"You lack a ship," Finn reminded him.

"But we have you," Jace pointed out.

Raider straightened, an evil grin lighting up his face. "And as you said, the ships are coded to your kind."

"I'm needed here," Finn said through gritted teeth. "I have no intention of helping you escape."

Raider watched Finn carefully, his expression considering.

"Don't even think it," Kira warned.

The rest looked at her.

"You attack him, and you'll have to deal with me," she told Raider.

CHAPTER NINETEEN

"That's if these three don't kick your ass first."

Raider made a tsking sound before settling.

"Some loyalty you have there," Noor said, eyeing the human with dislike. "We're the reason you escaped."

"Don't fool yourselves," Raider said. "We had an exit strategy within fifteen minutes of being placed under guard."

"This isn't our fight," Blue said bluntly. "It's yours. Can't blame us for wanting to make it home in one piece."

"Your people have certainly done the same in our place," Tank observed. "Or did you forget how four of your kind snuck out of Atlas during the bombing. They could have helped those people. They didn't because they deemed their own safety more important."

The Tuann glared at the humans.

Kira stepped in before things could degenerate further. "You're not going to overpower these three, so give it up."

Jace's expression darkened. She took it as a good sign when he didn't argue. It meant he hadn't been seriously considering that path.

"But it does make sense to split up," Kira continued. "I know Himoto has a ship out there. Signal it and let them know what's happening. We may have need of them. If nothing else, they can send a drop ship for you if things get too heated."

Jace's nod was grudging. He'd probably have come up with the plan himself if he wasn't so bent on antagonizing the Tuann

"Send one of your people as guide with the Curs. The rest of us will find Graydon and warn him," Kira said. She looked at Finn. "You're so convinced he won't betray us—prove it."

Finn nodded, flicking his fingers at the other two. Kira waited as they dipped their heads in agreement.

The two groups began splitting apart as they prepared to separate.

Jace walked toward her. He hesitated when he reached her, his back to the Tuann. "What will you be doing while the rest of us are trying to prevent an invasion?"

Kira debated how much to tell him. In the end, she decided to keep

337

her plans to herself. There was too much risk he'd try to stop her. "I'll be doing the same."

The look he bent on her said he didn't believe her, but he didn't plan on wasting time by arguing.

"Good luck with whatever scheme you've cooked up," he said.

"You too," Kira said. "Try to make it out of this in one piece."

He gave her a crooked smile. "Somehow I think you'll be the one in more danger."

True.

Jace didn't move for a long moment. Kira could tell he wanted to say something and waited, her expression curious but patient.

He sighed and shook his head. "Try not to die or disappear again. There are things I need to say to you."

She didn't speak for several moments, her throat tight with suppressed emotion. She jerked her head in an affirmative.

He nodded, hiding any emotion before ducking his head outside the door and looking each way.

"Coast is clear. We're Oscar Mike."

Blue and Tank followed seconds after him.

Raider stopped next to her. He sighed and shook his head. "You don't have to do whatever you're planning."

Kira's smile was humorless. "Yeah, I kind of do. I have promises to keep."

He gave her a long look before sighing again. He adjusted the makeshift pack he was carrying and started to follow the rest.

"Raider," Kira said before she could stop herself.

He looked at her, the normal sly sarcasm there in his expression.

"Keep your head on the swivel," she said. It was what they'd told each other every time they left on a mission. It was a reminder to stay alert and on task, and not take stupid risks.

"Try to keep your powder dry." He gave her a small chin jerk before stepping through the doorway, his posture changing to wary alertness as he disappeared after the rest of the Curs.

CHAPTER NINETEEN

Noor stole after him, the *oshota*'s passage silent.

She stayed where she was, wishing she could go with them, while realizing it never got easier sending your team into danger.

At least, she wasn't sending them onto a battlefield this time.

CHAPTER TWENTY

Finn and Isla conferred in quiet voices behind Kira, their voices a low buzz of sound as they discussed their options. She wasn't overly surprised when neither thought to include her. She might have taken charge when the Curs were there, but now that they were out of the equation again, the Tuann had slipped back to treating her like a pretty ornament—something she would never be.

That was all right. She could follow their lead for now. They were more familiar with the terrain and more likely to have an idea of what they faced.

Kira waited with Jin, keeping watch, even though it was a mostly unnecessary exercise.

Finn and Isla were intent on each other as they discussed options. She suspected their single-minded focus was an illusion. Both were well-trained soldiers. It would be ingrained in them to keep a situational awareness at all times.

She had no doubt that if she were to take a single step toward the door, they'd drop what they were doing and tackle her. They'd probably end up tying her to them afterward—not that she had any intention of disappearing into the Citadel. Not for the moment at least.

Finn looked up then, as if sensing her thoughts.

"What's the plan?" Kira asked, trying for innocent.

"Neither of you can show your faces," Isla said, her face grave. "Roderick's men will guess who helped the humans escape. They'll be

CHAPTER TWENTY

on the lookout for you. As soon as you're spotted, you'll be arrested for treason against your House."

"And you'll somehow escape the same fate?" Kira asked. Isla was right there with them when they'd rescued Jace's team. She'd be as recognizable.

She and Finn shared a look of amusement. "I'm not Luathan. All they see when they look at me is my armor. They'll know two of the commander's people helped in the escape but not which two."

"You're taking a chance they won't arrest all his people on sight," Kira said.

Despite her argument, Isla's assessment matched hers. She doubted Alma and the other conspirator realized she'd eavesdropped on their plans. They'd think the Curs' escape worked in their favor—odd timing or not.

If she was caught and immobilized, her credibility would be stripped and they could easily kill her. Freeing the Curs had made her situation more precarious, but it was worth it.

"Some risks are worth taking," Isla said as if reading her mind.

Finn offered his hand to Isla. The two clasped hands before slapping each other on the shoulder.

"I'll see you when this is done," Finn told her.

"I look forward to it. Don't forget you still owe me a drink," Isla said before slipping out the door without a backward glance.

Kira waited, her senses straining for signs Isla had been spotted. Clear so far.

"What will we be doing while she's locating Graydon?"

"*You* will stay close and follow my every order," Finn said, the words terse. "If I could, I'd secure you somewhere safe."

His dissatisfaction over not being able to do exactly that showed.

Once the Tsavitee battle cruiser landed and the planet descended into a warzone, there would be no safe place left.

"That still doesn't answer my question," Kira said.

Finn's voice was grim. "There's a chance Graydon is no longer at the ceremony. He's probably noticed your absence and has gone in search of you. While Isla checks the gathering, we'll try other places."

"And me? What should I do?" Jin asked. He did a figure eight in the air. "I can scout ahead or manage comms."

Finn jabbed his finger at Jin and then Kira. "Stay with her. Don't go wandering off. In fact, how about you stay quiet for a little bit."

Jin's sphere dipped in disappointment. "Rude."

Finn shook his head at Jin before checking outside the door to see if anyone was coming. With one last disgusted look at the drone, he made his way silently out into the hallway.

Jin tucked himself into the crook between Kira's neck and shoulder, his metal casing warm and comforting against her skin as she followed Finn.

"Just like old times," Jin whispered.

"Let's hope we don't leave behind the same body count," Kira said.

The three remained silent as they moved through the Citadel. This wasn't the time for idle chitchat or distractions.

The last time Finn had given her a tour of the Citadel, the artwork and carefully designed architecture had seemed coldly impersonal, despite its beauty. Tonight, it felt like those same statues and paintings watched Kira's every move, setting the spot right between her shoulder blades to tingling. She could almost anticipate the cold metal of a blade in her back.

Every twist and turn of their path came with an increased feeling of pending disaster, a perfect place from which to stage an ambush.

Tension sat heavy in the air. In war, you got used to the never-ending strain as you waited for the next awful thing to happen. You learned to ignore the ever-increasing tightening of your nerve endings as your entire body attuned itself to the possibility of what was coming.

Himoto had once called war ninety percent boredom so extreme you'd do anything for relief and ten percent sheer, unrelenting terror.

By now, everyone in the Citadel likely knew of her betrayal. They

CHAPTER TWENTY

would come looking for her, if they weren't already. All she could do was wait and hope she survived the ten percent of terror.

Kira was content to let Finn take the lead, remaining several feet behind him. His knowledge of the terrain was greater than hers. It made sense for her to follow.

As they approached another intersection where their hallway joined with several others, Kira's shoulders tightened, her senses hyper-alert.

Finn held up one fist, signaling a stop.

She nodded, placing her back against the wall so she could see in both directions. She remained in place as he disappeared around the corner.

She held her breath, straining to pick up even the faintest of sounds. She released the air when there wasn't an immediate furor. Good, that meant the coast was clear—for now.

"If you're going to put your plan into motion, the time is now," Jin said into her ear, several minutes later. "There are four heat signatures moving toward us from our three o'clock."

Kira hesitated, torn.

Finn rounded the corner. "Run."

Kira didn't wait to be told twice, turning and sprinting back the way they'd come. Jin flew before her, taking the lead, Finn pounding after them.

"This way," Jin yelled.

Kira followed, the sound of pursuit spurring her to greater speeds.

There was a screech of sound and then long, needle-thin arrows of green blazed down the hall. One hit inches from Kira's face as she made another turn. It burrowed into the wall leaving a thin pinhole behind.

She chanced a glance behind her, catching a glimpse of a woman in green synth armor adopting an archer's posture, holding a strange-looking contraption. In her left hand, she had a long-curved piece of wood. It looked like the front of a bow but lacked a string. As Kira watched, the woman drew back her right hand, energy coalescing at a point in front of her pointer finger until a long thin energy arrow took shape.

So that was what was being shot at her the first night.

Finn shoved her out of the way as the arrow flew free, shattering against the wall.

"Move," Finn yelled.

Kira scrambled to her feet and darted after Jin.

He disappeared between a set of double doors. Kira dashed after him, Finn close on her heels.

He whirled, slamming the doors shut behind them.

"Go, I'll hold them here," he said.

Kira hesitated. It didn't feel right leaving him to face them alone.

"Kira, come on," Jin yelled.

Her mouth firmed.

"Go, these two won't be a problem for me if you're not here to protect," Finn snarled.

"Since you're being an ass, have it your way," Kira said. She turned to leave, saying over her shoulder. "Try not to die. Otherwise, I'll have to make sure all the other *oshotas* know a few puny Luathans brought you down."

"Smartass," was his faint response as Kira jogged after Jin, a cold rock in her stomach despite the levity.

Only minutes passed before there was a giant crash and then a roar that told her the Luathans had made it through the doors.

Kira didn't try to be quiet as she pelted after Jin, the need for distance and speed outweighing the desire for subtlety.

She was lost within minutes as he led her through a maze of rooms, through halls and courtyards, and over more than one sloped roof.

Her legs burned as she followed, sprinting toward a garden retaining wall, running up it and grabbing the top. She pulled herself up, dashing along it as Jin took another shortcut.

Reaching the end of the wall, she leaped off it, trusting him to warn

CHAPTER TWENTY

her of danger. She landed, turning her forward momentum into a roll.

She found her feet again before sprinting down a stone walkway sheltered by an arboretum covered in pale, silvery flowers.

Jin paused at a set of doors leading to a glass-covered conservatory before moving inside. Kira cautiously followed.

It was a greenhouse, similar to what she'd come across on Graydon's ship. The darkness inside, coupled with the vines crawling up the walls and the overgrown trees and plants, shielded her from the outside, while giving her a 360-degree view.

"Where are we?" Kira asked, catching her breath as he made a circuit of the room.

"A little spot I discovered. From what I can tell, it's mostly abandoned. I've only ever seen one person visit, and that person wasn't a warrior. We should be safe enough for now," Jin said.

Kira spied a change of clothes on one of the workbenches tucked to the side. She headed over to them, shrugging out of the rags of her dress. Much as she loved the dress, she needed attire more suitable for fighting.

"How far are we from the Nexus?" Her voice was muffled as she pulled the shirt over her head. Her head popped out of the collar.

"Not far as I fly. It'll take longer for you given your big body."

Kira rolled her eyes before pulling on her pants.

"Why?" he asked, suspicion threading through his voice.

"Because that's where we need to go. If they intend to bring down the defense network, the Nexus is the best place to do it from," she said.

It was time to go on the offensive. Enough running around the Citadel searching for Graydon. There were too many buildings. They'd never find him in time.

If they wanted a chance at stopping the Tsavitee attack, they needed to go straight to the source.

Jin let out a gusty wheeze. "Why is it your asks are never easy?"

"Face it, if they were, you'd get bored."

He'd probably end up destroying half of civilization as a result.

"You keep telling yourself that, Kira. Somehow, I don't think it's me in danger of boredom," he muttered, trailing behind her as she left the glass building.

* * *

Finding the Nexus was easy. Not a single patrol hindered their progress.

The lack of security made her anxious. If she'd been in charge of security, she would have sealed the Nexus—the military command hub of the Citadel—first.

This didn't make sense, Kira thought as they approached the unguarded door to the Nexus. Its large frame reached for the ceiling high above. There were no signs of the Luathans anywhere.

Roderick might have been lazy and slightly dumb, but even he couldn't have been this inept. Right?

"What do you want to do?" Jin asked, no happier at the ease of their passage than her.

"I don't think we have a choice, do you?"

His silence was answer enough.

Kira pushed the heavy door open a crack and peered through. Inside was as deserted as the hallway.

Curiouser and curiouser.

She slipped inside, careful to keep her movements smooth and silent.

The emptiness of the massive room felt oppressive, like even her surroundings waited with bated breath for something horrible.

"I don't like this," Jin stage whispered.

Neither did Kira.

"Did you ever find it unattended during your patrols?" Kira asked, taking in their surroundings.

CHAPTER TWENTY

The room, like the rest of the Citadel, was one of incomparable beauty. Cathedral ceilings arched overhead, paintings and carvings drawing the eye up. Elegant columns marched down either side of the massive space and in the middle, two stone steps led to a sunken section of the floor in the shape of an octagon, a pattern etched into it.

The shape of the octagon was mirrored overhead by gold lines that intersected and weaved into a dizzying pattern that looped in on itself like a kaleidoscope if one stared at it too long.

Like much of the Citadel, there was an overwhelming feeling of airy lightness, the stones in the columns and floors white and flawless. An impressive feat given the lack of windows.

At least now she knew if there'd been a battle, the evidence of it would be written all over this room. Blood would have stood out in stark relief against all the white.

Kira took all this in from her place next to the door. She was careful not to intrude deeper into the room until she'd assured herself they were really alone, and no invisible assailants waited behind those columns.

The room felt almost holy, the air still and somber, silent as if unnecessary noise feared intruding. A great well of power crouched beneath the surface, deep and vast and mind-bendingly ancient. Kira could see now why it was called the Nexus. It was the meeting point between the planet's soul and the surface, reality stretching and bending until it felt like you could reach out and touch the intangible with little effort. She hadn't felt the Mea'Ave so vividly since her first encounter.

It was unlike anything she'd ever experienced, and she got the feeling if she didn't tread cautiously it would be the last thing she ever did.

"No, never," Jin said, answering her previous question. "There's always at least two guards posted inside the room and two outside."

Which meant someone with the authority would have had to recall the guards from their post. Something Kira found unlikely. The first general order any soldier learned was a variation of "I will guard everything within the limits of my post and only quit my post when properly relieved."

It was part of a set of rules sentries through the ages had abided by—long before humanity had spread through the stars, when it was a collection of countries at war with each other. The basic order's wisdom had endured for good reason.

Kira couldn't see the Tuann being any different. You didn't abandon the military command center of your base for any reason short of death.

Either the guards on duty were part of the conspiracy or something tragic had happened to them.

Both instances would have resulted in enemy combatants taking control of the Nexus.

Instead, it lay empty. Stranger and stranger.

"Hello, anyone here?" Kira called. "The door was open."

"What are you doing?" Jin hissed.

"They wouldn't have just abandoned this place," Kira said distractedly as she moved further into the room.

"Instead you decide to announce our presence to whoever might be waiting to kill us?"

She shrugged. "No one answered. I think we're safe."

"Unbelievable," Jin muttered. "I'd like to say I'm surprised, but nothing you do surprises me anymore."

Kira ignored his grumbling as she moved deeper into the room, not bothering to step lightly as her footsteps echoed in the large space. There were no soft surfaces to muffle the noise of her passage. The acoustics were amazing. A choir singing from the sunken section would sound like they had the voices of angels as their music reverberated through the space.

She approached the octagon and walked a long circuit around it as she eyed the two steps leading to it.

CHAPTER TWENTY

If she remembered correctly, this spot was where Liara had been standing when she was looking at the starmaps.

How did it work?

Kira saw no evidence of controls, and no way to manipulate it. It was an octagon someone had sunk into the floor.

The presence of the Mea'Ave strengthened the closer to the octagon she got, the pressure from the planet squeezing Kira's mind under its immense weight.

"I don't suppose you caught a glimpse of how to work this thing in your snooping," Kira said, straightening from where she'd bent to take a look at the floor.

"I may have seen something of that nature," Jin said nonchalantly.

Kira's glare told him to get on with it.

He made another grumbling sound and then a hologram appeared in front of him. Liara stepped onto the floor and raised her hands, her mouth opening as she sang several low notes. The air around her shimmered before stars spun into view.

Jin's hologram faded.

"That's it? That's all you've got?"

"What else do you need?"

"I don't know—something useful."

"I can't do everything for you," he shot back. "You figured out how the Tsavitee ships worked. I have faith you can do this too."

Kira's snarl would have once made junior enlisted military members quail. Jin didn't flinch.

"You're a pain in the ass," she said.

"Then we're a matched pair."

Kira muttered about insolent scraps of junk as she studied the sunken floor.

She didn't step onto it. Not yet at least. There was a possibility of hidden traps designed to attack unauthorized users. If this had been a Tsavitee ship, she would have counted on it.

Acting rashly could trigger an alert of a breach to their system.

Kira rubbed her hands together as she considered her options. If she'd had the time and an attack wasn't imminent, she'd spend several days studying this setup, testing and probing to see its reactions.

Time was the one thing she didn't have.

She bit her lip as she considered stepping into the space and just seeing what happened.

A hard hand grabbed her arm and jerked her to a stop just as she had psyched herself up to take that final step.

Graydon's furious eyes glittered at her. "Mistake. The Mea'Ave would fry your mind as soon it realized you weren't the Overlord or her heir."

Kira looked from him to the octagon in dismay.

"Good advice," she finally said.

She let him pull her back several steps. She sighed in relief before trying to remove her arm from his grip. His hand tightened to the point of pain.

His harsh expression finally registered. There was none of the warmth or heated promise from earlier in the night. She couldn't see the resigned annoyance that had characterized their first exchanges.

Instead, she saw a glittering hardness, diamond-like, lacking any trace of emotion besides fury.

Something was wrong. She knew this look, had been on the receiving end before by those she trusted.

A tight ball formed in her stomach.

It was the type of stare you gave someone when you realized they weren't the person you thought they were, when you found out they'd betrayed you on such a fundamental level there was no hope of forgiveness.

Graydon's jaw clenched so hard she feared he might crack a tooth.

Her gaze went over his shoulder. "Where's Isla? Didn't she come with you?"

Graydon's frown deepened as he asked, "Now, why would she have come looking for me when she had orders to stand watch over your

CHAPTER TWENTY

friends?"

"Ah." That explained it.

He cocked his head, fury deepening in his expression as his voice lowered ominously, sinking a wealth of fury into his words. "I've got it. Perhaps because you attacked the Luathans and freed their prisoners."

"I take it she didn't get the chance to warn you about the Tsavitee attack under way," Kira guessed.

This could complicate things.

Graydon let loose a sound dangerously close to a growl, a low rumble warning people to escape before the cold grip of death came for them.

Kira stayed where she was, fascinated in spite of herself, at the way his eyes darkened as he visibly battled for control.

"I have proof," Kira offered when it looked like he might give in to his urge to throttle her.

"That would be lovely," he said through gritted teeth. "But first, we need to get you out of here. If the Luathans catch you here, they'll execute you."

He didn't give her time to argue, forcibly marching her toward the door.

"But—"

Graydon ignored her protest.

She craned her neck to look at Jin. "A little warning would have been nice."

"I didn't sense his approach. He somehow fooled my sensors."

Kira stared at the side of Graydon's face. It would have been handy to know how the Tuann kept doing that.

"We can't leave," Kira said, struggling to escape Graydon's grip. It wasn't easy, especially since she didn't want to risk hurting him or further escalating the situation.

After an aborted movement, she gave up. His fingers were like bands of steel, tight and unbending unless she planned on breaking

351

them.

"Graydon, listen to me. There is a Tsavitee warship waiting outside the system. Someone is trying to bring down the defense network so they can land." Kira fought to slow his progress, desperation tinging her voice. "Unless we do something, people are going to die."

He turned to her, his nostrils flared. "Do you understand what they'll do to you if they catch you in here?"

Kira stared at him. It dawned on her he might be furious for reasons that hadn't occurred to her. That maybe it wasn't as simple as him assuming she'd betrayed him.

"Does that matter, if we can save them?" she asked. It was the only response she could think of.

She was no martyr. She had no intention of sacrificing herself for the Tuann. She'd seen too many people die, carried their souls on her own. She wouldn't dishonor them by throwing her life away recklessly.

Those same souls would rip her apart when she met them in the afterlife if she didn't try everything in her power to stop this, not when they'd sacrificed their lives on similar causes.

Eternity stretched between them as he studied her.

"Show me your proof."

Relief fluttered in her chest.

He was giving her a chance. That was all. She'd have to make it count.

"Jin."

Jin played the recording without any further prompting.

Kira took the time to study Graydon as he watched it. His expression remained closed, giving her no hint to his thoughts beyond a slight tightening along his jaw.

"You're here to see if the defense network has been tampered with," he said flatly.

She nodded. "Close enough."

He released a frustrated breath. "That is an excellent plan. Truly."

CHAPTER TWENTY

She sensed sarcasm in that statement as he pinched the bridge of his nose before looking at her.

"You have no clue how it works. It takes talent along with years of training to handle the stress it places on the mind."

Kira's lips firmed.

He nodded at Jin. "Your drone can handle a hundred tetrabytes of information at a time, right?"

"Two hundred," Jin boasted.

"The melding sends double that every second. Even if you'd succeeded in not killing yourself within seconds, you would have activated the secondary defenses."

Kira frowned pensively before shrugging. "I'd have figured something out. If nothing else, we would have waited for the traitors to show themselves. Killing them would have worked just as well."

"Yes, and you would have been executed immediately after. Brilliant plan," he snarled.

"I would have stopped the attack. I count that as a win." She gave him a thin smile. "You seem to think I'm easy to kill. I'm not."

"This is a true statement," Jin agreed. "She's like a cockroach, only hardier."

Graydon didn't react to that statement, never taking his attention off Kira as he scowled at her.

"A hundred different ways to address this and you chose the most dangerous," he muttered.

"Also, a trait of hers," Jin pointed out. "You get used to it."

"Are you going to help or continue to poke holes in this plan?" Kira asked Graydon, lifting her chin.

He curled his lip. "Follow me."

Graydon approached the octagon, stopping on the first step and going no further. He raised his hand, his forehead creasing with strain.

Before him a field of stars came into view, some dull and faded, others bright and almost blinding.

"Woah," she said, looking around her in awe.

The stars zoomed by as Graydon played with it.

"There, that's the Tsavitee ship," Kira said, pointing.

It was barely noticeable, an easily overlooked blip if she hadn't suspected its presence.

"It's heading toward the planet," Kira said.

Probably the only reason they caught it.

Graydon muttered several unfavorable curses.

"What about the defense network?" Jin asked urgently. "Can you tell if it's been tampered with?"

"No, I don't have access."

"Not even as the Emperor's Face?" Jin asked.

"Every House maintains their section of the defense network. Their codes vary. Under normal circumstances I could demand access, but there is little chance of that, given what you've done."

It was a dig at Kira. One she ignored, focused as she was on studying Graydon's motions and the stars in front of her.

The technology was cerebral based, relying on the strength of the mind controlling it. Fascinating. There must be some type of mechanism to prevent just anybody from accessing it. Maybe it was programmed to recognize brain patterns or the DNA of those coded into it.

The planet's spirit pulsed under her, its strength sending lancing pain through her head.

Graydon made several small motions and the starfield faded, a schematic taking its place.

"Is this one of the schematics for the defense net?" she asked.

He studied it with a resigned expression. "Yes, I asked to be shown the last thing accessed and this was what was pulled up."

"They wouldn't have something like that up unless they were doing a system or weapons check," Jin said, drifting closer to the hologram.

"Stay out of the octagon," Graydon warned. "You're as likely to be fried as her."

CHAPTER TWENTY

Jin backed up several feet. "Of course. My bad."

"I doubt they would have done a systems check so close to the ceremony. Not with so many high ranking Luathans here," he said, returning to their conversation.

Which meant this was probably the work of their enemy.

He stepped from the platform, slight beads of sweat dotting his forehead.

"Are you all right?" Kira asked.

"Manipulating the melding is more of a Luathan talent. I've never had a knack for it," he said, straightening, the brief flash of weakness already gone.

"Let's go," he said.

"Wait, we're not done. We haven't determined the extent of the damage," Kira protested.

"I've confirmed your theory. We need to leave before anyone finds us here."

"It's too late for that," Liara said from the doorway.

She stepped further into the room, her guards swarming into the room behind her, cutting off their exit.

CHAPTER TWENTY-ONE

"Again?" Kira muttered, glaring at Jin.

He made a strangled noise, managing to sound both sheepish and defensive at the same time. "Don't blame me. They obviously have some sort of technology to block my sensors."

"Uh-huh." She let her voice show how much stock she put into his excuse.

"Focus," Graydon muttered, not taking his attention from the others.

Liara strode forward, her face set in the icy, haughty expression Kira remembered from their first meeting. "Cousin, I'm disappointed. I opened my House to you, welcomed you to my family, yet you betray me at the first opportunity."

"She does know Graydon essentially kidnapped you; not to mention you've survived two assassination attempts since arriving, right?" Jin muttered.

Kira ignored him, too busy watching Liara's soldiers, considering and discarding a dozen different scenarios.

"I warned you to be careful of snakes in the grass," Alma said, appearing from behind Liara. Her eyes were filled with scorn as she looked Kira over. Kira was sure she was the only one to spot the glint of victory in Alma's eyes. "Nothing good ever comes of raising serpents. They always bite you in the end."

"You'd be one to know," Kira said.

Alma didn't respond to the insult as she turned to Graydon. "We will send you to your emperor in pieces as an example. After you, he

CHAPTER TWENTY-ONE

will know Luatha won't stand for his meddling. Your betrayal will be the spark that turns the rest from him."

Kira pressed her lips together at the threat. Graydon didn't move, motionless as he watched the Luathans.

Kira needed to do something before the Nexus erupted into violence and they lost any chance of convincing Liara of the truth.

"Jin, if you'd be so kind."

"Gladly," Jin said, gliding forward. The recording started up.

A harsh buzz ripped through the room. Electricity crackled and Jin gave a pained grunt. He hit the ground with a crash, his metal body bouncing before going still.

"Jin," Kira screamed, fear coating her throat.

For a long terrifying second, she couldn't feel the slight shadow of a presence in the back of her mind she associated with him, a thin thread barely noticeable most of the time. Right now, the connection vibrated with pain, the wounds of the weapon leaving it raw and exposed.

An eternity of agony lay before her as she faced the thought he was gone—forever beyond her grasp in the afterlife.

Darkness yawned wide inside. The thin bindings keeping her monster from laying waste to everything and everyone threatened to snap.

She forgot who she was, forgot the honorable person she fought to be. All she knew was rage and vengeance.

The transformation tingled along her skin, pain biting deep as she struggled to contain it. Her blood heated and the urge to kill her enemies gnawed at her.

The connection snapped into place. Kira could feel Jin again, hurt and scared, but alive.

She took a deep breath and settled, physically shaking herself as she grabbed for the gossamer-thin tendrils of composure.

When she opened her eyes again, her vision wasn't red-tinged and she no longer thirsted for destruction.

She stared at Ayela's sweet face, innocent and serene where she stood over Jin's body. The woman didn't know it yet, but she was already dead.

"What did you do to him?" Kira asked calmly.

She amused herself by envisioning leaping across the small distance and grabbing Ayela by the throat. In her imagination, she tore Ayela's deceitful head from her shoulders before kicking it across the room.

Graydon and Liara stared at her, awareness in their gazes, both sensing how close they'd come to dying.

"I defended my Overlord by removing the threat," Ayela said with a peaceful smile. "I couldn't let the abomination endanger her."

Kira sucked in another breath. In and out. In and out.

Killing Ayela fast was too good for her. Better to draw it out. Kira could rip her arms off, one at a time, then each leg. Ayela's screams would be glorious music.

When she finally grew tired of the sound of Ayela's suffering, she could rip out her tongue.

Only after she'd exacted every ounce of revenge and left the woman a quivering mess of insanity would she kill her.

"Your advisers are plotting against you," Kira said, the very lack of emotion in her voice a warning.

Graydon shifted so he was partially facing her as well as Liara's people. He suspected what she was.

She ignored him, not finding it in herself to care.

Right now, the objective was simple. Inform Liara of the impending attack then kill Ayela.

"Enough of these lies," Alma said impatiently. She nodded at Roderick.

Kira's muscles coiled with readiness.

"Hold," Graydon snapped. To Liara, he said, "Why were no *oshota* guarding the Nexus?"

Liara hesitated, unease touching her expression.

A slice of Kira's bloodthirstiness eased. There might be a way out

CHAPTER TWENTY-ONE

of this.

Ayela shifted closer as Kira ignored her. The other woman wouldn't be so foolhardy to attempt something without her overlord's command.

Kira waited, watching Liara expectantly as the other woman worked through the different possibilities and the tension in the room lessened.

Ayela shifted again, bringing her arm up. Pain blazed through Kira, fire sizzling her nerve endings. She hit the ground with her knees, her mouth opened on a silent scream.

The world around her turned to white noise as agony surged through her nerves again. Indescribable pain ate at her until she became aware again, her face pressed against the stone, her body convulsing slightly.

Stupid mistake, Kira. Not seeing Ayela as a threat even after what she'd done to Jin.

Gradually the sound of an argument came into focus as she smacked her lips together, the dull taste of copper in her mouth.

"Try it again, and I'll separate your head from your shoulders," Graydon threatened in a silky voice.

"I'm doing what's in the best interests of my Overlord," Ayela said politely. She pointed the weapon at Kira, preparing to fire again.

Graydon roared as he charged. He reached Ayela and struck, his fist crashing into her chest. Ayela's body crumpled under the blow, flying backward.

Kira knew that voice. She recognized it. Ayela was the unknown conspirator from earlier. How had she missed that before?

Liara and Alma argued near her.

"They pulled up the defense network. They must have planned to bring it down," Alma said. "We need to reset the key to ensure its safety."

"There's no way they got in. Neither one of them are coded into the system," Liara argued.

"She shares the same blood as you," Alma snapped. "Her tie to the Mea'Ave is strong despite her long absence. She's more human than Tuann. There's no telling what dirty tricks she's capable of."

Liara was quiet as she considered Alma's words.

Kira tried to sit up, to speak over the buzzing of her ears. Her entire head rang from whatever Ayela had done to her. Even her vision was slightly fuzzy.

"Don't," she croaked, the word almost soundless.

She rolled onto her stomach. It took her three tries to push herself upright. She reached out, knowing before she touched him, it was Graydon standing over her, his legs spread as he protected her prone form.

She blinked up at a blurry Graydon. "Trap."

Realization donned as he noticed the two women near the octagon, he shouted, "Wait."

His warning came too late. Liara stepped into the octagon. Lights shot from her, coalescing into thousands of symbols dotting the space around the Overlord.

"It's done. The codes have been changed," Liara said in relief.

Not good. Not good at all.

Kira struggled to stand. A hard blow on her shoulder sent her to the ground again.

"Stay where you are, traitor," one of Roderick's men said.

"Touch her again and I'll tear your arms from their sockets and beat you with them," Graydon threatened.

"Sir, the Emperor's Face is impeding our orders."

Roderick looked over, his expression unsurprised. "Deal with him accordingly."

Kira stiffened, Graydon tensing next to her.

Battle cries pierced the air as men and women in black synth armor poured into the room.

Suddenly the numbers were even, Luatha's people fighting for their lives as they tried to contend with Graydon at their front and his

CHAPTER TWENTY-ONE

warriors at their backs.

Amila and Solal surged through the clamor to appear beside Graydon.

"I hope this means you accomplished your mission," Amila said with a sassy smirk.

"That and more," Graydon responded, catching a blow on his forearm before bringing one fist on his opponent's shoulder. The man crashed to the ground.

"Good, maybe we can go back to civilization then," Solal grumbled. He sidestepped as a man rushed him, sinking the pommel of his sword into the man's head, knocking him unconscious.

"And Kira?" Amila asked.

"Bring her. She's the reason we're going home," Graydon said from where he tangled with three soldiers.

Easier said than done as the Nexus descended into chaos.

Graydon's people were better trained, but outnumbered five to one. They were also hampered by the fact they weren't trying to kill their opponents, opting to disarm or knock unconscious those attacking them.

The Luathans weren't under the same constraints.

Graydon roared as he challenged three warriors, his form lithe as a cat as he toyed with them.

Armor crunched on one as Graydon sank his weight behind a kick. He whirled catching the other guard's hand, before jerking him close as he picked him up and threw him at another.

In the melee, Kira lost track of Liara and Alma.

Kira stood, her limbs shaky, the furor of the fight all around her. She waited, not joining in the fight.

Graydon had the Luathans handled. She needed to find the instigators of this little debacle if she truly wanted this to end.

She turned and nearly ran into one of the cloaked strangers. She ducked, evading his grasp.

"*Azala*, you need to come with us," Silas said, his expression urgent.

"There's a lot of things I need; that's not one of them." Kira backed slowly away from the two as they spread out to trap her.

Graydon and the rest were busy with the Luathan guards, leaving her on her own.

A woman cried out in pain. All fighting in the Nexus ground to a halt.

"Liara!" Roderick screamed, starting toward his Overlord.

A thrum filled the air. A thin sheet of shimmering light bisected the room, cutting him off from his Overlord.

Graydon surged forward, grabbing Roderick around the neck and yanking him to a stop. Kira and the rest had no chance to evade as sheets of light surrounded them, creating a large box around the battling Tuann. The Tuann went from fighting each other to eyeing their prison of light with shock and dismay.

"A Caldon field," Kira murmured, holding her hand up to the light. The barest tingle warned her. Try to push past that tingle and unimaginable pain would shoot through her. Push a little further and it would burn her flesh until nothing was left.

"This is Tsavitee tech," Silas said thoughtfully.

Amila came to stand beside her, her eyes wide, a hint of fear in them.

Graydon's face was furious as he paced a line along the wall of light.

The only Tuann not in the light cage were Alma, Ayela, and Liara.

Alma looked around her in horror, her expression slack as she stared at the rest of them, trapped like flies in amber.

Guess Kira didn't have to ask herself whether Alma knew the full extent of Ayela's plan.

A pained sound escaped Liara as Alma supported her, huddling over her Overlord protectively. Liara touched her shoulder, grimacing as her hand came away bright red with blood.

"What is the meaning of this?" Alma demanded, as she stared at Ayela.

Ayela smiled at her, the expression no less serene than when she'd

CHAPTER TWENTY-ONE

addressed Kira. "The final phase of our plan."

"This wasn't part of my plan," Alma snapped. "The Overlord wasn't supposed to get hurt."

Ayela shrugged. "Maybe not your plan, but this was always my end goal. Thank you for resetting the defense codes. The Tsavitee waiting in the ship above will be very pleased about that. Won't they, pet?"

"As you say, mistress." A Tsavitee warrior stepped into view.

Shock and horror devastated Alma's expression as she faced the full extent of her betrayal. Somehow, the seneschal had believed she could turn the situation to her advantage, Kira knew. Now she was learning the error of her ways.

Kira focused on the Tsavitee. A general. Damn. That wasn't good. This operation must have been important to his superiors for them to send him. The Tsavitee rulers fielded the generals only when absolutely necessary.

He towered over the others, his form massive and built for power and speed. Kira knew he'd be fast and deadly. He had skin as dark as the void; the red symbols etched into one side of his chest proclaiming his rank and status.

What was he doing here? She'd only ever seen them leading invasions, content and safe on their ships as they directed the lower form Tsavitee.

"A Tsavitee," Silas said. "I was wondering what that stench was."

"Not just one." Kira's voice was soft. "That's a general. They wouldn't have sent him alone."

The stranger gave her a sideways glance. "Yes, I can see you're right."

More Tsavitee stepped into view. All of them much smaller than the first.

For all a general's individual strength, his primary purpose among the Tsavitee was to act as the military strategist behind the rest.

Because of that, he was the most dangerous person in the room.

The others might be vicious and savage, but ultimately, they were dumb. Left on their own, they'd probably have killed off their species.

It was only when the general and those above directed them in battle, they became a true threat.

It's what made the hierarchy of the Tsavitee horde so interesting. They weren't just one species but many.

There were several theories on how that occurred. Some thought they'd integrated conquered races into their horde, while others believed the Tsavitee high forms had engineered the lower forms to fit their specific purposes and roles.

The last argument was supported by the fact the DNA between all forms except the generals was strikingly similar. It pointed to a common origin.

Which theory was true didn't really matter. The end result was the same—a military force capable of breeding soldiers with enhanced combat skills faster than humans could keep up.

Kira knew some on the human side toyed with the notion of developing their own enhanced soldiers, bred specifically to fight the Tsavitee. There were rumors they'd started testing their theories.

All that stopped once the treaties with the Haldeel and the Tuann were signed. The treaties made it clear any further genetic modification for the purposes of war was forbidden and would result in full-on war with both.

"Cannon fodder," Kira said, taking in the array of Tsavitee as they moved closer.

Humans called them that because they were more numerous than the other species. They were usually sent directly at the enemy, overwhelming them with superior numbers and a single-minded intensity.

The lowest of the lower forms. Cannon fodder or puppets, as some called them, were little more than feral cannibals. They had no conscience and little intelligence from what Kira had seen. They'd crawl over the still-warm corpses of their brethren if it meant a

CHAPTER TWENTY-ONE

chance at human flesh.

She also spotted a mantis, its long lean form towering over the puppets beside it, and a telepath. The telepath looked sickly and gray, its limbs spindly as it stared at the room with a blank gaze.

Kira stepped back, moving so she wasn't in the general's line of sight.

"Put them in with the rest," the general ordered.

The Tsavitee swarmed the two women, herding them toward the light cage the rest of them were trapped in.

The Tuann pressed close to the front, eager for a chance to act once the Tsavitee dropped the light field to force Liara and Alma in.

Kira knew better than to get her hopes up. This wasn't her first time on the wrong side of one of these cages.

She let the others push their way forward, as she drifted to the rear of the cage. The cloaked strangers helped, stepping in front of her, their larger forms blocking her fully from sight.

She had a bit of a reputation among the Tsavitee. If they caught sight of her, things would probably not go well for her.

Roderick and another of his men dragged Liara to the cage, settling her on the ground not far from Kira. Liara's face was waxy, her eyes glazed with pain, her lips sealed tight against her whimpers, and blood coated her right shoulder.

"Your shoulder is severely damaged," one of the cloaked men said, kneeling by Liara's side. He pressed a bandage against her shoulder, ignoring her flinch and low moan. "We need to stop the bleeding so your body can put itself into a restive state and start to heal."

"Get away from her," Roderick spat, reaching for the man to jerk him away.

Kira got there first, knocking his hand away. "Stop being an ass. Take a look around; your enemy isn't in here."

Roderick snarled at her, his face a mask of rage. "You're wrong. Maybe my enemy is standing right in front of me. This started when you released the humans."

Graydon's people voiced their anger as the cloaked men kept their silence. Kira noticed Silas as he shifted closer, a hand disappearing into his cloak.

Violence threatened. Again.

You'd think the great Tuann would be smarter than this.

Kira sighed and glanced down.

Roderick's lips twisted in a smug smile.

Kira punched him in the throat. She hooked one leg around his and shoved, dumping him to the ground as he choked.

Graydon and Silas surged forward, forcing the Luathans back. Kira kneeled at Roderick's side. She grabbed the collar of his armor, jerking him up to sitting.

She pinched the tip of his ear. A high pained sound escaped him as she gripped his chin and forcefully turned his head toward the Tsavitee moving around the Nexus.

Their enemy was busy barricading the door as they dug in for a protracted siege.

"Look out there. That's a Tsavitee general. They lead invasions and aren't known for being merciful. Right now, they have the codes to your defense net, which is a bad thing since a Tsavitee warship waits outside your territory," Kira snarled, articulating each word carefully and calmly.

Things were bad. She needed him to understand just how bad they were. Maybe then he would stop this pointless posturing so they could all work together. That was the only way any of them would survive.

"Not quite," Liara said in a strained voice. She tried to sit up but only made it a few inches before her face whitened and the stranger pushed her down.

Kira waited for awareness to return to Liara's eyes before asking, "What do you mean?"

"I didn't change both sets of codes. I only changed the outer net. They won't be able to access the one around the planet. The curtain

CHAPTER TWENTY-ONE

remains intact," she said.

"If they approach the planet, the defenses will shoot them down," Kira said thoughtfully. She slid her cousin a sideways look. "Sneaky. I like it. Nicely done, cousin."

Liara's expression lightened with the barest trace of a smile before it turned regretful as she faced Graydon. "I set it to the highest level of alert. It'll destroy anything trying to approach."

"Leaving every ship outside the net on their own against the warship." Graydon's expression remained closed off, grief and resignation hidden there.

The same emotions were reflected in the faces of his soldiers.

"Our ship is out there as well," the cloaked stranger attending Liara said.

There was a long silence as they considered the gravity of that situation.

"Can you order them away?" Kira asked.

"The field blocks our communications," Silas said.

"My ship wouldn't leave anyway," Graydon said. "Not while we're here."

Kira frowned in thought.

"None of that matters while we're trapped in this cage," she said. "Liara's subterfuge works in our favor, but they'll figure it out eventually. Then they'll find a way to bring it down."

"The net can't be brought down," Roderick sneered.

"Only an Overlord's authorization will disarm the net," Liara said around a pained breath. "I'll never give it to them. Not even under threat of death."

Kira's smile was humorless, never touching her eyes. "What about the death of everyone else in the Citadel?"

The Luathan looked at her with horror. None had considered that possibility.

"They'll work their way through every single person they can get their hands on until they find your breaking point," Kira said. "Can you watch child after child be put to death? Your friends?"

Liara didn't speak, but Kira saw the answer in her face. No, she couldn't. Eventually the Tsavitee would find the one person Liara couldn't bear to see die, and they'd have her.

Everyone had a breaking point. It was just a matter of finding it.

"We have my men out there," Roderick said. "They'll stop the Tsavitee."

"You're assuming they're alive," Silas said. "One of your own betrayed you. The Tsavitee know how you operate. They'll know your evacuation routes."

"Either way, they don't need to take all of the Citadel, just some of it," Kira said. She looked at Liara "Am I right in thinking Ayela served as your personal aide? She'd know those closest to you?"

Liara closed her eyes, a wordless assent.

Kira turned to Roderick. The fight had run out of him, her words hitting home. Still, she needed to be sure he wasn't going to be a problem later on.

"You're going to cooperate, or the next time we have a little chat like this, you will be neutralized." Her hand squeezed the soft part on either side of his trachea, leaving no doubt how she intended to accomplish that.

His nod was grudging, but it was enough.

She released him and stood, carefully backing away in case he changed his mind and attacked.

Roderick's people helped him stand, pulling him away.

"That was nicely done," Silas said, his eyes on the Luathan marshal.

Kira grunted.

"I agree," Graydon said. "Where did you learn to take command like that?"

One side of her lips twitched up. She answered where she would have ignored Silas. "I was a squad leader by the end of my second year." Promotions happen fast when the people above you kept dying. "I looked like a teenager and most under my command thought they

CHAPTER TWENTY-ONE

were older than me. The only way to get them to listen was to appeal to their better nature."

Graydon quirked an eyebrow at her. "Meaning you beat your authority into them."

Kira grinned at him. "Humans can be hardheaded at times."

"As can Tuann," Silas murmured.

Kira made a sound of agreement before moving off. She approached her cousin and kneeled beside her, watching the second cloaked stranger as he carefully treated Liara's wound.

"How bad is it?" Kira asked.

"She will live. The wound didn't hit anything vital," the stranger told her. To Liara, he said, "You should take the primus form. It'll help you heal."

Liara's head moved, her gaze aimed at the floor.

She was hiding something. Kira wasn't the only one to notice either.

"I can stop you from attacking anyone if that is your worry," he offered.

Liara curled further in on herself.

"Primus form?" Kira asked, taking pity on her cousin and directing the man's attention away from her.

"It is the most powerful form our soul's breath takes. Most overlords of the major Houses have one. They have more capacity to harbor and harness the soul's breath. It's one of the reasons why they are overlords," he said simply. "Others in the House might have a primus form if the House is blessed. The number of members in a House who can achieve primus form is a sign of the House's power."

"Roake's overlord doesn't have a second form," Roderick pointed out. "Nor any in his House."

"Their situation is unique. He is the acting overlord and holds the position for another," the stranger said mildly.

"House Roake makes up for the lack in other ways," Silas said.

Kira ignored the hidden undercurrents in the exchange, sensing there was more to it than she understood. Now wasn't the time, the talk of primus forms, while interesting, especially in light of her own inner monster, wasn't relevant to their current situation.

Liara's face was slightly shamed as she confessed, "My primus form has not yet presented itself."

"How is that possible?" Graydon asked, undisguised shock on his face.

"There is no rule that the Overlord must have a second form," Alma said, defending Liara.

"It is greatly encouraged," Graydon said. "How does the emperor, at least, not know of her lack?"

Alma lifted her chin, the line of her jaw stubborn.

"We lied," Liara said, her gaze resting on her former adviser. "Another House was trying to merge with ours. Alma and Rayan could not hold it for much longer. I had to ascend to the position or we would have lost many things."

"If the Tsavitee knew of this, it might be why they decided Luatha was a good target," the stranger said. "They may have seen the lack as something they could exploit."

"No one in our House knew except my advisers," Liara said firmly.

Alma flinched the slightest bit.

Roderick rounded on her. "How else did you betray this House, Mother?"

"It was not my intention. You know that," Alma said, her expression pleading.

"Mother?" Kira muttered.

It explained some things, including how Roderick got his position.

"Roderick's father was the former marshal," Liara said quietly. "When I ascended, Alma asked that I make him the next marshal. She said it would look good, like the next generation was taking up the mantle."

"And it never bothered you his loyalties would always be to her first?" Kira asked.

CHAPTER TWENTY-ONE

Liara grimaced. "I didn't have many choices. Many of the *oshota* owed much to his father and his family. I saw him as the lesser evil."

Kira made a hmm as the drama before them unfolded.

"How could you do this?" Roderick shouted, his expression devastated.

"This wasn't how it was supposed to be," Alma cried. "You were supposed to fight them, retake the Citadel and strengthen our position. Not this."

"Our people would have still died," he roared.

"But your title would have been secured and our Overlord would have been known as the one who defeated the tsavitee," Alma said.

Kira winced as Alma admitted to not caring about what happened to the rest of them. Roderick and the rest of his people shook their heads, their expressions a mix of shocked dismay and disgust.

As imperfect as Roderick was, he and his people fulfilled the role of protector for the Luathans. To hear one of their own sought to exploit that would carry the harsh sting of betrayal.

With a muttered curse, the stranger attending Liara stood and took several steps toward where Roderick and his mother squared off.

Kira lowered herself to sitting beside Liara. They were as alone as they were going to get.

"The tsavitee will try to sacrifice some of your people to make you give up the codes," Kira said softly.

Liara jerked to look at her.

Kira hesitated, not liking this next task but not having much choice. It made her feel dirty to contemplate. It was emotional manipulation of the worse sort.

The situation was dire, and not just here. She had to take any advantage and use it, no matter how slimy it might make her feel.

"I can stop this," Kira said.

Hope shown on Liara's face.

Kira looked at her carefully. "But I'll need something from you first."

Liara's expression dimmed. "What do you want?"

Now or never, Kira told herself.

"Ten ships for the Consortium," she said in a rush. "And you rescind your House's claim."

In front of them, the stranger's head turned slightly. Kira narrowed her eyes at him. Could he hear her?

"I can't do that," Liara said. "I would be doing you an unimaginable disservice."

Kira gave her a crooked smile. "You seem to think I want a part of all this. I don't. This is a good deal. You lose nothing but a few ships."

Liara was quiet for several seconds. Kira let her think, knowing pushing wouldn't garner her the results she wanted.

"You might not be one of us now, because you don't understand who we are, but one day that might change," Liara said.

"Maybe, but it won't be today," Kira said.

The arched doors burst open and several Tsavitee strode inside, dragging small figures with them. They dumped their cargo in front of the cages.

Kira's heart gave a painful thump at the sight of Ziva and Joule, their faces terrified as they scrambled to their feet.

"It seems your Overlord was smarter than we gave her credit for," the general said, addressing those inside the cage. "We've brought incentive for her to give us the codes."

He gestured at the six children. Only Ziva and Joule had gained their feet, facing the Tsavitee with determined expressions.

"Your window is quickly shrinking, Liara," Kira murmured, her gaze locked on Ziva and Joule.

Their bodies were coiled tight.

Don't do it, she mentally warned them. Blend with the others.

Her words didn't reach them. Joule stepped in front of a Tsavitee when it would have reached for a child where she cowered on the floor.

Damn it, Kira cursed. He was brave. As the oldest, he'd feel it was

CHAPTER TWENTY-ONE

his place to stand before the rest. At least he had that part of being an *oshota* down.

She wished he'd had a little less backbone in this moment.

"A volunteer," the general said silkily as he watched Joule. "Very well. Bring him."

CHAPTER TWENTY-TWO

The Tsavitee grabbed Joule and hauled him over to the general. "Let him go," Ziva screamed, throwing herself at the Tsavitee.

She became a dervish, furiously attacking with no regard to her safety. Kira thought she recognized some of the moves as ones Kira and Graydon had taught her. What Ziva lacked in skill and precision was made up for by enthusiasm.

Kid had a gift, if she lived long enough to cultivate it.

One of the Tsavitee swiped at her, his large paw sending her crashing to her knees, her screams abruptly silenced.

Something in Kira broke. She stood. *"Lothos, I am hurt you didn't recognize me."*

The Tsavitee words rolled off her tongue. She hadn't spoken the language in over a dozen years, but her work on their ships had kept it fresh in her mind.

The Tuann in the cage turned incredulous expressions on her, all but Graydon and the two cloaked strangers drawing back as if they sensed a snake in their mist.

Kira didn't let their doubt affect her, remaining focused on the true enemy.

The Tsavitee around the cage peered closer at her before hisses of dismay rose. There were screams and screeches of fury as recognition spread.

The general had gone still.

"Perhaps I have not killed enough of your kind to make a true impression,"

CHAPTER TWENTY-TWO

Kira said. *"I will be sure to correct that oversight today."*

"What are you doing?" Graydon asked.

Her eyes flicked to him and she gave a slight shake to her head. He needed to let her do this and not interfere.

His lips flattened and his eyes narrowed to slits. She had a feeling he wasn't going to let her walk out of here. This could be a problem.

Graydon based his entire notion of self-worth on protecting those around him. He was a leader in every sense of the word. If he knew how she planned to sacrifice herself, he'd try to stop her.

He might ruin her plans—possibly even get himself killed. Neither option was one she could allow.

She tensed, prepared to drop him.

He flicked his fingers as if to say he was waiting.

She released a breath when he moved a half-step away, not far, but enough to show he was trusting her. For now.

"The scourge," Lothos said in human standard. There was little emotion in his voice. "We thought you were dead."

Kira tilted her head and waved her hands. "Surprise."

He stared at her thoughtfully, taking in the rest of the group then looking at the children.

Kira stiffened.

No, don't look at them. Look at her. She was the real threat. The children meant nothing.

"Leave them and bring her," he said in Tsavitee.

Kira's breath whooshed from her. Good. He'd taken the bait.

Liara grabbed her leg. "Protect all Tuann here, including yourself, and you have a deal."

Kira looked at her cousin. Liara's face held understanding. Of all those in the cage, she understood what Kira meant to do.

Funny how her cousin knew the inner workings of her mind the best. Maybe there was something to this family thing after all.

"Would you really deny them the ships if I die?" she asked.

Liara's licked her lips, her gaze going to the Tsavitee then to Kira.

"I wouldn't put my goodwill to the test."

Kira's small smile touched her eyes. "Then I guess I'd better stay alive."

Kira's warm expression disappeared as she faced the cage again. She stepped forward, Graydon moving beside her.

To her surprise, he didn't try to stop her. It seemed she'd underestimated him.

"I do not like this," he informed her.

"That gets me right here." She pointed at her heart. "Really."

The look he bent on her was unamused. "I will be most disappointed if you die."

"As will I."

He stopped her before she could reach the edge of the cage where the Tsavitee were massing in front of it. All of them eager to be the one responsible for bringing the Phoenix to her knees before death.

This was going to be bad.

Warm lips pressed against hers, distracting her from the madness she was about to face. Tingles skated across her skin as the kiss ended almost before it began. He drew back from her, his gaze full of thunderclouds. He gave her a cocky smile. "To give you something to live for."

"Arrogant man," Kira murmured.

He winked at her. "*Coli*, live and I'll show you I'm worth every bit of my arrogance."

"Hold onto that thought," Kira said as the light dropped to form a small doorway.

She squeezed Graydon's hand where he held hers. The joking distracted her from the gravity of what was about to happen, but it didn't quell the shaking in her hands or the knowledge she might soon be dead.

"Give them hell," he said. A second later, "That is the right phrase, correct? Human slang is so confusing."

Kira stepped forward, looking over her shoulder at him for one final

CHAPTER TWENTY-TWO

glimpse, wishing things had been different and they'd met earlier. "It gets easier with time."

His eyes held shadows as the light formed, cutting her off from the rest.

She faced the Tsavitee again, taking a deep breath. *Here we go.*

She didn't fight when the Tsavitee caught both arms and dragged her toward the general.

"What are you doing?" Ayela paced next to the general. "The children are a better bargaining chip. The Overlord will never give up the codes for the mongrel."

"The Phoenix's presence necessitates a change of plans. She's too dangerous to be left alive. Once she's taken care of, we may proceed," Lothos said, more diffidently than Kira had ever heard from a Tsavitee general class.

She frowned at Lothos. It was almost like he was submitting to Ayela's will, like she controlled him. That couldn't be. No one controlled the generals but the rulers.

"I'm ordering you to forget this nonsense," Ayela demanded. "You will listen to me. That was the deal we struck."

The general's face reflected irritation.

Kira wondered if this was why Ayela thought she could control the Tsavitee, because of a deal. It was possible. The Tsavitee kept any bargains they made. It was a weird dichotomy in such a backstabbing race.

Maybe because Tsavitee bargains never really worked out for anyone but the Tsavitee in the end. They were tricksters. You had to be very careful in the wording of your bargain or they'd drive a battlecruiser right through it.

"I have orders that supersede yours. Any Tsavitee who catches the Phoenix knows what they have to do. It doesn't matter what bargain you struck," the general said with forced patience.

Kira thought this might be the first time he'd had to explain himself. Their own kind didn't second-guess a general. They accepted his word and authority as the highest form of law. That he did now was darkly amusing.

"This woman is the single biggest threat on this planet. The capture and execution of the Phoenix is more important than anything else."

Ayela's expression was incredulous as she glanced at Kira. "Her? An untrained mongrel who hasn't gone through her majority?"

"Many Tsavitee have underestimated the Phoenix," Lothos said mildly. "They have all lived to regret it. I will not make the same mistake."

Ayela snorted, the sound inelegant and out of character for the diffident servant Kira had known. "Perhaps your kind are not as fearsome as I was led to believe."

The general bared a carnivore's sharp teeth at her. "I'd be careful, Tuann. We're not your pets. Push too far and you might find yourself dropped into a cage with your former comrades. I'm sure their justice will be swift and brutal."

Ayela's face paled slightly as Lothos stalked away.

Kira leaned as close to Ayela as the tight grip of the two Tsavitee holding her would allow. "Guess you're not quite as in control as you thought you were."

A sharp crack split the air and Kira's face turned slightly from the force of the smack.

She dabbed her tongue at her lip where a spot of blood welled. "I can see why they didn't let you advance in your training. You're weaker than the children. Should have used a fist. It would have hurt more."

The Tsavitee on her left moved to intercept Ayela before she could hit Kira again.

"Ignore her. She's trying to get under your skin," Lothos ordered from where he stood next to the octagon as the Tsavitee around him worked to hook up several lines.

Ayela settled back, her mouth pressed into a tight line and her eyes narrowed to slits.

CHAPTER TWENTY-TWO

"I'd say it's working." Kira's smile was nasty as the Tsavitee dragged her forward.

"Put her on her knees," Lothos said without turning around. "And if she speaks again, you may punish her."

There were hissed chuckles above her. One of them grabbed her shoulder, a blast of psychic power sending agonizing pain screeching along her nerve endings as it ripped a scream out of her.

Kira seized, her body shaking violently as they dropped her, letting her flop on the ground unhindered. The sound of their amusement a taunt above her.

Finally, her seizures slowed. Blood filled her mouth. She must have bitten her tongue at some point.

"You're supposed to wait until I've said something," Kira snarled at the two above her. To the general, she spat, "Your standard for cannon fodder has really gone down in the years since the war."

Another touch from the Tsavitee sent Kira to the ground, drool leaking out her mouth as her entire body protested the abuse.

The Tsavitee glared at her before one of them spat a glob of spit at her.

Lothos didn't even spare her a glance as he worked on melding his technology with the Tuann's. "You're right about the quality. Unfortunately, we had to grow them too quickly to replace the forces humanity decimated. Mistakes were made and it resulted in a decrease in intelligence. We'll correct the oversight in the next batch."

The Tsavitee above her didn't react to the insult. Kira couldn't tell if that was because they really were little more than obedient attack dogs, or if they truly didn't care.

Kira picked herself up off the ground, pushing herself to her knees as she glared at the general. The Tsavitee above her didn't attempt to grab her arms again.

"It seems you can learn," Lothos observed when she didn't say anything. "I had my doubts. My brothers told me you were incredibly stubborn. Almost impossible to train."

Kira held her silence. All the generals of the Tsavitee called themselves brothers. He could have been referring to any of them.

"Of course, many of them are dead by your hand, so perhaps they spoke truer than they knew," he said.

Feeling was gradually coming back into her arms and legs and the shakiness was passing.

Good.

"I will admit to being surprised to find you here. Last we knew you were dead or so close to it you didn't matter," he said. "Tell me, are you still capable of the burst?"

Kira stared at him.

"Answer me or they'll use their psions again," he said calmly.

She caught a glimpse of the Tsavitee to her left reaching for her.

"Stay and find out," she said.

He studied her, tapping his fingers against his leg in thought. "I don't think you'll use it even if you can. Too many emotional attachments to those in this room."

Kira struggled not to react to the surprisingly on-target assessment. She didn't want him to see how close he was to the truth.

"Does it surprise you that we know your weakness?" he asked with a sly smile.

He would have been considered handsome if not for the horns and strange markings on his skin or the fact he was the enemy.

"After our last failure, we made sure to study you and your habits. You've been quiet since using the burst on Rothchild. Only using it once more during the Falling. Some might even say you've been in mourning," he said, his black eyes fixed unwaveringly on Kira's. "Tell me, how many of your friends did you kill there?"

She kept her chin lifted as she forced boredom into her expression. "There's a lot of repressed emotion in this little chat. If you're not careful, I'm going to think the generals feel something for one another."

CHAPTER TWENTY-TWO

He bared his teeth. They were those of a meat eater, pointed and sharp. The incisors longer and capable of tearing into flesh or breaking bone.

"Your death will bring much joy to the Tsavitee. The best part is when we inform her of your defeat at our hands. You know, she sometimes screams for her Phoenix."

Everything in Kira went still. Her heart clenched painfully.

"I didn't know," Kira said, her words slow. "Thank you for that. We weren't sure if she lived. I promise to visit the full measure of my vengeance on your brothers as I let them know you're the one who sent me."

It was a promise, to herself and the general. Everything she'd done for the past seven years had been aimed at finding out what had happened to Elise and if she lived. This validated all that work.

The cold-blooded monster within the general peeked out. The need to tear out her throat and bathe in her blood was easy to see. He'd done a good job hiding it until now, almost seeming refined and civilized. That's how they destroyed the first human colonies, by pretending a façade of elegance and honor. Humans had soon learned the truth about them.

She smiled. Try it, she urged.

"Lothos, it's up," one of the Tsavitee said into the quiet. This one wasn't one of the cannon fodder. His eyes were intelligent and bright as they flicked over Kira.

A reaper—the shock troops of the Tsavitee. Dangerous and powerful and similar in form to the generals.

The general straightened, his height impressive. He would have towered over Graydon.

"Connect me to him," the general said as he turned to face the platform.

The Tsavitee rushed to obey as Kira settled to wait.

Battles were as much about moments as they were tactics and weapons. Strike too soon and you gave up the advantage, wait too long and you've lost before you could turn the tide. It wasn't her moment yet. She needed to wait.

A niggle of awareness drew a line from her to where Jin was lying inert on the ground. His thoughts busy and desperate. She didn't know what he was working on, only that it was important. She'd buy him what time she could.

She chanced a glance at Ziva, Joule, and the other children. They huddled in a group in front of the cage, the Tsavitee poking at them every once in a while and laughing when the children cried or screamed.

Joule, Ziva, and another boy, slightly older than Joule, protected the front of the group, defiantly facing down their captors.

Ziva and Joule looked devastated as their eyes caught Kira's. Shame moved through their expressions, both blaming themselves for her predicament.

She winked at them before smiling. It didn't work, their faces becoming more morose, Ziva's eyes welling up with tears.

Guess her reassurance needed work.

Kira sighed and shifted on her knees trying to relieve some of the painful pressure. This had turned into a clusterfuck of a situation.

When she assured Liara she'd be able to save the Tuann, she might have been a little overconfident in her abilities.

Right now, she had two main sources to protect. The children and the adults. At least the adults were behind a forcefield. The Tsavitee would have to open it and chance being overwhelmed by those inside before they could use them as hostages. The children weren't as protected.

It made Kira's promise complicated.

If this had been ten years ago, before Rothchild, before Epiron, she wouldn't have questioned herself. That was before she'd used the first burst, before people had died while under her protection. Before her body started destroying itself.

The general had been right about her not using the burst, but not

CHAPTER TWENTY-TWO

for the reasons he thought. The burst was a wave of energy her body generated when under duress, capable of annihilating everything around her, friend and foe.

It was a powerful weapon but came at a steep cost. Using it put her close to death. Last time she'd used it she ended up in a coma for years. Her body was recovering slowly, but she was nowhere near what she'd once been.

Her huff was sad. Poor children, their only chance of survival was a dysfunctional Tuann and a half-fried drone that may or may not come back online in time.

She inhaled sharply.

A screen formed above the platform, liquid ribbons of silver condensing to form a mirror.

A Tsavitee general peered out of it, his expression remote. He looked as young and ageless as the rest of his kind, his eyes red instead of black. The tip of his left horn was broken, the edge jagged and white.

Neron.

Interesting choice on Lothos' part. Neron was high ranking, but he wasn't the highest. Not even in the top five, unless things had changed more than she knew.

This general had a history with her. She was the one who'd broken his horn, which was considered a bit of a status symbol in his culture. He held a wicked grudge about the whole thing, even though he'd been doing his utmost to kill her at the time.

"Lothos, why are you calling me?" he asked.

Lothos bowed his head and touched his fist to his chest. "There has been a development."

The red eyes narrowed. "What kind of development?"

Lothos stepped to the side, giving Neron a clear view of a kneeling Kira.

Neron went still. His expression hardened, becoming even more remote. At last, he relaxed into his chair. "Phoenix. Like the human myth, you have once again risen from your own ashes."

By then Lothos had backed up until he was standing behind Kira and her two captors.

Several seconds passed as the tension in the room built.

"Nothing to say to your old enemy?" Neron asked, his voice a silken menace.

Kira pretended to think. "Just a message for your masters. You can tell them I'm coming for them. I plan to keep the promise I made you the first time we met."

Hisses of displeasure came from those around her. The only ones who were silent were Neron, Lothos, and another slim figure Kira had just noticed.

The new general was young, barely out of his maturation phase from what Kira could tell.

Neron's gaze shifted to Lothos and the two shared a long look. "You know what to do."

Lothos inclined his head. "Of course, consider it done."

Lothos looked at the two Tsavitee, his expression flat. "Kill her."

There were pleased chortles from the Tsavitee as those in the cages erupted. The Tsavitee dragged an unresisting Kira closer to the octagon, forcing her onto her knees where Neron would have a front row seat to her death.

His face was set in the same impassive lines she associated with the generals, no recognizable emotion rippling across its surface.

Kira held his gaze as the Tsavitee next to her prepared, one of them readying a laser ax, the quiet hum sizzling through the air. The other grabbed her hair, forcing her head down and exposing her neck.

This was it. Death had come for her.

The blade neared her skin as the Tsavitee lined up his stroke. Distantly she noted their feet resembled a goat's, hoof-like with no shoes.

The blade lifted. A deafening roar sounded from the cage as something threw itself against it, again and again.

CHAPTER TWENTY-TWO

Kira couldn't turn to see what.

She slipped her hand along the top of her boot, palming the finger-length blade hidden there.

Sloppy of the Tsavitee not to secure her hands.

The ax descended.

Kira grabbed the arm of the Tsavitee holding her hair. She rolled into the other Tsavitee pulling the first into the path of the descending ax.

There was a scream as blood sprayed, the blade cleaving his shoulder in two. Kira twisted, not bothering to find her feet, sinking her blade into the executioner's leg, searching for an artery.

Blood gushed. She couldn't tell if she'd hit it or not. Best to make sure.

The executioner lifted the blade again. Kira surged up, staying close to his body. His swing missed. She trapped his arm against her side and swiped her blade across his neck.

Warm blood hit her face as she held him against her, not letting his dead body fall.

Kira maneuvered him so his dead weight was between her and the rest of the Tsavitee.

"This is your only warning. Those who wish to live—run," Kira said in Tsavitee.

Neron's image clicked off.

Kira spared one glance at it before focusing on the force in front of her. There was no going back now. The Tsavitee higher-ups knew she was alive. They'd view her as a threat and come for her before she could come for them.

She sighed and shook her head. Thoughts of future problems could wait. There was too much in the here and now to take care of.

The sound of a slow clap came as Ayela stepped from between the ranks of milling Tsavitee. The two generals stayed where they were. They might want Kira dead, but they had enough experience to know with her loose it was better to let the cannon fodder wear her down before striking.

The younger one looked stunned, his mouth agape. Lothos stared at the two dead Tsavitee with a blank expression.

"Congratulations, you've managed to survive for another minute," Ayela said sarcastically, pushing through the Tsavitee. "But you're still alone with no weapon besides that blade and you face an army."

Pity moved across Kira's face. "That's where you and the Tsavitee always seem to go wrong. I rarely face your kind alone."

Confusion reflected on Ayela's face, before realization descended. Her mouth opened to shout orders.

She was too late.

Sound ripped through the air. "The Ride of the Valkyries" playing as Jin shot up from the ground.

Kira used the dead Tsavitee as a shield against Tsavitee fire as she dove for cover.

Jin drew a drunken path through the air as the Tsavitee turned their weapons from her to him. He returned fire, the laser gun she'd installed mowing down the dozen Tsavitee between him and Kira.

An explosion rocked the room as part of the ceiling caved in. Rope descended seconds later, several forms rappelling down them. Guns barked as those above fired into the horde.

The Curs. About damn time.

Kira abandoned her cover, tackling the Tsavitee closest to her. She buried her blade in its neck several times, leaping off it before it hit the ground. She caught another, knocking its weapon away. It fired on its allies instead.

The Tsavitee was dead in the next second.

Raider and Nova were careful to keep their lines of fire away from the hostages.

"Jin, tell me you recorded Liara's promise," Kira shouted over the chaos.

"Of course, I did. What do you think I am? An idiot?"

Kira smiled, relieved beyond words to hear her friend—even if

CHAPTER TWENTY-TWO

his voice was full of sarcasm. "Then get working on that cage and protect the Overlord and her people at all costs."

He grumbled about being given obvious orders as he made a beeline for the hostages, the song blaring. It was a little on the nose, but Kira couldn't complain given its distraction had saved her ass.

Raider burst out of the dust next to her, lifting his face shield.

"You're late," she told him.

"You're lucky we came at all. That Tuann who protects you was near frothing at the mouth when he found us. You're lucky Blue put a tracker on your ass. The other one tried to stuff us in a closet once the Tsavitee started running rampant," Raider griped.

Noor appeared beside him, removing the head of two Tsavitee in a single swing of his sword. "You are not a truthful human."

Raider rolled his eyes as he fired at several of the enemy. "Yeah, yeah. Tell it to someone who cares."

"Jace and Maverick are working on calling our ship," Raider told her after he'd taken care of another batch of enemies.

"Jin is working on the cage. We need to protect them until he finishes," Kira said.

"You never ask for much," Raider said before turning to call out orders to his troops.

Finn appeared beside her like a ghost, his eyes glittering and blood coating the front of his armor. "We are going to have a talk when this is over."

Kira didn't bother acknowledging that statement.

"Protect the children," Kira told him. "They're the most vulnerable right now."

He exhaled through his nose, his eyes approaching slits before he stalked off, the other Tuann trailing behind Raider.

Kira killed anything that came near her. She searched the melee but both generals were long gone, having disappeared as soon as the ceiling came down.

Kira spotted Blue fending off three Tsavitee. Kira sprinted toward her, landing in the middle as she ducked one swing, delivering three carefully placed strikes in seconds.

"Help Jin," she ordered as soon as the other woman focused on her. Blue's chin jerked in a nod and she hurried off.

The firefight intensified, the Tsavitee rallying enough to recover from their earlier surprise.

The Curs had shifted the tide, but the battle wasn't yet won.

She checked on the others, her gaze snagging on a Tsavitee as he crept along the wall, his blaster aimed at Raider's back.

"Raider," Kira screamed a warning. She'd never reach him in time.

He began to turn, dropping to one knee, the Tsavitee already firing.

Kira reached for the tangled, thorny vines at her center, the source of power that had once obeyed her without question. It surged forward, easier than it had in years, the power bright and hot in her mind as she threw it out from her, wrapping Raider in a protective layer.

The blast hit it and faded. The shield disappeared in the next second.

Raider fired, hitting the Tsavitee in the chest and killing him.

Kira smiled in relief as he turned to face her with a thanks on his lips. His expression shifted, horror dawning.

His rejection stung.

A sucking pain lanced through her chest in the next instant. Choked gasps did nothing to relieve it as Kira glanced down. Vague surprise filled her at the sight of a sword point sticking out of her chest.

A Tuann en-blade, she noted distantly, touching it in dismay. Red coated her fingers.

Ayela stepped around her, her expression gloating. "Guess I'm not so useless after all. I killed you, didn't I? Even the general failed to accomplish that."

Kira blinked at her, unable to talk, her thoughts stilted and weak.

Her gaze shifted to Raider as she tried to force sound out. Bubbles of blood formed at the corner of her mouth.

CHAPTER TWENTY-TWO

The sword had punctured her lung. Speaking would be difficult.

"Run," she mouthed.

He took off.

"Protocol Phoenix! To me, to me. Jin, get that cage down!" Raider screamed.

Jin swung toward Kira but at Raider's order, he focused on the cage with a foul curse.

The Curs streamed toward him and the cage, herding the children in front of them.

Ayela laughed as she yanked the blade out of Kira's back. "These are who you chose to ally with? Cowards?"

Kira didn't respond, she couldn't. Blood poured out of her wound as she pressed her hands against her front.

Her vision wavered.

Raider and the rest were almost at the cage.

She needed to hold on. Just a little longer.

Ayela walked toward them, not bothering to hurry. Her prey had nowhere to go.

The cage dropped. Finally.

The Curs pushed the children inside. Raider and Blue yanked Finn and Noor after them as they dove for its safety. Jin turned the cage on.

Kira smiled. Finally.

She let the darkness consume her as she toppled forward.

CHAPTER TWENTY-THREE

Graydon roared, the sound the embodiment of denial and rage as the tip of a sword burst from Kira's chest, the shock and surprise on her face echoing Graydon's. The bright flicker of her spirit guttered.

The cage fell and Graydon's muscles bunched as he prepared to drench the room in his power. It answered his call, a cold so intense it burned.

The children and humans piled in, the cage flickering into place.

"What are you doing?" Graydon shouted.

He grabbed the human closest to him and shook him, the human's head wobbling like a doll's.

"Open it," he roared.

"Easy there, hoss," a man said from next to him.

Graydon thought it might be the one called Raider. He couldn't be sure since he hadn't taken the time to learn all their names. He struggled not to rip the man's head from his shoulders. The urge was difficult to resist.

"You don't want to go out there right now, believe me," Raider said, his expression cautious.

A long menacing sound rumbled from Graydon's chest, primal and terrifying.

He hadn't thought these humans so devious they would leave one of theirs behind to die.

"Maybe you do," Raider said, correcting himself. "Just wait a moment."

CHAPTER TWENTY-THREE

"Drop the cage, human," Graydon ordered, his voice eerily calm.

"We've adjusted the energy barrier. It'll protect us from what's outside," the woman with blue hair said. "This is the safest place right now."

"Except not everyone is in it," Liara pointed out, struggling to sit.

"Believe me, lady, everyone who needs to be is," Raider said, turning to stare out.

Graydon narrowed his eyes. The humans were worried. It was more than the Tsavitee. Until Kira went down, they'd been holding their own. Now, they stunk of stress and fear.

"Shouldn't it have already happened?" Blue muttered to the big man next to her.

He grunted, his eyes narrowed on Kira.

Raider paced in front of the cage wall as Ayela continued toward them, her lips curled up in a satisfied smile. The humans didn't spare her a look.

Graydon was known for his discipline. He was a stalwart stone when others let the eddies of emotion carry them into the rapids. He reached for that side of him. It was harder than it'd ever been before.

The humans had stopped seeing those outside as a threat. There was one thing that worried them, and it wasn't the Tsavitee.

Graydon was silent as he watched the humans stare at Kira's fallen body.

"Look at this, so many lovely sacrifices," Ayela murmured. "Bring me one of them."

The Tsavitee flanking her moved to obey. Graydon's muscles tightened as he prepared to attack, the rest of his warriors doing the same.

The Tsavitee's face reflected confusion when the cage refused to obey.

"What's the holdup?" Ayela demanded.

"It won't open, mistress."

Jin chuckled. "We own this space now, bitch. Prepare to be

disappointed."

Her eyes narrowed as she turned to give him a look of dislike. She shrugged graceful shoulders. "No matter. I'm sure my companions can figure out how to reverse what you've done."

Jin got close to the cage's barrier. "They're not going to have time to do much of anything. You shouldn't have done that. Now you're all going to die."

Ayela's head tilted with confusion.

Behind her, Kira rose, her hair covering her face as she straightened so very slowly.

"That was a mortal wound," Quillon murmured, rising from where he tended to the Luathan Overlord. His cloak whispered into place around him.

It had been. Graydon was sure of it.

"Kira," Joule and Ziva shouted in relief.

"Guess again," Raider said in a soft voice. "It's something much more dangerous."

"The Phoenix," the blue-haired woman whispered, her voice hushed as tangled notes of fear and awe ran through it.

The figure finally lifted her head, her expression feral, her entire focus locked on Ayela, the rest of the world forgotten.

Graydon saw what he and the rest of the Tuann had missed.

It wore Kira's shape, it had her face, but there were subtle differences. The pale creaminess of her skin was replaced by a dark gray. Violet symbols etched themselves across every exposed piece of skin, lines linking them in swooping patterns only the oldest of the ancients would be able to decipher.

To the uneducated eye, some might have mistaken her for a female Tsavitee general, but Graydon knew her for what she really was. Primus. Precious and rare.

Her eyes opened at last, glowing violet as she focused on Ayela's head.

"Primus form," Graydon said in stunned understanding.

CHAPTER TWENTY-THREE

"What are you looking at?" Ayela asked with a frown.

Kira's hands appeared on either side of Ayela's head. They closed on it and wrenched, a crack piercing the room. Ayela's body slumped to the floor, her neck broken. She stared sightlessly up at the ceiling.

Kira stepped over the body, her attention turning to the occupants of the cage for the first time.

"Weapons up," Raider said.

Kira struck in the next second, the cage shuddering from the force of the blow. The walls of the cage crackled as she continued to press her hand against it, the smell of scorched flesh reaching Graydon.

She was damaging herself as she tried to break into the cage.

The humans had their weapons trained on her, fear and pheromones flooding the air.

"Will the cage hold?" Raider snapped.

"Probably." Jin didn't sound convinced.

"Not good enough," the human snarled.

Jin snorted. "That's the best you're going to get. I'm not a magician. I had seconds to switch the polarity to give us this much protection. Next time give me more of a head's up if you want a more quality product."

"Can our weapons pass through?" the big man asked.

Both Graydon and Jin voiced an immediate denial.

"Look, we don't like this any better than you," Raider said, irritation making him snappish. "But she's in berserker mode. It's kill her or let her kill us."

"Your weapons won't do anything to her in that form," Graydon said, forcing reason into his voice. He stepped nearer, placing his hand in front of hers. He ignored the sting of warning, the small snap of pain as he waited for her to meet his eyes.

It took several seconds before she lifted her attention from the humans. When she did, it was like being punched in the chest. Her gaze cut through all the noise, as if seeing into the deepest parts of himself. It settled him even as he yearned to lose himself in her.

There was awareness in those eyes. Intelligence. Feeling. She was in a battle rage, yes, but she hadn't let herself be lost to it.

"You are so beautiful," Graydon said in Tuann.

Kira blinked at him.

"It's time for you to protect yourself now," he said, his voice adopting a soothing cadence.

She drew one sharp claw down the cage wall. A streak of pale yellow followed.

"She's writing," Blue said in a stunned voice.

Graydon gritted his teeth and told himself that strangling the humans might set her off again.

"In primus form her instincts are close to the surface, but she isn't an animal. She's capable of thought and reason," he said, struggling for patience.

Although it was rare for one so young to possess enough discipline to gain control so quickly after the influx of *ki* necessary to achieve the transformation.

Ships as promised. Jin has recording. Protect all.

Raider's lips thinned as he considered. He seemed torn between duty and loyalty. That struggle was what saved him and the rest from a painful death at Graydon's hands later.

Raider gave a jerky nod. "You heard her. Get to work on the exit strategy."

"Roger that," several of the humans said.

They moved quickly, bending and placing putty in a ring on the floor.

"Graydon, you're not going to let this happen, are you?" Silas asked urgently.

His former mentor wasn't going to leave her side willingly.

"I'm not leaving either," Liara said. Her face was pale and slick with sweat. Her objection mostly for form's sake.

A derisive snort escaped him. She should have thought about her cousin's health before making that asinine deal with her in the first

CHAPTER TWENTY-THREE

place.

Graydon met Kira's expectant gaze. He let out a low sound of frustration. "I'll do it. I'll get them out safely," he told her.

She inclined her head.

There was really no other choice. He had a duty to his people and the Luathan Overlord. As much as he'd like to stay and fight, some things came first. "Follow the humans."

His first task was to see those assembled to safety. He'd come for her after that.

He chanced one final look behind him, mentally ordering Kira to stay safe until then. She'd better be alive by the time he returned.

"Do it," he ordered Raider.

Raider nodded. "Take cover."

Raider and the other humans crouched, curling in on themselves, covering their ears and tucking their heads down.

He looked up at Graydon. "You should do the same."

Graydon rolled his eyes. "We're not as weak as you."

Raider shrugged. "Suit yourself."

Graydon wrapped his soul's power around him and the others, creating a small bubble of protection seconds before the small space exploded.

The group disappeared into the gaping hole, gone in seconds.

* * *

Kira felt the vibration from the explosion.

The Curs might be human, but they knew what was at stake. They'd protect Liara and the others to the end.

Throw in Graydon and the others were as safe as she could make them.

She bared her teeth, ones every bit as sharp as the Tsavitee general's had been. She looked over her prey.

Now that the others were out of the way, she could take off the chains keeping her in check.

Time to go hunting.

* * *

A short time later, every Tsavitee in the chamber was dead. She stood over their bodies victorious, covered in blood. She tilted her head up and basked in the moment.

A slight warning beep from the platform shook her from her exultation.

She opened an eye and scowled at the offending sound. It ignored her displeasure, merrily beeping away.

She growled and stalked over to it, her clawed feet clicking against the stone. At some point she'd lost her shoes, not that that bothered her. Her feet were more powerful this way, and shoes irritated the claws.

Kira eyed the space. A small button glowed in midair.

Someone was hailing the command center.

She stared at it for several seconds, the urge to go back to enjoying her kills strong.

The beeping continued.

She jabbed her finger at the button.

"What?" she snapped.

"Tuann ship the *Valiant* hailing the Luathan Overlord. This is Commander Kai requesting immediate assistance."

Kira struggled to think past her immediate needs, the berserker rage of this form making difficult.

"Please come in," Kai said, some of his strain getting through to her.

Kai. She knew him. He was one of Graydon's people. She liked Graydon. He'd called her beautiful and kissed her. She sometimes wanted to bite him then force him to chase so she could run. He brought parts of her to life, made her feel whole and safe.

CHAPTER TWENTY-THREE

"What do you want?" The words were stilted and unnatural, not sounding like Kira in the least. This form wasn't meant for long conversations, it was meant for killing.

"Your second line defenses have gone online and are targeting my ship anytime we get close. There is a Tsavitee warship bearing down on us. My ship is a diplomatic ship. It's not equipped to withstand the firepower of a dreadnaught. Let us pass through your defenses so we can land."

Kira looked at the array. "Don't know how to do that."

Silence crackled over the line. "This is Luatha command, isn't it?"

"Yes."

"Then you should be able to turn the defense off or at least point them toward the enemy," the commander said in a strident voice.

Kira's head tilted. "Impossible."

"What do you mean impossible?"

"Incident down here. Overlord set defenses. Can't be undone."

"Then find her," he shouted.

"Not possible."

There was another length of silence as she could feel him considering, weighing her words.

"Are you Luathan?" he asked suspiciously.

Kira chuckled. "No."

"The enemy then," he said it as a statement. There was resignation in his voice.

"Not the enemy," Kira said.

She could feel his interest. The longer she stood near the Nexus, the more she thought she understood it. Graydon had said it was controlled by the strength of your mind and will.

That was before the Tsavitee had run their lines and hijacked the link. She might not know Tuann tech, but she knew Tsavitee technology.

It might be enough.

She wasn't weak-willed. She might be able to help the ship above, or she might burn her brain up trying.

She paused. Would Liara consider being brain-dead a breach of their promise?

The concern floated away as quickly as it had come. Emotions were fleeting and hard to reach, locked behind a barrier of ice.

"Stand by, trying something," she told Kai.

"Of course, it's not like I'm going anywhere. There's just a warship heading my way," he said sarcastically.

Kira stepped onto the platform and waited. A force clamped on her mind, slicing through any natural barrier she might have had like it was butter.

She grunted at the feeling, gritting her teeth as she rode the pain. It was easier in this form, insulating her from the worst of it.

When it eased slightly, she found her mind split. Half of it was high above, standing on the bridge of a Tuann ship. The rest was standing in the stone room, her expression frozen.

She lifted her hand and stared at it as the Tuann near her jolted back, their eyes wide. She ignored them as she rotated her hand, fascinated by the slight translucence. She held up her other arm, seeing the same ghostly, insubstantial effect, her body shimmering in and out of view.

Someone cleared their throat next to her. She looked up to find the captain's eyes fastened on her, his gaze nonplussed.

He seemed to be able to see her. Fascinating.

She dropped her arms. "Can't bring down the defenses without risking the planet."

And she wouldn't do that.

He shut his eyes. "Then we're dead."

"Not necessarily," Kira said.

He leaned in, a reserved hope in his expression.

"Full ahead. You need to take the fight to them," she said. "I'll guide you in."

His lips parted and then he gave a nod, barking orders at those

CHAPTER TWENTY-THREE

around them. She could feel the ship accelerate, or maybe she saw it accelerate. Here in this space, it was hard to distinguish what input was from her senses and what she was picking up from this strange melding.

Something streaked across her right shoulder. The ship shuddered as a Tsavitee weapon punched into it on the right side.

Interesting.

Her body seemed to have taken the place of radar, telling her where the next attack would hit.

"Shift vector by five degrees," Kira called.

She didn't pay much attention to the frenetic activity on the bridge, concentrating on the surrounding space instead.

The defenses grew small behind them as they barreled toward the Tsavitee ship. An angel class six. A world killer. Even with the Tuann's considerably powerful technology, it would be a difficult foe.

There were thousands of Tsavitee on that ship. The Tuann ship contained at most fifty. Even with the other Tuann ship up here following them, their odds weren't good.

Both Tuann ships were fast and maneuverable, but they weren't meant to meet an angel head-on.

Her collar bone and the side of her arm tingled.

"Six degrees port side and two degrees up," she said.

"How is she predicting their movements?" someone muttered.

"I'm reading the energy of their ship," Kira murmured, her gaze focused and distant. "It's quite easy when you know what to look for."

And after several years spent sifting through the wreckage of every Tsavitee ship she could get her hands on, she knew exactly what to look for.

A spot on her stomach burned.

"Roll," Kira shouted.

The ship jerked around her incorporeal body, shuddering when one of the blasts glanced off the mid-section of the ship.

"Hull breach in decks six through ten," someone shouted.

"Increase acceleration," Kira said.

Distantly she noted a string stretching from her intangible body out into the void. It was faint, barely there, more suggestion than reality.

Curious, she tugged on it, faintly surprised to find it attached to something.

While the *Valiant* raced toward the Tsavitee ship, cutting through space as it dodged and swooped, returning weapons fire when it could, she investigated the ghost string, feeling along its length.

Ah, so that's what it was.

The plan that had been coalescing in her brain took shape.

"The enemy ship is charging all weapons," someone on the bridge called.

"We're not going to make it," Kai said.

Kira didn't respond, still busy with the ghost strand.

Kai closed his eyes, making a decision. He straightened. "Ram the ship. It might buy the planet enough time to mount a defense.

"Belay that order," Kira barked. "Prepare for a hard turn."

There was a silence on the bridge as everyone considered her.

"I'd do it now," she said mildly.

Kai's jaw locked as he considered her, judging how much to trust her. "Do what she says."

The deck bustled with movement.

The ship began to turn, the force of its momentum screeching through the hull as it threatened to cleave it in two. Even here in space, the laws of physics wanted to be obeyed, and what they were doing threatened to tear the ship apart.

"Almost there," someone called.

"The cannons on the Tsavitee ship are realigning. They'll lock onto our new position in ten seconds."

"It was a good try," Kai told Kira. "Don't blame yourself for it

CHAPTER TWENTY-THREE

failing."

She didn't glance at him, a faint smile on her face. "You need to learn to have a little faith."

The Tsavitee ship's weapons prepared to fire. Those on the bridge braced, their hands dancing across the controls as they fought until the last second.

The ship completed its turn.

"Second ship detected," someone shouted.

"An enemy?" Kai asked.

"No. Human."

Kira's smile felt strange in this form. The flinch of those closest to her told her it wasn't a welcoming sight. Understandable since primus form looked more monstrous than beautiful. The more time she spent in it, the less she resembled the Kira and became something else entirely.

The human ship appeared on the Tsavitee's other side, firing into it, their weapons already targeted and locked.

Good, they'd gotten the firing package she'd sent.

The Tsavitee were caught off-guard, largely unprotected on that side, their cannons having rotated to lock on the Tuann ship.

"The humans are firing at the Tsavitee ship," someone said in excitement.

A voice came over the comms. "Tuann ship. This is Admiral Grant of the *CSS Reliance*. Please unload everything you've got. We'll do the same."

Kira tied the two ship strands together, linking them. She wasn't sure if the action would help or hinder, but it felt right. That would have to be enough.

Her consciousness faded from the Tuann diplomatic ship.

She stumbled, her body weak and tired as the symbols faded from her skin, the gray turning to normal pale creaminess as her second form deserted her.

She resisted the cold pull of rest. Her job wasn't done quite yet.

Lifting her arm, she used one fingernail to peel off the small, nearly invisible dermal micro storage device she carried on the inside of her bicep.

The color of her skin, it was designed to stay attached through everything, short of being burned to death. It was her backup if she ever got caught somewhere without her normal supplies.

Carefully, she stripped the wires of the Tsavitee device before wrapping the patch on the exposed metal.

Her hands shook as she sifted through the Tuann database. Trillions of pieces of data at her fingertips. She hoped the patch could download everything she needed.

Ah, there. That's what she'd come all this way for.

She downloaded what she needed into the patch before disconnecting it and smoothing it back onto the underside of her upper arm.

Done. Finally.

It looked like Odin was getting what he'd asked for after all.

Kira took a step and stumbled, ending up on her ass. She leaned against the cool stone of the Nexus, too exhausted to do anything else.

Her chest ached from having a sword rammed through it and the cells of her body felt like they were about to tear apart.

Warmth flowed up into her from the ground, the planet pouring its power into her, bolstering her. It was seconds before that warmth turned sharp, burning a line through her as her body struggled to accept the power.

She didn't know if it was going to be enough. She'd done too much. Was too injured.

She might not be able to keep her promise to Liara after all.

That was her last thought as exhaustion and pain pulled her down.

* * *

CHAPTER TWENTY-THREE

Kira blinked up at a familiar ceiling. It took several seconds to remember where she'd seen it before. She was back in the healing room.

She shifted her head, expecting Finn's morose expression as he stood guard. Instead, Graydon looked down at her, a pensive expression on his face.

"You got them out," she croaked.

"Yes."

She cleared her throat. "Thank you."

The words seemed to insult him, his gaze going wintry. "You're an idiot."

She blinked at him. That was harsh.

"One against nearly thirty. What could have possessed you to think those were good odds?" he said, his jaw granite hard.

Ah-ha.

She looked around the room as if searching for an explanation or maybe some patience. Finally, she glared at him. "It worked. Everyone survived."

"Pure luck," he said.

She scoffed. "It was many things, but it wasn't luck."

He raised an eyebrow. "Now who's being arrogant?"

A small sound of frustration escaped her. The two remained locked in a glaring match until a small sound came from the door.

Finn cleared his throat and then glanced between the two of them with a placid expression. "I'm glad you're awake. Your humans won't shut up, perhaps with you awake we'll get some peace finally."

"Unlikely," Graydon muttered.

Kira aimed a glare at him. "You should be a little nicer. They helped save you after all."

Even the ships in orbit had benefited from their interference.

Graydon's eyes never left hers as he said, "Funny coincidence, the human ship lurking outside our borders happened to enter our space just when the *Valiant* needed help most."

"How fortunate for them," Kira said.

"No one can figure out how the humans knew exactly where and when to appear," Graydon said slowly.

She shrugged. "Have you asked Raider? He and the others were trying to contact the Reliance when we split up."

"Noor said they never got the chance," Graydon responded.

"Then your ship was lucky they showed up when they did," Kira said.

"Lucky indeed," Graydon murmured, his eyes narrowed.

Kira leaned forward in bed looking over the two men. "What happened to the Tsavitee who survived?"

"Any we've found, we've executed. We're searching out any survivors," Graydon said.

"The generals?"

He shook his head. "Gone. We haven't found them."

And they weren't likely to. The generals were experts at survival. They were probably halfway to rendezvous with the rest of their forces.

"The admiral on the human ship has offered his assistance," Finn said.

Kira nodded. "I'll find him and brief him, but I doubt we'll remain long."

Graydon went still. "You plan to go with them."

Kira met his gaze, sensing an undercurrent of danger. "That's always been the end goal."

And her deal with Liara made it possible.

"You could stay here," he said.

Her stomach tightened.

He didn't know how tempting his offer was. To feel companionship once more, to delve into the potential between them. It was more than she ever thought she'd have again. She wanted it so badly she was willing to do almost anything to keep it.

That was why she had to go.

CHAPTER TWENTY-THREE

If she stayed, how long before she lost herself in him and the rest of the Tuann? How long before she forgot the purpose that had driven her for so long?

She wanted him and the promise he offered more than she wanted almost anything else in her life. Those feelings were what gave her the strength to refuse.

"No," she said. She couldn't bring herself to explain, to tell him there were things only she could do. If she survived, maybe she could return.

She said none of that. He deserved to come first for whoever chose him. He deserved someone whole, not some barely functioning shell who might not survive the next year.

"No," he repeated slowly. He nodded, his expression emotionless.

Finn looked slightly alarmed from his post at the door.

Graydon stood in an abrupt movement.

Kira knew what he would do almost before he did it.

Graydon bent down, his eyes dark spears as they locked on hers. She let the kiss come, knowing it was probably the last and wanting to cling to it, to hold it close so she could remember and cherish the feeling later.

She fell into all that he was, fighting to imprint herself on him as anger and passion rose between them.

His lips left hers, leaving her cold and achingly alone as he straightened, his face once more an expressionless mask.

"I'm leaving," she told him.

"We'll see," he said before turning toward the door.

Finn shook his head at her when they were alone.

"What does that mean?" she asked.

His gaze was sympathetic. "It means things might not go the way you planned. The commander doesn't often give up his quarry."

Kira flopped back unable to think of any response.

CHAPTER TWENTY-FOUR

Kira cursed the size and torturous length of the Citadel as she dragged her bag along yet another set of steps into another long hallway.

Would it have killed the Luathans to build a city with a rational layout?

She could have asked Finn for help, but the last time she'd asked which way the landing field was, he'd given her a beatific smile and a vague response.

She'd stopped asking after that.

A headache pounded at her temples.

The sunlight streaming in the windows stabbed at her eyes, despite her sunglasses.

It'd be several days before her eyes could take the sun's piercing light again. A side effect of the primus form. Until then, they were extremely sensitive, leaving her craving the cool comfort of dark, something in distressingly short supply in the bright, airy Citadel.

Right now, she felt like a herd of alien horses had trampled over every part of her body, leaving her feeling like one giant bruise. Another lovely side effect of the transformation.

While it gave her unimaginable power for a short while, it also sucked up an immense amount of energy and resources. Until her body recovered, she was left as weak as a human newborn.

It was one of the reasons she was forced to drag the duffel along after her rather than carry it. She couldn't bring herself to care about the damage she might be doing to the floor.

CHAPTER TWENTY-FOUR

If they had a problem with that, they should have provided someone to carry the bag instead of refusing her any help.

The same Luathan healer who had attended her on her last visit to the medic had been furious when Kira said she was leaving on the next shuttle.

She'd ordered Kira into bed for another week of rest.

Kira had declined. She couldn't chance being left behind. The Tuann didn't often journey to human space. If she missed this shuttle, it could be a long while before she found anyone willing to give her a ride to O'Riley.

She wouldn't put it past Graydon to bribe Jace with more ships to get him to leave.

That left her schlepping her own gear to the shuttle landing zone, even though she felt like she was experiencing the most extreme form of the dreaded hangover humans so often complained of.

A glimpse of forest appeared through a doorway, and Kira made for it, spotting Raider and the rest. She pulled her duffel next to theirs and let it drop.

She was in the act of collapsing beside it when she spotted two small figures watching her through one of the arched windows on the second floor.

Joule and Ziva stared down at her with morose faces, looking like they thought she was abandoning them.

Kira struggled to shrug off her guilt. She'd told them she wasn't staying. She'd warned them over and over. It wasn't her fault if they hadn't listened.

"Perhaps you should talk to them," Jin suggested.

"It would just prolong the inevitable."

He made a small hmm. "The Luatha canceled the rest of the tests to search for you when you went missing that night. It could be a while until they're rescheduled given the current state of their House. The children will be in limbo until their status is settled."

"They'll be fine. I asked Liara to intervene on their behalf. She's promised to get Joule the training he needs to become an overlord. She won't let anyone in her House stand in the way of his goal," Kira said waspishly.

Her cousin owed her and she knew it. It had taken some convincing, but Liara had agreed to Kira's request. She'd even volunteered to take in the rest of Joule's surviving House until such time as he became an overlord.

"Somehow neither of them looks particularly satisfied with that outcome," Jin observed.

"I can't help it if they got attached," Kira snapped.

"I think they're not the only ones," Jin murmured as Kira collapsed beside her duffel bag. She was done with this conversation.

"Wake me when the transport gets here," Kira mumbled before sticking her face into the crevasse between the bag and ground.

An answer came, the words garbled.

She drifted, half-asleep until someone kicked her foot.

She lifted her head, staring bleary-eyed up at Raider. "Transport here?"

"They said it's not coming," he said, gesturing at two Luathans, their faces apologetic.

"What?"

"Apologies, lady, but the human shuttle was waved off," one of them said.

Awareness filtered in and Kira felt a little more alert. "That's not right. Liara gave her word we could leave."

"The Overlord is the one who refused its landing," he said.

Kira stared at him, unable to form intelligent words.

Raider was not so constrained, letting a few choice words slip loose.

"Language," Jace snapped, striding out of the Citadel.

"They yanked our window," Raider said, hands on his hips as he glared at the Tuann.

"I'm sure there's a good reason," Jace said. He turned to the two messengers. "Can we speak to your lady?"

CHAPTER TWENTY-FOUR

They spared a glance to where Kira had flopped down, curling into her duffel as she judged being upright too difficult. Finn watched with an impassive face.

"Yes, we can take you to her," one said.

Jace gave them a polite nod. "You do that."

He bent to Kira and shook her shoulder. "You need to be part of this."

"I'm sure you have it handled," Kira mumbled, already half-asleep.

Her duffel was yanked from under her. A cry of protest burst out as she landed on the hard ground.

A caramel bar appeared in front of her face.

"Let's go," Jace said, no sympathy in his expression. "I have a feeling you're the reason for this change of plan."

Kira snatched the bar from his hand, ripping it open and stuffing half in her mouth. She glared at Jin. He was the culprit responsible for jerking the duffel away from her.

"Don't look at me," he protested. "We both know this was the only way to get you to move."

"I want two more candy bars once this is done," she told the two of them.

"Fair enough," Jace said.

He and Raider helped her to her feet, their assistance more necessary than she let on.

"Lead on," she told the two watching Tuann.

Finn trailed behind as their escorts set a quick pace that gradually slowed when they saw Kira making no effort to keep up.

"You know anything about this?" Kira asked Finn.

"I have an idea."

She scowled at him. "You want to share?"

"I think it's better for you to find out for yourself," he said.

She gritted her teeth and stomped into the Citadel.

Kira entered the room her escort pointed to, ready for a fight. Anger was the only way she was going to get through this without collapsing.

"Would someone like to tell me why I'm not on a shuttle heading home right now?" she barked.

The sight of Graydon seated at the table, his gaze calm and amused temporarily threw her off-balance.

She gave him a hard look. What was he up to?

She took the time to look over the rest of those assembled. Liara sat on one side of him and on the other, the two strangers. This time they weren't wearing their cloaks, their dark gray synth armor with midnight blue detailing on proud display.

They weren't Luathan. Another House perhaps?

"Kira, we've been waiting. Please have a seat," Silas said. "Your friends too."

Kira bit back her impatient words.

Kira and Jace shared a glance before the two of them, along with Raider, Tank, and Blue settled themselves at the table. Nova and Maverick had remained behind to guard their belongings.

Kira pushed down her frustration. The mood in the room called for patience and intelligence. She might have been able to bully Liara into keeping her promise, but the two in the strange House's synth armor were largely unknown entities. Better to watch and wait.

She narrowed her eyes at the healer at their side.

"Why have you refused permission for my shuttle to land?" Jace started.

"We have matters we need to clear up before we let you go," the man said.

"Here it is," Jin muttered.

The man's gaze lifted to her friend, but he refrained from commenting. "Before we start, I feel the need to introduce myself. My name is Silas. This is Quillon. We're House Roake."

Kira didn't respond beyond a wary nod.

"What misconceptions did you want to clear up?" Jace asked, smoothly taking the lead. "I was under the impression you were

CHAPTER TWENTY-FOUR

grateful for our assistance against the Tsavitee."

"We are," Silas said with a gentle smile. "You and your people have proven worthier than we could have ever hoped."

"Is this about the ships then?" Jace asked, his back straight and his expression guarded.

"No, you will get what you were promised," Silas said.

A sigh of relief came from the humans present. Kira watched and waited. She didn't feel easy just yet.

"However," Silas said. There it was. The catch. "They will not be as helpful as you think. They require an ability to manipulate soul's breath to power them. They're useless without it."

No one moved on Kira's side—the news freezing them in place.

Kira's stomach dipped sickeningly.

Humans needed those ships to fight off the Tsavitee. She wasn't going to be enough this time. The Tsavitee knew she was coming. They knew her strengths and weaknesses. There would be no advantage of surprise.

"We're willing to lend you the individuals needed to make them work," Silas said.

Hope leaped onto the faces of the Curs. Kira felt numb.

"You would?" Jace said, blinking rapidly.

"We would," Silas confirmed. "We just require one thing."

"What's that?" Raider asked, suspicion already on his face.

"Me." Kira's gaze locked on Graydon as his gaze shifted to meet hers, the look in his eyes saying "gotcha."

Silas bowed his head in confirmation.

Kira's gaze swung to her cousin. Liara was pale but looked a hundred times better than the last time Kira had seen her. "You released your claim on me. So much for trusting your word."

Liara met her eyes defiantly. She took a deep breath. "I will keep my word. However, there are subtleties you may not have considered."

Kira waited.

Silas leaned closer. "While your mother's people may have rescinded their claim on you, your father's did not."

Kira blinked rapidly at them, her gaze shifting to Jin. How had they not considered this possibility?

"Uh," Jin said dumbly. "That was not in your code of laws."

Silas's smile was small and humorless. "There are many codices. This is an old law, one rarely invoked since few are born with equal claims on multiple Houses."

"What does that mean?" Kira asked.

Graydon's smirk said checkmate. "It means you're not going anywhere. You're ours, and we mean to keep you."

Discover More by T.A. White

The Broken Lands Series
Pathfinder's Way – Book One
Mist's Edge – Book Two
Wayfarer's Keep – Book Three

The Dragon-Ridden Chronicles
Dragon-Ridden – Book One
Of Bone and Ruin – Book Two
Destruction's Ascent – Book Three
Shifting Seas - Novella

The Aileen Travers Series
Shadow's Messenger – Book One
Midnight's Emissary – Book Two
Moonlight's Ambassador – Book Three
Dawn's Envoy – Book Four

CONNECT WITH ME
Twitter: @tawhiteauthor
Facebook: https://www.facebook.com/tawhiteauthor/
Website: http://www.tawhiteauthor.com/
Blog: http://dragon-ridden.blogspot.com/

About the Author

Writing is my first love. Even before I could read or put coherent sentences down on paper, I would beg the older kids to team up with me for the purpose of crafting ghost stories to share with our friends. This first writing partnership came to a tragic end when my coauthor decided to quit a day later and I threw my cookies at her head. This led to my conclusion that I worked better alone. Today, I stick with solo writing, telling the stories that would otherwise keep me up at night.

Most days (and nights) are spent feeding my tea addiction while defending the computer keyboard from my feline companions, Loki and Odin.

Printed in Great Britain
by Amazon